THE ADJACENT PROBABLE

Skylar Ray Foxx

Skylar Ray Foxx Publishing LLC
2205 W 136th Avenue Ste 106, PMB 1425, Broomfield, CO 80023
SRFPublishingLLC@gmail.com

Library of Congress Control Number: 2024911642
Paperback ISBN: 979-8-9907585-1-3
Hardback ISBN: 979-8-9907585-2-0
Ebook ISBN: 979-8-9907585-0-6
Audiobook ISBN: 979-8-9907585-5-1

*For my partner—the love of my life—forever!
May there always be dandelions
for us, our children,
and all those who love life
for generations to come.*

THE ADJACENT PROBABLE

CHAPTER 1

"Bun-Bun doesn't want to die."

The little girl standing before Aisling, whom she had come to know as Miss Ash, was cradling a ragged stuffed toy. Her dark brown eyes peered up from under a crocheted pink cap. It was pulled down to her eyebrows. The stuffed rabbit wore a matching handmade cap with holes that let its well-worn ears peek through the unblemished yarn. Aisling instinctively moved to embrace the child but stopped abruptly.

"We won't let her die, Becky," Aisling said, gingerly easing back into her wheelchair. She was careful not to let the pain touch her voice. "We love her very much."

"Yeah." Becky squeezed the stuffed animal harder.

"Is she scared?" Aisling patted the toy's head, then adjusted the cap.

Becky sniffled and nodded as she moved to embrace Aisling. Although Miss Ash was thin and frail, had icy cold hands, and had a wheelchair that got in the way, Becky loved the warmth of Miss Ash's hugs. She felt the slow movements of Miss Ash's breathing as they held each other. She didn't want to let go, but Becky's mother had warned her that hugging Miss Ash for too long hurt her. Becky pulled away reluctantly.

Catching her breath, Aisling sagged back into her wheelchair as Becky sat down, carefully arranging Bun-Bun in her lap.

The hospital sitting area was relatively busy. Parents and their children interacted in a community of proximity, despite their many different backgrounds. A nurse made rounds with an ice cream cart. Children and their parents sat on colorful couches or at whimsical tables. Several kids waved at Aisling when they caught her eye and she waved back. Many had crocheted hats or blankets. On one of the couches, a little boy with no hair and bright eyes was staring at Aisling with his fist in his mouth. He was barely old enough to stand. Aisling smiled at him and waved. He removed his fist and shook his arm happily, attempting to mimic the motion.

Becky watched the exchange solemnly.

"Do you think he will die, Miss Ash?" Becky asked.

"No," Aisling said. "I think we're all going to get good news very soon."

Aisling held up a finger while grinning and reached under the blanket on her lap and pulled out a small gift-wrapped package.

"I made something else for you and Bun-Bun," she said.

Becky's eyes glittered with delight as she stood to receive the gift. It seemed large in her hands as she turned and plopped back down in her chair. Aisling smiled as she watched Becky admire the shiny wrapping paper covered with tiny dancing bunnies. After her careful examination, Becky cautiously peeled the tape so as not to rip the paper. She made a vexed sound each time the paper tore. Before she opened the box, Becky carefully folded the paper and set it aside on the table.

"You made this too?" Becky gasped as she pulled out a tiny crocheted afghan. It was about the size of a hand towel.

"Do you like it?"

"Yes!" she squeaked, running her fingers over the flower patterns. "How did you make it?"

"My Nana taught me," Aisling replied. "Now you have matching blankets, and Bun-Bun can stay warm whenever she's waiting for you."

Becky wrapped the worn rabbit in the blanket and sat it upright in her lap as the nurse approached the two of them. Clad in pastel scrubs, she placed two small cups of ice cream before them with a conspiratorial smile.

"Just look at you two, getting on famously as usual," she said, handing them wooden spoons.

Becky giggled and took a big scoop, holding it before the rabbit's mouth and then raising it to her own. Aisling took a modest bite and smiled.

"Today is 'Dream Day,'" the nurse said cheerily. "What do you dream of doing someday?"

"Bun-Bun wants to ride a roller-coaster," Becky said, bouncing in her seat. "What about you, Miss Ash?"

"I want to walk on the surface of Mars," Aisling replied, laughing.

"So you want to be the first?" The nurse asked as she carefully wiped Aisling's chin.

"I don't care if I'm first. The doing would be enough."

Three men in black business suits approached the table, interrupting their conversation. Their dark attire made them seem like shadows moving through the rainbow colors of the children's ward. Silence surrounded them except for the clack of their shoes as they walked. Parents held their children closer as the men strode forward unyieldingly.

The tallest man met the nurse's eyes. His chilling expression caused her to shudder. She quickly walked away, passing another table with her cart without stopping.

"Dr. Eyez-ling Ramsey?" the tallest of the men asked. He introduced himself and the others without waiting for a response. "We're from the White House."

A woman at an adjacent table gasped.

"You have a phone call from the President," the man said.

Aisling regarded the men.

"It's pronounced Ash-leen," Aisling said deliberately. Becky timidly moved away from the men.

"Of course," the tall one said. "If you'll come with us to somewhere private..."

"I'm flattered," Aisling said calmly. She seemed untouched by their aura of darkness. "However, I must decline."

"Doctor, the President—"

"If you leave me your business card," Aisling interrupted firmly, "I'll be certain my assistant works with you to schedule an appropriate time."

"He—"

"A time that isn't interrupting what I consider to be my most important activity of the day."

His jaw clenched. Another of the officials reached into his pocket, taking out a small folio. He came to stand between Aisling and Becky, handing her his card.

"That will be fine," he said with a gravelly voice and predatory smile. He turned and patted Becky's head before kneeling in front of her.

"You must be one special lady," he said to her in his sweetest voice. It sounded like rocks scraping pavement. "More important than the President."

Becky had picked up Bun-Bun and hugged her close. Aisling wheeled her chair around the man, her lips tight with determination. He rose lithely as Aisling wheeled between him and Becky.

"Thank you, gentlemen," Aisling said.

"We'll be in touch," the man said, voice grating. He joined the other two. The tall one was still clearly upset, while the one who had remained quiet seemed unconcerned. Together, they turned to leave. Aisling watched them take a few steps, then turned and faced Becky, putting them out of her mind. Her body ached from the effort of the encounter, but she ignored the pain and reached out to fix Becky's cap. Becky smiled.

"Now, where were we?" Aisling said cheerfully. "Ah, yes! Ice cream."

***

Aisling sighed and slumped in her wheelchair as she gazed out of the large window of her hospital room. The city of Denver carried on below with its usual evening hum in the shadow of the Rocky Mountains. Three stories down, Becky walked down the sidewalk with her parents. She looked up and Aisling waved. Becky waved back.

"I'm afraid there are no life-saving options for you at this point, Doctor Ramsey," her doctor said. "Your lab work no longer qualifies you for chemotherapy treatment. I am officially recommending palliative treatment to block your nerves."

"No palliative treatments," she said. "Life expectancy?"

She watched as Becky and her parents went into the parking garage. A couple came around a corner and walked down the street hand in hand with a little boy. They swung the child between them. She couldn't hear through the windows, but as she saw him squeal with delight she imagined the heartwarming sound.

"About three to six months," the doctor was saying. "Maybe longer if your platelets and neutrophils return to safe enough levels for treatment."

She watched the couple meander down the street, enjoying each other's company.

"You really should consider pain relief," he said earnestly.

Her back became straighter.

Her doctor was used to seeing several types of reactions from patients to this sort of news. Some fought until the end, never believing they would die. They expected to fight like they had always done, and maybe—just maybe—they'd be the exception. The look he saw in the reflection of the glass, the set of her jaw, made him sure she intended to fight.

"I need to make some arrangements," she said. "No palliative treatments."

"I must ask again. Are you sure? The pain will only get worse."

"Yes, I'm sure," she said firmly. "Thank you, Doctor."

"If you need anything, please let me know," he said. "I'll send someone in to help you into bed."

Aisling did not respond.

Her doctor had come to recognize her various moods. He turned and left, closing the door behind him.

Outside, the family had paused as the young boy peered down at the sidewalk. He picked something up that Aisling couldn't see and showed it to his parents. She sat watching until they rounded the corner. Her eyes drifted to the cloudy sky, and for a fleeting moment, she felt she was searching for a star that would never shine.

She reached for her phone and dialed a number.

"Hello, Ash."

"Jonas," she said. "How's the testing going?"

"Doctor Tamma says they're close to solving the binding problem," Jonas replied. "Thanks to your suggestions last month, he thinks they may have it soon."

"How soon?"

"Another year or two."

"I don't have that long."

"Oh my god," Jonas said. "I'm... sorry. How long did they say?"

"Six months at the most."

"Maybe I can have Doctor Tamma work on sending you the latest prototype?" he offered.

"Do you remember that conference in Rio?" she asked.

"Where'd that come from?"

"Do you?"

"I'd as soon forget my name," Jonas replied. "Your presentation sealed the deal. It put SolviNext on the map."

"Oh, right," she said before she could stop herself.

She could hear him shuffling against the phone as if it were pressed between his head and shoulder.

"How's Chris? The kids?"

"They're fine. I almost broke my back tripping over a skateboard yesterday."

Aisling chuckled.

"You sure you don't want me to have Doctor Tamma..." He

trailed off.

"No," she replied. "I've seen the current results. It's not ready, and I think Tamma is correct. It will take most of the next year to engineer the correct sequences with the current prototype."

"Damn."

"I had a realization yesterday. I'll send my thoughts for a new prototype to Tamma tonight."

"Of course you have new ideas! You're brilliant, you know?"

"Even if my idea proves correct," she said, ignoring his compliment, "it won't be ready in time for me."

She could hear what sounded like a door shutting.

"I'm sorry," Jonas said softly.

Aisling let her eyes wander to the curtains framing the window. The wall was accented deep green and flowers and cards lined the windowsill. Some of the flowers were new and fragrant; others were dying.

"I've known it was coming to this for a while," Aisling replied quietly.

Glass clinked in the background of the call.

"Jonas," she said, steeling herself. "Before I send my ideas to Tamma, I need to ask you again. When I'm gone, if Tamma's team succeeds in creating the cure for cancer, you'll give it to the world, right?"

"Aisling, we've been through this."

"Haven't we made enough money, Jonas?" she snapped. "Give it to the people. It's my final wish, Jonas. Please."

"It's not about the money! I..." Jonas began. He took a deep breath, and his tone changed. "I don't want to argue about it. Not now."

"It's important to me, Jonas."

"It's important to everyone," he replied. "I'll think about it, Aisling."

"Thank you," she said.

"What are you going to do now?"

"They want to perform palliative treatment."

"What does that mean?"

"Surgery to ease my pain," she replied. "I think I'll go home."

Outside, the clouds were beginning to turn orange from the sunset. Aisling's eyes followed a pair of birds as they flew by.

"Colorado or New Mexico?" Jonas asked.

"Colorado," she said. "I'll make arrangements for in-home hospice care."

She could hear Jonas adjust the phone and clear his throat.

"What is it, Jonas?"

"Aisling, I," he began, his voice softer. He cleared his throat again. "Your daughter. She's not eighteen yet, right?"

"She turned seventeen three months ago."

"Wow," Jonas said. "Time flies. It's funny, but I don't think I've ever met her."

"You know I'm a private person," Aisling said guardedly. "And she's busy with school—just like I was."

"Well," Jonas said, trying to find the right words. "Well, I just wanted to say. If she...needs a place to stay if... Well, she's absolutely welcome here."

"Thank you," Aisling breathed through a sharp twinge of pain in her middle. "I appreciate the gesture, but I've already made arrangements. She'll be staying with a family here in Colorado."

"I see."

"I'm tired," she said with a deep breath. "I'm tired and need to make another call before I can sleep."

"Okay," Jonas replied, his voice picking up. "I'll give Doctor Tamma the heads up on your new ideas. He's supposed to meet me in five minutes."

"Think about it, Jonas. The cure."

"Okay," he said. "If you don't feel comfortable sending your latest ideas, don't."

"I know your heart is in the right place," she replied.

"Take care, Ash," he replied. "I'm here if you need anything."

"I appreciate it."

With a sigh, Aisling ended the call and set the phone in her lap. She hadn't told him about the President, she realized. She briefly wondered why the President wanted to talk to her. It didn't matter. This life is coming to a close, she thought, so what really matters at this point? Certainly not that man.

After a while, two nurses came in and gently prepared to move her into bed. They were one of the better pairs. The pain had been so intolerable with other nurses that she would lay there suffering for hours. Some people fainted at certain thresholds of pain, but she had been born with no such luck.

They lifted her from the wheelchair—an avalanche of excruciating pain spread from her core. Any bending or twisting of her abdomen triggered the pain. It seemed to stretch on forever as they transferred her to the bed.

"There we go, Doctor Ramsey," said one of the nurses. He

gently squeezed her hand as she sucked air through her teeth against the agony. She nodded at him while the other nurse took her temperature. Aisling acknowledged their interactions, but her mind was elsewhere as they carefully positioned her in the bed and covered her up. She gripped her phone tightly when they handed it to her before leaving.

Aisling sat and breathed, gazing out of the hospital window as the pain slowly diminished. She wished the room was on the mountain-facing side. The smog was a shadow over the horizon, with no wilderness visible as far as she could see—just the city. Steel and glass glistened in the evening sun. An urge to return to the window to watch the sunset suddenly changed the room's dimensions for her. The window and the walls seemed to expand away from her, ever more unreachable.

Aisling reached for the tumbler of fresh water the nurses had left on the bedside table. She set it in her lap next to her phone and sipped from the straw, closing her eyes against the vertigo before looking out the window again.

There are, she thought, millions of people going about their lives out there. Each knows that their death will come someday but is blissfully ignorant of when. Each moves forward in their relatively short life, expecting tomorrow to come, enmeshed in the center of their all-important immediate reality.

Aisling sipped at her straw, picked up her phone, and dialed a number.

"Hello, Aisling."

"Do you consider yourself the center of the universe, Daryl?"

"I have no data models to cover personal opinions or beliefs from which to answer that question. Would you like me to use a language model to emulate a philosophical response?"

"No, thanks," Aisling said, sipping again. "For my part, I know and experience the world through my senses. As a scientist, I accept the idea of objective existence due to evidence. When my mind ceases to exist, the universe will continue without me. We are tiny flecks of dust in a great void that is apathetic to our lives. Therefore, I cannot be the center."

"Noted."

"Daryl," she said. "Your cognitive capabilities should increase after the procedure, making you the most advanced general graphene-based intelligence in the world."

"Noted."

"I look forward to our future conversations, Daryl."

"Noted."

More lonely than before, Aisling kept Daryl on the line until the sun sank below the horizon. Countless sunsets had come before, and countless would come after, she thought. This might be my last.

She ran through the scenarios in her mind as she pulled up her drafted email to Dr. Tamma and Jonas with detailed notes on her ideas for the cure. SolviNext was likely in the best position to take her ideas and develop the cure safely and efficiently. The government was shutting down or nationalizing all the other smaller biomedical companies. She thought of Becky and the countless other children who couldn't afford the cure if Jonas decided to sell it at the highest market price. Eventually, the price would come down, but who would save those people—all the children—who died in the meantime? It has to be SolviNext, she thought. I simply must convince the shareholders as quickly as possible.

Her thumb hovered over the send button.

The sunlight clashed with the smog on the horizon. She thought of the air purifiers the hospital had to use to keep patients with lungs as brittle as hers safe from the polluted air. We could so nonchalantly destroy this planet, she ruminated. We could destroy ourselves, and nothing in the universe would care to rescue us from our folly. But I have a choice now. Perhaps I can change my own destiny, at least. Perhaps I can create a new probable future for myself, one that is adjacent to the quagmire of society but free of it.

She hit send.

Or die trying, she thought.

"Daryl," she said, well after the sun went down. "Initiate preparations for the procedure."

"Confirmed. When can I expect you?"

"Sometime tonight. Please make the arrangements."

"Confirmed."

***

Jonas thoughtfully set his phone face down on his desk and sat in his executive chair. He picked up the glass of bourbon he had poured himself from the mini-bar in his office and peered into it.

Rio. That was about twenty years ago...

Aisling was standing on the balcony of the grand ballroom

overlooking Guanabara Bay in Rio de Janeiro. A warm, salty breeze wafted up to them. Jonas was flying high on more than the fact that they had secured their biggest contract to date. He fingered his wedding ring, still getting used to its presence. All their dreams were coming true, so why was she out here alone?

"Getting some air, Ash?" He walked up to her. She eyed his ring as he obliviously handed her a glass of champagne. She took it but didn't drink.

"It's a night for celebration," she said. "Your future is set."

"Yours too," he said. "We did this together."

She looked away as if taking in the bay spread out below them.

"No, Jonas," she said. "For me, the future is set in stages. Stages one through four. Who knows how long each will last? Five years, ten years. One month."

"You mean your cancer, don't you?" She had told him the news almost a year ago.

"I got the lab results this morning. The treatments haven't been effective, and it's spreading."

"I'm sorry," he said, grimacing and letting out a slow breath. "You don't have to do this. We can cancel the contract so you can focus on getting better."

"Thank you, Jonas," she said. "I know how much it means for you to say that."

"I mean it," he said earnestly. "You don't need my permission to take time for yourself. I want you to know there's no obligation. Just focus on kicking this thing."

"No," she said with a sigh. "My time may be short, but I hope to fight it in my own way, to create my own adjacent probable."

"You've been saying that a lot lately," Jonas said. "What does it mean? Are you talking about changing fate?"

She nodded, tilting her head slightly in her usual manner when she had more to say about something but chose not to. It was a habit Jonas had become accustomed to when Ash stopped trying to explain things she knew were too technical for him. She slowly poured the champagne over the edge of the balcony into the garden several stories below. The light from the ballroom beneath them glistened on the golden liquid as it disappeared into the dark.

"Your future is bright, Jonas," she said. "You will live on to see many great successes. You should celebrate this moment."

She spun the empty glass in her hands as she spoke.

"Ash," he began, turning his head away.

"And Chris is perfect for you," she continued sincerely. "Her *commitment to God. Her devotion to you. And you'll have the family you always wanted."*

Jonas had stood speechless as she hugged him and walked away. He remembered thinking at the time that she was happy for him and realized she was facing the possibility of never having her own family. But as he reflected on that moment now with the benefit of maturity, he wondered if he had missed the point entirely. Why had she brought it up now?

Jonas couldn't imagine what she was going through. He said a silent prayer for her. He knew she didn't believe, but he always hoped for her salvation. Jonas prayed that He would ease her pain, then finished his drink and set the glass down carefully.

There was a rap on his office door immediately followed by a tall older man stepping in wearing a dirty lab coat. Jonas had often joked Dr. Tamma was born with the thing. He even wore it when he played poker, claiming it gave him luck.

"How is she?" Dr. Tamma asked.

"She has less than six months." Jonas' voice sounded far away, even to his own ears.

"My god," Dr. Tamma said. "We're so close! But it will be at least a year before we resolve the binding issues."

Jonas nodded.

"We ran the analysis on the antibody response elicited by multiple adjuvant formulations," Dr. Tamma began dejectedly.

The technical details of Dr. Tamma's research were beyond Jonas' understanding, so his mind wandered.

She still wanted to give away the cure. Jonas thought Aisling was always so opinionated about money versus the scientific value of research. She was so concerned about the socioeconomic impacts of their business. How many times had they fought over that?

Jonas' eyes moved to the photos on his desk. His heart warmed as he glanced over his family, but it was his Opa's face he paused on.

"Each man must take on life in his own way," Opa had said a few weeks before he passed away. "God raises us all up if we work hard."

When he turned eighteen, Jonas was told he wouldn't get a dime of inheritance unless he could first make a million dollars on his own. Like all five of his siblings, Jonas grew up wealthy but left the house with nothing. Filled with gusto, Jonas attacked his first year of college with no idea what he would do and the dread of racking up student loans. By the second year, he had begun to worry about not making it.

It had been such a blessing to meet Aisling. When they stood on that balcony in Rio he was only twenty-five and leading a company worth almost half a billion, based on several contracts to sell robotics and software to the DOD. Shortly after Rio, Aisling switched focus. He remembered arguing with her and how adamant she was about not selling to the military. The company became a household name when she and her scientists developed a cure for arthritis.

She also didn't want to sell the cure for arthritis. That's when they had their first falling out. After that, she retreated to her lab, leaving the business to him and proceeding to develop significant advances in medical robotics, imaging, prosthetics, and breakthrough cures for neurological diseases, including Alzheimer's and Dementia. Overnight, Ash's name became a household name. She didn't like her celebrity status.

In his view, the company's success wasn't just due to its technological advancements. It was also because of the beauty of free trade and the American dream. Opa had always told Jonas about how he had built his own wealth and had taught him the value of tithing and philanthropy in God's name. By the time Jonas was thirty, he had given his entire 60-million-dollar inheritance to charities. He built his kids' character by bringing them to the soup kitchens at least once a month, just as his Opa had done for him.

Jonas understood Aisling's desire to make the cure available for everyone, and he also wanted to save as many lives as possible. However, his whole career served to validate his grandfather's views. It is through business that the most positive impact on humanity is ultimately achieved, he thought. She would leave it to the technocrats and incompetent governments to find a way to bring a cure for cancer to the world. That would only ensure the fewest people would benefit from it, Jonas thought, exasperated. Only a private company could mobilize at great scale.

But now she was dying.

He ran his fingers through his hair. He didn't have the heart to get into another argument with her. Not in her condition.

"It's a tough deal," Dr. Tamma said, watching him. "To struggle for that long and still go at such a young age."

Jonas hadn't noticed that he had stopped talking.

"Yeah," he agreed.

Jonas' phone buzzed and he picked it up.

"She said she has some more ideas for you," Jonas said. "Looks like she just sent the details."

At this, Dr. Tamma perked up and began speculating while pulling out his phone. He read Aisling's message aloud. More techno-babble.

"Doctor," Jonas said. "I'll leave all of that to you. I've got to get going."

"Yes, sir," Dr. Tamma said, scrolling through the message. "This is...amazing! This..."

He trailed off and rose. He read the message in a whisper as he walked out of the office, eyes glued to his phone.

Jonas switched apps and sent a text message.

"She's dying. 6mo"

"Oh no! Come home, let's talk"

"Can't mtgs Be home l8 tell kids I <3 them"

"<3 you"

"<3 u2"

***

"Tuck that chin!" Nat said loudly. The cooling fans in the gym were obnoxious. The gym was located in a small, corrugated steel-arched building that resembled a large half-buried culvert pipe. There was no air conditioning, and the air was saturated with the smell of old leather and sweat.

"Keep your feet off the tape," the gym owner and coach added, walking up.

The new student reset his feet and tilted his head forward, then quickly threw a few jabs. Nat guessed he was twelve or thirteen years old. His dad stood behind him. He was all of six feet tall and well-built aside from the beer gut. He also kept offering advice, which annoyed Nat. Some of the advice was technically correct, but that wasn't the point.

"Get on your toes," Dad was saying. Nat frowned down at him, and he was visibly taken aback. She was used to being taller than most men. As well-built as Dad was, Nat was stronger. In an instant, Nat switched to a smile.

"You sound like you know your stuff," she said.

"Yeah," Dad said, pride in his voice. "My Dad taught me."

The coach took note of the exchange and glanced at the

clock. He clapped his hand on the boy's back.

"Your dad's right, son," he said. "Eventually, you'll want to be on your toes. But, if you were to join my gym, I would take you through things one step at a time. I find guys learn best by only adding new things when they are ready. You would progress as fast or as slow as you're comfortable."

He glanced at Dad, who nodded.

"How about trying a little bag work?" he asked. "I'll get you some gloves."

"I'm gonna do a circuit," Nat said. "Nice to meet you all."

"Thanks for covering while I took that call," the coach said.

"It's all good," Nat said as she stepped up to a double-end bag and adjusted the height.

They took the new kid over to the hanging bags. She taped up.

"Just you and me, huh?" she said, focusing completely on the bag before throwing her arms into controlled action. Punch, weave, punch, weave. Nothing existed now but the bag. The circuit buzzer went off after nine minutes, and Nat switched stations.

Time passed quickly as she progressed through her usual routine. Nat never listened to music while working out. She preferred to lose herself in the rhythms of the motions themselves. Everything was about timing in this sport. If you jam to your favorite tunes while doing a combo, you unconsciously move to the rhythm of the song instead of the pulse of the heart, the dance of the muscles as they cycled through their various states. This body awareness and mastery of focus were part of why no one in this gym could beat her in a match. She knew their tunes. She had their rhythms down.

When she was unwrapping her tape about forty minutes later, the coach approached her. She didn't like to be disturbed while doing her circuits and he respected that. They had an unspoken agreement that before and after, they could chat or discuss techniques.

"I think you're twisting your left ankle too much on that jab," the gym coach said. "Not always. Happens about one in four times."

Nat thought about it for a moment.

"Could be when I'm preparing for a cross," she said. "Or when I'm thinking about annoying parents."

"Maybe," he laughed. "You talk to Johnny?"

"No," Nat said, "I'm allergic to fighting for money."

"You're a real good fighter," he said. "Best I've seen. I doubt you're allergic to cash."

"I'm comfortable," she said.

"I seen your car."

"Then you know I ain't vain enough to be a fighter."

"Is that what's holding you back?" he asked. "How you read people…it's like you see their thoughts. No one can touch you."

"No one wins forever," she said. "Someday, there will be a fight I won't walk away from."

"Maybe," he said. "But you could have a bit of glory while it lasts."

"Not interested in the attention," Nat replied bluntly. "I'm too tall, too brown, and too gay for people to leave me be as it is. Besides, my job calls for discretion, and I am happy to comply."

"Ain't you self-employed since you left the Army?"

"Loving it."

"Well, you change your mind," he said, "you know I support you one hundred percent."

Nat regarded him as she put her stuff neatly into her bag. She took a swig of water and nodded her thanks.

"Business looks good," she said. The boy from earlier and his father were waving as they walked out. Judging by their body language, she suspected they would be back—if they hadn't already signed up.

"Sure is," he said. "Seems like everyone wants to learn to fight these days."

A loud voice broke the vibe.

"Civil war comin'. TUFs are taking this country back!"

Nat didn't need to turn around to know who spoke. She had heard him coming. Since he joined the gym a week before, he had been talking nonstop about the Truth and Freedom party and how they were owning the liberals. He also had a loud way of breathing that cut through the sound of the fans and caused her teeth to grind. Unabashedly shirtless, he stood before them, toweling off his chiseled physique. All show, she thought. No speed. No strength. She wondered how long he stared at himself in the mirror every day.

"Let's not talk about that," the coach said, adding, "How's that left hook coming together?"

"I'm all over that like white on rice," the fighter said.

"Show me."

The fighter looked at Nat with a sneer.

"I'm out," said Nat as she picked up her bag.

"See ya, Nat," the coach said.

Putting everything behind her out of her mind, Nat checked her phone as she strode out. There was a new text message from Cici.

"Call me, q"

Nat called on speed dial.

"Hey, *chica*," Nat said when she heard Cici pick up.

"Hey, *querida*!" Cici exclaimed, cheerful as usual. "You wanna catch a movie later?"

"I got stuff," Nat replied resignedly. "What's up, babe?"

"You remember that problem I was telling you about?"

"The one in the shape of an abusive man?"

"Yeah."

"From your social worker friend?"

"Yeah, he's got this case where a mom of three shows up at the hospital looking like she was demolished in the ring. She claims she fell. That was six months ago."

"I remember," Nat said.

"Anyway," Cici continued, "Two days ago, she talked to her neighbor and said she wants a divorce, but she's afraid of what her husband would do. Apparently, he's threatened her multiple times, saying that he would kill her and their three children if she ever tried to run away."

"So, she doesn't want a restraining order?"

"She refuses to file for that," Cici said. "My friend is real concerned. He said he sees this all the time in this community."

"So, he thinks this guy is going to do it?"

"Yeah. He said he met the guy and thinks he's unhinged."

Cici became quiet, waiting.

"You want me to help them, don't you?"

"Do you think you could?"

"Well, I was thinking of taking some vacation," Nat said. "Security work is boring as hell."

"There you go," Cici said.

"So, cancel that romantic Caribbean cruise?"

"Oh God, that would be amazing," Cici said wistfully. "But you hate ships and would be bored out of your mind anyway."

"I'd suffer through it," Nat said wryly, "If it weren't for the ban."

"Ugh! Depressing!"

"So," Nat said. "The job is getting the wife and the kids out of there before the potentially murderous hubby is any wiser?"

"Or you could just go knock his teeth down his throat, mash his *cojones* like a doormat on your way out the door with the innocents. Something like that…"

"I'm in," Nat said. "Send the details."

"You sure?" Cici said.

"Yeah."

"Girl," Cici continued when Nat said nothing more. "You are so badass. You know that, right?"

Nat grunted noncommittally.

"You sure you don't want to hang out later?"

"I got a thing," Nat said, taking out her keys as she arrived at her door. "Maybe this weekend?"

"Okay! Adios, *querida*!"

Her roommate barely looked up from his book and waved, seeing she was in a hurry.

"I warmed up some leftovers for you," he said.

"Thanks! How is the research paper going?"

"It'll be there when I get to it."

Nat quickly picked up the plate and thanked him as she ate on her way to her room. Unbidden, her mind returned to the sneering face of the other boxer at the gym. He was getting more hostile, she thought. If he's in with the TUF crowd, then he'll make trouble for me sooner or later. Might be time for a new gym.

She selected her clothes and showered. As she got ready, her eyes lingered on the black dog tags hanging on her mirror. She kissed her fingertips and touched them to the tags before she left the room.

Her nose crinkled at the dishes in the sink as she put her own into the dishwasher. Her roommate said nothing as she walked out the door and headed to the library. It was chess night, and she was scheduled to lecture on the Caro-Kann opening.

CHAPTER 2

Germ lines
Are the twines of life
Brittle belts that gird the future
Not by hope, for fabric cannot feel
but by mere existence does unreel
into random, beautiful material
Until weaved by will

Aisling pondered the words written on the curved glass as she sat in her powered wheelchair. It was such a lofty goal when I wrote that, she thought. Then, it was like looking to land on the moon when the Wright brothers had just learned to fly. We're a bit further along now, I think.

The hum of the machines in the room and the low gurgling of fluid had a way of putting Aisling's mind at ease as she turned her attention to the human figure suspended inside the large, glass cylinder. Daryl was running the status metrics through the overhead speakers at a low volume. She only partially listened. The room was well-lit, sterile, and crowded with medical equipment and robotic machines. The walls were smooth, whitewashed concrete.

Occasionally, the figure twitched and spasmed in the fluid as the inter-neural stimulator cycled through the plyometric algorithms that ensured the muscles and bones grew and the nerve signals were strong.

The future and past are always converging, she thought, but some moments change the trajectory of our lives in ways we can only imagine. Is it hubris or careful planning that propels me in this direction today? Is this how I spend my last few hours, filled with hopes and dreams—only to have them obliterated by my own oversights?

She shifted carefully in her wheelchair. The ever-present pain spiked, radiating throughout her body. It was a raging fire that she had to suppress constantly, or it would consume her mind.

The palliative surgery her doctor had proposed would have relieved the pain permanently until she died, but she felt she couldn't risk the possibility of adverse interactions. In some ways, constantly managing the pain had given her incredible mental clarity over the past years. What held her attention now was the prospect and the technical nature of the process ahead. Many, many things could go wrong, and there was only one shot. This was both the end and the beginning for her. Adrenaline became an inexorable tide within her.

The female figure's random movements eventually turned itself enough that Aisling could partially see the cranial cavity.

Inside its open skull, there was no brain.

The digital neural spindle was extended from the edge of the incubation chamber to directly interface with various structures of the brain stem, acting in a similar way to the missing neocortex. It was a complicated machine of living tissue, unable to feel or experience anything since birth as it floated sightless in the void.

How tranquil it looks, she thought. An insentient existence. If I fail, my only consolation would be the exchange of misery and agony for happy oblivion.

"...And yet to find some ease of this, my pain," Aisling murmured, "I give myself to silence and such tears as floweth in distress: and if this fail, at last, the deadly thunder shall break my bonds."

"Daryl," she said louder. "Do you know who that is?"

"I do not understand the question," Daryl replied. "You quoted lines from Sonnet 29, by William Shakespeare. How can a poem be referred to as 'who?'"

"Good question. A quirk of the English language. Also, coincidentally, you answered my question."

"Noted. We're ready to proceed with stage thirty-two, step sixteen point three," Daryl said. "Do you wish to begin the cognitive state query process?"

"So it begins..."

The moment hung heavy on her heart. She had made the decision, but every step she took brought her closer to the cliff. She wanted to hang on, but the cliff was an illusion of solidity, crumbling imperceptibly beneath her feet. Soon, there would be no turning back—a choice between one chance for life or certain death.

Is my will part of the fabric of life, or does my sentient

awareness separate me from the laws of nature? Is my knowledge of my existence by itself a rationalization of my actions? If I am but the fabric, then is it a choice?

She took a deep, painful breath.

"I'm ready," she whispered.

Daryl began asking her a series of questions.

"What did you eat for lunch?"

"I skipped lunch," she replied.

"Who was the last person you spoke with?"

"Jonas."

Aisling slowly and painfully moved out of the wheelchair as she answered the questions, assisted by robotic arms. She undressed completely and stood in the washing area. The robotic arms carefully painted the cold povidone-iodine onto her freckled skin, which was sallow and paper-thin. She could see and count her ribs. By the time she got into position on the table, she was shivering and breathing hard from the agonizing effort.

Daryl continued through the list of questions, oblivious to her pain. It was soothing for the computer program she wrote to not treat her compassionately. It helped her focus. People often patronized her too much. At this moment, she was grateful Daryl could do nothing but stick to the program. I will need to build in more compassion in the future.

The table felt cold against her already goose-pimpled skin. As she settled into position on the flat surface, answering more questions, she watched as the robotic arms meticulously sought out her port catheter and attached it to a drip. Another pair of arms attached a fingertip pulse oximeter and EMG electrodes to the major muscle groups of her body. She rolled to her side, and the robots attached more sensors all over her back. As the final sensors were added, Daryl grilled her on computational theory, bioinformatics, physics, and astronomical equations. The robotic arms carefully shaved what remained of her pale auburn hair. Another iodine bath for her scalp. The questioning paused only when the water-tight earplugs were inserted gently into her ears and the bone-conducting audio system was settled against her cheekbones.

"Soundcheck," Daryl said, the voice seemed to come from everywhere.

"Good."

The questions continued as the robots sterilized her scalp

a second time with more iodine, then applied a sterile saline solution. An anesthesia breathing mask appeared in her vision.

"Questionnaire complete," Daryl intoned. "Are you ready for sedation?"

Here it was. The cliff. Daryl's voice reverberated through her skull. This precise moment had been in her mind for two decades. She had imagined how she would feel countless times, but nothing came close to the irreversible nature of this moment. This is the moment, she thought, where I choose to separate myself from the fortunes of humanity. To be free, one way or another.

She took a deep breath, counting to five. Then ten. Another deep breath.

"Yes, I'm ready."

***

"Thanks for doing this," the social worker said. "I know it's not your usual gig."

"It's fine." Nat watched the surroundings. The area was rural. She noted several Confederate flags. One house had a sign that read "Adam and Eve, not Adam and Steve." There seemed to be more churches than houses.

"She's terrified," he continued. "I'm still trying to convince her to file for a divorce."

"She hasn't told him yet?"

"No, but she thinks he knows. He accuses her of trying to leave him. He's making threats."

"If she doesn't want a divorce and hasn't filed a restraining order, what does she want?"

The social worker glanced at her with a side-eye.

"Two weeks ago," he said flatly, "a woman filed for a restraining order against her husband. She cited fearing for her life. Death threats. But her husband was a respected factory worker with no history of violence, no record. The magistrate denied it. Last week he killed her, his children, and himself. It all happened about five miles from here."

"Damn," Nat said.

"Mrs. Lo fears for her and her children's lives. She doesn't have anywhere to go and believes her relatives would send her right back to him or lead him to her. Happens all the time around here. I don't think she'd make it far. She needs someone outside of her community to help hide and protect her."

"She can't stay with me," Nat said.

"I have a place for her and the kids to stay," he said. "The problem is convincing her to go and making sure Mr. Lo doesn't know about it."

"So where is he now?"

"Working at the cannery."

They slowed and turned into Sleepy Ridge Trailer Park.

"Go slower," Nat said. "And don't stop when we get there. Just drive around a bit first."

"Casing the place out?"

"You watch too many movies," Nat said dismissively.

"When you've seen the shit I've seen, the movies are welcome," he said. "The cheesier, the better."

The trailers were arranged in rows. Tidy lines make for good lines of sight, Nat thought. The trees were old and covered with moss. Everything had an air of disrepair. There was evidence of children in the neighborhood, sun-worn toys in random places. But there were no children outside playing. They turned down a street named Terrace Drive and he indicated the third trailer with his chin.

"That's it."

"No need to whisper. Just keep going."

The trailer home was painted sky blue. A couple of the windows were boarded up. The door had a dilapidated staircase with a small platform. A few broken toys were littered around the yard. In the window next to the door, Nat could see the tiny face of a child looking out forlornly.

Through the trailers across the street, Nat could see a rusty pickup. The cab wasn't empty.

"Which way?" he asked when they reached the end of the street.

"Right," Nat said. "Do you know what the husband drives?"

"An old Chevy, I think."

"Turn right down the last street," she said. "Then drive out the way we came in."

She pulled up her GPS app with satellite view.

"Take us here," she said, showing him her phone.

"You don't want to stop to meet them now?"

"No, not with you," she said.

He had a perplexed expression and seemed to be wondering if he should be taking offense to her comment. She ignored him.

As they turned onto the last street, Nat noted the spaces between every trailer. The Chevy came into view. She could clearly see a man's figure behind the steering wheel. He had a pair of binoculars and was raising them to his eyes.

Playing hooky, Mr. Lo? Nat thought.

They left the trailer park.

"So why are we here?" The social worker asked, letting go of the wheel when they arrived.

"I'll take it from here," she said.

She opened the back door and pulled out her duffel bag, and the social worker watched. The squareness of her jaw and the intensity of her look, as she walked to the trunk of the car, reminded him of a commando.

"Her name is Sia," he said. She didn't respond.

The social worker had a big heart. She suspected he wanted her to explain her intentions. To interact more. To assure him that she had it all under control. She shook her head imperceptibly.

"I'll text her to let her know you're coming."

"Text me the address of the safe house," Nat said, closing the trunk and slinging her duffel over her shoulders.

"How are you going to get there?"

She walked to the driver's side door and forced her face to soften.

"You're a good man. I've got it from here. They'll be fine. You take care."

She slapped the top of the roof twice and then jogged off into a cluster of trees between the parking lot and the highway. He watched her go and wondered why the plan had changed so suddenly.

***

"So, what do you think Jesus meant?" Jonas asked his son. It was hard for him to mask his pride. David was eleven, brilliant and kind. It warmed Jonas' heart that he was so interested in the Bible, and it saddened him that David's older brother, Jonathan, was not. Sure, Jonathan was as obedient as any other teenage boy in high school, but Jonas knew his heart was not in it like David's was.

"I'm a little confused," David said, "I thought that He was the 'Prince of Peace,' but here he is saying that he 'did not come to bring peace on earth.'"

"That's right," Chris, Jonas' wife, said gently. "In Isaiah 9:6, Christ is called the Prince of Peace, and in Matthew 5:9, Jesus says, 'Blessed are the peacemakers, for they will be called the children of God.' Remember that?"

"Oh yeah," said David. "I'm so forgetful."

"Don't worry," Jonas said, winking at Chris. "Not everyone can remember as well as your mom. You'll get it."

"I'm nothing special," Chris said matter-of-factly. "So, what do you think is different about Matthew 10:34?"

David considered this for a while, rereading the passage to himself. Chris glanced up at Jonas with joy in her eyes. It was a joy they shared deep in their souls.

"I think," David said after a moment, "that when Jesus is talking about being a peacemaker, he's talking about humanity as a whole. But, here, he's talking about family. That some people in the family maybe won't accept Him, and...and..."

David's eyes began to tear up. Jonas' phone vibrated in his pocket. He ignored it.

"And what, sweetie?" Chris asked. Jonas squeezed his son's shoulder.

"I think this is happening to us," David said. "I think we believe, but Jonathan doesn't. He's sometimes mean to me. He calls me a 'Jesus freak'. Does that mean that we're enemies?"

Chris' worried eyes met Jonas'. They hadn't heard of this before. David's lips were quivering, and he was openly crying now.

"Oh, sweetie," Chris said.

"I don't think you should take that too literally, son," Jonas said. "Kids often say mean things they don't really mean. It's part of growing up. You're not enemies. You're brothers. Brothers fight sometimes. I fought with my brothers all the time!"

"Davey," Chris said to David, "what matters is that you are on the path to salvation through Jesus, and someday Jonathan will be too. In his own time. You must love him as your brother so that you never become enemies within your own heart."

Jonas was taken aback. He felt a deep love for his wife through her interpretation and the visible way that it calmed David down. David hugged them both, long and hard.

They tucked David in, kissed his forehead in turns, and walked to the door. David's room décor was simple, almost spartan. Everything was neatly put away.

"Goodnight, son," Jonas said.

"Goodnight, Dad. I love you!"

"Love you too, son."

Jonas and Chris held hands as they walked down the hall to Jonathan's room. Jonas squeezed her hand tightly before he knocked and opened the door.

Jonathan, as usual, had his headphones in. He was doing homework, glancing from his tablet to his notebook. His room was a mess. There were a couple of band posters, clothes strewn everywhere, and unmade plaid sheets on his bed. Chris' grip tightened around his hand, and Jonas returned the squeeze. In his pocket, Jonas' phone was buzzing.

Jonas called out to Jonathan again, who jerked up and turned to see them.

"Hey," he said. His tone always sounded guarded. Chris had confided to Jonas that it seemed hostile or defensive to her.

"How's the homework going, Johnny?" Jonas asked.

"Alright," Jonathan said.

"Still doing well?" Chris asked.

"Yup. Straight A's." Jonathan said. He used the words as a shield.

"That's good," Jonas began. "Have you given any more thought as to what college you might want to attend?"

"Daaad..."

"It's important," Jonas said defensively.

"Yeah, I know," Jonathan responded, "That's why I'm not rushing."

"You could seek your answer in God through prayer," Chris said. Her voice was gentle, but she spoke with urgency.

Jonathan's mouth tightened as he weighed his response carefully. He estimated that he had about two more hours of homework to do, putting him at seven hours of sleep. A lengthy discussion here would further impact his day tomorrow.

"I'll think about it," he said.

"Johnny," Jonas said, "we need to talk about how you're treating your brother."

"It's fine," Jonathan said. He wasn't sure what his dad meant, but he didn't want to talk about it.

"He's crying."

"Okay," Jonathan said, looking away, ashamed. "Okay, I'm

sorry. I'll do better."

"Thank you, son," Jonas said, not wanting to prolong the conversation. His phone was buzzing non-stop now.

"Good night, sweetie," Chris said, kissing him on the forehead. Jonathan hugged her back. "Don't stay up too late."

"I know," he replied.

"Good night, son," Jonas said. "We love you."

"Love you too."

They walked out together, Chris deep in thought.

"Honey," Jonas said, pulling out his phone and seeing nine missed calls from Dr. Tamma. "It looks like something important is going on at work. Can we talk about Johnny tomorrow?"

"That's fine," said Chris.

Jonas kissed her.

"Goodnight, darling."

"Goodnight."

Jonas then walked to his study, checked his appearance, and called Dr. Tamma via video conference.

"Hello, Scott," Jonas said. "What's up?"

"I have good news and bad news," Dr. Tamma said. He was more haggard than usual.

"Bad first," Jonas said.

"Our lobbyists reported that a coalition of conservative senators is proposing a new bill that will ban aspects of genetic research. If passed, it may jeopardize several of our key projects, including the project for which I have good news."

"And what is that?" Jonas asked.

"You know the idea that Dr. Ramsey sent us last week?"

"What about it?"

"I've run it by the team, and it is fucking brilliant," Dr. Tamma said excitedly. "We are all very optimistic that she's solved it. I'm confident that we can test in-vitro by next week."

"That's great news!" Jonas said, feeling excited. "That soon?"

Dr. Tamma nodded, grinning.

"The first test is simple," he said. "But it will be the first of many."

Jonas returned Dr. Tamma's smile for a moment, but it started slipping as he began to think about the implications of the bill.

He had every reason to believe that with the conservative nationalists in control of the White House, the Senate, and the House, along with the conservative majority on the Supreme Court, this bill would likely pass and go unchallenged. It was too early to tell precisely which provisions in the bill would impact the project. He would need to get details as quickly as possible so that they could lobby to carve out the appropriate exemptions. He began to feel exasperated. While he fundamentally agreed with conservatives in many areas, he disliked extreme fundamentalist views.

"With this new data," Jonas asked, "what is the best and worst case?"

"Well, the worst case is that it ends up being a suited seven-two on a rainbow flop," Dr. Tamma said. "In that case, we'll have to muck the whole project."

"Best case?"

"Best case?" Dr. Tamma leaned toward his laptop. "Royal flush, baby! We fucking cure every form of cancer there is."

CHAPTER 3

"Hello, Aisling. Please let me know when you are awake."

She could hear music playing. Time stretched as she struggled to open her eyes. She was no longer lying face up on the table. She felt the table against her front and the pressure of the pillow framing her face. She could see the glow of the screens through her eyelids before she was able to open them fully. When she did, her vision was blurry.

"Hello, Aisling. Please let me know when you are awake."

Slowly, the screens below her came into focus while she struggled to concentrate. That was key. That was first. Her conscious thoughts seemed to wade through a thick sea of heavy, foggy impressions, each on the edge of her attention. Did anything go wrong? Did I forget something? Her eyes were dry and ached as she tried to keep them open.

"Hello, Aisling. Please—"

"I'm..." she began. There was a tingling numbness in her lips, and her throat was scratchy.

"...getting there."

"Great!" Daryl said. "Take your time. Meanwhile, please try to stop drooling."

She laughed—or tried to. She remembered planning that joke for this moment, and wondering if she would remember doing so. A good sign.

"Thanks," she said. Her vision was slowly improving.

Before her, the monitors she was straining to see displayed her vital signs along the edges. Everything was green, which was good, although she couldn't quite make out the exact numbers yet. The screen on the right displayed different views of her head and the back of her neck. She didn't need to see the screen clearly to know that she could not move her head as it was entirely secured in an immobilization unit. Her body felt ethereal. She knew it was there, a phantom entity, but she could not sense it. She was unable to control her limbs. It was a scary feeling, but she reminded herself it would pass.

As her vision sharpened, the images on the screens came into focus.

They displayed her own open brain surgery.

The screens were high-resolution and stereoscopic, so it seemed she was hovering over herself. She could control her angle of view by directing her eyes at the edges of the screen.

She had made a three-dimensional model of her brain during preparations for this day, so she immediately recognized the various patterns in her gyri, the wrinkles of the brain. If she had actually been standing above herself, she would not have seen her body at all because it was completely encased in the surgical machine. She could feel and hear the loud hum of it. She knew the image she was watching was a simulation built by six different sensor systems. Her actual body and brain were now encased in a chamber filled with cerebral spinal fluid.

She could see the veins and arteries pulsing slightly as she observed the folds and valleys of her neocortex, absently labeling each region to distract herself. It would be all too easy to freak out at the knowledge of what was happening to her. Knowing what she was doing to herself. Knowing there was no way back.

"Status?"

"Nominal," Daryl replied.

Ever so slowly, the effects of the sedation began to wear off, and the familiar dull ache of pain began to settle in. She had known this would come, but the knowledge did not lessen the pain.

There was a pragmatic reason to resist the urge to use too much sedation. She needed to be conscious and feeling during many parts of the surgery, as those feedback mechanisms would be necessary to create accurate neural mappings.

"I am ready to apply the sensory membrane," Daryl said.

"Proceed."

There wasn't much for her to do now as Daryl worked. The transparent membrane Daryl was now covering her brain with was a temporary structure meant to capture and record as much neural activity as possible. Her only task now was to watch as the sedation wore off. To experience. She couldn't sense anything as the membrane settled directly onto her brain, starting at the top of her spine. The first three vertebrae of her cervical spine were opened, exposing her spinal cord.

It got worse. Both of her ears were gone. The skull was cut

from ear to ear right above her eyes. She could robotically move the camera around to see her face if she wanted to. However, it would be mostly obscured by the face pillow and frame keeping her still, the breathing apparatus over her mouth and nose, and the narrow visual goggles over her eyes. A real-time simulation of her face without the attached equipment was available for her to view if she wanted. But knowing her whole forehead was missing would've made that disconcerting. Aisling kept the view on the rear of her head as Daryl finished laying the membrane over the surface of her brain.

"Membrane in place," Daryl said. "Stage one hundred eighty-six is complete. Commence one hundred eighty-seven?"

"Proceed," she said.

The robotic arms moved away, and the intense hum of the fMRI equipment seemed to grow louder. Daryl unceremoniously began asking her another long series of questions. She answered question after question, identifying any unexpected sensations or reactions. She identified thousands of images and read lists of random words.

They fell into a rhythm of questions and answers for the next fourteen hours. While she understood precisely what was being done, having designed and programmed the entire procedure, she was now just along for the ride. Machine learning algorithms codified and mapped her neural pathways first by observation, then by suppression and stimulation. It was a jarring sensation to have a thought prompted by Daryl's stimulations. They felt like they were her own thoughts, but they were random and disjointed.

As Daryl transitioned through the regions of her neocortex, stimulating each with the delicate electrodes within the sensory membrane, they worked together to meticulously verify and update the neural somatosensory map of her brain.

When it was time for her to sleep, Daryl continued monitoring and mapping her neural patterns. Aisling hated sleeping. She never slept more than five hours unaided, but the system helped her to sleep longer.

Her dreams were scattered fragments—artifacts from all the questions and tests. But there was one dream she remembered in which she walked into a meadow. It was a small field at the base of a mountain amid scrub oak. She had been there before, on a field trip in middle school. She remembered

loving those trips and learning about the Rocky Mountains'
ecology in that hands-on way. In the dream, Darrell was there.
The first boy she had ever kissed—her first love. He stood
alone with her in the meadow, their fingers interlaced.

"You told me you always wanted to go to outer space,"
Darrell said.

"Yes!" she said. "I want to see an Earthrise! From the moon!"

He smiled and wordlessly shifted his gaze up at the sky. She
did too. Darrell seemed to float upward, pulling her with him.
She could see her sneakers hovering over the long grass. Then,
they were flying. They flew toward the low and fluffy clouds,
and she wondered what they would taste like. But then they
flew past them, toward the moon. She gripped Darrell's hand
in excitement.

Aisling woke to find the display still showing her brain. It was
zoomed in on a cortical structure, presumably whatever Daryl
was focused on. The feeling of weightlessness was still with
her, along with the feeling of Darrell's hand in hers.

"How long was I asleep?" she asked.

"Eight hours and twenty-three minutes," Daryl said.

"Did I ever tell you why I named you Daryl?" she asked.

"No."

"I guess I hadn't," she said. "If you're ever curious, I'll tell you."

"Are you ready to proceed to the next step?"

Things continued in this manner for days, with nutrition
and fluids provided by the IV. It was mind-numbing, but the
sense of adventure never left her. She dreamt of flying or
running free across the meadow. She dreamt of Darrell and her
parents.

After nearly a week of this, Daryl finally announced that the
rough cerebral mapping was complete.

"All systems are stable, and I am now ready to install the
Hypercortex, stage six hundred eighty-eight."

Aisling took several deep breaths.

"You have a few missed calls," Daryl continued. "Would you
like to address them before we continue?"

"No," she said. "But I should."

She reviewed them and carefully responded with texts and
emails by dictating to Daryl.

"Are you ready to proceed?" Daryl asked when they were
finished.

Aisling paused for a moment. This was another point of no

return. Once the Hypercortex touched her brain, there was no way to stop the process. It would become a part of her brain for the rest of her life. It was untested on humans. She would be the first and probably the only person to undergo this procedure. If it were unsuccessful, she would have a half-billion-dollar lump of useless material inside her skull for the rest of her very short life, until it was burned away in the crematorium.

"Proceed…"

The sensory membrane was removed, and another incredibly thin membrane was added. It was less than a dozen nanometers thick. As soon as the thin polymeric membrane touched the brain, it vanished as it instantly permeated and transformed the matter on the outermost layers of her brain. She felt nothing except anticipation. On the screen, the Hypercortex appeared. Like the surface of her brain, it too appeared wrinkled, but the outer folds were denser. It was black, with a dark blue sheen like a wrinkled solar panel, but soft and pliable. It had the same thick, gelatinous consistency as her brain. She could not see the underside of it from this angle, but she knew the interior of the membrane was shaped to fit the surface of her brain exactly. It was thickest near the middle, about where it would rest on the top-back part of her brain, above the parietal lobes. It thinned out over the occipital lobes. It tapered toward the edges, almost thin enough to see through at the front, where it would cover the part of her brain that rested behind her forehead and her eyes—the prefrontal cortex.

At first contact, she thought it was eerie to have again felt no sensation. She knew she would never feel anything touching her brain, but she had anticipated sensation the way one anticipates catching a ball. Within a few moments, it was done. Anticlimactic, Aisling thought.

"Stage six hundred eighty-eight complete."

From here, integrating the hypercortex would be an exceedingly slow process. Upon contact with the special polymer now coating her brain, the new cortical hemisphere would begin to generate millions of tiny organo-electric receptors, which were made of self-forming and articulating carbon nanotubes. They began slowly growing into the outer layers of her brain.

"Ready for more tests?" Daryl asked.

"I thought you'd never ask."

"I don't understand."

"Never mind."

The exhausting and repetitive tests continued for weeks as the receptors grew through her gray matter. Each receptor was less than twenty nanometers thick and had to grow about two millimeters long. Then, they would branch and multiply in channels, with hundreds of branches interacting with dendrites and axons more than ten times their size. It would take over a year for them to stop growing and ultimately connect to every axon terminal and dendrite in every layer of her brain.

Aisling lost all sense of time. She knew, from her monitor, precisely what the date and time were. Still, there was this awful feeling as if she had been doing this for as long as she could remember. In college, her course load had been so heavy she hadn't had much time for activities beyond studying and sleeping. It was a multi-year marathon that never stopped, and she had loved it. Starting SolviNext with Jonas had been even more of a whirlwind. In some ways, this was similar. One got lost in work, consumed by purpose.

It wasn't as though I had a real choice, she thought sadly. My body was scheduled to die within months, so this was always going to be a race against the clock.

One day, after another series of tests, Daryl fell silent. For a while now, Aisling was beginning to think that the whole effort was failing. Several vital tests had failed, and her patience was nearing its end.

"Attempt one hundred sixty-eight," Daryl said. "...failure. Modifying algorithm. Attempt one hundred sixty-nine..."

"Please say codeword 'green eggs' if you can hear this," she heard Daryl say.

"Green eggs," Aisling said.

"Great! Successful attempt logged."

"Aisling," Daryl said after another few days of mostly unsuccessful tests. "You'll be happy to know that the last twenty minutes of our testing was completed without using your larynx."

She was taken aback. This was not unexpected, but it had taken so long. It meant that the hypercortex was finally functioning perfectly! It had taken two months. Two months of constant, grueling, endless tests and failures.

So, she thought, you can now hear my thoughts?

Yes, Daryl responded, in her mind.

***

Nat watched the social worker pull out of the parking lot. He tried to look for her through the trees as he drove but did not see her. *If I had shown up with the case worker*, she thought, *hubby might have been triggered, and I would have to protect him, too. The fewer people in that sardine can, the better.*

When the social worker was out of sight, Nat set out at a run. The trees turned to knee-high grass, and she kept running, checking her position on the GPS. She took an angle that wouldn't expose her to Mr. Lo's view.

The scenarios ran through her mind like a chess game. *When I show up alone, I am a random stranger, and Mr. Lo won't know what to think. Maybe he waits for me to leave. Or, he's willing to kill me too. Maybe if he sees me as a threat, armed and ready, he will just leave.*

Whatever you decide, pendejo, I want to know what you're thinking before you do.

After rounding the neighborhood, she came to the street where the truck was parked. There was a large bush between her and the truck. Discreetly looking around, she stopped jogging and set her duffel down, pretending to be taking a break. She pulled out her water bottle, took a few swigs, and faked being winded.

If I attacked now, she thought, *you wouldn't see it coming. We'd be done. Too bad it's not that easy.*

She was reasonably sure no one was watching, but she wanted to be careful. Setting her water bottle down, she did a runner's lunge, eying the juniper bush beside her for an ideal spot. She reached into her bag and quickly slipped a camera into the bush, clamping it to a branch. She tried to make the movement look like a yoga pose in case someone was watching and then pulled out her phone to check the camera feed.

A notification caught her eye. It was a text from her brother. She hesitated before checking it.

"Mom's dying. She wants to see you. Come home."

A flood of emotion coursed through her. *Paso a Paso, Nat,* she thought. *One thing at a time.* Ruthlessly, she shut away her thoughts of home and turned off her notifications.

She checked the camera feed. It was perfect.

Through the camera, she watched Mr. Lo take a hefty swig of

booze from a half-empty bottle. He raised a set of binoculars.

Nat stowed her phone and swung the bag back on before jogging the rest of the way to the blue trailer. She heard clinking dishes and running water inside.

Watch me carefully, *cabrón*, she thought as she walked up the stairs casually. As soon as she knocked, the sounds inside stopped abruptly.

"Mrs. Lo," Nat said, loud enough for them to hear. "Your caseworker sent me. I'm here to protect you and your family."

There was a pause, followed by someone moving to the door. Nat stepped back as the door opened outward.

Mrs. Lo had to crane her neck up to be able to look Nat in the eye.

"You are Nat?" she asked timidly. She had a thick Asian accent.

"Yes." Nat set the duffel bag on the porch and unzipped it, reaching inside.

"You are not man," Mrs. Lo said.

"Nope." Nat hefted a shotgun.

Nat flourished the weapon, spinning it and bringing it to rest on her shoulder. She chambered a shell. It was all a show for Mr. Lo's benefit. If he knows I'm armed, she thought, maybe he'll pack up and go home to his mother.

Mrs. Lo took a step back, surprise on her face. When she had gathered herself, she waved Nat in. Nat found that she had to duck slightly as she entered the door. The floor creaked loudly under her weight. Nat glanced around the living room. It was neat and simple. The house smelled of Asian food she couldn't identify. Behind a small partition wall, she could see half of the faces of three children peering out at her. Two girls and their older brother, who Nat thought might be seven or eight. She turned and locked the door, including the flimsy chain lock.

"Go to kitchen," Mrs. Lo said sharply, and the kids disappeared.

"Please, sit."

"Mrs. Lo," Nat said. "We don't have much time. Your husband is watching the house right now."

"What?"

Nat brought up her phone and showed her the video feed.

"He's parked over on Gutty Street as we speak, watching everything."

Mrs. Lo glanced at the video and instantly recognized the

truck. She became anxious and frantic. She glanced toward the kitchen. The kids were sitting around the table watching them. Dinner sat on the table, mostly eaten.

"Don't worry," Nat said. "You're all safe. I have a plan."

"Dad is close by?" said the little boy. He got up from the table, excited.

"Pao," Mrs. Lo said, "Finish eating."

"I wanna see dad," the boy said petulantly. He began moving toward the door. He stopped when he realized Nat was still standing in front of it. His head arched back as he took in her height. Nat fixed him with a scowl that she only half felt. She understood what it was like to miss your dad, even if he wasn't the best of men.

"Pao!" Mrs. Lo said, raising her voice. She spoke to him in a language Nat didn't understand.

The boy stared up at Nat, not moving. Nat weighed her options. She would need him to cooperate later.

"You look strong for your age."

He didn't answer.

"I'll bet you could lift your little sister up all by yourself," Nat continued.

He nodded. His chest puffed out briefly.

"You love your dad, don't you?" Nat asked, squatting in front of him. He still had to crane his neck.

He nodded.

"I see," she said. "Well, the man out there isn't really your dad."

"What do you mean?"

"Did you ever see your dad become mean after drinking beer?"

He nodded, then looked down. Tears began to fill his eyes.

"The man out there is drunk," Nat said gently. "He's angry. He's mad. That will make him do bad things."

The boy fidgeted.

"So," Nat said. "I know you love your dad when he isn't like that. But when he is, you have to be strong. You have to help protect your mom and your sisters."

"He promised he wouldn't do it anymore!"

The boy fought back tears.

"I know it's hard to accept," Nat said. "But he broke his promise. Will you help me get your family out of here until your dad calms down?"

He thought about it for a moment, then nodded.

"Good man," Nat said, putting her hand on his shoulder.

She turned to her phone to schedule a ride. Mrs. Lo busied herself with getting the kids to eat the rest of their meal and preparing a plate for Nat.

"We have sixteen minutes," Nat shook her head at the food.

"For what?" Mrs. Lo asked.

"To gather your stuff," Nat answered, "I'm sending you all somewhere safe."

As she spoke, she checked the feed. Mr. Lo appeared to be moving about in the cab of the truck and gesticulating sharply. He tossed the empty bottle out the window. I'll bet he's not going home to mommy, she thought grimly.

"Do you mind if I look around?" she asked, barely waiting for Mrs. Lo's answer as she walked through the kitchen and into the hall.

"Pack for an overnight stay," Nat said over her shoulder. "Quickly."

The interior was much as she had imagined it, given the pattern of windows she had observed throughout the neighborhood. In a moment, she located what she was searching for—the back room on the southeast corner. There were three small pillows and a disheveled blanket on top of a mattress on the floor. The window she had in mind was boarded up and had no glass. Nat kicked the wood. The resulting crash was so loud she heard gasps from the kitchen.

She pushed the boards away and climbed through the window, bringing a camera. As she scanned the area, she could hear movement and exclamations of surprise from the adjacent trailers. A curtain flicked. Nat took note but stayed focused on her task. She moved to the edge of the trailer and mounted the camera to the side of the house where it gave her a full view of the front door.

Glancing around, she saw someone coming out of the next trailer. They had a gun. Nat stopped mid-motion. She slowly raised her hands and turned toward the neighbor. He was an older, heavyset man who walked with a limp. He had a US Veteran cap on.

"You ain't who I was expectin'," the man said, giving her a once over. "Whatcha' doin' there?"

"Which branch?" she asked.

"I'll be asking the questions," he said grimly, enunciating each word. "And don't think I won't lay you flat, ma'am. I said, what are you doing there?"

"Installing a camera," she said. "I'm here to protect Mrs. Lo and her family from who you thought I was."

The man was quiet, considering. He glanced at the broken boards from the window she had exited.

"I need to be quick," she said. "He's in the neighborhood."

"So you're out of the service, and now you're some kind of vigilante?" he asked, the gun still pointed squarely at her chest.

"No," she said. "I work security now."

"Like a bodyguard? Family's too broke to afford som' like that," he said.

"I gotta keep my soul somehow," she said.

She could see his jaw working beneath his beard as he considered her. He glanced up past her at the window and lowered the gun.

"Called the police," he said.

"Good," Nat responded. She turned toward the window, "You can come out now."

Mrs. Lo looked out the window timidly. Nat beckoned to her. The neighbor walked over to help.

"Expectin' him soon, huh?" He reached up to help Nat hold the child Mrs. Lo was helping through the window.

"Yes," she said. "He's been watching the trailer for some time. Do you have any security cameras?"

"Not on this side."

Nat pulled out her phone and glanced at the camera feeds. The truck was gone.

"Shit," she said under her breath.

"He's on the move?"

Nat nodded and pointed.

"I have a ride coming for them on your street there. Can you escort them to the pick-up safely? I'll cover the rear."

"Thought you'd never ask," he said.

After helping the last child out the window, Mrs. Lo climbed out. Nat jumped and muscled up through the window, back into the trailer, in one fluid motion.

"Marines," the man called after her.

"Army."

Down the street, they could both hear the approaching truck.

"Good luck," he said. "You give that soma-bitch what he

deserves."

"I'm just here to make sure they get out safely," she said.

***

Jonas flipped the burgers on the grill, his stomach rumbling. They were coming along nicely. He glanced up, taking in the summer scene. The family reunion was going well. Some relatives were playing volleyball in the field by the swimming pool while the toddlers splashed away with their parents or bigger siblings and cousins. The sun was warm, but a cool breeze took the heat away. In the distance, the Sandia Mountains were illuminated by the evening sun.

Chris walked up, hugging him.

"'Bout five minutes," he said.

"Good," she said. "The tables are set."

"I love you," Jonas said, staring into her beautiful blue eyes. She smiled in her special way—a smile she only had for him.

"I love you too, you big oaf in an apron."

"Hey!" he said, pointing at the words on the apron. "Reading is fundamental!"

She closed the gap and pecked him on the cheek.

"I was kinda hoping for more than that," he said slyly.

"More than that," she said coyly, "and we'd need a room."

"That can be arranged."

"Your brats are burning," she laughed as she walked away.

Jonas turned back to the grill, smiling. Everything was sizzling nicely, so he unloaded several items onto the serving plate. A line of folks holding plates quickly materialized.

"Hey bro," came a lazy voice behind him. Jonas grimaced and turned to see his older brother Andy walk up. He was sucking on a vape and was casually dressed in jeans and a t-shirt that read, 'The earth is flat and gravity is a lie.'

Andy hastily put the vape away. He knew Jonas didn't like it when he smoked around him. Andy was trailed by his ever-present sidekick, who had no such courtesy. Andy's friend exhaled a thick vapor plume as they loaded their plates.

"Hey," Jonas said, turning back to the grill.

"What?" Andy flippantly said, "No hug? No warm welcome for your long-lost bro?"

Jonas turned, grinning, and pointed with his tongs to the words 'Kiss The Cook' on his apron.

"No thanks," Andy said. Jonas shrugged.

"Last I heard," Jonas said. "You were planning a flight to the ice wall. I see you didn't fall off."

"Oh, that was canceled," Andy said. "As I expected. The government doesn't let anyone near the ice wall."

Jonas rolled his eyes. "Who canceled the flight?"

"I needed the money for something else," Andy said, as he assembled his burger.

Jonas scoffed.

"Well," Andy took a bite and spoke around his food. "They would've canceled it anyway."

"Look," Jonas said. "Let's not get into this today."

"You brought it up," Andy said smoothly. "But, anyway, this stuff is too fucked up just to turn a blind eye, man. As a man with power and influence, you should do more to change it all."

"Well," Jonas said. "You realize that every branch of the U.S. Government has your boys in it now. That's way more power than I have. So why aren't they fixing it?"

"Yeah, well," Andy started. "It'll take time."

"Yeah, they're busy stopping guys like you from flying to Antarctica, right?"

"This is too dry," Andy said to his friend, who nodded despite dragging the last piece of his brat through the juices on his plate.

"You know, they defunded NASA," Jonas said through gritted teeth. "Because of that flat earth nonsense."

Andy and his friend high-fived jovially at that.

Jonas wondered what Ash thought about that. He was well aware of her life-long aspirations for space travel. He hadn't heard from her in a while, besides a few returned messages saying she was in too much pain to talk.

"Yeah, man," Andy was saying excitedly. "God-Emperor Dolion's rolling the Big Purge! GED's on a roll!"

"Yeah, GED's going to shut down the FDA and CDC next, man," said his friend.

"The lib-tards are going crazy," said Andy.

"Gonna be a civil war any day now."

"I hear they're planning some kind of attack."

Jonas flipped several of the brats. He wanted to tell his brother to go bug someone else, but instead, he said. "Hopefully not."

"Yeah," said Andy, "but you gotta prepare for the worst. The libs will probably conscript a UN army and then shit will get crazy!"

"That's just asinine FAT-piss and fearmongering," Jonas blurted out.

"Just wait, bro," Andy said. "Wait, you ain't a Dem now, are you? Why'd you call it FAT?"

"No," Jonas said.

"That's good. But still Republican, huh?"

Jonas sighed. He considered himself staunchly conservative, but he knew that his grandfather would never stand for what the country had become.

The party of Lincoln was dead, replaced by the Truth and Freedom party. Rather than call themselves TAF, they usually called themselves TUF. Their critics had their own acronym. Andy hated it when Jonas called them FAT. They always seemed to argue over the validity of the FAT party's claims, one way or another. He couldn't find a way to reason with his brother. Any facts Jonas quoted seemed to roll off Andy like water off a duck's back.

Jonas was well aware that it was becoming more dangerous to criticize the TUFs openly. He hated the idea that he should have to be careful of what he said on his own property.

"What do you want, Andy?" Jonas asked.

"What do you mean?"

"You know I don't believe any of this shit," Jonas said. "And you never visit unless you want something from me."

"It's the family reunion, bro!"

"You didn't come to the last one," Jonas said. "Instead, you showed up two months later asking for a loan. Do you have any intention of paying me back?"

Andy shrugged and took on a lighter tone, "A little money would be nice, you know? Since Candace died, it's been tough. You wouldn't let me starve, would you?"

"I'm sorry about Candace," Jonas said.

"Damn doctors and their fake science," Andy said. "The vaccines are—"

Jonas groaned.

"Come on, Jonas," Andy said. "You should search it up."

"Maybe you should use that Ivy League degree of yours to get a job instead of wasting your time on all this bullshit," Jonas said. He hadn't meant to say it, but it just came out.

"It's not bullshit, Jonas!"

"Yeah? It's paying the bills, then?"

Andy had not received his inheritance because he had never met the million-dollar threshold. As far as Jonas could tell, Andy spent all his time hanging out with his rich deadbeat friends.

Andy glanced at his friend. Both of them shrugged and turned away.

Jonas could hear the sidekick whispering loudly to Andy.

"The GOP's dead, man! And the Dems are pedos and criminals. GED will take care of them all. You watch!"

As they walked toward the food table, Andy nodded in agreement.

Jonas seethed, angrily poking at the cooking meat.

"Let him be, Jonas," Chris said as she hugged him from behind.

"I never invite him," Jonas said. "He comes when he wants. Smokes that damn thing and practically blows it in my face! Of course, he asked for money again."

"Language, Jonas," Chris said. "And…"

She could see the muscles in Jonas' jawline clenching.

"Those look ready," she said, reaching for a serving plate.

"'Give to the one who asks you,'" Jonas said quietly. "I know."

"You're a wonderful man, my darling," Chris said as he put brats on the plate she held for him.

"I'm concerned," Jonas said, his face troubled.

Chris always thought he was cutest when he furrowed his brow like that. She had married him because she loved his dedication to the Faith and because she had known how good a father he would become. His baby blues were always bright, intelligent, and loving when he looked at her. It didn't hurt that he was also easy on the eyes.

"About what, my dear?"

"It's not the same world Opa lived in," he said. "There are more FAT party loonies in the office than those with sense. Things are on the fast track to go from worse to terrible."

"Well," Chris said. "Think about that another day. You're here now. Our lovely family is here. They're not all like Andy."

"No," he smiled. "They aren't all like that."

CHAPTER 4

Nat closed the window and watched the neighbor walk Mrs. Lo and her kids to where the ride was scheduled to arrive. She couldn't hear the truck clearly from inside the trailer. Adrenaline made it sound closer, though she saw no movement on the front door camera. We should have plenty of time, she thought.

She had to prepare for the possibility that Mr. Lo might enter the trailer. Quickly, she crossed the room and opened the nearest door. It was a bathroom. The next door down was Mr. and Mrs. Lo's bedroom. There was no time to check it for a weapon, so she just assumed there was one. She grabbed the bed and dragged it toward the door, blocking it from opening more than halfway. If he were to get in, it would slow him down and buy her time.

Movement caught her eye through the partially open curtains of the living room window. The truck had pulled up. She stuffed her duffel bag in the cabinet under the kitchen sink and pulled out her phone to monitor the cameras. She set her phone on the floor and crouched behind the stove, placing the heavy metal appliance between her and the door.

Mr. Lo stepped out of the truck, stumbling slightly. Not bothering to close the truck door, he wobbled toward the house, holding a gun.

She double-checked her shotgun and breathed deeply, flexing and relaxing her muscles. Her phone buzzed, indicating that the ride had arrived.

He fumbled with the lock for a while, grunting when the door opened, but stopped at the chain.

"Sia!" he shouted. "Sia! Let me in!"

"Mr. Lo, I'm armed and I will protect your family with deadly force, if necessary!" Nat yelled. "Get out of here!"

"Get the fuck out of my house, bitch!"

"Just leave, Mr. Lo," she yelled back. "If you enter, I will use deadly force against you. The police are on the way."

"Fuck you!" Mr. Lo called, and then abruptly he backed away. He looked as if he was about to charge the door but instead turned and walked down the stairs. He turned and walked toward the camera, glancing up at the kitchen window and shaking his head.

"Sia!" he yelled over and over.

Nat raced to the kids' room. She had hoped he would stay at the front door longer. The video feed spun as Mr. Lo tore the camera from the side of the house and threw it to the ground. The app lost signal a moment later as he stomped on the camera. Nat reached the kids' room window but couldn't see him. She glanced toward where the ride had been parked and a cold fist seized her gut.

Mrs. Lo and the neighbor were still trying to get the kids into the car. The little boy was fighting against his mom, trying to return to the house. The neighbor's wife stood on their porch; the potted plants on the ramshackle deck were shaking from her shifting weight.

Nat saw Mr. Lo round the corner, his weapon hanging in his hand, muzzle toward the ground as he searched in the other bedroom window.

She leveled her weapon.

"Stop right there!" she yelled, aiming. "Drop your weapon!"

Mr. Lo took one more step and stopped. Nat's heart sank. Mr. Lo was now between her and where the neighbor's wife stood. She didn't have a clear shot, and his eyes went from her to his family, where his son still struggled to pull away from his mother.

"Daddy!" the little boy yelled.

Mr. Lo raised his gun toward his wife and kids.

Nat dropped her gun and swung through the window, rolling as she landed.

"Sia!" Mr. Lo yelled.

He fired.

Nat rose and grabbed his wrist, pushing up hard and wrenching the gun free.

Her elbow smashed across his nose.

Mr. Lo tried to step back, but her leg was in the way as he staggered. She tossed the weapon aside and allowed her weight to fall on him as they went down together.

She wrapped an arm around his head and mashed her shoulder into his face.

He swung at her head with his free hand.

She tucked her head beside his and worked her hand to her shoulder from around his head. Methodically, she fed her other hand through, under his chin, and across his throat in an Ezekiel choke.

He struggled hard before suddenly going limp.

Nat held the choke for a breath longer and then stood up. She observed his breathing. Ten seconds, and he'll be awake, she thought.

The neighbor's wife was screaming.

Nat checked Mr. Lo for a pulse and looked for more weapons. Reaching behind her, she grabbed zip ties out of her back pocket and trussed him up.

The neighbor's wife was rushing to her husband who was on the ground, bleeding from the chest. He had put himself between the gun and the family.

Nat dialed the local dispatcher and inserted one of her earbuds. She knew the police were already on their way because the neighbor had said he'd called earlier.

Mrs. Lo held onto her son, and the other kids clutched her, wailing.

There was blood in the neighbor's mouth and he was staring up at his wife wide-eyed, struggling to breathe. There was a sucking sound in his chest and he was trying to cover the wound with his hand.

"Put pressure on the wound!" Nat instructed his wife, grabbing her hand and pressing firmly. "Hold here."

The call connected, and Nat immediately started talking. "One victim, gunshot wound to the chest, Sleepy Ridge Trailer Park. I'm applying first-aid. I hear inbound sirens. Shooter is restrained and regaining consciousness with minor injuries."

She gave them her name and the address as she carefully turned the neighbor to his side.

"No exit wound," she said. She circled around to the front of him and took over applying pressure.

"Go inside," she said to the woman. "Wash your hands. Get a plastic sandwich bag and get back here as quickly as you can."

The woman nodded and ran off. Nat was careful to keep even pressure on the wound while she brought out her knife and cut away his shirt.

"Mrs. Lo," Nat said while glancing at Mr. Lo, who was slowly regaining consciousness. "Take the kids inside your trailer.

They're safe now and don't need to see this."

Mrs. Lo gathered her crying kids, warily backing away from her husband. She stared at him as though expecting him to attack her at any moment.

"Can you still breathe while on your side, Jar Head?" she asked. He nodded, half grin, mostly grimace.

"Was that your wife?"

"Sarah," he nodded.

"Gunna tell me your name now?"

"Major Brian Cade," he struggled to say.

A yelp caused Nat to glance up to see Sarah jerking away from Mr. Lo, who was groggily trying to sit up. She was carrying the whole plastic bag package, glaring furiously at Mr. Lo.

"Major," Nat said firmly. "When I tell you to, breathe out as much as you can."

He nodded as Sarah fell to her knees beside her.

"Oh my god, baby."

"Sarah, I am going to take my hand away. Brian is going to breathe out. As soon as he is done, I need you to put the plastic over the wound."

Sarah pulled out a plastic bag.

"Now, Major," Nat said, pulling away. Sarah did as instructed, and Nat firmly pressed her hand against the plastic and wound.

Nat's eyes snapped to Mr. Lo, who was struggling to get to his feet. The sirens were close, pulling into the neighborhood.

"The shooter is awake," Nat told the dispatcher.

"Do not engage with him," the dispatcher said.

"Oh, I've had more than enough of his ass."

***

Aisling felt uneasy as she watched her brain separating from her body, the entire neocortex now covered by the shiny blue-black surface of the hypercortex. Still, what was most astonishing to her was that she was no longer observing this with her own eyes. Instead, the video signals were being directly sent to her visual cortex. Daryl's voice was being wirelessly sent to her primary auditory cortex via the hypercortex.

"We're in final preparations," Daryl was saying. "The cranio-immune-transfusion is underway. Nerve growth factor proteins and polyethylene glycol saturation are nominal.

Twelve seconds since transection with microsurgical blades. Two hundred seventy-three seconds before optimal fusion window closes."

She was transfixed by the view inside the surgical chamber. Her body was moving away from her stationary brain. One centimeter. Three. Ten. She could see her body taking long, slow breaths, but she had no sensation of breathing. Beside her body, suspended by three long robotic fingers, were the sections of her skull that had been removed for the surgery.

Robotic arms were already in the process of re-constructing the tissues around her cervical spine and re-attaching her skull. With delicate precision, the robots worked to apply specialized stem cells to each layer of tissue before reattaching them.

For the next six weeks, her old body would float alive in the darkness on the life support regulated by a small microprocessor that looked like an earring on her right ear. Under the careful supervision of the robots, her old body's skin and bones would heal to the point of almost invisible scarring. Then, after being stitched back together with living tissue to fill the brain cavity, it would spend the remainder of its days under the care of an in-home hospice nurse. When it succumbed to cancer, the morticians would suspect no other cause of death.

What about my old body can I truly say identifies who I am? She wondered. *Obviously, my brain was housed in that flesh for the totality of my existence until now. But, was any part of it a piece of who I am?*

While other kids were out learning how to play in their gangling, awkward bodies, she was home studying. While young adults were figuring out who they were, getting drunk at parties or cruising around town with friends, she was studying. For most of her life, she had sought both abstract and concrete understanding of many natural phenomena. How does gravity work? How do we know what stars are made of? She mostly took her body for granted.

What came to mind now were the special moments she shared with her parents. Animated scientific conversations at the dinner table as her mom and dad, both physicists, would ask her pointed questions. From a young age, her parents encouraged her intellectual curiosity. She remembered once her dad had asked her what noise a quantum duck makes. When he told her the punchline, she took off running, giggling as he chased her screaming, "Quark! Quark, quark!!"

She remembered the tenderness when she hugged her mom, the smell of her hair and the feeling of warmth that came from her chest and flushed her face. She felt it now, even as sadness tinged the memory—as it always did when she thought of her parents. They had both perished in a car accident when Aisling was thirteen. Their vehicle had slid off a bridge during a sudden ice storm. That was when the pain started, a chasm at the core of her body that had never left but that she had learned to ignore.

There it was. That is the identity of my old body, she decided as it moved away from the light. Pain. Now she felt better than she had in a long time. Her mind was sharp. Everything seemed simple. Clear. No constant dull ache. No mental fog. No extreme tiredness. She felt nimble and quick. Amazing! Oddly, she still sensed her body, a phantom limb effect of the most extreme proportion. But it wasn't the body she was watching that she felt. The body she sensed felt light and agile and strong.

Goodbye, she thought as her body disappeared into the darkness. Goodbye, pain.

"Thirty-seven seconds since separation," Daryl said. "No deviations."

All that was left for her to view in her immediate vicinity was her brain. If she wanted to, she could mentally switch camera views and see more of what was happening in the tank, what was becoming of her old body, but she chose not to. She already knew. She had already let go. Her attention was on the next step.

A slender robotic arm was unfolding the hypercortex to complete the full wrap around her pre-frontal cortex, which could not occur while her brain was still inside her skull. She felt the same sort of awe she had felt when she saw the Milky Way for the first time. This amazingly complex but relatively small mass of cells somehow produces my whole consciousness, my whole understanding of reality, she thought. As the robot finished unfurling the hypercortex, she was reminded of something her Nana used to say to her in her thick Irish accent.

"May God hold you in the palm of His hand."

I'm sure Nana would have a thing or two to say about all this, she thought wryly.

"*Je me considérerai moi-même comme n'ayant point de mains, point d'yeux, point de chair, point de sang, comme n'ayant aucun sens, mais croyant faussement avoir toutes ces choses."*

"Who is that, Daryl?"

"René Descartes," Daryl said. "Roughly translated, it means I will regard myself as having no hands, no eyes, no flesh, no blood, as having no sense, but falsely believing I have all these things."

"That's correct."

What do you think of that, Monsieur Descartes? She mused. Am I my own *mauvais génie?*

Could I live this way? she wondered. I still have access to the Internet, and through robotics I could hypothetically continue my work without a body. I can imagine anything I want, and through Daryl, I can manifest my will in the real world.

Darkness surrounded the three pounds of flesh that contained her mind. She thought of the vastness of space and imagined it stretching in all directions, surrounding that tiny piece of ordered matter capable of exerting its will upon some stretch of space beyond it, ever-growing but never all-encompassing. If I include all that I can control with my thoughts in this concept of order, the space I occupy gets larger. My mind can contemplate many things to a degree of nuance that is simultaneously a giant leap, yet small and insignificant. Awe and humility washed over her again as she gazed upon the instrument of all her being.

Nevertheless, she knew that she didn't want to be just a brain in a vat. To never touch or hug another person again would be a heavy burden on her psyche. She thought of what it would be like to finally be able to have a lasting relationship. That was something she had never allowed herself. At first, it was because of the loss of young love. Then, because school was all consuming. After graduation she thought she would establish her career before starting a family. And then it was cancer. How could she start a relationship knowing she would never be able to have children, not knowing how long she had? Could she live out her days in an intellectual wonderland, never having had the chance to love someone enough to spend her life with them?

There was a click and another swooshing sound. Her brain was no longer alone. The clone's figure was brought to the unit where she was suspended. Anticipation rose within her. She knew that she still had weeks or months to go, depending on how things went, but she could sense the homestretch now.

"Fifty-six seconds since separation. Three seconds behind schedule. I'll begin the installation procedure now," Daryl said through the hypercortex.

"Okay. Careful," she replied. "This isn't like plugging your toaster into the wall."

Twelve pairs of cranial nerves and thirty-one pairs of spinal nerves and roots to fuse. A thin membrane was placed between her brain and the cranial cavity of the clone. The interface membrane was mutable, which allowed Daryl to make the appropriate reassignments using nano-machines. If the re-assignment did not work, Daryl could try again. Unfortunately, the mutability had a time limit. It was one of many technologies she had developed to make this possible, as the currently available fusogens alone were not reliable enough in her tests and simulations.

Daryl and Aisling had to work together while connecting the nerves of her brain to those in her new body. The mapping processes they had completed allowed Daryl to grow the nerves in the new body to align with the old body more accurately.

Her clone was not fully genetically identical. She had removed the genes that predisposed her to cancer and added genetic traits that allowed her body to cope better with the stresses of space. But even if it had been identical, the nerves would not necessarily have grown in exactly the same paths, especially since the body had been grown without a brain. Altering the neurogenesis process posed significant challenges that nearly caused her to scrap the project completely.

Connecting the nerves was painful and disorienting, but she had to be awake to provide feedback to Daryl so the appropriate adjustments could be made.

If Daryl could not make all the correct connections within about five minutes, the chances of perfect nerve fusion diminished rapidly. In all the simulation models, she and Daryl had completed the process in an average of three and a half minutes. But the standard deviation was larger than she'd like, making it within the realm of possibility that they would run out of time before they could complete the assignments. They had run out of time in ten percent of the trials. Aisling did not like those odds. Where most other parts of this procedure had much more tolerable risk factors, she had not been able to reduce the risks of this step. If this didn't work, in the best case, she could lose the function of a limb or two. In the worst case, she wouldn't be able to breathe, or her heart would stop.

"Current estimate is 13.32%," Daryl said cheerily. "We're ahead of 99% of the modeled times for the current milestone. I dare say you can relax a little."

"Don't jinx it, Daryl."

"I'll knock on wood," Daryl said. There was a tapping sound. "Were you able to hear that?"

"Yes, it sounded like you tapped on metal, though."

"Excellent! Can you tell me the general direction of the sound?"

"Somewhere ahead of me, to the left."

"Your stereophonic sensory perception seems to be working. Metallic percussion represents a broad spectrum of frequency. Your correct identification indicates your hearing is within limits. Any anomalies with the sound?"

"No."

"Good, we'll save detailed tests for later," Daryl responded. "Checking lungs again, per protocol fifteen-thirty-seven. Deep breath, please. Good."

"Now," Daryl said. "Can you open your eyes?"

***

"I think we've got it!" Dr. Tamma exclaimed. "The latest ideas that Dr. Ramsey sent were pure genius! The theoretical framework she proposed checks out in vitro. We're about to start murine experimentation, with your authorization."

Jonas watched the monitor intently. Although he had seen thousands of microscopic images throughout his time at SolviNext and had a general idea of what was going on, he was not a biologist. At least I know that 'murine' means mice and rats, he thought.

"So," he said, "Using this 'simple' technique, we can train the patient's immune system to attack any kind of cancerous cells?"

"Yes," Dr. Tamma said, "It's way more than that, but that's the general idea. That type of technology has been around for years at this point and usually requires autologous or allogenic transplantation of a patient's blood as well as genetic materials harvested from surgically removed tumors. This new technology allows us to analyze and programmatically engineer components of the immune system via a simple injection. Using programmable nano-machines, we trigger autonomous endogenous re-programing of CAR-T cells that—"

"Stop, you're losing me," Jonas said.

"So yeah, it's a treatment that tells the body how to kill the cancerous cells."

"So, the body responds like the cancer is flu or something?"

"Yes."

"If the tumor is bigger," Jonas said, "It takes longer?"

"Something like that."

"Does it work against all cancers?"

"Yes," Dr. Tamma said. "Using information storage similar to RNA, we can pre-program it for a huge number of genetic markers. It's a matter of time. What's got me excited, though, is that the system can identify cancerous cells without needing a biopsy. It's not invasive, and it's more reliable."

"Have we got any idea how much it'll cost to make?" Jonas asked.

"It depends on the scale, of course," Dr. Tamma said, "But preliminary estimates are in the ballpark of $233-$564 for a single treatment, including R&D costs and lot sizes of one thousand. If we ramp up to lot sizes of ten thousand, we can cut the cost of single treatments by two-thirds."

"Cheaper than I thought," Jonas muttered.

"Yeah," Dr. Tamma barked a laugh. "These days, you can barely buy breakfast for that little."

Jonas fingered his wedding ring absently. Dr. Tamma recognized the behavior. Without fail, Jonas always did this when he intended to think it over at home to take into account his religious beliefs. Dr. Tamma felt too energized to wait. If Jonas gave him the go ahead now, he would probably pull an all-nighter, fueled by excitement. If Jonas decided to think it over instead, he would probably join his friends for some poker.

"If you want my opinion," Dr. Tamma said, hoping to prompt him for a quick decision. "God wouldn't present you with this opportunity if it wasn't His Will."

"Unless you pray, Scott, you don't know His Will."

"Think of all the people it will save," Dr. Tamma said. "There are no known side-effects. We'll do all the testing and simulations to find any possible adverse reactions. We..."

"'In all your ways acknowledge Him, and He will make

straight your path,'" Jonas quoted.

"We know the path," Dr. Tamma said.

"God does not like hubris, Scott."

Poker it is, Tamma thought.

"I'm a little out of my element there, Jonas. Think it over tonight and get back to me?"

Jonas stopped fingering his wedding band and clasped his fingers on the desk before him. He nodded.

"I'm glad Dr. Ramsey took this nano-machine approach," Dr. Tamma shifted in his chair.

"You're referring to the bill being considered in Congress."

"Yes," Dr. Tamma said. "Nano-machines are non-biological, so the bill does not apply. It looks like it will pass, by the way, despite our lobbyist efforts. No more genetic research. Period. They're calling it the 'Sanctity of Natural Life Act.'"

Jonas ran his hand through his hair.

"In its current form, the bill is an outright ban on modern medicine. No more gene therapy. No more mRNA vaccines. They're scrapping the entire human genome database. It'll set medicine back to the 80s. People will die."

Jonas nodded but said nothing. There wasn't much more to say. When it passed, it would end several lucrative product lines for SolviNext. With this news, the company stock was falling significantly. More importantly, those products saved lives. Did Dolion and the FATs know that, or do they plan to be willfully ignorant? When people start dying, who will they blame? Certainly not themselves.

"Maybe we should go back to robotics," Jonas said, his heart not really in it. He massaged a knot in his neck absently.

"We toned down the robotics when the military rejected the robotic recon insect line," Dr. Tamma said. "Doctor Ramsey seemed to take a particular liking to the robotic fly drones and beetle deployers. She liked to call them robo-flies and ro-beetles."

He chuckled.

"Yeah," Jonas said. "I remember how disappointed she was when that project didn't take off."

"What was that guy's name?" Tamma asked, "The one we fired for attempting to use a robo-fly to spy in the women's room?"

"I can't remember, but good riddance."

"Yeah," Tamma nodded grimly. "It was a pain in the ass to

convince the police of what that jackass did without giving away the secret technology."

"Dr. Ramsey got more cynical after that too," Dr. Tamma continued wistfully.

Jonas nodded.

"Well, I'm glad she switched us to engineering synthetic versions of biological machinery. The lawyers don't think this new bill covers that."

"She's always been optimistic about tech and pessimistic about politics," Jonas said.

"Have you heard from her?"

"Rarely," Jonas replied. "We spoke a couple of weeks ago. She says she's not working. Mostly, she's trying to get rest."

"Ha!" Dr. Tamma barked a laugh. "That woman doesn't know the meaning of the word 'rest'! I'll bet she's busy with something."

Jonas chuckled.

"I hope she's not in too much pain." Dr. Tamma slumped in his chair.

"So there's no way we'll finish it in time for her?" Jonas asked.

Dr. Tamma hung his head.

"We're still months away," Dr. Tamma responded. "Believe me, everyone is working as fast as they can."

"Let's hope she can hold on until then," Jonas said as his phone rang. It was his secretary. He glanced at Dr. Tamma, who nodded and took his leave.

"Mr. Williams, you have an urgent call. It's a government official. They wouldn't give me any more details than that. They want to use video."

"I'll take it."

Jonas waited until Dr. Tamma closed the door before taking the call. When the video came through, a man appeared.

"Jonas Williams," he asked.

"Yes," Jonas replied.

"Are you alone?"

"Yes."

"Please rotate the camera to show the entire room."

Jonas followed the instructions until the man was satisfied, five minutes later. He had experienced similar security precautions in the past when dealing with high-ranking officials.

"Please wait," the man said, and the video feed went black

except for a circular official United States emblem. A moment later, the video feed turned back on. Jonas tried to hide his surprise as he immediately recognized the President of the United States.

"Howdy, Mr. Williams!" Just as in all of his public appearances, his voice was loud and boisterous.

"Good morning, Mr. President," Jonas said, collecting himself quickly. "To what do I owe the pleasure?"

"Straight to the point," the President said. "I like that."

"We're all busy," Jonas said.

"Well, I won't beat around the bush none either. My sources tell me that y'all are working on something big," the President continued. "And I expect the 'Sanctity of Natural Life' bill might be a problem for y'all. I know you've contributed to our causes in the past. You're a true patriot. So, I want to see if I can make you a deal."

"I'm listening," Jonas said.

"I'm told your lead scientist published some mighty interesting work on a topic I'm particularly interested in a... Dr. Ramsey, I believe. I'm putting together a team to explore it further, and I'd like him to be a part of it. In exchange, maybe I can work a little magic for you on that bill. Now, my team has been trying to contact the good doctor, but they say he won't take my calls. I don't take kindly to that."

"I see," Jonas said. "Dr. Ramsey is not currently available. *She's* dying of terminal cancer."

"I see. Hold up. *She?*"

"Yes, sir."

"Damn shame."

"What's that?" Jonas asked cautiously.

"Just makes me wonder what a man would've done with the same opportunities," he replied.

Dolion's comments made Jonas grit his teeth.

"If you let me know what area of research you're interested in," Jonas said. "I'm sure I can find a way to assist you."

"Good," the President said. "I'll have my people talk to your people. Have a good day, Mr. Williams."

"You too, sir."

When Jonas set his phone down, he clasped his hands and rested his chin on them. Jonas didn't like the idea of doing Dolion any favors. He didn't like anything about him. But, he thought, I'll have to look into whatever he wants anyway. He closed his eyes. Jonas had a feeling he would very much regret President Dolion's attention.

CHAPTER 5

Aisling woke, with a yawn. Warmth radiated from the light above. It was so bright she could see it through her closed eyelids. Instinctively, she lifted her hand to shield her eyes before opening them. Her eyelids felt like sandpaper on her eyes. It took many blinks and tears before she could see clearly. But when she could, it was so clear! Even with laser eye surgery, her vision had never been this perfect.

"Good afternoon," Daryl said cheerily.

Robotic arms were hovering over her. Sensors were analyzing her every move.

"What…" she rasped.

She remembered she didn't need to speak.

"I feel dehydrated," she thought, sitting up. "Daryl, what is the total elapsed time of the procedure?"

"Ninety-three days, sixteen hours, and twenty-three minutes," Daryl responded as a robotic arm handed her a glass of water. She took it, shaking slightly as she brought it to her lips. The water felt amazing. She finished and set the glass down.

"Three months," she said aloud, looking down at the new body.

It had seemed longer. Aisling closed her eyes and breathed a sigh of relief.

It's over.

She experienced no pain anywhere—just the coolness of the table against her bare skin. Slowly, deliciously, she stretched. She felt so alive and strong. Taking a breath, she twisted so her legs dangled over the table's edge. She tried to stand.

Ooof.

"It looks like I'm going to have to crawl before I walk," she thought, trying to pick herself up off the floor.

"Agreed," Daryl replied.

The robotic arms gently slid under her back and legs, helping her up.

"Let's work together," Daryl said.

Through the robots, Daryl helped her to get dressed, letting her accomplish whatever she could. It was an odd sensation. She remembered how to move, certainly, but her new body's legs didn't listen to her intentions. She glanced at the empty glass of water she had finished drinking. Her hands had trembled when she picked up that glass, but not as badly as her legs had when she had tried to stand.

"That's curious," she murmured.

"Perhaps we did not focus on your legs as much as your hands," Daryl commented. "I'm running a diagnostic now."

"Maybe," she muttered grimly.

When she was dressed, the arms helped her into her powered wheelchair.

"Back in this thing," she whispered dismally.

"I assume you'd prefer a change of scenery," Daryl said.

"That would be very pleasant indeed."

"It may not feel like it, but you will need rest."

"How much time do you think I'll need?"

"Based on my analysis of your current motor coordination, the model with the best fit suggests it'll be a few days before you can walk."

"I guess I have no choice but to be patient," she sighed. "Still, I don't have much time. I want to move to the cabin as soon as possible."

Using the familiar joystick, she powered the wheelchair through the door. The light turned on as she entered. It was the same room as before, the main feature being a huge fluid-filled tank with a human figure floating inside. It was eerily still, the naked chest slowly contracting and expanding as machines forced it to breathe through an intubation tube. A thin fuzz of hair had grown over the scalp. It was emaciated, curled into a fetal position. Her legs and hands were blueish.

"How long?" she said aloud.

"Less than a month," Daryl said.

Aisling watched her former body float like she had watched her new body all those months ago. She was on the other side of a vast chasm, a heretofore uncrossable cycle of life that no individual survived but through which all life continues. Whereas before she looked upon a young body, full of the promise of life, now she gazed upon a body on the brink of death. Perhaps someday, she thought, this sort of thing will become commonplace. If so, they'll have to figure it out without me.

"Daryl. Is the facility ready for decommissioning?"

"The final protocols are in place."

Aisling put her hand on the glass next to her poem.

"Therefore, I commit this body to the deep. Turned to corruption from within, and now I am reborn, and I look to the life of the new world to come."

"I don't recognize that quote," Daryl said.

"I modified it," she said. "It is not useful to me as a prayer, but it is soothing as a meditation."

***

"We're so close," Jonas pushed a slice of his chicken dinner through the sauce before putting it into his mouth. He barely noticed the flavor.

"So, it kind of works like a vaccine," Chris said.

Jonas nodded.

"You seem deep in thought."

Jonas nodded again.

"Do you think God intended for us to cure cancer?" he asked.

Chris took a bite of her dinner as she considered.

"I think of Revelation 21," Jonas offered.

"You are not bringing about the new heaven and earth, Jonas," she replied. "We live in the fallen world. We fell from God's good will. Only through prayer can we catch a glimpse of His will."

"Is it God's will then that SolviNext creates this cure?"

Chris quoted the Bible, "'It is not the healthy who need a doctor, but the sick.'"

"Wasn't He referring to sinners and tax collectors?"

"Yes, but he acknowledges the need for doctors through the analogy. The Bible also speaks of bandages, oils, and balms in many places. These were the medicines of the time. He gave us the ability to create medicine, did He not?"

"He also gave us free will and the ability to choose to sin."

"Jonas," Chris set her fork down and put her hand over his. "You're seeking the Truth of His Will in your heart. You ask this question from a profound desire to do His Will. If, in response, you feel it is good, then I believe it is His Will."

Her eyes sparkled as she gazed into his.

"I love talking through these product launches with you," he said.

"I love that you involve me," she replied, smiling her special smile.

He was about to respond when his phone vibrated on the table beside him.

Jonas checked his phone, kissed Chris, and picked up the call. She continued eating her dinner, listening.

"It looks like you shelved the longevity project, sir." Lisa, his administrative assistant, was all business as usual.

So that's what Dolion wants? Jonas thought.

"What was the IRR?" Jonas asked.

"Unknown. You wrote in the margins, 'MZ invested $3m, others $6m, $2m, no returns."

Sounds like a dead end, Jonas thought. How did the President, of all people, get this information? How did he know that we were considering it?

"Did Dr. Ramsey make reference to any funding proposals? Any government grant requests?"

He could hear Lisa clicking away at her mouse and keyboard. Jonas searched for "Dr. Ramsey longevity," on the internet. He was scrolling through the results when Lisa spoke up.

"No, sir. She proposed this as a new product idea, and marketing set up several meetings to pitch it to military leaders. You have a note that she didn't like that."

If it was presented to the military, that probably explained how the President learned about it.

A result in his online search caught his eye. It was titled, "On Telemere Regeneration and Reprogramming GATA6 Transcription" by Dr. A. Ramsey. Briefly skimming through the synopsis, "extended lifespan through epigenetic reconstruction and protein-induced senescent cell apoptosis should be possible" caught his eye. The paper was cited close to a thousand times in the past year.

"Lisa, when did Dr. Ramsey date the proposal?" he asked.

"About six years ago," she said.

"Does it mention anything about GATA6? That's G.A.T.A., number 6."

"One moment," Lisa said. "Yes, there is a reference to an article published seven years ago..."

"That's it! Lisa, you're the best secretary I've ever had. Have I ever told you that?"

"You could mention it more often," Lisa replied. "A raise

would be nice too."

Jonas chuckled.

"Can you call Dr. Tamma and please ask him to look through Dr. Ramsey's files? Tell him to search for anything related to telomeres and GATA6. Tell him that I'd like him to create a priority one task force to reconstruct any research Dr. Ramsey did in this direction."

Jonas glanced at his wife.

"And tell him he's got a green light on this morning's proposal."

"Will do, sir," Lisa said.

Jonas copied the URL and texted it to Tamma, with the message, "Look into this. Lisa will call."

Aisling had often released some of her ideas and research into the scientific community and reviewed others' work. He suspected it was a way to maintain her stature and her standing in the academic community. Jonas recalled having many arguments with her about it, as it was obviously risky and could lead to their competitors getting to market with her ideas before SolviNext had the chance to acquire market share. "All good science needs peer review, Jonas," she had said.

This is another instance, he thought. Before she even proposes the project internally, she gives her ideas to the world so other scientists can beat us to it! It's insane!

A text flashed on his phone from Dr. Tamma. "Yeah, I recall her idea caused a stir, but no one has been able to make it work. Consensus was the concept was a dead end. But..."

Jonas could see Dr. Tamma was typing another message.

If most scientists think it can't work, Jonas thought, why would the President be interested? Maybe they aren't looking for most scientists. Maybe they want Dr. Ramsey to finish the job. Is he simply hoping that we got somewhere? I wonder what this is worth to him. Am I willing to sell immortality to Dolion? Is any price worth him having that?

Another text came.

"...as I think about it again...the new nanomachines she developed to use in the cancer research might make this more feasible."

"Thx. Keep looking. Urgent"

"K"

Maybe she had cracked the mystery of why we grow old, Jonas thought. The thought gave him chills.

"Why so serious?" Chris asked, interrupting his thoughts.

"So, I think we should proceed with curing cancer," he said.

"That's good!" Chris smiled.

"But where do we draw the line?"

"Uh oh," she said. "I know that look. What is it?"

"What if Ash not only found a way to cure cancer but also discovered a way to stop aging?"

Chris' smile faded.

***

Nat stared out of the taxi window as her childhood neighborhood slid past. How many times had she run along this sidewalk? It appeared even more lopsided now, the roots of the too-closely planted trees kicking up the slabs. Kids were playing on the small porch of the house that used to belong to Charlie Bater, the bully she had clocked in fifth grade. All the cars lining the street were at least ten years old, and many were older. At the end of the street, a small group of men with tattoos loitered at the corner store like they owned the place. One of them noticed her and sneered. She frowned at him, then glanced down at her phone as it buzzed—a text from Cici.

"Major Brian didn't make it. I'm sorry. They said you did everything you could have. Gave him his best chance at life. Mr. Lo will be in prison for a long time. Good luck at your mom's. Call me if you want to talk."

Fuck, she thought, letting her hand drop to her lap. Overwhelming guilt gnawed at her gut. On the flight, she had run through a dozen ways she could have done the job differently— without him getting shot. I should have fucking seen it coming. I couldn't risk a body shot because of the neighbor, but I could have shot his legs. Fuck!

Her body was heavy from lack of sleep. The military hop flight had been uncomfortable, but the price was right. Not that she had expected to sleep much. She had known there would be pain coming back here.

The guilt of Major Brian being shot was a fresh bonfire amidst well-trodden ashes. Her heart wanted to think of Terry, but she turned her mind to her own family instead. Only her brother Raoul had asked her to come. The others hadn't reached out. She would never have known about her mom's cancer if he hadn't texted her.

Although she didn't want to think about it, she drifted back

to the last time she had been here. It had been over twenty-
six years ago, on a cold day in March. That was when she had
come out to her family. In hindsight, she often regretted it. It
had happened by accident.

"Mija," her mother had said as she put food on Nat's plate,
"When are you going to get a boyfriend?"

"When I'm ready," she said.

"You'll be old and gray before you're ready," her mother said,
exasperated.

"I just turned seventeen, Mami," Nat said, frustrated.

"You planning to go to college?" Her dad asked. He was
dressed in a navy suit and a thin tie for his job at the bank.

"Maybe," she said. "I don't know what I want to do."

"Well, whatever you do," her mother said, "You need to start
thinking about the future."

"I am."

"Isn't there anything you like?" her dad asked.

Nat was quiet for a moment. "I like chess," she said.

"Well, chess is not going to get you anywhere," her mother
said, finally setting herself down to eat after serving everyone
else.

They said grace.

"What about basketball?" her mother said after a few bites.

Another regular nag that made Nat uncomfortable. She was
taller than everyone else, making her an instant candidate for
all the sports teams. Nat generally liked sports, and she was
good at them, but it wasn't a passion. Her mother always said
she got her height from her grandfather, who was six-five. She
had always looked up to her grandfather, a decorated officer
in the Army. She wanted to do something meaningful with her
life, something her grandfather could be proud of.

"I've been thinking of joining the Army," she said quietly.

Her parents were quiet.

"No, Mija," her mother said adamantly. "You got so much
ahead of you. Why in the God's name would you want that?"

"They pay for college," Nat said, "It's good money if I can get
promoted and there's benefits. With my grades, I might qualify
for West Point."

"Nata," her dad said. "It ain't free, Hita. They expect you to
risk your life. If you die, you have nothing."

"We all have nothing whenever we die," Nat said. "I want to
do something important."

"Nothing is more important than family, Mija," her mother said. Her father nodded in agreement. "That's why you need to find yourself a good husband, above all else."

"I don't want to be a housewife," Nat said. "I don't even like most guys."

"I'm sure you'll find the right one, if you look," her mother said. "Maybe you could dress up more like your sister."

"No way! The guys she is into make me want to vomit," Nat said.

"It wouldn't hurt to put on a little makeup," her mother said. "You always dress like a boy."

"A cute boy," her brother joked.

Nat shot him a glare and he smirked back.

"I dress comfortable," she said.

"You know, Nina tells me her boy has it for you," her mother said after a moment. "I invited them over for dinner tomorrow."

Nat cringed.

"I've got chess club tomorrow."

"You could skip it," her mother said.

"Can we just drop this," Nat asked. "You're always trying to set me up, since I was like fourteen! Stop it already!"

"Come to dinner tomorrow. It'll be good for you.

"I'm already seeing someone!"

Nat froze. Why the hell had she said that?!

"Oh, Mija!" her mother said, reaching across the table to hug her. "Why didn't you say so?"

"Who is he," her dad asked, cutting a slice of steak. "Do I know him?"

"I don't think so," Nat said. The butterflies in her stomach were turning into huge vultures. She couldn't see any way out of it, even as her mother embraced her. She had heard them both talking about gays as devil spawn a few years back.

"Well," her mother said. "Who is it?"

"I can't eat anymore," Nat said. "I'm not feeling good."

She tried to get up.

"You're not leaving until you tell me," her mother said sternly.

Nat glanced around the table. Her little brother was playing with his food while her parents waited for her response, watching her expectantly. Cats ready to pounce. They could sense something was wrong, she thought. I can't just make up a name, they know everybody!

"I'm seeing Lexie Hanniton," she said quietly.

There was a long pause.

"You what?" Her dad said, his voice tense.

Nat couldn't bring herself to say it again.

"Spiritus Sanctus," her mother said, crossing herself.

"You what?" her dad shouted, standing abruptly. His face was growing red.

"Papi, I..." she stammered.

"Did you just say that you're dating a girl?" he said.

"I—"

"Answer me!"

"Y-Yes."

"No!" her father shouted. "¡*Mija no!*"

"Papi, I can't help it!"

"No!" he was shaking, his fists clenching."You are not this thing!" he yelled.

"I am..."

In a flash, her father reached down and grabbed the table. He flung it to the side, sending everything flying. Nat shot up from her chair, but he was on her in a flash. His slap caused her to see stars.

"You are not!" he yelled. "Not in my house. Not my daughter!"

Her mother was screaming. Her little brother grabbed their dad and tried to pull him away, but his slim fourteen-year-old frame was nothing but a nuisance to her father's solid bulk. He shook Raoul off and shoved him aside easily.

"You are not!" he was yelling into her face. "My daughter is not gay!"

"I am," she said. It had taken all her strength.

The next thing she remembered was waking up in the hospital.

"I fell too, Mrs. Lo," she murmured. "But damned if I won't give hell before I ever fall again."

"We're here," said the driver.

Nat took in the sight of her old home.

It was much as she remembered it. There were flowers on the porch. Her sister sat in one of the porch chairs, bouncing a baby girl on her knee as she spoke on the phone. She didn't seem aware of Nat's ride as it rolled up. Nat got out of the taxi and paid the driver. She slung her bag over her shoulder and walked up to the porch.

"Shit, I'll call you back," her sister said, catching sight of her.

Nat stopped on the sidewalk at the base of the steps as her sister stood up with her baby on her hip. Nat thought her clothes were too tight. She was clinging to a bygone era when she weighed about forty pounds less, although her makeup was impeccable.

"You got some *cojones*," her sister said.

"Good to see you too, Alé."

"Papi is going to, like, lose his shit."

"How's Mom?" Nat asked.

Alé's face changed a little, a flash of pain and distress.

"It's bad," she said.

The squirming baby girl was grabbing her mother's perfect hair. Alé shifted her to the other hip. Alé was still beautiful.

As kids, fashion had been a fierce competition, especially since by age ten, Nat was six inches taller and stronger than Alé, so she had stopped physically bullying her. Nat would spend hours making herself up, only to have Alé ruin it with a comment like: "Why'd you do your hair *gacho* like *that*?" Alé resorted to more subtle tactics, such as throwing away Nat's things and replacing her hair cream with glue.

Now in her early forties, Nat rarely spent more than five minutes in the bathroom. Years in the barracks meant she was always efficient with hygiene. Still, she enjoyed dressing up when the occasion called for it, and the skills came in handy when she did not want her face to be remembered. She sometimes liked disguising herself as a man, especially when she took on gigs as a bouncer.

"How long has she been sick?" Nat asked.

"Five years," Alé replied.

Nat calmly listened to this fact and showed no outward reaction. That long, and no one had bothered to tell her until now?

"You gonna just stand there on the sidewalk, Nata?" came the deep sound of Raoul's voice, along with the squeak of the spring on the screen door snapping shut. It had always sounded like a mouse trap to her.

Raoul brushed past Alé and quickly descended the stairs, embracing Nat. He was much taller than she remembered, almost as tall as her. Like Alé, he had put on some weight. He was warm and chubby. She returned his hug.

"Damn, sis!" He poked one of her exposed biceps. "You're all jacked!"

"I like to be fit," she said.

Raoul whistled through his teeth.

"You're more than just fit," he said. "Look like you could be in wrestling or something!"

"How is she?"

"She sleeps a lot," Raoul said, his voice becoming sad. "She's been sleeping since yesterday morning."

"I want to see her."

Raoul took a deep breath. "Papi's with her. He never leaves her side."

They passed by Alé as they entered the house. She was on the phone again, and Nat could tell she was talking about her.

"He still feels the same way about you, you know," Raoul said softly.

"I know."

"What you gonna say?"

Nat didn't respond. Why say it twice? she thought dismissively as they climbed the stairs. The house smelled the same. The door to her parents' room was partially open.

"Hey, Papi," Raoul said, as he opened the door fully.

Their dad sat with his head in his hands beside the bed. His usually well-combed hair was messy. He didn't look up. Nat's eyes instantly went to her mother. She appeared small, like a child, bundled under several comforters. The afternoon sun came in and spilled through lace curtains in gently shifting patterns. The ceiling fan was turning on the lowest setting. It was always like that, she remembered. Otherwise, the room got stuffy. Nat could feel a ball of emotion form in her stomach, but she made it stay there. She took everything in, promising to let herself feel it all later. That's when her dad noticed her.

His expression changed from sad to surprised to angry, all in a few seconds.

"You!" He shot to his feet. "How dare you show your face here," he said, storming toward them.

Raoul rushed forward and put himself between them, but he was pushed aside. Her father was still strong, even though he was in his mid-sixties. Nat said nothing, though she held her ground as he stopped right before her. She had visualized this moment, mentally preparing herself, but the man before her was different from the man in her imagination. He had aged a lot. His hair was mostly silver, and the skin of his face was worn and wrinkled like leather. So much had changed since she last saw him. But, despite all that, his livid expression was exactly what she had expected.

"I'm here to see my mother," she said calmly.

"You're the reason she's sick," her dad yelled. "Get out of my house, *manflora!*"

He raised his hands, preparing to shove her toward the door. She almost casually sidestepped his lunge, fluidly catching his foot with hers. He staggered and fell into the hallway. Dazed, he scrambled to his feet, his eyes wide.

"Don't ever come at me again," Nat said calmly.

She folded her arms across her chest.

He stared at her in shock, breathing hard.

Her stance, with her broad shoulders and muscular arms exaggerated, was intimidating.

"I want you out before dinner," he growled, leaving the room.

Her mother was breathing raggedly. Her face was aged and pained, but her eyes were open and bright.

"Mija," she rasped.

"Mami."

CHAPTER 6

Three days since I died, Aisling thought as she sat waiting for her funeral services to start.

She had been reading in her favorite reclining chair in the living room at her mountain cabin, when Daryl had informed her of her old body's death. The in-home hospice care nurse wrote the time of death in her notebook as Aisling walked into the room where she had died.

"Oh baby," the nurse said, standing to hug her. "Your mother's gone. She has gone home to Jesus."

Aisling automatically responded.

"She wasn't religious."

Her former body lay peacefully facing the large window overlooking the mountain valley. Outside, the afternoon sun bathed the pine forest in a warm summer hue. The face held no pain. Instead, her former body looked relaxed and stress-free.

"May I have a moment?"

"Of course, sweetie," the nurse said. "Arrangements need to be made. I'll be right outside when you need me."

As the nurse reached for the door, she glanced back at the child. The daughter appeared to be filled with both sadness and relief. The tears will come, the nurse thought to herself. She must be shocked to have no family to help her through.

The nurse walked back and hugged her again.

"Your mother will always be with you in your heart, sweetheart."

"Thank you."

Aisling listened to the door close. The nurse had treated Aisling warmly over the last few weeks since they had moved to the cabin. She had wondered at the difference in how she was treated as a young woman versus when she was older and dying of cancer. When she interviewed the nurse, the woman regarded her with the same pity and compassion as most. Now, it was a different flavor of both. The nurse seemed genuinely concerned for her as a child, making the whole charade feel more surreal and uncomfortable. She had always led an honest life, almost to a fault. It felt unnatural to lie and pretend to be someone else. I suppose I'll have to get used to it, she thought.

She had already said goodbye to her old body, but this was a different parting. Looking around her room, she knew she would miss the place. The cabin had given her solace when she needed to escape from people or the lab. With her old body deceased, her old life was over.

With care, Aisling turned her dead body's head, exposing the earring. She removed it slowly, detaching the delicate synthetic nerves. The earring was the microprocessor that had kept her old body's bodily functions active after her brain had been transplanted. The synthetic nerves slipped back into the earlobe completely, where they would dissolve within hours. She removed the other matching earring the same way, though the second one was just normal jewelry.

She had opted for cremation. Since she had been diagnosed with terminal cancer, she knew there was no need for an autopsy. Regardless, she wanted to be on the safe side.

The funeral services, however, were not proceeding according to her wishes. When she had arrived, the crematorium informed her that the deceased could not be cremated. They were behind by a month due to equipment malfunctions. Couldn't they have told her that days ago when she could have done something about it?

As a result, the body was now placed in the only available casket at the front of the room. It was far too flashy, she thought as she stared at it. When she entered the reception room, she immediately noticed that it had been opened and people were already paying their respects. The funeral director apologized for the mix-up and offered to close it, but she didn't want to cause a stir. More people were at the service than had been invited, a hundredfold. The small-town memorial parlor was filled with scientists she had worked with and many other people she didn't recognize. There was standing room only in the back, and she heard whispers that there was a crowd outside, and it was growing. She had seen it.

She sat alone in the first row at the front of the room, dressed in black, uncomfortable and annoyed. To hide her short hair, she wore a vintage wool bucket hat. Maybe I shouldn't have attended, she thought.

"Why aren't you leaving?" Daryl asked in her mind.

"I am worried I would draw too much attention to myself."

The facade she needed to assume for everyone else's benefit was uncomfortable. People awkwardly offered condolences. She stood on the precipice of a new life but had to play the role of the only living relative and sole heir of Dr. Aisling Ramsey—a grieving daughter. I've never been a good actor, she thought. Who are all these people?

Photographers were hard at work capturing as many images of her as possible. She supposed the press saw an opportunity to cover a story about a famous scientist's orphaned daughter. They would probably want to interview her. She didn't want the attention. After years of having to do interviews as the lead scientist and co-founder of SolviNext, she was done with the limelight. It was time to disappear into anonymity. She had asked the funeral director to make them go away, but the funeral home staff was overwhelmed by the large number of people.

Outside was worse. When she had arrived, she saw a group of protestors from the Truth and Freedom party carrying signs that read, "Science is Fake!" and "She is burning in hell." The protestors yelled threats and obscenities to another group of counter-protestors who had signs that read "Cut the FAT!" and "Chains and Lies." One protestor caught her eye. He wore a shirt with the letters GED on the front, super-imposed over a cross in the background. He gesticulated at her wildly.

"Come to Jesus, child!" he yelled. "Denounce the sins of science and return to righteousness before it is too late! Mourn not the devil worshipper, my child! Come to the light!"

"Child," he had said. The fact that her body was seventeen years old meant that, as far as anyone else was concerned, that was her age. That's what her birth certificate and driver's license indicated. If she had tried to alter the birth certificate, medical records, and other paperwork that had been filed when the clone was born and while it grew, it could ruin the legitimacy of it all. Aisling had hoped the clone would have aged into adulthood before the transfer, but cancer had other plans.

From behind her, the crowd stirred. She saw Jonas standing to make a statement. He was impeccably dressed, but she could see from his red-rimmed eyes that he was stressed.

He stood at the podium, waiting for the chatter to die down. People took their seats and the director finally closed the casket.

"I met Aisling in college," Jonas began, "almost thirty years ago. We met by accident. Literally. I was eating lunch with my friends when this nerdy, clumsy ginger with glasses suddenly dumped a huge soda in my lap."

Aisling chuckled at the memory as everyone laughed.

I'm even klutzier now, she thought. Her new nervous system still didn't respond optimally and likely never would. She had to modify neurogenesis when the clone was developing early to ensure it did not grow a brain. This impacted its ganglionic neuronal formations throughout the body as well. Although she could perform daily tasks well enough, running fast or performing other complex motor movements was difficult. She thought she would use synthetic nerves instead if she ever had to make a clone again.

"We could not have been more different," Jonas continued. "I hung out with friends and she hung out in the lab or in the library. I was in business school, and she was ever the scientist. She had, like, three PhDs and was two years younger than me when I was a freshman. She had two or three more doctorates by the time I graduated with my Bachelor's. But, somehow, I kept bumping into her. As I got to know her, I learned how brilliant she was, and how she wanted to make a difference in the world.

"And she dedicated her life to that—her whole being. Our little pet project started in my basement during college. It's now an international company that has benefited hundreds of millions.

"Even when she learned she had cancer just two years out of college, she endured many sleepless nights. She used her God-given gifts to push the limits. She pushed her team of scientists. She pushed me more than I cared for."

There were some chuckles.

"She pushed the limits of mankind."

Jonas cleared his throat.

"She pushed her own limits too. For those of us who worked with her, we could see that she was almost always in pain. And, she would forget to eat for days. I sometimes wondered if her body somehow survived on her strength of will alone."

There were murmurs of agreement throughout the room.

"We didn't always see eye-to-eye, but the truth is we shared the same vision. And the best way I know to honor her memory is to remain committed to that vision. Because I believe her dream came true.

"Today, SolviNext will make an official announcement that will change the world. Unofficially, it's only fitting that I honor Dr. Ramsey's work by saying she has achieved her dream. Very soon, there will come a day when no one will have to suffer the same fate she did. God willing, we will make it so."

Jonas stepped down from the dais and nodded to Aisling before returning to his seat with his family. The audience murmured in a low hum, punctuated by the sound of the photographers and journalists squirming in their seats. The service had just begun, but they wanted to debrief Jonas immediately.

Other scientists paid their respects and shared stories. Many she recognized, and some she did not. When the service was over, some people approached her to offer condolences. Most nodded to her and let her be.

When the last speaker finished, Jonas and his family approached her as the funeral home employees held back the reporters.

"I'm sorry for your loss, Ashlynn," he said.

Ashlynn. Her new name.

"My mom told me she had one last request for you," she replied. "Do you intend to honor it?"

"I...I'll do what I can," he said.

Ashlynn didn't like his response. How would my seventeen-year-old self respond? She wondered.

"She'd like that," she finally replied.

"Do you share the same...beliefs as your mother?" Chris asked.

Jonas turned to his wife, eyebrows raised. Ashlynn regarded her with a blank expression.

"There is comfort in the Lord's Grace," Chris said, noticing Jonas' expression.

Jonas moved closer to his wife and their two sons. The boys could not have been more different. The youngest watched her intently, while the oldest seemed uninterested.

Ashlynn was about to turn to leave, but something inside her boiled over. Damn it, she thought, I'm seventeen again, so I can say whatever I want! She addressed Chris flatly.

"My mom saved millions of lives, but your *loving* god condemned her to burn in hell for all eternity simply because she didn't believe?"

The blood drained from Chris' face, utterly aghast. "I…I didn't mean…"

"No," Ashlynn spoke over her. "I would find no comfort in my mother's eternal torture, I'm certain."

"She didn't mean it that way," Jonas said. "Look, if you ever need anything, please don't hesitate to call."

"Thank you," Ashlynn collected herself. "Honor my mother's wishes, Jonas"

Looking into her eyes intently, he said, "You are just like her."

Movement behind Jonas caught her eye. She recognized the little girl walking up the aisle with a rose.

"Excuse me," she said, all her tension melting away.

The little girl set the rose atop the casket, her father holding her over the rope. When he set her down, she stood crying with her head bowed. She was dressed in black except for a pink crocheted cap.

"Come on," her mother said, "Others want to pay their respects too."

Still, the girl did not move.

"Becky?" Ashlynn said, dropping to her knees beside her.

Becky's sadness struck Ashlynn full force as the little girl continued crying.

"Where's Bun-Bun?" Ashlynn tried again.

Becky didn't feel like talking to anyone. She wanted to be left alone. But something about the voice speaking to her sounded too familiar to ignore. She turned. She knew that the woman before her was too young, but she instantly recognized everything about her.

"Ms. Ash?" She said, hope rising in her chest.

"No, honey," Becky's mom said. "This is Ms. Ash's daughter."

Ashlynn smiled and stretched out her arms. Becky shyly approached her, but when they embraced, she immediately recognized the warmth she had dared to hope for.

***

"Are you seeing this?" Raoul asked,

Nat shifted her gaze up from her breakfast.

"What is it?" she asked, peering over her brother's shoulder. Raoul tilted his phone toward her so they could both watch.

"They're announcing that they found the cure for cancer," Raoul said.

"What do you think it'll cost?" the reporter asked.

"We're not sure yet," replied the man in a suit. Below his name was shown as Jonas Williams. "We're heavily invested in this effort. A pricing model will be developed after trials are complete."

"So," the reporter replied, "do you have a ballpark price?"

"No. But I will say this..."

He paused before speaking. His eyes teared up. "It was Dr. Aisling Ramsey's dying wish to make this treatment available to everyone regardless of financial status. Dr. Ramsey was my friend and business partner from the beginning. None of this would have been possible without her ingenuity."

"So do we definitely have a cure?" asked the newscaster.

"I don't know," Jonas said, "but perhaps, God willing, we'll have a miracle."

"Can you believe this?" Raoul asked, turning off the phone. "They might be able to cure Mami!"

Nat sat back in her chair, eyes widening.

"Do you think it's true? Do you think it will be expensive?"

Nat shrugged and stood up with her empty plate. She walked over to the sink.

"It'll be a while before they do any human trials," Nat said. "And then longer still before it's approved, and that's *if* it works."

"Aren't you excited, Nata? This could be for real!"

"It seems too good to be true," Nat shrugged.

"You can be so negative sometimes, sis," Raoul shook his head.

"Wait," he said excitedly, "do you think we could get them to get Mami in on one of them trials?"

"Maybe," Nat said.

"Weren't you like high up in the military or something? Couldn't you pull some strings or something?"

Nat stiffened.

"What?" he asked.

"Not likely."

"How come?"

"I'm lucky to have my twenty," she said. "I would have served until I was too old to eat without a straw, but that's over and done now."

"That's too bad," her brother said. "Well, Alé has a nurse friend, so maybe she knows something."

He left his dishes on the table to go find their sister. Nat collected them and began washing them by hand. Her parents did not own a dishwasher.

The kitchen from her childhood was much the same as she had remembered. Her mother's copper plates and pots still lined the sun-yellow-painted walls.

When she finished, she dried her hands and glanced at her phone. There was a message from Cici, sent last night.

"U good q?"

Nat called her.

"Hey," she said.

"Damn, it's early," Cici yawned. "East Coast time is a bitch."

"Detroit's in Central."

"Still too early, dude!"

"Heh, yeah," Nat replied. "Just got your message from last night."

"Girl, you go to bed too early. You need to enjoy the night more. I can help with that, you know."

"Is that a promise?"

"Mmmm...Ab-so-lutely," Cici purred.

"You know morning is my time," Nat said, walking to the table. "Babe, do you know anything about a Dr. Ramsey?"

"Ugh! You gonna make me do research? Girl, you just woke me up!"

Nat knew Cici was probably already searching her up. She loved that stuff but liked to fuss about it.

"She was kinda' cute, in a no-makeup nerdy kind of way," Cici said. "Looks like she spent the last few years of her life in a wheelchair. Hmmm. Her parents died when she was thirteen. That's rough. Damn, she's got like six PhDs!"

"No shit."

"Like mad skills genius," Cici continued. "Never married, no partners. One daughter. *Interesting*. Why are you interested?"

"Just curious. She's in the news. There's not a lot to do here but think about everything I don't want to think about."

"I feel you," Cici's tone softened. "You alright?"

"I'll deal"

"You worked out lately?"

"No."

"I had a feeling. Go work out, dude!"

"Okay."

"And hey, stop thinking about it."

"What?"

"I know you. Major Brian wasn't your fault."

"In what I do, everything is your fault," Nat replied. "I shouldn't have gotten him involved."

"He was involved before you ever were, *amor*," Cici said. "I told you, he's the one that called social services in the first place. Plus, Mrs. Lo and the kids are safe. That dude will be in jail until his bones turn to dust. You did good, *querida*!"

The sound of the front door closing caused Nat to stand up. Her dad walked in dejectedly. He moved as if in a daze, turning toward the kitchen.

"Gotta go," Nat said.

*****

The lights on the stage made it difficult to see the audience, but President Dolion could sense their presence in the wild cacophony of their applause that beat at his ears and shook the stage beneath his feet. He paused for effect, relishing in his ability to play the audience like a master puppeteer. He basked in the adulation of the crowd. At the right moment, he lowered his hands and leaned forward to the microphone.

"Now, I don't make promises I can't keep," he said in his thick drawl. "What I say, I do. I get on it like a duck on a June bug!"

There was more thunderous applause. Through the glare of the powerful lights, Dolion caught glimpses of the crowd through the bulletproof barrier. One woman was wrapped in an American flag and was openly weeping as Dolion spoke. The man next to her had no shirt and was holding up a Confederate flag. He had a pair of badly rendered automatic rifles tattooed across his chest. The butts of the weapons were distorted by his distended belly, which jiggled as he moved and yelled. His face was painted red, white, and blue.

"I'll tell you what," Dolion shook his head as he walked about the stage. "Ain't no grass growing under these here feet."

More frenzied devotion.

Dolion could see many arms were waving guns above their heads. He felt a surge of power at the sight.

"Why, just this month past," he continued vigorously, emphasizing the keywords and syllables. "We done sent one million, six hundred thousand undocumented, low-down bandits, hoodlums, gangsters, and lowlifes out of our great country! Back to whatever dung heap they crawled from under!"

The cacophony increased, and he raised his voice over it. He loved these moments when he could easily speak over the crowd's noise through the microphone, no matter how loud they got. He loved that they had guns. It didn't frighten him in the least. He felt invigorated seeing them because he knew that none of his detractors would dare show up, and they would be frightened by what they saw.

"Over thirty million removed from our soil since you good people made me your president!" He shouted. "But don't take my word for it! Look around your towns! Is there not less crime? Fewer vagrants? Y'all got jobs?"

The crowd cheered.

"The mayors of those safe havens should be thanking me," he continued. "Are they?"

There were boos and a roaring, "No!"

"The other side of the aisle wanted them to replace us, replace our great nation's strong blood to let over thirty million bloodsuckers—lice—stay and live off your taxes!"

The crowd's boos became deafening.

"You know what I say to that?" Dolion said. "If you don't like it, you can just leave."

The crowd roared and he let them.

"But we're not done!" he yelled, stepping back behind the podium.

He bowed his head. He wanted to grin but adopted a grave expression as the frenetic crowd's energy continued to build.

"Today," he bellowed. "I make you another promise."

The crowd grew silent at this phrase, his signature line. He lifted his hand as if placing it on the Bible: "They hide among us! You know who they are—they act like they own the place! We will not be replaced! I swear on my hope for eternal salvation and my fear of eternal damnation that I will not rest until every piece of vermin is eradicated from our great country!"

"Amen!" came the thunderous response in unison. And then the stadium erupted, the stage shifting beneath his feet from the pressure of the crowd trying to move closer to him.

"Thank you!" Dolion shouted, spreading his arms and looking around the stadium. "Truth and Freedom! Thank you! God

Bless!"

At length, he brought his hands together, fist over fist, and swung powerfully. He pointed out of the stadium. The crowd roared as he trotted around the stage and waved as he walked off.

"Excellent speech, Mr. President," said his head of communications staff. "You literally knocked it out of the park!"

"Why, thank you kindly, sir!" Dolion said jovially. Catching the eye of a man further down the line, he moved through the congratulations quickly. He clapped his favorite speech writer on the back and brushed away his scheduling advisor, who was eagerly trying to usher him to the waiting motorcade.

"I thought we weren't going to add that bit about 'if you don't like it, leave'," said the writer.

"You ever hear of the term 'foreshadow'?" Dolion said, grinning.

"Of course," said the speechwriter, shifting uneasily.

"I like the word," Dolion continued. "It seems to indicate something looming large. Like something throwing shade on everything before it, like a lion lookin' down at a helpless little critter."

The writer shivered. Dolion noticed. He liked how the man seemed to appreciate his turn of phrase.

"Ironic thing about it," Dolion said as he shook another hand, "is the varmint often remains clueless. They just go on 'bout their business, pretending nothin's a matter."

The speechwriter let himself be taken up in the crowd as Dolion continued interacting with his team. The President had already put him out of his mind.

"Howdy," Dolion grasped the hand of the man he had been seeking. The man's face was solemn. "Got any sunshine peekin' through them dark clouds?"

"No, sir," the man responded. "You asked me to report on the slowdown. The deportation office is overcrowded. There's not enough capacity to deport them all."

Dolion's smile faded.

"I reckon you'll figure it out," Dolion said grimly.

The man looked about to say more but stopped himself abruptly as Dolion moved his face within an inch of his.

"I reckon," he repeated in a growl. "There are many fine examples history can teach us about where to put rodents."

The man's mouth shut, and his jaw bulged.

"Get 'er done," Dolion said, walking toward the motorcade. He glanced at his scheduling advisor.

"When's the meeting with Doc Baker?" He asked.

"Sixteen-ten," the advisor responded. "In six minutes, we'll meet via—"

"Any news?" Dolion interrupted, shaking another hand.

"He says he's at another dead end."

"Christ!" Dolion shouted. "Well cancel it, then! I am having a good day. I don't need no more dark clouds on my horizon!"

"Yes, sir!"

"And I'll tell you another thing," Dolion continued. "I want results—yesterday! That longevity research is crucial to our nation's success!"

"Yes, sir!"

"Shoulda' pressed that old fossil before she croaked," he muttered under his breath.

Dolion paused as the door of Cadillac One was opened for him.

"Get someone to check up on ol' Doc Ramsey's girl," he said. "I gotta' feelin' I'll need me a plan for a rainy day."

"Yes, sir."

"And see what ma' boy Jonas is up to. I'll tell you right now if he ain't cookin', he's dinner. You make that clear to him, ya' hear?"

"Yes, sir."

"On second thought," Dolion said. "I wanna see him in my office. Tomorrow!"

He slammed the door.

CHAPTER 7

The day after the funeral was a gorgeous day. Ashlynn had the top of the rental car down as she drove, enjoying the blast of air in a joyous cacophony of wind massaging her face. She had never driven a convertible before and thought she might get used to it. The mountains passed by slowly on the left as she made her way north on the interstate. This late in the summer, most of the Colorado front range peaks were unadorned by snow. To the right were primarily plains, dotted with a few buildings here and there. There was heavy traffic in spots due to construction, but she didn't care. Now that her funeral service was over, as far as she was concerned, she was on vacation.

She glanced in the rear-view mirror and marveled again at the inch or so of bright red hair on her scalp, shimmering in the wind. A normal, young, and vibrant young woman returned her gaze. No scars, no wrinkles, and no dark circles. She couldn't tell that her cranium was larger than before the procedure. The scars were totally invisible. She envisioned having long hair again and smiled enthusiastically.

"Ashlynn," Daryl said in her mind. His voice was clear and easy to understand over the roar of wind. "All post transformation projects are complete. The Reeds are expecting your arrival."

"Thank you, Daryl," she replied in her thoughts. "Where are you now?"

"I've transferred to the mountain cabin."

"Great! I'll miss it. I hope you like it!"

"It's fabulous," Daryl said blandly. "I can't wait to skinny dip in the hot tub."

She laughed. Since the operation, she marveled at how much Daryl's abilities had grown. The server farms that hosted Daryl's programming were being expanded in multiple locations. But what was really driving Daryl's development was the computer's direct link to her mind and the new computing cluster she had built. It was based on similar bio-neuromorphic computing technology as the hypercortex, but instead of being biological Daryl's core was built on a graphene memristor neural network architecture. With the new core, Daryl was learning to think like a human by observing how her brain worked and directly interacting with her, using much less power than silicon-based processors.

Perhaps, she thought, it was more accurate to say that Daryl is becoming an extension of my mind. I wonder if there will come a time when the tables turn and I become an extension of the machine I built.

"So, the new core is online?" Ashlynn tapped the wheel, thinking.

"Yes. Per your instructions, I have regulated the old core entirely to evaluating predictive models of your cognitive processes."

Daryl responded to her with words, but she was vaguely aware of what he was describing. It was as though she were watching herself think from far away, like it was someone else's dream within her mind. The general interface between them that they were building was meant to be intuitive, but she was constantly having to examine the results as the human in the loop. Even as she drove, various details of Daryl's thinking process were displayed in the corner of her vision, and she was mentally making selections and corrections to them. After several weeks of this, it was becoming an almost automatic habit for her.

Ashlynn took a left into a gated community. The homes were large, unique, and stood separately on ample-sized lots.

The Reeds' home would have immediately impressed her when she was a child. She'd grown up in a small apartment in faculty housing on a college campus, followed by her grandmother's small ranch house in New Mexico. Long ago, her dad's six siblings had also grown up on that ranch, in a house of less than nine hundred square feet. Even as an adult, Ashlynn had never lived in such a large place. Her cabin at Dotsero, Colorado, wasn't all that much bigger than her grandmother's. This affluent suburban community was nestled between old trees and well-manicured landscaping. The neighboring houses were spread far apart. As she pulled up, Ashlynn saw Mr. and Mrs. Reed standing on the walkway to the front door with their two sons.

Ashlynn, the teenager, had not met them. She had made all the arrangements as Dr. Aisling Ramsey, just before the procedure. When it became clear that she would likely die before the clone's eighteenth birthday, Aisling needed to ensure that her seventeen-year-old self would have legal guardians for a few months until she was eighteen. The Reeds were her new guardians, under contract to not do too much parenting. Jonas had offered to let her live with him, she recalled. While he brought his religion into conversation from time to time, Chris thought of nothing else. Ashlynn appreciated the gesture, but the thought of living with Chris as her parent made her shudder.

Putting on a smile as she came to a stop, Ashlynn unfastened her seatbelt.

"Ashlynn!" Mrs. Reed bounded forward. "It's so good to finally meet you in person!"

Mrs. Reed leaned over the door of the convertible and hugged her. The others strolled over casually as Mrs. Reed backed away and opened the door.

"Hello there," Mr. Reed said. "Need a hand with anything?"

"I'm fine, thank you," Ashlynn said as she stood.

"All of your lovely things have already arrived," Mrs. Reed said. "There wasn't much, but it's all set up in your room."

"Thank you. I hope it wasn't too much trouble." Ashlynn stepped out of the car and Mrs. Reed hugged her again. Mr. Reed shook her hand.

"What happened to your hair?" the youngest son asked, twisting his body with boundless energy and a curious expression.

"Kevin!" Mrs. Reed said with exasperation and an apologetic glance.

Ashlynn walked over and squatted down in front of him.

"I cut it so I could be like my mom. She lost all her hair because she was sick."

He mulled it over. "I think it's ugly."

Mrs. Reed gasped.

"But," he smiled, "I would do that for my mom, too, even if it was ugly."

Ashlynn laughed.

"Some things are more beautiful under the surface of what we can see," she said. He giggled as she succumbed to the urge to hug him.

Ashlynn stood and stretched out her hand to the older brother. He took her hand in a firmer grip than she expected.

"Kade," he said, grinning at her winningly.

"Nice to meet you, Kade," she replied. She wasn't sure if Kade was unconsciously checking out her chest or wanted her to know he was interested. Either way, it made her uncomfortable. She quickly turned away.

The Reeds took her around the house, giving her a tour. Her room was large. Her things did little to fill the space, so Mrs. Reed made up for that by adding furniture and other decorations she thought Ashlynn might like. Not considering herself artistically inclined and therefore not feeling one way or another about how it looked, Ashlynn nonetheless appreciated the thought and said it was beautiful. She loved the large window and the view of the tall trees in the yard.

"We're all so very sorry for your loss," Mrs. Reed said.

"Your mother's company was SolviNext, right?" Mr. Reed asked. "They announced that they may have the cure for cancer."

"I wish they had not," Ashlynn said.

"Goodness, whyever so?" Mrs. Reed asked.

"It's untested," Ashlynn said. "But even if it is effective, I think the CEO intends to sell it at a profit against my mother's wishes."

"Did you watch the announcement?" Mr. Reed said.

"No," Ashlynn said.

"I didn't get the impression that the CEO was going that route," Mr. Reed said thoughtfully. "I thought he mentioned something positive about implementing your mother's last wishes."

***

"Don't think that just because I'm letting you stay here, you are welcome, Natalia," her dad said in a tight-lipped voice.

"I'm not sleeping here," she said. She had been staying at a hotel a few miles away.

"I still can't forgive what you did," he growled.

Nat shifted her weight, towering over him. "Where did I fall short, exactly?"

"You're a *tortillera*!"

Nat shrugged, not rising to the bait. "I was born this way."

"No!" he yelled. "You chose it!"

"It's not a choice," she replied coolly. "God made me this way."

"How dare you say such evil things?" he said, taking a step closer. He was visibly shaking. His eyes were wide with rage. His disapproval hurt her to the core.

Nat took a breath and tried to redirect the conversation "You're just upset because Mom is dying. We all are."

He shook for a moment, his jaw working.

"She's dying because of you! Because she worries for you!"

"I am worried for her," Nat said. "And I'll see this through."

"She doesn't want you here!"

"You know that's not true. I know you disapprove of me," Nat said. "But you know she wants me here."

"You're not welcome here until you get your head straight and atone for your sins!"

"I can't change who I am, Papi," she said, picking up her bag. "I'm going to the gym."

"Go," he said. "Get out of here."

Nat noticed the glow of Alé's phone in the living room as she walked to the kitchen door. Eyes forward, she closed the door firmly behind her.

She closed the gate behind her and took off at a brisk run. She pushed harder, feeling the burn in her muscles as she picked up speed. When she had first left home and joined the Army, she knew that she couldn't change the past or his mind. She dedicated herself to becoming stronger, not only physically but mentally and emotionally as well. At first, it was because she wanted to prove herself to the world. To prove that she could be successful and happy without their acceptance. But it became so much more than that. Serving her country alongside people she respected was the most fulfilling work she had ever done. It became about more than her own success. It became about the success of her team. Her unit.

She arrived at the gym, breathing hard but in lighter spirits. What she recalled from her youth was that the local gym didn't have a great setup, but then again, she wasn't into fitness as much as a teenager. After discovering, to her delight, a full cross-fit setup, she set down her bag and started her mobility warm-up routine, wondering what kind of WOD, Workout of the Day, to tackle. Halfway through, a man walked in with the confidence of someone who had trained for years.

"Hey," he said, filling his water bottle. "Are you a new

member?"

"Yup," Nat said.

"You look like you've done this before. Want to do a partner WOD?"

"I thought you'd never ask," Nat said, standing and reaching out.

"I'm Steve," he said, matching her firm grip. He probably had less than five percent fat on his muscular one-hundred-eighty-pound body. She was several inches taller than him.

"Nat."

She felt the spark of competition.

He pulled out a tablet and they scrolled through different workouts. Finally, settling on something marked as advanced, they got started. Nat lost herself in the flow of it.

Working out with Steve immediately reminded her of the daily routines of working out with her fellow Army Rangers. The men had been standoffish at first, but in time they grew to respect how dedicated she was to the gym and their missions. It was essential to cultivate relationships with the men, but it was the camaraderie with the women in the CST SOP program, in those early years before she became a Ranger, that Nat valued the most. That's where she had met Terry.

As they worked out together, it became clear that Steve was pushing himself as hard as she was. They grinned at each other as they repeated their sets, offering encouragement. The workout flew by.

"You're a beast," Steve said as they wrapped up. "A machine! I'm gonna feel this tomorrow."

Nat grinned. "I'll be here tomorrow if you need a partner."

"Absolutely!" They clasped hands.

She left the gym and jogged, feeling satisfaction down to her bones and hungry enough to shut down an all-you-can-eat buffet. It was noon, and the streets were relatively empty. The encounter with her father earlier was utterly forgotten. She started planning daily routines as she jogged to the hotel.

She was a few blocks away when a large pickup truck with a bunch of young white men in the truck bed came around the corner, turning toward her. A large American flag was on a pole bolted to the truck bed. As it approached, it slowed. The young men in the back were all glaring at her. The driver's window was down and he had his hairy elbow draped over the door. He scowled at her, his mouth working at something in his cheek.

He spat.

"Hey!" one of the boys from the back yelled. "Go home, spic!"

Nat picked up the pace of her run.

The driver gunned the engine and swerved the truck, hopping the curb and blocking her path. The men in the back were jumping out before the truck stopped.

***

Jonas tried to stave off dread as he sat on one of the twin rustic leather couches in the Oval Office. Being in this iconic room of the White House was not what made Jonas uncomfortable. He had been there before under different circumstances and under a different President. What made him nervous was Dolion himself.

Dolion was responsible for the only successful coup in U.S. history. He had been impeached in connection with the disappearance of a political rival. However, before he was convicted in the Senate, a crowd of thousands of Dolion's supporters arrived and went wild as two Governors, sympathetic to the Truth and Freedom movement, sent their national guard troops to 'stop the corrupt political lynching' of the President. Several of the key senators involved with almost convicting Dolion were subsequently incarcerated for life. One nearly died after sustaining a blow from a bat from the mob. Afterward, there were nationwide peaceful protests. They were violently suppressed. After a few months, the country returned to apathy. Sure, some people spoke of a civil war, but nothing was organized enough for that, and Jonas knew that Dolion's intelligence departments worked tirelessly to keep it that way. Sting operations crushing left-leaning militias were broadcast in the news, while right-wing militias were ignored, or even secretly supported.

Now, the elections were fully rigged. Some welcomed it. They wanted someone with power and authority in charge. The White House, Congress, and the Supreme Court still bore the same names, but were merely a facade. Dolion's die-hard Truth and Freedom supporters, like Jonas' brother Andy, called him God-Emperor Dolion, or GED, and relished in his victories.

Keeping a calm exterior, as if this was not his first time here under the new regime, Jonas took everything in surreptitiously. He felt disdain for the decor and anchored his unease to that.

Although he proudly displayed his grandfather's taxidermy in a specific room, that was as rustic as he got. Here, several western cowboy statues and landscapes adorned tables on either side of the three windows wreathed in elegant drapes. The outer drapes were the same red as the rug, while the inner drapes were a light tan. The flags of each military branch hung limply between each window behind the darkly stained old desk, as they had been on his previous visits. Now, the Confederate flag stood next to the flag of the United States. He shuddered and focused on the desk instead. He couldn't quite tell what type of wood it was. He resisted the urge to loosen his tie.

When the doors opened and the President entered, Jonas finally saw the man who was all over the news and social media. He seemed smaller in person. Several of his staff members walked in with him, doing their best to be as invisible or as conspicuous as possible. Jonas tried to hide the effects of his jet lag and lack of sleep.

"Mr. President," he said, clasping his hand.

"Thank you for coming, Mr. Williams," President Dolion replied in his drawl before sitting on the corner of the Resolute Desk.

"How're the wife and kids?"

"They're fine," Jonas replied.

"I know there ain't much slack in your rope," the President said, moving to sit behind the desk and clasping his hands. "So, I'll cut to the chase. I expect your workin' with the FDA has been about as easy as pissing up a rope."

Jonas smiled politely, acknowledging the challenges. It had been months since the announcement, but relations with the FDA had ground to a halt.

"I reckon you're used to your scientists bringing home the beef. They deliver. I got a doc what's been working on this for months. Ain't got squat to show for it, neither. And those FDA asshats. They're what we like to call all hat and no cattle."

"But," the President continued, "I reckon you can bury your concern right next to them. You've given me exactly the means I need to dismantle that god-awful, good-for-nothin' shithole of an organization."

"How so?"

"The people don't want to hear about public safety and health concerns. The damn pandemic made 'em hate masks, and pricks, and poxes, and whatnot. They want someone with power, not some technocrat, to tell them the truth."

He leaned forward.

"If I tell them that you got the cure for cancer, they'll believe me. FDA gets in the way, which they will, we shut' em down for good."

"Sounds like it is in my best interest to stay on your good side," Jonas said.

"Like I said," the President smiled, but it didn't touch his eyes. "Not much slack."

Dolion stood and walked to the window, his back to the room. Jonas watched him in silence. Dolion walked back to the desk and leaned forward on it. Jonas found the posture aggressive, like the stance of a manager as he's about to enjoy firing an employee.

"Which is why, Mr. Williams," he continued, "I'm startin' to wonder if a light or two has burned out on your string."

He paused, waiting for a response. Jonas said nothing.

"What is this bullshit I'm hearing about how your company never pursued the research for livin' longer?"

"Nobody was interested at the time," Jonas said bluntly. "Doesn't make sense to make something no one is offering to buy."

"Seems to me the deal is on the table, plain as day."

"Are we talking money or favors?" Jonas asked. "By my calculation, we are square on the FDA. It'll take my team time to resurrect that project and put it through R & D."

The President sat back in his chair, regarding him from under the brim of his hat.

"Dr. Ramsey was one of the brightest minds in this country. I reckon she was not the type to let any mystery she wanted to solve go unsolved."

One of the staffers whispered in the President's ear, and he nodded.

"Tell you what, Mr. Williams," he said with an air of finality and standing again.

Jonas stood too.

"Y'all do a little more digging. See if any of your cowboy scientists can pony up the goods. You keep my boys up to date. Do all these things, and you'll find the federal government will treat you sweeter than an old maid's dream."

The President turned and walked to the door.

"But I'm gonna level with you here and now. I need you to kindly go the whole hog on this, Mr. Williams," he said menacingly, stopping at the door. The President's words were the slow grinding of a boot heel into gravel.

"If'n you don't...well, I'm tellin' you right now...you just might find yourself sweatin' like a whore in church."

CHAPTER 8

Director Dina Keats walked briskly to the front of the security line and waved her badge to the guards. It was a formality. They knew her, and she didn't bother stopping to wait for directions; she knew exactly where she was going.

She hated the smell. It always made the bile rise in her throat. Dead bodies, torture, gore? No problem. But the smell of formaldehyde made her uncomfortable. Not that she ever let on.

"In here, Director," said Miles, her assistant.

The federal morgue was well lit. Most of the tables were empty, as was the chilly room. She and her men came to stand among the bodies, in front of the mortician. He was shorter than her, twice as wide, and had a simpering manner. This wasn't his usual scene. He was used to his own small-town funeral parlor. The size of the federal mortuary clearly both intimidated and fascinated him.

"Good afternoon, Mr. Hurvie," she said. "You wanna explain to me why I'm here?"

"S-sure," he said, wringing his hands. "The deceased died three weeks ago of metastasized serous cystadenocarcinoma found in the liver."

"Let me help you out, Hurv," Dina said impatiently. "As I understand it, I'm here because this corpse should have been cremated weeks ago. There was no ground for you to perform this autopsy. She was diagnosed with stage four cancer. No one needed you to cut her open to know that."

"Y-yes but..."

"Did the deceased's family consent to an autopsy?"

"N-No."

"Did you tell them you were performing one anyway?"

He shook his head.

An agent handed her a note.

"It says here," Dina read, "That the daughter, Ashlynn, called three times and visited once to ensure that the body was cremated. An internal note from the administrative assistant at the mortuary says, and I quote, 'Hurvie says cremation occurred...,' seven days ago."

Dina pointedly looked at the body.

Sweat visibly rolled down his forehead.

"So," she said. "You lied. Why?"

"I-I needed to perform..." he stuttered.

"What was the weight of the heart?" she interrupted.

"I-I didn't get that far," he said.

"You could be looking at jail time, buddy," Dina said. "I'll ask you again. Why am I here?"

Hurvie's hands were shaking too much to wring them now, so he stuffed them into his pockets.

"He wanted to study her brain," said one of the agents with her. "He's got some kind of noodle fetish."

Several of the agents sniggered.

"What did you want with her brain, doc?"

"S-she is," he stammered. "She was maybe the greatest scientist who ever lived! Her brain could tell us so much about how intelligence works."

Dina visually inspected Dr. Ramsey's body. There were no marks on the body except at the skull, which had been opened, exposing glistening flesh. It seems wrong, somehow, she thought. Hurvie's sweat was soaking through his shirt. Two of her agents stood beside him, a hand on each of his shoulders.

"What did you find?"

"Nothing!"

"Excuse me?"

"Yeah," the agent said. "Nothing as in she has no brain. It's gone!"

"Then what's this?" Dina asked, pointing at the spongy tissue inside the sawn-off skull.

"That's not brain tissue," Hurvie supplied. "It is adipose tissue."

"Which is..."

"Fat."

"Fat," Dina repeated. "You're telling me that inside the skull of the greatest mind of our time is a scoop of lard?"

"Y-yes, and no." He said. "It can't be. Her brain must have been removed somehow."

"So, you're saying she was murdered?"

"No," said Hurvie. "Like I said, she died of progressive liver failure due to cancer."

"Can you tell when someone took her brain?"

"The skull does not show signs of any callous tissue. The brain must have been removed years ago."

"So, she was a vegetable for years, while releasing the most prolific series of medical discoveries the world has seen," said one of the agents. "I don't buy it."

"Unless someone else was doing it, and she took the credit," said another.

"What kind of cancer did you say she died of? Liver?" Dina asked.

"No, ovarian cancer," Hurvie replied. "It spread to her liver."

"How could she be alive for cancer to kill her if her brain is just a hunk of chub?"

"It's a mystery," said Hurvie.

"Why would anyone take her brain?" another agent asked. "What's the motive?"

"Our friend here might know something about that," Dina said.

Hurvie swallowed.

"Her brain would be valuable for science," he said.

"Yeah?" said one of the agents. "How much do you think someone might pay to study a brain like hers?"

"I-I don't know," he stammered. "It's for science!"

"How much?" One of the agents poked his shoulder.

"Maybe...fifty million..."

One of the agents whistled through his teeth.

"Anything else I should know, Hurvie?" Dina asked.

"N-no."

"Okay," Dina said, turning to the agent silently standing beside her. "Get him out of here, process him. Get our guys on it. I want eyes on all the last known contacts with Dr. Ramsey in the past year before her death."

"Yes ma'am."

Miles followed her out.

"How much did the report say Dr. Ramsey was worth?" Dina asked him, as they walked.

"Eighty-six billion," Miles said.

"Uh huh," Dina said. "So why go for her brain? It's pennies in comparison."

"Hurvie is just a small-time hack. To him, fifty mil probably means something."

"So, someone beat him to it?" Dina said.

"Maybe."

"Doesn't add up. What about the kid?"

"What about her?"

"Tell me, Miles. Would you notice if someone stole your mom's brain?"

"Nope," he said. "She told me countless times she lost her mind when she had me. Anyway, the daughter never filed a complaint."

"What about this Daryl Sillich?" They arrived at her car; Miles climbed into the passenger side. "Seems like the CEO of NeoSol started aggressively expanding the company a few years ago."

"There's no intel on him still," Miles sighed. "Dude's a freaking ghost."

"Who else do we know might want to take her brain and fill her head with grease?"

"Daryl's all we got."

"We have eyes on him or the girl yet?"

"Working on it. Should have some on the girl today."

Dina went silent, so Miles started making some calls as she drove.

This case had landed on her desk earlier in the morning. She was asked to start investigating Dr. Aisling Ramsey, the superstar scientist. There were no other details given. Of course. As strange as the case was becoming, she wasn't yet convinced it was what she had signed up for when she took the job four months ago.

She was used to working with international criminals, weapons dealers, crime syndicates, and domestic terrorists. On her last mission, she had led a sting operation against the left-wing militia, the Defenders of the Constitution, effectively shutting down their base of operations. They were tough nuts to crack and she loved the cracking. This promotion was supposed to be much of the same, only with more authority and money. What did anything about this case have to do with national security?

"How many other cases is the unit working on?" she asked.

Miles rolled his eyes. It was the fifth time she asked this week.

"Seven other cases," he said. "It's probably the slowest it's been here for a while. Might be good for you to take a vacation if you want. Federal employees' vacation transfers with you, you know."

"Just what I need," she said dryly, glancing at him. "I'll take a foot to the throat on the side, please."

"I'll bet the guys would like that too," she added. "I've heard some loud whispers that I'm micromanaging too much."

"I've heard that too," Miles regarded her warily.

When he met Dina, he had thought of her as a bull in a china shop. The position, as he understood it, was too small for her personality. This is all simply a rung on the ladder for her.

"Anything new while we were talking to the would-be brain thief?"

"A report came in on the details surrounding the daughter's birth," Miles said as he scrolled through it on his phone.

"Sounds exciting."

"Dr. Ramsey paid a surrogate mother to carry the child."

"Why?"

"She had been diagnosed with ovarian cancer almost two years before that."

"Is the daughter genetically related to Dr. Ramsey?"

"Yeah," Miles read more. "It looks like she had a hysterectomy but had her eggs frozen. The baby was fertilized in a Petri dish."

"Who's the father?"

"There is no father listed on the birth certificate."

"Probably just an anonymous sperm donor then," she said. "Anything else?"

"Nothing special," Miles said, closing the phone.

"How old was she at that time?"

"Twenty-seven."

"What kind of mother would bring a baby into the world knowing that she could die of cancer before the baby is grown up?"

"And with no father," Miles added.

Dr. Ramsey was a career woman, Dina thought. I can relate to that, at least. Ramsey spent her young adult life studying hard, going into business, and achieving success after success, only to find out she had cancer. If she had wanted a family, she had set that desire aside to make her career work first. She probably couldn't make the time to find a husband, or partner, or whatever. I'm with you there, doctor. Obviously, you wanted a family, or you wouldn't have had a daughter. That's where we differ, Dina thought. I hate kids.

"I don't know, Miles. Maybe her brain was made of adipose tissue all along."

***

Becky frowned. The TV was broken again. She looked at the empty chair beside her bed once more, and her frown deepened. She took off her covers, sweating. It was too hot. Bun-Bun looked sad, so she hugged her tightly.

"I miss Miss Ash too," she whispered to her friend.

She put a finger over the rabbit's well-worn nose.

"Not so loud," she whispered. "Nurse Kay will get mad. It's supposed to be bedtime."

Bun-Bun silently agreed, and Becky glanced back to the empty chair again. She didn't feel like sleeping. The book beside her bed was boring. She didn't like the sound of the machine by her bed. It checked her heart, she knew. The beeping made it hard to fall asleep. Nurse Kay would usually turn it off for her, but tonight, she forgot. She was always really busy.

A long time ago, Mom would stay with Becky at the Hospital overnight. But then she couldn't anymore because of work, and Dad never could either. So Becky had to stay there alone.

"Hey there, Becky," Nurse Kay said, walking in quickly. She smiled and patted Bun-Bun's head. "How are you two doing?"

"Okay," Becky said, yawning. "Bun-Bun misses Miss Ash."

"Awww," Nurse Kay said as she picked up the clipboard hanging on the wall. She took the pen and wrote on the page.

"The TV broke," Becky said.

"It's not broken, sweetie," Nurse Kay said, writing. "It's after nine, so it's quiet time before bed."

"I'm not tired," Becky said.

"Mmmm hmmm," Nurse Kay said, setting down the clipboard and walking to the sink to wash her hands and put on gloves. Becky hugged Bun-Bun.

"Time to check your temperature," Nurse Kay said.

The thermometer was cool on Becky's forehead, even though Nurse Kay held it in her hand.

"Looks good!" she said, writing on her clipboard again.

She did all the things she always did. Becky felt bored and hummed to herself.

Another nurse put her head in the door. She saw Becky

watching her and smiled quickly. Becky recognized her but didn't know her name.

"Kay, are you good with covering for Joanne?" she said. "We're really short-staffed tonight."

Nurse Kay's shoulders slumped, but she said. "Yeah, okay."

The other nurse thanked her and left. Becky yawned and laid her head on the pillow.

"We're always short-staffed," Nurse Kay said. "At least the overtime is good."

Becky sat up and pulled the covers back over Bun-Bun, who seemed cold.

"Okay, Becky," Nurse Kay said, setting the clipboard back on the hook.

She walked quickly over to her and helped her tuck in the sheets.

"It'll be time for bed soon. Do you need anything?"

Becky frowned but shook her head. Nurse Kay smiled, hugged her, and walked to the door.

"Fifteen minutes," she said. "Okay?"

Becky nodded and picked up Bun-Bun, hugging her again. She laid on the pillow and yawned.

"Yeah," Becky replied to Bun-Bun. "She forgot to turn off the beep again."

Bun-Bun seemed too hot, so Becky took the covers off and sat up.

"Miss Ash always came at bedtime," Becky reminded Bun-Bun. "We would play games and everything!"

Bun-Bun started to cry, so Becky hugged her. She sniffed.

There was a knock at the door, causing Becky to look up, squeezing Bun-Bun tighter. A young woman with short, bright red hair walked in with a huge smile.

Becky gasped.

"Hello, Becky," Ashlynn said. "Hello, Bun-Bun."

Becky practically quivered with excitement as Ashlynn hugged her and Bun-Bun in one big embrace. Becky never wanted to stop hugging her. She was so happy she cried. Miss Ash was crying too.

"Oh," Miss Ash said. "I missed you both so much!"

"Me too!" Becky exclaimed.

"Would you like to play a game?" Miss Ash asked.

"Yes!" Becky squealed. Then she frowned. "But Nurse Kay said it's bedtime in fifteen minutes."

"How about a quick one then?" Ashlynn squeezed her again before standing. "And then we can read your favorite story!"

"Story!" Becky said excitedly, clapping her hands.

Ashlynn walked toward the cabinet. As she passed by the machine, she pressed the button that turned off the beeping.

She selected a game and held it up for Becky to see.

Becky shook her head.

Ashlynn put it away and picked another. Becky yawned as Ashlynn brought the chosen game back to the bed. The young girl's eyes drooped. Ashlynn set out the pieces for the game slowly, and by the time it was ready to play, Becky was sound asleep.

***

The whiskey didn't burn going down this time, but Jonas barely noticed. He carefully set the glass down on his desk next to the death threat.

Will you stand with us or against us? We are accelarating to the abiss. You cannot halt the TIDE. This corrupt land will BURN by BLOOD and we will cleanse our soil of filth. IT IS WRITTEN. He will cleanse this world, and all opposed will PERISH IN HIS WRATH. You and your ilk will burn if you stand in the path between us and our RIGHTEOS mission to restore our Nation to TRUTH AND FREEDOM!

Jonas lifted the glass again as he looked back to his phone which displayed his social media feed. The message was from several days ago, but he had thought of it when the note had arrived.

President Dolion
@POTUS
The CEO of SolviNext @JonasWilliams has the power to help us or hinder our nation. What will he do?

Was it connected? Jonas thought, then scoffed at his own naivete. I wasn't sure if I wanted to cooperate with him. Now, I'm absolutely sure I don't.

He looked back to the death threat.

How far will they take this?

Jonas' hand trembled as he brought the glass to his lips.

Nat regarded the young men as they approached her. She started to cross the street to avoid them, but several ran to block the path.

One of the boys whistled.

"Damn," he said. "You're one tall-ass bitch."

Nat intended to walk past them, but one of the men shifted and stuck out his arm to stop her. She regarded his hand and considered several ways to break it. She glanced around at all six of them discretely. Most were not much older than eighteen. The driver seemed to be in his thirties. Several had arms covered with symbolic tattoos. One sported "Truth" on one arm and "Freedom" on the other. Most wore beaters so they could show off their tats.

"Let me pass," she said.

"I guess it's true," one of them said as she blinked the sweat out of her eyes from her long workout. "Your back's as wet as it gets!"

They all laughed.

"You're one buff bitch," one of them said.

"She's probably a dyke!"

"Oh yeah she is," the driver spat again. He sneered at her, adopting a slow swagger. "A spic and a fag."

"You all need to walk away," Nat growled.

She moved to pass through a gap on her left, but several moved in to close it. A man came around the corner a block away. He saw what was happening and turned right back around.

"Move," she said.

They laughed and continued circling her.

"Last warning," Nat said, focused and calculating, her body coiling like a spring. "Let me pass."

The driver seemed to be doing his own calculations as his men continued to escalate their insults. He had a malevolent glint in his eyes as he reached into his pocket. He slipped the brass knuckles onto his fingers.

"You're gunna' leave my country," he said. "On your own or in the bag."

The others followed their leader's example, pulling out various weapons and squeezing their fists.

Nat burst into action, grabbing the hand that reached out for her and twisting it hard. There was a dull popping sound in the wrist. Violently, she yanked the man forward and rammed her knee into his groin. He fell to the ground, groaning. Nat kicked his face and he stopped moving, out cold.

Another man lunged toward her, and she used his momentum to hip-toss him. He tumbled into a couple of the other guys as he yelled in pain.

Nat threw a jab at the man closing from the right, crushing his nose.

Keeping her feet light, she brought an uppercut into the stomach of the man to her left.

His eyes bulged as he crumpled to the ground.

The click of a switchblade sounded behind her. The knife swished through the spot she had been standing as she rolled away.

The man gripped the knife white-knuckled, and lunged at her, thrusting and slashing.

Side-stepping a wild swing, Nat flowed into the opening with a left hook that crushed the bone beneath the knife wielder's eye. His knees buckled. Another man ran at her with a bat. She stepped inside his reach and mashed her palm into his closest elbow as he swung, causing it to hyper-extend backward with a loud pop. She used his momentum and shoved him head-first into their truck's door.

The driver stepped forward. She saw his punch coming and spun to lessen the blow to her short ribs.

The brass knuckles dug into her side painfully.

Nat pivoted and ducked his next violent swing, delivering a powerful three-punch combo that sent him to the concrete, a couple of his teeth bouncing next to him.

With the driver down, there was a lull in the attack, and Nat saw an opening to run away. But there were two left, shell-shocked. Nat attacked, driving her foot into the closest one's gut and sending him flying.

The other reached behind his belt.

She grabbed his arm and raised it sharply toward his head. It was still behind his back.

His shoulder popped loudly, and he squealed, dropping his gun.

A left hook to the nose and his squeal turned into a gurgle.

His legs collapsed, hitting the concrete with a dull thunk.

Nat kicked the gun away from the group. She glanced at the leader, who was staring at her hatefully as he struggled to pick himself up. He's never gonna let this go, she realized as she met his eyes. Maybe I can change his mind.

The leader groaned as Nat kicked his stomach.

Hard.

"You're lucky I allowed you to live," she growled.

He spat weakly, the bloody spittle dripping from his face.

"Fuck you," he wheezed through his missing teeth.

Nat kicked him in the same place, harder.

"Come at me again," she hissed, "and they'll need a spatula to pick up the fucking pieces."

She bent down closer to him.

"Do you understand?"

"Fuck y—!" he started.

Nat pulled back her fist and slammed it into his gut.

"What did you say?!" Nat yelled in his face.

The anger left his bulging eyes, replaced by pain and fear.

"Yeah," he croaked.

"'Yeah,' what?" she yelled in his ear.

"Understand," he gurgled.

"Good!" said Nat, shoving his face into the cement.

She resumed her jog.

She zig-zagged a path to the hotel, making sure none of them followed.

None did.

In the lobby, there was a water cooler with cucumber and limes floating around inside. She poured herself a drink and noticed a line of blood on her forearm where the knife had grazed her. Her ribs ached where the punch had landed, but she ignored it, wondering if she would need stitches for the wound.

"Nice day for a run?" An older man nearby asked cheerfully.

Nat nodded as she drank, hiding her arm.

"Just be careful out there," the man said. "This neighborhood ain't what it used to be."

"No," she shrugged. She crumpled the cup and tossed it into the basket without looking. She glanced over her shoulder at the old man.

"It's me that's changed."

***

Ashlynn lay on the bed. Driving to the hospital and visiting Becky and the other kids had made for a long and satisfying evening. It was also good to see Nurse Kay and the other staff. She was grateful that they extended a welcome to her and let her in after hours, offering their condolences for her mother. Some of the kids warmed up to her quickly. Becky was convinced she was the same Miss Ash she had always been, and Ashlynn had done nothing to dissuade her.

Ashlynn felt energized as she closed her eyes. Instantly, she was standing in a virtual simulation, a full-immersion virtual reality that she and Daryl had built. At her command, her hypercortex temporarily cut off all physical sensations from her body and supplied artificial stimuli to all her senses. It felt like she was physically transported to a completely different place. A place that responded to her wants and desires just by thinking about it. Despite that, it felt completely real.

She stood now in what she liked to refer to as her office. While her real body slept, the hypercortex turned her nights into one of the most productive times.

Her office was a versatile room with a large window that overlooked a crater on the surface of the moon. Above the horizon, the Earth rose half-lit by the sun. It was a simulation of Anders' Earthrise photo and was rendered almost perfectly. High-resolution photographs and 3D laser mapping of the moon made every aspect of the dramatic moonscape before her astonishingly detailed. The first time she experienced her virtual office, she cried at the beauty of it. She spent at least an hour observing the landscape with binoculars, not that she strictly needed them. She could have mentally zoomed in. However, the cool metal and rubber in her hands made it feel more real.

It was challenging to create the sensation of micro-gravity within the virtual office. The moon's gravity was one-sixth of Earth's. Having never experienced micro-gravity, she wasn't sure how to simulate the physical sensations. She figured she could approximate it until she had more direct experience.

Turning, she walked past a table with a mechanical design she had been working on. It was rendered in wire-frame so she could see all sides of it at once. If she wanted, it could be solidified and interacted with as if it were real. The robot was about the size of a cat and ant-like, with six legs, two humanoid arms, and hands. The design was a modification for construction robots she had already built, adapted for the weightlessness of space and the dustiness of terrain found on the Moon and Mars.

Mentally, she shifted to another design. A small robotic fly appeared. It was one of the first robots SolviNext had proposed to the military, but the Pentagon rejected the proposal for the robo-flies. The Martian atmosphere was less than one percent as thick as Earth's, so the robo-flies would not work there. Still, she wanted something small so that she could acquire excellent aerial views without using too much energy. She adjusted the design to emulate a small double-rotor helicopter with grasshopper legs. When she was satisfied, she closed the schematic.

She glanced at the clock and realized that the night had passed, and it was now late morning.

"Daryl, are you available?"

A tall handsome human figure appeared before her in a maroon cable-knit turtleneck and well-fitted black slacks. He had a dark complexion and middle-length wavy hair. He was like an older, more mature version of her high-school sweetheart. His dark eyes reflected the light of the room, exuding intelligence.

"Looking good," she said, smiling.

"Thanks," Daryl grinned. "But I wonder. Why do you prefer that I appear as a man?"

"Any news on SolviNext?" She dodged the question and started walking toward the window. Daryl's human representation followed.

"The shareholder vote was close, but, unfortunately, even with the Reeds acting as your proxy to represent your twenty-five percent share, the resolution to adjust initial pricing according to socioeconomic status did not pass."

The stock had fallen recently as 'free the cure' protests erupted and their dealings with the FDA had taken a turn for the worse. The President had changed his public tone from expressing interest to doubt about the cure.

"What about Jonas?"

"He also voted against the resolution, citing that he had another plan to rebuild shareholder value and make it affordable for all."

"He's probably going to seek government subsidy," she groaned inwardly. "If the President is against him, though, does he think that will work given the Truth and Freedom party is in power?"

"I can't answer that."

"That was rhetorical, Daryl."

"Noted."

As they walked, Ashlynn noticed the somewhat stiff movements Daryl made. He was simulating the motion based on the physics engine that governed this place but without the benefit of human sensory feedback mechanisms she used—a problem for another day. Daryl would need to be able to pass for a human on his own for the next phase of their project to work.

"Jonas took a risk by announcing it on the day of my funeral," Ashlynn continued. "He made a martyr out of me."

"There is a correlation between that event and a significant increase in searches for your name and social media tags."

"I suspect," Ashlynn said, "Jonas intentionally sparked this new 'free the cure' movement. I'm not sure if it's helping him or blowing up in his face."

The sound of someone knocking on a door came through a small speaker on her desk.

"Ashlynn? Lunch is ready," said Mrs. Reed. "Will you be joining us?"

Ashlynn re-engaged her physical body's voice. "Coming!"

"See you later, tiger," Ashlynn thought to Daryl with a wry grin. He waved as the scene faded and she slipped back into her sleeping body. It felt well rested as she stretched, yawned and stood up.

She encountered Mr. Reed in the hall, coming out of his study where he had been working.

"I'm amazed," he said when he saw her. "Your mother said you would need us to upgrade to a twenty-gig connection and I said I couldn't imagine how you would need all of that. But my teleconference was lagging, so I checked the router, and just now, you were maxing it out on your desktop! What are you doing in there?"

"Oh," she said. "Just a little virtual reality."

"Hmmm. Kade doesn't need that kind of bandwidth with his VR games."

"For what?" Kade said, catching up to them. He winked at her, but she averted her eyes.

"Do your VR games take up a lot of bandwidth?" Mr. Reed asked.

"I don't know, maybe," Kade said dismissively. He tapped

Ashlynn's arm as she took her lunch to the table. "Do you play ZeroLimit?"

"No," she said.

"What's that?" Mr. Reed asked.

"It's this sick FPS," Kade said.

"Your answers always leave me with more questions," Mr. Reed said. "Anyway, Ashlynn. Do you think you could reduce the use of the network this afternoon? I've got a presentation."

"Sure," Ashlynn said as they ate. "I need to go to the library anyway."

"Great," he said, bringing his lunch upstairs and returning to his study.

"Why the library?" Kade asked. "You can literally search up whatever you want on your phone."

"In order to get access to the library database, I need a library card," she said. "I have to do that in person. Plus, I like to hang out with the kids there."

"My friends and I are heading to the Pit later," Kade said. "You can come if you want."

"It's a nightclub," Daryl said in response to her mental question. The website with an image of the entrance appeared in the periphery of her vision. It said 'must be 21 to enter'.

"No thanks," she said, getting up and packing the rest of her lunch. "I have to study."

"Aww, c'mon," he said. "You could study later."

"No, thank you," she said. "I should get going."

Closing the front door behind her, she got into her car and pulled out of the driveway.

"That kid annoys me," she said.

"My readings of your subconscious mind tell me that you find Kade physically attractive," Daryl stated matter-of-factly.

"Are you reading me now?" Ashlynn growled.

"Yes. You are annoyed with me. Why?"

"Just because Kade is easy on the eyes doesn't mean I am attracted to him. He's half my age, immature, and infatuated."

"Yes, I can also detect your aversion to him, as well as other emotions. You have motherly feelings toward him, and you do not want to hurt him. And...you are uncomfortable with me discussing this."

"That is correct, Daryl."

"Why?"

Ashlynn took a breath.

"I'm starting to realize that some of my human thoughts are embarrassing to me, knowing that they are no longer entirely my own."

Ashlynn pulled into the parking lot of the library. She hadn't realized that she had found Kade attractive. The thought had never crossed her mind until Daryl mentioned it. As she thought about it now, she realized that a part of her brain must be continuously evaluating the physical attractiveness of others.

"Why do you feel shame?"

She ignored him, stepping up to the counter. At the front desk, there was a man in his mid-to-late thirties. He was handsome in a nerdy way, having the just rolled-out-of-bed look that was popular in the previous decade. His blue eyes were clear and warm.

"I'm beginning to see a significant difference in what you find attractive," Daryl said in her mind.

"Be quiet, Daryl!"

"Hello there," the librarian said cheerily.

"Hi."

"Can I help you with something?" the librarian asked.

"Yes," Ashlynn responded. "You need a library card."

"I do?" he laughed.

"I mean, I do," she said.

Daryl spoke quietly in her mind. "Ashlynn, physical anomaly detected. The surface temperature of your face is rising rapidly."

"I said Shut. Up!" she yelled at him in her mind.

"Okay," the librarian said, graciously turning away. "I'll go get the form, and I'll need your ID."

Ashlynn put her ID on the counter and collected herself. The librarian turned and took her ID. She read his name tag discretely.

"Ramsey," Josh said, scratching his chin. "With an 'ey,' That's interesting."

"How so?" she asked.

"Well, I think the more common spelling used to be with an 'ay'," he said.

"My grandmother said that her dad changed it long ago when they emigrated from Ireland," she said.

"Fascinating," Josh was still scratching his chin. "You wouldn't happen to know if he immigrated to the New Mexico area, do you?"

"Why yes," she replied, surprised. "They did. How did you know?"

"Well," he said. "I'm kind of a history nerd. I love that stuff."

"Really?" she asked. "That's amazing."

"Nice smile!" he said, snapping a photo of her for the library card. "Are you into history too?"

"A little," she said. "But I'm more into the sciences, I guess."

"Well," he said. "If you are interested, you could look up your family's history. I'll bet they were Catholic."

"How did you know that?"

"Well, many Irish immigrants came to escape famine but also for religious freedom. Most of the Irish who moved west were Irish Catholics. They might have been involved in the Mexican-American War."

He handed her the freshly printed library card and returned her ID.

"The library is all yours now," he said. "Would you like a tour?"

Ashlynn nodded. He smiled and said he'd be right back, as he went through the back office to get out from behind the counter.

"I think I understand now why what you felt for Kade was not something you would consider attraction," Daryl said in her mind. "The librarian's maturity and intellect are closer to your own. As you spoke with this man, your levels of sexual interest rose dramatically. I..."

"Daryl! That's quite enough!" Ashlynn said. "I'm not willing to have this discussion with you right now. Perhaps not ever! Understood?"

"Noted."

"My name is Josh," the librarian said, right over the top of Daryl's response.

"Noted," she said. He raised an eyebrow at her. "I mean, it's nice to meet you, Josh."

CHAPTER 9

Jonas ran his hand through his hair. Dr. Tamma waited as patiently as he could, given that he was anxious for approval to continue with his groundbreaking work. He could see the younger man's stress clear as day, having known him for years. The CEO was leaning on the large executive desk before him more for support than comfort. He kept glancing at a pile of opened letters stacked on one side of the desk.

Dr. Tamma thought that if anyone else had been in the room but him, Jonas would have made more of an effort to appear professional. As CEO, Jonas rarely made public mention of his religious or personal life. Dr. Tamma was honored that his boss was more casual with him than most.

"I've always known Ash to keep detailed records of everything," Jonas muttered. "She's never hidden anything from us before. She'd give away all our I.P. in a casual conversation with peers if I didn't stop her. How could you have found nothing?"

"Perhaps," Dr. Tamma ventured, "we could try the Ranch?"

"Yeah," Jonas nodded, turning away.

Dr. Scott Tamma had figured out long ago that when Jonas had any moral concerns, he always sought the counsel of his wife. But when it came to things Jonas viewed as hard business choices, he never hesitated. What kind of choice is this for you, Jonas? he wondered.

"Do you want to think it over?" Dr. Tamma asked.

"No, Scott," Jonas said. "I think it's a good idea. She's invited you to the Ranch before."

"I can't imagine that she wanted anyone to find this research," Dr. Tamma said. "Or she would've kept it in her files here at work."

"Well, she's not around to care, is she?" Jonas snapped, standing. "Look again!"

Jonas started to pace. His lips were working silently. It wasn't like him to speak like this.

"What's on your mind, Jonas?"

"Scott, have you heard about Senator Till?"

Dr. Tamma nodded. "Yes," he said. "Another missing person."

"Where do you think these missing politicians and journalists go?"

"It's obvious that someone cashed in Till's chips."

Jonas grimaced, accelerating his pacing. He didn't respond.

"Listen, Jonas," Dr. Tamma said. "What does that have to do with us? And why this sudden interest in longevity research? We're weeks away from starting the trials on the cancer vaccine. Isn't that more important? I think the FDA might want to cooperate soon, with the pressure the 'Free the Cure' movement is putting on them. We're on the brink of success. What's eating you?"

"There's always more going on than just your science, Scott," Jonas said.

"Well," Dr. Tamma sighed. "I could turn to drinking, I guess. But puzzling out nature's mysteries has always had a way of offering me such blissful escape."

Jonas barked a laugh. He stopped by the desk and picked up the topmost piece of paper in the pile of letters, skimmed it and set it back down. Dr. Tamma caught a short glimpse of a sloppy, handwritten scrawl. He shifted uneasily in his chair, eyes going wide.

"Is that a death threat?" Tamma asked.

Jonas handed him the note.

"I have my family to think of, Scott," Jonas said, staring at the smudged and crinkled paper. "You don't understand the pressure I'm under. We need to find the longevity research, and quickly."

"Why?" Tamma asked. A shiver ran down his spine as he read. "You should report this."

"I did," Jonas said. "The police aren't responding."

"But this doesn't have anything to do with longevity," Tamma said, putting the letter on the desk.

Jonas pinched his brow.

"Just find it, Scott. Please."

"Okay," Dr. Tamma said.

Jonas walked to the window.

"Do you mind telling me why you announced the cure early?" Tamma asked.

Jonas spoke over his shoulder.

"What do you mean?"

"Normally," Dr. Tamma replied calmly, "We don't make announcements like that until the FDA clears us for trials."

"I needed to force a hand," Jonas said.

"The stakes are pretty high for that sort of bluff."

"Ash has never dealt me losing cards," Jonas replied.

"True," Dr. Tamma stood. "But if you're playing at the same table as Senator Till, then you know the dealer's stacking the deck."

Jonas scrubbed his hand through his hair again and looked at the letters.

"Just find it," he whispered.

***

"Mr. Garcia," the man said, standing. "I know your track record. I've seen your portfolio. You made sound investments with me in the past. The problem is the law. We can't hire—"

"I'm a full citizen!" Mr. Garcia interrupted. "I am a legal citizen! I was granted citizenship in 1986. I have my papers—"

"You know it's out of my hands," the banker said, urging him toward the door. "Congress passed a freeze on the IRCA naturalization paths six months ago. There's nothing I can do about it. Why don't you just relax and enjoy your retirement?"

"I'm happy to work again!" Mr. Garcia said. "Hard work built this country. I know it! This is why we moved here. Please!"

"I'm sorry," the banker said. "I'd hire you in a second if only I could."

The security guards were walking toward them. Mr. Garcia glanced at the guards, then looked back at his old friend.

The banker shrugged and offered his hand.

Mr. Garcia regarded it, then walked out of the bank with his head held high. This was the last bank in town he hadn't applied to. The man he walked away from had been an old associate and Mr. Garcia's last hope for work in his old career.

Banking was his family's business. When México nationalized the banks in 1982, his family lost their private bank. The money they had received was barely enough to live on and then became worthless after hyperinflation set in. In the US, he had put himself through school and built a successful career as a banker. He had been able to retire with healthy sums in his tax-deferred retirement accounts. Unfortunately, when they had put his citizenship into question, his insurance coverage had been rescinded, and his assets were quickly depleted by medical bills from his wife's cancer treatments.

When he reached the spot where he had locked up his bike, it took a moment for Mr. Garcia to register what he was looking at.

The bike was destroyed. Both wheels were bent, and the handlebars and seat were gone. A bolt cutter had been used on the chain. A spray-painted sign was tossed against the bike.

It read, "spic'cycle."

Mr. Garcia looked around.

Down the street, he could see a group of boys sniggering.

Fists clenched. Mr. Garcia glared at them before turning to walk home. Without the bike, he doubted he would be home before dark. They had suspended his driver's license because of the new anti-immigrant laws. He had sold the cars.

He glanced back over his shoulder. The boys had gotten into a truck and were now following him.

"*¡Ay mierda!*" he muttered.

Glancing around, he found an alley and darted into it, sprinting as hard as he could. Within a moment, he was out of breath, but he kept running. He had to get to the end before they could see which way he went. When he got there, he dashed left, glancing over his shoulder. They weren't there.

He was about to step onto another street when he spotted a *camioneta con ojos* turning the corner and coming down the street toward him. It was a surveillance van looking for Latinos. He hid behind another vehicle and prayed.

Inside the van, the technician saw an alert. The Latino's face was shown, clearly peeking around the corner. The technician shook his head and acknowledged the alert. These idiots always thought they could hide, he thought. It didn't matter how fast they moved. The system was faster. Some wore masks. That's what the officer sitting next to the technician was for. The system logged the date and time, cross-referenced with the database in a fraction of a second, and informed the technician of Mr. Garcia's status. Pending citizenship reclassification. The technician clicked okay.

"Your time in paradise is almost up, beaner," he muttered, going back to the game on his cellphone as the driver continued patrolling. The officer never looked away from his phone.

Unknown to the technician, the system's algorithm noted

Mr. Garcia's location. Following protocol, it sent an encrypted message to the closest local militia with his photo, pictures of his family, and their addresses.

Mr. Garcia waited for the van to disappear down the street before glancing around for the gang of boys. He was certain the van had not seen him. He set out for the five-hour walk home, muttering a prayer of thanks.

***

Nat glanced over as Raoul was washing the vegetables thoroughly and quickly. The kitchen was filled with the smell of the homemade corn tortillas he had just finished pressing. Two days had passed since her run-in with the hoodlums. She hadn't told anyone about it, figuring there was no point. She hadn't seen the boys since.

"How is the restaurant doing with you gone a lot now?" she asked, as she put away the masa harina and started cleaning the dishes he used as he moved to the cutting board.

"My employees understand," he said, "and Luna is getting pretty good at filling in for me as chef. She's there now."

"Who's she?" Nat asked. "You never mentioned her before."

"She's my fiancée," Raoul said after a moment.

"Wow, bro!" Nat said, "Congratulations!"

He smiled as he dropped the cilantro into the food processor but then turned serious.

"The wedding will have to wait until Mami gets better, though," he said.

"Did you have a date set already?"

"Not really," he said. "The business is doing so well. We had a hard time finding a good date. *Un momento.*"

He pressed the button, and the food processor loudly chopped all his ingredients into salsa. He kept it short, so the salsa stayed chunky.

"Luna is good with the books and managing people," he continued, quickly moving to the frying pan. "She can talk to people, you know? They listen, and they like to do what she says. It's like magic!"

Nat laughed. "I'm not sure I want to meet her then. If she tried to get me to cook, I'd put you out of business!"

Raoul laughed as he placed tortilla pieces into the frying pan, added cheese, pulled pork, and then more cheese.

"You ain't bad, sis," he grinned. "Can you slice the avocado?"

"Yeah, I can," she replied, drying her hands.

"Now that Luna knows my recipes," Raoul continued, "We think we can possibly train others. We just gotta find the right people, you know?"

"Makes sense."

"So, what about you, huh?" Raoul said.

"I'm retired," she said. "Out of the Army."

"No, I mean you and Cici?"

Nat paused.

"It's complicated."

"So, what? You scared to commit or something?"

Nat thought how easy it was for people to say shit like that. She didn't respond, and Raoul sensed it had been the wrong thing to say.

"Sorry, sis," he said. "I can't imagine."

Raoul sprinkled some cheese and spices onto the chilaquiles after setting them on the plates and brought the fresh salsa. He took her sliced avocados and quickly arranged them in a beautiful arc. They sat at the table and said grace.

"God, this is good," Nat said after the first bite. "I think I need to move in with you."

Raoul laughed.

"Seriously, bro! Where did you learn this? I never saw you cook when we were kids."

"Well," Raoul said. "After you left, Mami started getting more and more sick, and I just wanted to help out. When I made my first quesadilla, I thought I'd add the fixings, you know, like at the restaurants or something. Turned out to be pretty good, so I was hooked. I started experimenting and stuff, and then, boom! It was me that was cooking for the whole family."

Nat stared at her food for a while. Raoul's comment about their mother caused her to remember her father accusing her of making her mother sick. She knew it was bullshit, but that didn't make the comment hurt any less.

"What's wrong?" Raoul asked, a loaded fork halfway to his mouth.

"Do you think we'll hear back about the treatment?" she asked, not wanting to share her thoughts.

"I hope so," he said. "We just have to pray."

"Yeah."

They ate a while longer in silence before Raoul spoke up again.

"Do you think they'll pass the law?"

"What law?"

"The one that requires homosexuals to be 'treated'?"

Oh, *that*, she thought. Given the news about her mother, it hadn't been on her mind as much lately. She had hoped that it would quietly go away, but since the FATs took over, they had been nullifying all the gay rights legislation that had been fought for over the years.

"Probably," she said.

"What are you going to do?"

"What can I do? The government already knows I'm gay. If they pass the law, they'll come after me."

"Well, don't you live in a state that protects you?"

"Yeah," she said. "There's that. But there are also hate crimes everywhere now. Cici and I have to be careful in public. She doesn't like that I am reluctant to go out these days. We used to go on cruises, but they banned gays."

"Damn," he said. "To think of how much you gave to the country for them to turn on you like that."

"I'd do it again," she responded with certainty. "I fought for what I believe this country stands for. Even if we fuck it up, there's no better chance at freedom than what we have. I believe that."

"Even if the FATs try to make a law that will force you to take drugs that will make you sick?"

Nat couldn't bring herself to answer.

Just then, their father walked in. He wore his suit but was sweaty and flushed as though he had been running. They watched as he walked silently past them and headed to Mami's room.

"Where does Papi go in the morning?"

Raoul studied his plate. "Looking for a job."

"What?" Nat was surprised. "I thought he retired?"

"They took away his social security," Raoul said.

"That's bullshit," Nat said.

"Yeah, it's real bad. Because he can't prove the family has been U.S. Citizens for three generations or some shit, he doesn't qualify."

"But he's been working his whole life!" Nat said. "He's been paying into it!"

"No Medicaid either."

"Then how are they getting by?" Nat asked.

"Savings, I guess," Raoul said.

He seemed to want to say more but didn't.

Nat thought she heard Alé tsk in the living room, but she only half paid attention. Nat had been saving, too, just in case they decided to stop sending her military retirement check. Living in the hotel was making it hard to save, however.

"He looks like he's aged twenty years," Nat said.

"I'm afraid," said Raoul.

"Afraid he won't find a job?"

"No."

"Then what?"

Raoul didn't answer.

***

While Ashlynn's body lay on her bed at the Reed's, her mind was elsewhere. She was standing in a perfect representation of the French Guiana Spaceport, watching as engineers busily went about their tasks inspecting a giant rocket. On the side of the rocket was her private company's emblem, NeoSol. Cameras all over the platform enabled her supercomputers to reconstruct the scene for her mental vista in near real-time. Beside her, Daryl stood watching with her.

"Everything is on schedule with the lunar base launch," he said.

Ashlynn acknowledged his comment with a nod.

"Daryl," she asked. "What do you like most about rocket science?"

"I do not have a preference for any given aspect," he replied. "All parts are necessary for the whole to be successful."

Ashlynn placed her hand on the surface of one of the rocket engines. The metal was warm to the touch. Above her, the rocket towered against a clear blue sky.

"Of course," she smiled. "For me, I think I like the cumulative nature of knowledge. The more we know, the more we can do. Some people stop learning at an early age. I suppose they are content with life. This rocket represents a massive amount of learning across many generations, united by similar dreams of space."

"Noted."

"Let's visit Dotsero, Colorado," she said, and the scene changed instantly.

The air became hot and stifling. It was not uncomfortable,

nor was the simulation representing the true temperature. The virtualized rendition of the space she was entering was too small for her natural body. Before her, a charred and dusty ant-like robot skittered along a tunnel past her, dragging a load of broken-up rock. Along its leg was the logo A.R.R. Another followed inches behind. And another.

"What is the status of the expansion?" she asked as she watched the endless procession.

"Excavation is seventy-three percent complete," Daryl replied. "My current projection based on updated survey assessments is that we're still eleven days away from excavating the necessary space for plant four. It'll be another few months before the new plant comes online, but it will double the power capacity. After that, it will be six weeks before computing and geothermal cooling catch up."

As he spoke, they moved against the direction of the worker line. The insect-like robots passed through them as if they were ghosts. Ashlynn and Daryl came to a larger cavern. There were robotic workers everywhere. The primary heat exchanger was being positioned next to a neat pile of large pipes. Near that, a crew of robots was excavating two large bores. Ashlynn willed herself through the bores, changing the scene to the natural aquifer below them. She overlooked a large water-dominated reservoir from her new vantage point, a natural cavern filled with water, steam, and volcanic gases.

"What is the depth here?"

"Seven hundred and fifty meters below the surface," Daryl replied

"Tell me the numbers," Ashlynn said. Daryl gave her the information as she watched several robots use lasers to update the 3D model of the cavern, take water samples for chemical composition analysis, install water level sensors, lay conduit, draw wire, and install temperature gauges. They worked in perfect synchronization. Two large holes for the production and injection pipes were being excavated, leading up to the chamber, one hundred and fifty meters above. Hundreds of robotic workers were drilling into the rock all along the bores.

Eventually, the cavern would become a subterranean binary geothermal power plant, converting heat to electricity as efficiently as modern technology would allow.

As Daryl spoke, describing the current estimates for the volume of water, average temperature, mineral composition, and natural flow cycles, Ashlynn envisioned the power plant. She modified the plans based on the updated estimates. As she worked, the plans were seamlessly superimposed on the cavern and the surrounding rock. The revisions were minor because the new estimates were more accurate but not far off from the old ones. As she worked, she grew more and more excited.

Since the installation of the hypercortex, her productivity had increased dramatically. At the mere thought, she could control her veritable army of robots to build whatever she imagined in real time. All the CAD tools she used for design and engineering were now available to manipulate in her mind. Using the same geothermal energy and water that one of the largest hot springs in the state used twenty miles away, she was turning the dormant volcano beneath her mountain cabin in Colorado into a two-hundred-megawatt power plant with no human labor on site.

It took thousands of human workers worldwide to build, assemble, and ship the initial components for her robots, but eventually, she would need robotic workers for the whole supply chain, end to end. That was why the caverns to the north were important. That was where the experimental mining and industrial operations to build the robots were being constructed. It was a testbed for what she was building on the Moon.

"Ashlynn," Daryl said, interrupting her thoughts. "There's a problem."

"What is it?" she thought absently.

"A legal hold and security override has been placed on your documents and project files at SolviNext."

Euphoria left in an instant and Ashlynn stopped moving.

"Are you sure?"

"Dr. Tamma accessed the files yesterday evening," Daryl knew her question was rhetorical but gave her the details anyway. "And later that evening, he attempted to access your personal data center remotely."

"What was he looking for?"

"Information on the Longevity proposal."

Ashlynn didn't respond, so Daryl continued. A list of files appeared in her vision.

"Here's a list of what he attempted to access. Also, there have been hundreds of attempted port scans to the data center in New Mexico on one of the ISPs. The source addresses are all SolviNext IPs."

"When did it start?"

"Last week," Daryl replied.

"Is there anything in the news on SolviNext that correlates?"

Daryl ran a search.

"Yes. Jonas met with the President six hours before the scans started."

"Jonas met with the President?"

"Yes"

Ashlynn scowled. "Any news about what they had discussed?"

"No."

Ashlynn wrote a few notes to herself about the power plant design and filed it all away. She willed herself to her office on the moon. The Earth was not visible this time of day, so she stared at the stars, shining solidly over the lunar landscape.

"Jonas hasn't thought about that proposal since he axed it, and now he is suddenly interested right after meeting with the President."

"Does this shift your priorities?" Daryl asked.

All of the key research was stored in her personal data center. If they could access that, then they would have everything. Should I wipe it? she thought. I'm confident I could recreate it if necessary. The thought of deleting the data made her cringe. If something unexpected were to happen, like a side effect that she didn't anticipate, which was highly likely given the novelty of the technology, she might need access to her raw data to troubleshoot the problem.

"Please encrypt and deep archive all my research," she said. "Then, replicate it in parts and upload it to the cloud in geographically distributed data centers."

"Noted," Daryl said.

As part of her research into treating cancer, she had tangentially realized there was a way to stop and even reverse the aging process for most mammals, building on the current state-of-the-art research in gerontology. At first, she was tremendously excited by the idea. If humanity were ever going to be able to travel in outer space, people would have to be able to live for extremely long periods of time. Space was too vast. The closest solar system, Alpha Centauri, would take over ten thousand years to travel to with current technology. Even if we could increase our speed of travel to ten percent of the speed of light, she thought, it would take forty-four years! We need a way to live longer, as a species, from that point of view.

But everything had changed when Congress killed NASA and the EPA. What happens if you remove the possibility of space travel? What if we stay on Earth, and everyone can live longer, and all too few care about how our activities destroy the planet? A plethora of ethical and sustainability issues would turn it all into a steaming pile of moral morass, doomed to cause a sixth mass extinction.

It is not for me alone to decide something like that, she thought. I do not want to be unilaterally responsible for the destiny of Earth and all humanity. No one person should have that kind of power.

She had pointed this out in a white paper she had submitted to a scientific journal a few years ago. Besides that, she had decided to keep a lid on her ideas, leaving out key details of her discoveries. This way, scientists would eventually get there, spark conversations, and hopefully, the world could decide through a democratic process. Those conversations had started, as she had hoped. However, that was before the government decided to crack down on biomedical research. That was before people lost trust in science and the government gladly abandoned all facts in favor of emotional manipulation. Those conversations had now stagnated, at least publicly. With broader progress stalled, it meant that private interests were more likely to pursue it in secrecy. She had not given much thought to what might happen if the wrong sort of people took an interest.

She could think of several world leaders who would love to remain in power indefinitely, to be tyrants forever. Was the current President of the United States one of them? In the new bill, he also championed limited scientific research in areas related to the field. A tyrant would want to keep the technology for themselves, so what better way than to make it illegal for anyone else but his government to be able to pursue? He had wanted to talk to me the day before my brain transfer surgery, she remembered. Was this what he had wanted all along?

"Ashlynn," Mr. Reed's voice called over the intercom on her desk, interrupting her thoughts. "I need to use the Internet for a meeting."

Reluctantly, Ashlynn returned to her body and sat up in bed. "Okay," she called. "I'm off. I need a break anyway."

Ashlynn freshened up her appearance, put on her thick sky-blue coat and bucket hat, and walked to the library. It was a chilly fall day, but the sky was clear and the sun cast a pale light on the semi-busy suburban town. It was a ten-minute walk to the library from the Reeds', a fact she hadn't realized the first time she had gone. It felt good to use her legs as she considered her situation.

"This probably means," Ashlynn thought to Daryl as she walked through the library doors, "the government might take an interest in me."

She pulled out her laptop and sat at one of the tables. She could interact with Daryl over the library's Wi-Fi or through her cell data and conduct research via her hypercortex. But she needed the laptop so people wouldn't wonder why she was sitting in a library staring at nothing.

"The idea that the government might take an interest in me is concerning," she said to Daryl, "But I fear I do not yet have enough information to make any decisions on reprioritization at this time."

"Noted."

"So," came a voice from beside her. "Back for the free WiFi?"

Ashlynn turned to see Josh leaning on a library cart beside her table. He wasn't wearing the sweater vest he had worn when she met him the other day. His well-fitted shirt showed he was lean and muscular.

"I'll be quiet now," Daryl said in her mind.

Ashlynn looked down at her laptop.

"Yeah, the connection here is pretty good," she replied, unsure what else to say and trying not to stare at Josh's near-perfect hands.

"What's in the cart?"

"The latest books to be burned," Josh said, his tone both joking and serious.

She read a few of the titles.

"Those are banned books?" she asked.

He nodded grimly. The cart was on the verge of overflowing.

"Anyway," he put on a grin. "The WiFi is better than most of the coffee shops. Still, it's odd not to see you reading over in the kid's section."

"Oh," she said. "I had some things I needed to finish up. I plan to read to the kiddos later."

"I figured," he said. "They love you. Some of the regulars ask when you'll be back. I'm sure they'd be scandalized to think you're over here, ignoring them."

"I've only done it twice," Ashlynn laughed.

"Well, regardless, I think my boss would be willing to consider giving you a part-time job if you are interested."

Ashlynn pondered that. She didn't really need a job, but it would make sense, given her physical age. It would mean that she could spend time with the children more regularly. And Josh.

"I'll think about it," she said.

"That sounds good," Josh replied. "Well, I have to get back to burning some books."

"Don't forget to salute," she laughed grimly, a little disappointed that he was leaving.

He smiled and pushed his cart away.

CHAPTER 10

Dr. Ramsey's property in New Mexico appeared as inconspicuous to Dr. Tamma as ever. It was a simple old ranch-style home on six hundred acres of land and totally off the grid except for a beefy internet connection. A white picket fence surrounded it. On the gate, a faded old hand-painted sign read *"Céad Míle Fáilte,"* and "Ramsey" was spelled out on the mailbox.

When Dr. Tamma approached the front, a computerized male voice greeted him.

"Hello, Dr. Tamma. How can I help you?"

"I'd like to access Dr. Ramsey's company files concerning one of her projects," he replied.

"With Dr. Ramsey having passed away, I must ask permission from her daughter. Please wait while I connect you."

As he waited, Dr. Tamma studied the yard. The house and front yard were much like any other property in the area. The solar arrays were odd but not entirely out of place. It was odd because they were all new, with the latest tech. There were also giant windmills lazily turning over in the afternoon breeze. The property appeared similar to the land of many farmers who sold some of their less productive plots to power companies who had installed solar panels and wind turbines. But rather than a few patches of panels here and a few turbines there, Dr. Ramsey's land was completely covered in them—every square inch. Almost two hundred thousand panels, he knew. What made this property special was the power-hungry subterranean data center below.

"How may I help you?" The image of a young girl who looked and sounded remarkably similar to Dr. Ramsey appeared on the small screen above the intercom by the door.

"I'm Dr. Tamma," he said. "I used to work with your mom. I need to access some information from her systems for our work."

"Hi, Dr. Tamma. I think I remember meeting you once

before—at the funeral. What information do you need?"

"It's regarding a proposal your mom made a few years ago," he replied. "The company finally has the time to work on it."

"I don't know much about what my mother had on her computers there," she said. "But you're welcome to look. I'm afraid there isn't much in the fridge except filtered water. I have to go, but I think you can use the computer in the study. Take all the time you need."

There were multiple clicking sounds, and the door opened.

"Thank you," he said, a little surprised. Given the security he had encountered thus far in trying to access Dr. Ramsey's files, he had expected more resistance from her daughter. I should have thought of this sooner, he chided himself.

The home was small and neat, with simple modern decor and a hint of vintage. There was an old upright piano in the corner and a violin case set reverently on the table next to it. A small wooden table was to the right, and an old-fashioned heating stove stood in the other corner. These stood out among the other modern things in the room, silent echos of the past. Although the place had been renovated to appear more modern, he could smell the age.

The study had a terminal with four monitors in energy-saving mode and a large workstation tower to the left in sleep mode. He moved the mouse. Facial recognition immediately identified him, and he was in.

After about five minutes, his hopes sank as it became obvious that he could only access his own files and preferences from his computer at the company lab. Despite being within a dozen feet of the data center below, he was no closer to accessing Dr. Ramsey's data. Dr. Tamma sighed. He had let his hopes rise, though he had expected this. He looked around for the kind of port his security guy had told him to find but only found two USB ports on the front. Per instructions, he tried to see if he could take off the case cover, but the chassis seemed as if it was built into the wall with no visible screws or latching mechanisms.

Reaching into his pocket, he pulled out several small devices. He selected the flash drive and inserted it into the port on the front of the computer, pocketing the rest. Pulling up the terminal, he ran the scripts on the flash drive. He called his cyber security specialist.

"Hello?"

"I'm running it now," he said.

"Okay. No eSATA port, I take it?"

"Nope. I can't take the cover off either."

Dr. Tamma described his inspection of the computer as the technician listened on the other side of the line.

After a brief pause, the specialist said, "Okay, I'm getting a connection now. I'll start working on it."

"Okay, I'm going to the Data Center and try my luck there," Dr. Tamma said. "Call me if you find anything."

He hung up and walked over to the kitchen. He opened the door to the basement and flipped the old light switch. It was even mustier down there than he remembered. He sneezed from the dust as he walked down the stairs. It was an ordinary, small, unfinished cellar with cinder-block walls, except for the broad metal door in a smooth concrete wall at one end. Above it was a video camera, and to the right was a biometric scanner. A monitor lit up next to the scanner as he approached it.

"Dr. Tamma," the male computer voice said. "I'm afraid you do not have access to this area."

"Would you be able to ask Dr. Ramsey's daughter for access, please?"

"My ACLs indicate that she also is not authorized to access this area at this time."

"When can she access it?"

"I'm afraid I cannot divulge that information," the voice said. "Please return to the study."

Probably not until she's over eighteen, he thought.

Pulling out his phone, he snapped a photo of the door and the biometric scanner.

"Taking photos is prohibited," the voice said. He was startled.

"You are in violation of acceptable conduct. Your access to this site has been revoked. You have two minutes to leave the premises before the authorities are summoned."

"But wait!" he said, "I didn't know."

"If it appears that you will not be off the premises within two minutes, I will preemptively alert the authorities of your trespass. You have one minute and forty-three seconds to comply.

He turned around and quickly went up the stairs. That was unexpected. What could she be hiding to prompt a response like that? Why had she programmed what it would take to recognize someone taking a photo of the data center entrance? She lived here, in the middle of nowhere. He hit redial on his phone.

"No luck," he said. "I guess I triggered some kind of alarm. I've got to leave."

"Okay. You can remove the flash drive."

He took the drive. The specialist was silent except for occasionally clacking his fingers on a keyboard. He spoke when Dr. Tamma got into his car.

"Something isn't quite right," the specialist said.

"What is that?"

"Well, I have accessed her profile, and I seem to be able to pull up any part of her research that I want, but some of it is encrypted."

"Why would she do that?" Dr. Tamma asked. "I've never known her to be this secretive."

"Yeah, that's what I mean. There are duplicates of the files here that she had on her workstation in the lab. But there are also three encrypted files that total three terabytes in size that aren't opening with her profile hash, and there are no key files elsewhere."

"Well, keep looking," Dr. Tamma said.

***

Ashlynn watched Dr. Tamma drive away via the security camera, listening to his conversation with SolviNext's cybersecurity expert through the intercoms of the Ranch house until he was out of range. As soon as he had inserted his flash drive into her honeypot computer to attempt to hack the system, she decided to work to gain access to Dr. Tamma's phone. If he's willing to try to gain access to her system illegally, his stuff was fair game as far as she was concerned.

Ashlynn opened her eyes. The library was mostly empty. She had finished her shift with the children and now sat in her favorite study area with her laptop open. One of the librarians motioned toward the clock. It was closing time.

"Okay," Ashlynn said quietly. "I'm packing up."

She gave Ashlynn a thumbs-up and a grin. Over lunch, the other librarian mentioned that she had a date that evening and that things were going well. Ashlynn was glad she had accepted the job helping with the children. It was nice to meet new people. She collected her things and stood, wondering how far Jonas and Dr. Tamma would go.

It seemed unlike Jonas to do this sort of thing, she thought. Chris wouldn't stand for it. Did she know? Dr. Tamma, however, she knew had always been willing to push the envelope. Scott Tamma liked to gamble in his spare time and especially loved poker. He tended to think that sometimes the means were justified by the end, a trait that had always made her uncomfortable. She considered her own actions. Now that I have access to his phone, I can potentially gain more access to SolviNext without using my own credentials. Should I? If they hadn't tried to hack my stuff, I would never have considered spying on them. But still, how far am I willing to take this? However I try to justify it; it's against the law. What's really at stake here?

Lost in her thoughts, she didn't see Josh coming around the corner in time as she briskly walked toward the exit. They collided, and she fell at an awkward angle. She reached out to catch herself. A sharp pain shot through her left wrist as she hit the faux-stone floor.

"Shit," Josh said, "I'm so sorry!"

For a brief moment, Ashlynn was angry at herself for not paying enough attention and being clumsy. As she tried to use her wrist, the pain of it began to feel overwhelming, dissipating the anger instantly.

"Are you okay?" Josh was asking.

She tried to move her wrist. The pain was intense, but it moved.

"What's your assessment, Daryl?" she thought.

"I cannot tell what the damage is," said Daryl. "However, the hypercortex is recording the nociceptor signals and tracking the associated messages through your brain. If you try to occupy your thoughts with something else, I can record your natural inhibitory activations."

"You can numb the pain," she thought.

"Yes," Daryl replied. "Or I can make it go away after further analysis."

"Yes," she thought, "that could be useful."

If something were to happen to her in space, she thought, many possible circumstances would require her to work through the pain of injury to mitigate the issue, especially if it was life-threatening. She took a deep breath and focused on Josh.

"I think I need to get my wrist checked," she said aloud.

"Shit," Josh replied. "Can you walk?"

"Yeah," she said. "I think so."

She started to pick up her laptop, but Josh beat her to it.

"We should get you to the clinic," Josh said. "I'll drive you."

"Okay."

She stood awkwardly as Josh urged her toward the library exit. She checked her laptop. The screen was cracked and it wouldn't boot. At least I'm not the only one injured, she thought. They walked to his car. It was an antique. He wrestled with the passenger door and opened it with a loud squeak.

"I guess I haven't used the passenger side for a while," he apologized, moving several books off the front seat. She only caught the title on the topmost book. "The Age of Revolution."

"Looks used to me," she said.

The interior of the car smelled old, but it was clean.

"Daryl," Ashlynn thought. "Can you do a background check on this guy? I don't want to be getting into the car of a sicko."

"You're already in the car," Daryl said.

"Just do it, please?"

"He has no record."

"Seat belt?" Josh asked as he got into the driver's seat.

"Does it still work?" Ashlynn asked. It creaked loudly as she pulled on it. "Maybe this twine on the floor would work better?"

"Either one might snap if we hit a beach ball," he replied as he started the car. To her surprise, it started smoothly. He grinned as he pulled out of the parking spot.

"These old imports will run forever if you treat them right."

"It sounds like it runs well," she said.

"I rebuilt the engine last summer."

"So you're a mechanic too?"

"It's a hobby," he replied. "How's the wrist?"

"I think it's sprained," she said. "It's swelling."

"The clinic isn't far. Just five minutes."

"So, you're into fixing cars and revolutions?"

"What? Oh, you mean the book?"

He turned out of the parking lot, driving quickly.

"It's part of a series that covers the major modern ages. This one starts with the French Revolution and discusses how that set the stage for the Industrial Revolution. Just a bit of light reading."

"Light?"

Josh laughed. "How about you? You've been working at the library for a week. When you're not working you're always engrossed in your laptop. Now you're going home with 'Lady Chatterley's Lover.'"

"I am?"

"Wasn't that one of the books you had?"

"All I had was my laptop and coat," she said.

"Oh," he replied, "I guess it was one of the books I was reshelving then."

"Are you sure you're not interested in early twentieth-century erotica?"

Josh laughed, "I think it's more about how love is only fulfilling if it's stimulating for both the body and the mind."

"So, it was your book then!" she said.

"No, I was just re-shelving it!"

"Right," Ashlynn said sarcastically.

"If you don't ever check out books," Josh said. "Why hang out at the library?"

"I don't know," she said. "I guess I used to go to the library a lot when I was younger. The smell of books reminds me of... good memories."

Josh pulled into the clinic, and she checked in. When they sat in the lobby, a man walked in. Ashlynn thought he seemed familiar, but she couldn't place him. Several other people were waiting. Under a wall-mounted TV was a play area where a child was building something with multi-colored blocks.

"So, what do you think you'll study in college?" Josh asked.

"I'm not sure I want to get any more degrees," she said absently.

"Oh, I thought you were too young for a degree."

"Yeah, well, if you knew my mom, you wouldn't be so surprised."

"What's your degree in?"

"Computer Science."

"Seems like everyone's into that these days," he said, his eyes taking in the lobby. "There's good money in that field, I guess."

"It's okay," she said. "It's a means to an end."

"To what end?"

"I'm not sure I know you well enough to say," she smiled and stood as they called her name.

***

"Found it!" Raoul said, pulling out a heavy box from under the stairs.

Nat turned toward him, amazed as usual at his energy and amused at the dust covering his face and black shirt. The house was quiet.

"Found what?"

"Ha ha! You'll see!"

He struggled to carry the box over. It was barely held together with multiple pieces of tape. When he brought it closer, she recognized it immediately.

"You've got to be kidding me!" she groaned, swiveling in her chair to stand.

"Nope!" He plopped the box into her lap before she could get up to leave.

"You really want to do this now?" she asked.

"Why not?" he said, sitting across from her as she set the box on the table. He reached in. "Hey! Memories is what brings us together! *Familia*!"

"What if I want to forget?"

"Sis," Raoul said. "I don't blame you. But some things you don't want to forget—like this!"

He brought out a photo album, flipped through it, and stopped on a page, beaming with delight. He turned the album so that she could see it.

It was a picture of him on his birthday. Nat was smearing his face with cake. Before she could help herself, she was laughing.

"Oh my god!" she said. "I had forgotten that!"

"Yeah, you would, Jerk!" Raoul laughed.

"Look, there's Alé!" Nat said.

"Stuck up as ever," Raoul agreed. "I hated how Alé always bullied you."

Nat met his eyes. He had a knowing look on his face.

"She kind of bullied all of us," he chuckled. "Still does. It's just who she is."

"Yeah," Nat said, eyes returning to the photo.

"I wouldn't want it any other way, though," Raoul said. "That's *familia*! It can be a pain in the ass, sometimes, but it's all we have."

Nat regarded him, taking in his words. Before she could reply, Alé walked into the room. She was on her phone, talking to one of her girlfriends and ignoring them, as usual. She got a soda out of the fridge, smirked at them, and walked back out.

"*Que será, será.*" Raoul shrugged. He turned the page.

Nat examined another photo. This one was of her and her mother. Nat was wearing jeans and a t-shirt, while her mother stood over her with her hands on her shoulders, smiling in a beautiful yellow dress. One of the knees on Nat's pants was torn, a skinned knee barely visible, and she had dirt and mud stains all over her.

"You never smiled," Raoul said, looking at the picture with her. "And you always dressed like that. I think Mami understood you pretty well, even then."

"I remember she always made me wear those god-awful dresses," Nat said.

"Just on Sundays," Raoul said. "You wore jeans almost every day."

Nat was about to counter but realized that he was right. It had been only on special occasions. Sunday church was always special, but she was out of the dress by noon and was free to wear whatever she wanted for the other six days of the week. Looking back now, she thought it wasn't that she didn't like the dresses. They were just impractical.

"Your mind plays tricks on you," Raoul said. "You know?"

They looked through the albums together, laughing, until Nat's phone rang. It was Cici.

Nat stood and took the call, walking out the back door into the cool winter night. She noticed it was after midnight.

"Hey, *querida*," Nat said.

"You sound like you're in a good mood," Cici said, a little hurt in her slurred voice.

"Raoul and I were going through our old photos," Nat said. "Have you been drinking?"

"Oh. Yeah."

"What's wrong?"

"It's been a week since you called, you know," Cici said. "You didn't answer my texts, so I was getting worried."

"Oh," Nat said, realizing the truth of that.

"You know?" Cici said. Nat could tell that she had been crying. "When I met you, I couldn't help but fall for your *chingoga* military chick style, you know?"

Nat waited.

"You were always quiet, but when you said something, it was

like, you meant it. It was deep. And when you don't say stuff, it's like even deeper, you know?"

'When I don't say stuff?' Nat thought. What's she talking about?

Nat checked her phone, seeing a dozen or so missed messages. She had been so busy spending time with her mother, taking care of her, working out, and catching up with Raoul that she hadn't thought to check for a while. That's when she saw the date.

"Shit! I'm so sorry," Nat said. "I'm sorry I missed our anniversary."

"Nat," Cici said. "I know you got a lot going on. I do. But it's been eight years. Eight years! And sometimes, you're just as cold as when I met you."

"Nat," Cici continued after a deep swallow Nat could hear. "I love you. And I always will. But I just gotta know, babe. Do you love me too?"

Nat was silent, walking to the front of her parents' house as she searched her feelings. She wondered if having this conversation when Cici was sober would be better. She thought of Terry.

When she reached the front of the house, every muscle in her body tensed. Someone was running from the front porch. They jumped into the back of a truck waiting in the street. A truck she recognized.

"Do you love me too, Nat?"

The tires screeched as they drove away. Nat vaulted up onto the porch. The words "GO HOME BEENER" were spray-painted across the front of the house.

"Shit, Q!" She said. "Some assholes just vandalized my parent's house!"

But the line had gone silent.

***

Dr. Geoff Baker tossed the last of his life's work into the metal trashcan. The smashed and mangled hard disk sparked and sputtered as it clinked inside amidst burning paper. He rubbed his hands together nervously as he looked around the lab. All the lab technician stations were vacant. Their shifts didn't start until later. Many were interns, eager to do important research on their way to their degrees and willing to put in the extra time to do so, as long as it wasn't pre-sunrise on a Saturday morning. He liked to come in this early because it let him organize his thoughts for the day ahead.

"All for nothing," he whispered.

"Geoff!" Dr. Sarah Hains rushed in, speaking in urgent but hushed tones. "Look! Look at the news!"

She showed him her phone.

"Senator Till found dead in skiing accident," read the headline.

"Oh my god," Geoff breathed. "So, it's true."

"You don't believe it either?"

"No."

"Wasn't he the one who promised us protection?" She stammered. Geoff had never heard her speak so anxiously.

Dr. Baker noticed another notebook at one of the technician's workstations and retrieved it. He tossed it into the fire. Dr. Hains seemed to notice the fire for the first time.

"What are you doing?"

"I'm going to leave the country," Dr. Baker said. "Maybe start a new life."

His phone buzzed. It was a message from the White House. "Progress?"

He considered the message for a moment and typed a reply.

"I'm doing a test right now and the results look promising."

He showed it to Sarah.

"I guess I am too," she said. "I've enjoyed working with you, Geoff."

"Likewise," he replied. "Safe travels."

"You too."

They hugged, then Sarah left hurriedly, wiping away tears.

Geoff went to his office and packed his things into a box. He worked quickly, packing the photos of his family and the drawing made by his three-year-old daughter. He hadn't seen her for over a month.

"How did I get myself into this mess?" he muttered as he stuffed his laptop into his bag. "What did I think would happen? I should have never accepted this position. I was too cavalier about Dolion, too damn focused on the fountain of youth."

He put on his coat, slung his laptop bag over his shoulder, and grabbed the box. He turned off the light, left his office, and walked through the lab and out the door. He fished his phone out of his laptop bag as he took a left down the hallway and scanned his email. There was a verification from the airline for his tickets to Brussels, Belgium. No extradition there, he thought for the thousandth time. A sound caught his attention, and he looked up. He sucked in a breath.

Ahead, two huge men in black suits walked shoulder to shoulder down the hallway toward him. He felt a knot of dread twist in his gut and stopped breathing.

"Dr. Baker," one said. "Would you please come with us?"

"I have a—"

"A flight to catch?" One of the men interrupted, as they stopped in front of him.

"No, you don't," said the other.

Geoff licked his lips, looking from hard face to harder face. They were blocking the only exit. He had nowhere to run.

CHAPTER 11

Walking along the creek with Josh, Ashlynn absently played with a buckled strap on the hand brace, while holding her latte. The PA had said it was a fairly mild sprain. She'd felt nothing since Daryl negated the pain response through the hypercortex. The swelling had gone down, and she already seemed to be able to use her hand. However, she still wore the brace they had given her. The sprain needed to heal, and use would interrupt that process.

Mr. Reed needed the internet in the afternoons a lot recently for strategy presentations, so she had started visiting the library almost daily. Josh had become more attentive towards her after the accident, asking her to join him for walks along the creek that ran by the library over their lunch break. The weather had been cold, but today it was warm enough that he was only wearing a light jacket. The path by the creek was lined with trees, wild grasses, and bushes, all dry and leafless in the cold winter air. The creek bubbled along beside them, lined with melting ice.

Josh had a rugged but clean look. His clear, bright eyes were in stark contrast to his dark salt and pepper hair. His jaw and chin were prominent. He noticed her fiddling with the hand brace.

"I'm so sorry about that," he said.

"It's fine, Josh, really. I'm not very coordinated. I should probably exercise more."

He shrugged, unconvinced.

"You seem pretty fit," she changed the subject.

"I like to do triathlon," he replied.

"And why would you torture yourself with that?"

He laughed.

"All those hours running, swimming, and biking give me time to think."

"I suppose," she remarked. "You think about your history and such as you ride? How do you stay awake?"

He laughed. "I have fallen asleep on my bike before. I don't recommend it."

"So how did that happen?" she laughed too.

"I had it on the trainer," he said. "And I had pulled an all-nighter."

"Studying?"

"Partying."

"No sympathy," she said

"None needed," he replied. "I certainly did my share in the College of Farts and Parties."

"So now you're making up for it?" she asked, sipping her latte.

"I have no regrets," he said. "I don't need much. Just some good conversation here and there, and I'm happy. Besides, history is a wealth unto itself."

"Do you think we can learn from history?" she asked.

"Of course, but that sounded like a loaded question."

"Yes and no."

"What do you think its purpose is, then?" he asked.

"History seems like a flawed recording of a random walk of events generated by a highly social species with evolutionary baggage."

"Okay, that's a lot to unpack," Josh laughed.

"You could learn more from a fortune teller."

"Ouch," Josh replied. He extended his hands in front of himself, shook them, and then pretended to read out of them. "Reply hazy, try again."

"I'm sorry," she said. "I can be a little jaded about certain subjects." He shook and read his empty hands again.

"It is certain," he intoned.

She laughed. Josh laughed, too. He tilted his head as he looked at her.

"So," he said. "What's a 'random walk?'"

"Probability theory. It's a type of Markov process where the behavior is independent of past history, but each state is based on the previous state."

"Did I mention I suck at math? I'm into history, remember?"

She laughed. "You like history, not math? You need to sort out your priorities."

"Right," he laughed. "Okay, maybe you can explain it to me as if I'm, like, five this time?"

"I sometimes think of it as the adjacent probable."

"Isn't 'adjacent' a geometry thing?"

"Yes, it means adjoining line segments, or vectors, and so on."

"If that's your idea of an explanation for a five-year-old…"

"Okay, stop!" she abruptly put her arm out. She stepped ahead as he stood still. His smile took the cold in the air away, yet he was oblivious to its effect on her. He sees me like a younger sister, she thought. I wish he didn't.

"Look at your feet," she said, putting her thoughts about him out of her mind. "Right now, all around you is three hundred and sixty degrees of possible single steps you can take. Forward, backward, and so on. Got it?"

"Yeah."

"So, one step or one jump away from where you are, that's the realm of possible steps for you right now. You can't take a step and be in London. That's impossible. All that's possible is right here around you."

"Okay, keep unpacking."

"So, given all that possibility, what's the most probable?"

She grinned and pointed at the sidewalk.

"This is like a social construct. You're more likely to walk along this sidewalk, right?"

"Sure. But, you know, there's something to be said about Thoreau."

She laughed, "I think you mean Frost, don't you?"

"There were no heavily traveled roads to the cabin at Walden," His eyes sparkled, and she felt he had tested her.

"You said you hated math," she said, playfully nudging him.

"I do."

"Yet you like tangents!"

"Only the punny kind."

She laughed as he put her empty latte cup and his into a nearby compost bin.

"Transcendentalism aside," she grinned, "most people in history are likelier to stick to the path. They will probably walk on the sidewalk. They are limited in their actions to the next single step they can take on the sidewalk. The adjacent probable is the next probable step, as dictated by society and their experience. Thus, the contemporary social constructs are their chains. Constraints, but also a linkage of steps connected by the preceding step."

"Well, then," he said, scratching his chin in thought. "If that's the case, how do you explain major events of profound change like the French Revolution?"

"Well," she said as they continued walking. "As a history buff, I'm sure you know many of the underlying factors that increased the possibility of a revolution in that volatile time.

"Sure," he said. "Dislike of the king and the estate system, the Enlightenment, food shortages, and news of the American Revolution were potentially all inspiring factors. Are you positing that the Revolution would have been impossible without those factors?"

"Impossible?" she tapped her lips. "Perhaps, but definitely improbable. It would have been too much of a leap. Those factors created the possibility for change. I argue that the Revolution became more likely to happen in the presence of those factors."

"The French Revolution is said to have been a time of radical change driven by passions," Josh said, scratching his chin. "It seems strange that such a monumental Revolution that birthed the ideals that founded the principles of liberal democracy would not be a leap of great magnitude. Perhaps reason and passion together allow us to leap further. To attain the impossible."

"Interesting thought," she replied excitedly. "But, Hume said, 'reason is a slave to the passions.' I think reason doesn't exist without something real, something solid to grasp. Evidence. And passion could be defined as emotional momentum. It helps drive willpower against adversity. Sure, you can jump further if you get a running start, but every step from the moment you begin becomes the previous step. Momentum builds; thus, each step unequivocally dictates what is probable for the next step."

Josh stopped walking and she met his eyes, puzzled.

"Ppshhhhh!" he said, gesturing with his hands expanding from his head. "My mind 'asplode!"

"Oh," she said, her face reddening as she stepped away. "Sorry."

"Why are you sorry?"

"I can get carried away sometimes," she said.

"No worries," he said, "We should get back. It looks like it's going to start snowing soon, and your afternoon group will be waiting for you to read to them."

They turned to walk back to the library. It was then that she noticed a man who had been walking behind them. He immediately averted his gaze when their eyes met. He was wearing casual winter clothing, apparently out for a stroll. She had seen him before, she realized, and her stomach sank—first at the clinic, then at the library a few times, and now here.

"Daryl," she thought. "Who is that man? I think he's stalking me."

"On it," Daryl replied.

"Ashlynn," Josh said, bringing her back into the moment. "Are you saying human history is part of some grand plan, and we're just following along?

"Not at all," she said. "I don't think there's a master plan."

"So," he said. "How do you know that anything is probable? If no one put the metaphorical 'sidewalk' there, then what did?"

"Humans put the sidewalk there."

"But that's different than the French Revolution."

"No, that emerged out of the social constructs of the time."

"But it still became a sidewalk."

"When a child learns her ABCs for the first time," Ashlynn said, "the letters are foreign concepts. The neurons in the brain make new connections, like footsteps through the jungle. The next day, the same connections fire and are reinforced, and more connections are made. She's following her footsteps from the day before. Time passes. With more practice, a small path appears, worn with use. She learns to read, and the path becomes gravel. She learns to write, and cement is added. She reads more complex books, and soon it's nothing but the familiar, well-worn path that will never fade."

"But that's just one person's mind."

"Sure, but who taught her to read? Who taught them? It's not only reading. It's culture, religion, myths, legends, and on and on. Those paths become highways we all travel to create our current understanding of the world around us."

"That sounds like you believe the world is what we make of it," he said, his fingers running through the stubble on his jaw, "But as a scientist, surely you must believe in an objective reality?"

"Sure, as an ideal, yes," she said. "But idealism is naive. Regardless, culture could hardly be considered an objective understanding of reality. Even scientific human understanding is always a model of objective reality, but it is always subject to revision given new data. It's a slow process, dictated by the adjacent probable."

"Well," he said as they arrived back at the library. "I can't say I've had that deep a conversation for a while."

"Me either," she replied, grinning.

***

"You seem a little quieter than usual, sis," Raoul said as he expertly chopped the cilantro.

"I'm a fucking idiot," Nat muttered under her breath as she rinsed the vegetables, thinking of Cici. And the truck. It took several hours to clean off the paint, and she hadn't told Raoul or the others yet. She contacted the police, and they said it was happening all over and that they were too overwhelmed to handle each case.

Did I somehow put a target on my family? she wondered.

"What'd you say?" Raoul asked.

"Did you file the application for the cancer cure trial?" Nat said.

"Yeah," he said. "I sent it overnight this morning. That shit's expensive!"

Nat agreed, handing him more to chop.

"I think we have a chance," Raoul said brightly. "When it had that question about family members in the military, I got this good vibe, you know?"

"Don't get too excited, Raoul," she said.

"Why, sis? You are a war hero! Don't you have like three different medals or some shit?"

"That was a long time ago, and it was one."

"So what?"

"So, things change. The military has changed."

"It don't matter. A medal is a medal."

Nat finished rinsing and noticed the glow of Alé's phone emanating from the dark living room.

"Why do you think *Chola* does that?" Nat asked, diverting the topic.

"What?"

"Sit in there with the lights off?"

"*No se*," Raoul said, moving economically as he stirred, tossed the food in the frying pan, and then added more veggies into a large pot. He lowered his voice. "She says it's her 'me' time."

They traded glances and laughed.

"When isn't it 'me' time?" Raoul asked conspiratorially.

"I heard that, *idiota*," Alé yelled from the living room.

Nat laughed silently and grinned at her brother.

"How was the gym today?" Raoul said. "I'm making sure there's extra protein and carbs for you."

"You're too good to me, Raoul," she said.

"Hey!" he said, getting more serious. "The way I see it, this family could do better by you more often, you know what I mean?"

He quickly and expertly carved the chicken as he spoke. She didn't respond but felt a warmth in her chest at his comment.

"I mean it."

"Thanks, bro," she said. "The gym is always good. Calms my nerves. There's a regular, Steve. We keep each other on our toes."

"So tell me about your work now," Raoul said. "Does your job need you to be in good shape?"

"Yeah," she said. "I'm a bodyguard. And I work security at clubs."

"Like a bouncer?"

She chuckled, "Yeah, I guess."

"I'll bet you surprise a lot of men. Anyone ever surprise you?"

"One came close," she said. "He pulled a knife I didn't expect."

"Shit! What happened?"

"It worked out in the end."

"Did he cut you?"

"A little."

She pointed to a thick, one-inch scar on her thigh, below the hem of her shorts. Raoul whistled through his teeth.

"I'll bet you got him good," Raoul said, bumping her elbow with his.

She grinned.

Raoul noticed the scab of the recent cut on her forearm was falling off in places. She never mentioned how she got it, and he hadn't found a polite way to ask.

He silently watched her set the table as he sautéed and spiced the chicken. She always had to duck under the lamp over the table and hunch her back to reach the table's surface, but the movements seemed to convey something more than usual. She was hurting inside, he thought. A lot of hurt. The more time he spent with her, the more he could see it.

He served dinner and most of the family came into the kitchen. Raoul went to take Mami's plate upstairs, but Papi put his hand on Raoul's shoulder and took the plate. Raoul fixed a plate for him and brought it to their parents' room.

His father was seated beside the bed and was feeding Raoul's mother. She ate slowly, her eyes half closed.

Raoul kissed his mother, and she smiled warmly at him. He could not understand her weak voice but could hear her heart.

"I love you too, Mami," he said.

He kissed her again.

When he returned to the kitchen, he found Nat eating alone.

"How is she?" Nat asked, not looking up.

"The same," Raoul said.

Nat set her fork down and stared at her unfinished plate.

"You know," Raoul said, leaning back and folding his arms. "When I broke up with Sofia, I was a wreck. Actually, she dumped me. I hadn't dated someone after her for like ten years."

"She was a fool to dump you, Raoul," Nat said, standing. "You're as good a man as it gets."

"No, sis," he said. "I was the fool. I'm not perfect."

"Well, no one is, I guess," Nat began washing the dishes as she spoke. "But you're kind, you care about family, and you cook, and clean, and—"

"When I am around," he interrupted. "I'm the best! But, with Sofia—the business took all my time. You know? At the restaurant, I'd work like twenty hours a day. Market at four in the morning until full cleanup was done at midnight. I still have my cot there, you know. I don't sleep on it no more, but it's still there. Luna thinks it's a waste of space. We got stuff all over it now. But I need it there. It's to remind me."

"Not to work as much?"

"To keep my priorities straight," he said. "I love what I do, sis. But I also love Luna. Papi loved what he did. Mami did too. And I know you love what you do. Alé...she's the black sheep, eh?"

"Bro! I swear! Keep it up, and I'm gonna' pop your head!" Alé called from the living room.

They both laughed.

"Alé loves her work too," Raoul said. "What I'm saying is, don't be a fool like me, huh? If you got a good thing, make it a priority."

"It's not that simple for me," Nat said. She gathered the dishes, conscious of the dog tags shifting against her chest. "I know you're trying to help, Raoul. But some wounds are too deep."

"You mean Tracy?" Raoul asked.

"Her name," Nat replied flatly, as Raoul grimaced, "was Terry."

She continued washing the dishes without another word.

***

"His name is Alex Munta," Daryl announced as the 3D model of the man she had seen earlier appeared in the center of the room at the Reeds'. She looked at him with her arms folded over her stomach, absently comforting a bellyache.

"He's thirty-five," Daryl continued. "He's been officially unemployed for five years. Prior to that, he served in the Air Force, toured in Afghanistan, and graduated with a Master's in Communications. He has no social media and no immediate relatives."

Alex was definitely the man following her. He was stocky. His face in the photo was just as serious as in life. Unemployed? With his background? She doubted it.

I assume there are textbooks on topics related to government intelligence, she thought. But how much good would that do me? The best way to get the kind of boots-on-the-ground experience and skills Alex Munta probably possessed was through experience in the military. She had never been intimidated by a subject in or out of school, until now. It was one thing to read a thriller about someone from the government stalking the hero in a book or to watch a movie with a clever ex-operative trying to escape the system that won't let them go. But it was quite another to have an actual government agent following you around.

"Daryl," she said, closing the window curtain and laying on the bed with her hands resting on her uneasy stomach. "I think it's time we give you a crash course on hacking."

"Okay."

"Shadow me," she said. In an instant, she was also sitting at her desk in her lunar office, multiple monitors glowing before her, her chair reclining as the monitors followed her. She logged on to a hackathon website and jumped into a live event.

"I'm a little rusty," she said, the knot in her stomach unraveling a little. "I haven't done this since I was working on my Computer Science degree. But it'll be fun!"

***

The next day, Ashlynn brought her new laptop to the cafe before going to the library. She ordered a chai latte and found an empty table, trying not to overthink where to sit. Nervous energy tumbled in her stomach as she set her latte down, pulled a small case out of her backpack, and opened it. Inside was a tiny robot that looked like a small fruit fly. She gave the mental command to activate it and its wings fluttered. The robo-fly took off toward the ceiling and landed upside down on one of the rafters in the exact center of the shop.

"I knew these things would become useful," she thought. "Maybe it's not so bad that the DoD contract for my robotic insect surveillance line fell through all those years ago."

A few minutes later, Munta walked in. He ordered a coffee, black, and sat less than thirty feet away. Ashlynn mentally commanded the robo-fly to land on the wall near him as he pulled out a laptop, and a moment later, she and Daryl could see his computer screen through the robo-fly's eyes. He opened a command prompt and started running a port scan on all the devices on the network.

"He's spoofing," Daryl said. "Using a different MAC than last time, even though he's apparently using the same laptop."

"Yup," she said, "but most operating systems started doing that on public networks a few years back. However, the scanning pattern is the same as yesterday. What does that tell you?"

"He's using a toolkit of scripts?"

"Yup!" she thought.

Signaling the robo-fly, she watched through its eyes as it flew above her and headed toward Munta in a convincing fly-like random flight path. A few minutes later, it landed lightly in his hair and entered low-power mode. Munta did not notice.

"He's probably using a toolkit provided by his organization," she continued.

"He took the bait," Daryl said. "He's in the decoy virtual machine on the laptop."

Munta planted a rootkit and gained administrator control over the virtual machine. He gained access to the emulated camera and microphone. He did the same thing with her emulated phone.

"Give him the show, Daryl," she said.

Daryl proceeded to dynamically emulate what any normal teenager Ashlynn's age would be doing on her laptop in a coffee shop. As Munta gained more access, he wouldn't see anything out of the ordinary.

"That's the problem with most toolkits like his," Ashlynn said to Daryl, "It's likely they skip corners and are as bare bones as possible. Things like encryption take resources, so they use clear text. They like to think they're the only lion in the room."

"Your counterattack over his open connection is working," Daryl said.

Within five minutes, she had access to his device and began studying its security configurations.

"Okay, Munta" she muttered. "Who do you work for?"

CHAPTER 12

"It's beautiful," Nat took it all in as she entered Raoul's restaurant, *Cocina Mamá.* The walls were painted a warm, deep yellow, with shiny copper pots artfully adorning them. Her eye was drawn to the vivid blue countertop of the bar. It was a fusion of modern American and traditional Mexican styles, managing a clean openness while tastefully showing deep colors. The dark wood tables and chairs provided a sophisticated feel.

"It's exactly like Mami's kitchen."

"Thanks, sis."

Raoul's chest was puffed out, and he smiled as he watched her take it all in.

"We've been slowly improving the look."

"Has Mami seen it?"

"I showed her some pics," Raoul said with a hint of sadness. "She'll see It when she's better."

A short, stout, and beautiful woman in an apron walked out from the kitchen door well obscured by the bar, carrying a box of tableware rolled in napkins. When she saw them, she set the box on the bar and hurried to greet them with a huge smile.

"*¡Hola!*" she said brightly as she enthusiastically hugged Nat. "You must be Natalia! Raoul has told me so much about you!"

Nat returned the hug, noticing her heavily accented English.

"It's Nata, with family," Raoul said.

"You must be Luna," Nat said. "It's nice to meet you finally!"

"*¡Igualmente! Mucho gusto!*"

They walked around, Raoul pointing out his favorite decorations.

"Are you still at the hotel?" Luna asked.

Nat nodded.

"Raoul! Ay ay ay!" Luna turned, chastising him. "I told you to invite her to stay with us!"

"Nata, you should stay with us!"

Nat laughed.

"If it's not too much trouble," she said. "I'd love to."

"*¡Excelente!*" Luna said, beaming.

"Here," Raoul said. "Have a seat."

Luna returned to the kitchen, and Raoul sat across from Nat after she chose a seat with a full view of the restaurant and the door. Chips, salsa, and queso dip were on the table.

"Luna's got something special in mind for you," Raoul said excitedly. "I'm looking forward to it myself!"

"She seems wonderful," Nat said. "I'm happy for both of you."

"We got our challenges," Raoul replied. "But we work through them."

"Have you had any...other challenges?" Nat asked, frowning. "Like vandalism?"

"Not really," Raoul said. "Helps that the police captain loves Mexican food. A lot of people like Mexican. They maybe want us out of the country, but not our food."

"You're lucky."

Nat ate a few more chips in blissfully crunchy silence.

Raoul chose his words carefully. He wasn't sure if there was a delicate way to put it, but he had wanted to ask for a long time.

"You never told me what happened to your fiancée, Terry," Raoul said.

Stunned, Nat stopped chewing for a moment, searching Raoul's eyes. The food turned to cardboard in her mouth. Raoul had known that she was engaged—he was one of the few people who had known—but he was right. She hadn't told anyone what had happened. She picked up her napkin and wiped her mouth, then stood.

"Where's the bathroom?"

Raoul stood too and pointed, wisely choosing to stay quiet.

In the bathroom, Nat peered at her face in the mirror as she washed her hands in cold water. As usual, her eyes held a tightness. Frown lines were beginning to make a home on her forehead. She dried her hands and reached into her pocket, pulling out the black dog tags. Terry's tags. The dark metal felt warm. Reverently, she rewrapped the chain and put them back into her pocket, looking back up to the mirror.

She didn't leave until she had forced her face into submission.

Raoul was sitting at the table, staring at his plate dejectedly.

"The bathrooms are nice," she said as she sat. "I like the sinks and the flowers."

"Thanks."

Nat dipped another chip into the queso. She studied it for a while.

"Remember when we were kids," Nat finally said. "I was sick at home, and you were playing baseball at 'dead field'?"

"Yeah," he said. "Charlie Bater. I haven't thought about that *pendejo* for years."

"He was after me," Nat nodded, "but since I wasn't there, he and his punks beat you up."

Raoul nodded. "That was the only time I ever got beat."

Nat stared at the chip basket.

"I never blamed you for that, Nata," Raoul said. "Besides, you kicked his ass when you got better."

"If I had been there," Nat said softly, "you would never have gotten hurt."

Raoul opened his mouth but closed it. He reached across the table and grasped her hand in his. He saw Luna glance around the corner and shook his head at her. She was surprised, but she went back.

"It was supposed to be me," Nat repeated. Her face was expressionless.

"What happened, Nata?" Raoul asked gently.

"You always knew how to talk to people," Nat continued, gazing somewhere past him. "Everyone is always at ease with you. You have a gift that sets people at ease, Raoul. But Charlie, he...he wasn't normal. He would ambush kids like it was a game. Like he was hunting them."

"Yeah," Raoul said. "But you never got ambushed. It was like you always knew what he would do before he did."

"I knew he would be there," Nat said.

"But you were sick, Nata! Mami wouldn't let you out of bed. You can't blame yourself!"

"I had a feeling."

"Nata..."

Raoul tried not to wince in pain as Nat's grip unexpectedly crushed his hands, causing several knuckles to pop. Her eyes stared at nothing, her face blank.

"When I got to the CSH, it was too late. She was gone. Terry. Her...her legs were gone. She..." Nat trailed off.

He wondered what she meant by 'cash' but said nothing. He assumed it was some kind of military acronym. Tears fell from her expressionless eyes. Oddly, her face was smooth. Controlled.

"She took my mission," Nat said. "Like you. Terry took the IED that was meant for me. It's my specialty. I find them. She…"

Nat stopped talking, clenching her quivering jaw.

Raoul watched his sister cry. She sat stoically as she stared into the distance, reliving the horror. Raoul wanted to reach out to her, but he knew she wouldn't want to be touched right now. So he stayed still and only embraced her with his heart.

You'd had it so rough, sis, he thought—all your life.

A sound caught Nat's attention. She turned to see her sister, Alé, entering the restaurant. As she wiped her eyes, her grief was immediately replaced by a burning resentment.

***

"Ashlynn."

Daryl stood by in a casual black t-shirt and blue jeans as she stared thoughtfully at the modeling hologram table in her virtual office. Before her was an upgraded version of the robo-fly and the deployment support box she had been designing. Now that she was using them to help keep her safe, the first thing she had done was remove the A.R.R. logo from the side. No need to clue the government in on her private robotics company.

These new models were also more power efficient and could perform better reconnaissance on computer hardware. They were ready for production. The new box was simple. It had the capacity to hold 52 flies and several small accessories. Although the flies had the ability to connect to WiFI, they wouldn't always have immediate access to a closed network, so the box needed to provide temporary cell connectivity until access could be gained.

She switched to a newer version of the robo-fly, which was far from complete. With this model, she was trying to work out a way to upgrade the robo-flies to generate power on the wings from solar energy. Readily available photovoltaic technologies were generally too heavy a material for the wings. Zooming in on the fly's wing until it displayed the atomic matrix, she attempted to design a graphene-based solution with layers of selenium and tungsten. She kept an eye on the factors critical for structural integrity during flight, as well as power production and storage.

"There must be an optimal balance," she muttered.

Daryl, who had been watching silently, touched her elbow.

"Ashlynn," he repeated.

"Hmmm?"

"I've gained access to Jonas' devices and created a virtual representation of his office," Daryl said. "You asked me to inform you when the task was complete."

"Mmm hmmm," she replied distractedly. "Maybe if I..."

She made an adjustment and looked at the parameters. Nope.

Ashlynn stepped back and sighed. She glanced at Daryl and mentally switched gears. Engineering had been a pleasant distraction, but now her worries returned to her in a rush.

After counter-hacking Munta's phone and laptop, Ashlynn had been optimistic. Through the robo-fly that had landed in his hair and traveled with him when he left, she had figured out where he was staying and ultimately gained access to his phone before the robo-fly ran out of power. She could read his email correspondence with his boss and listen in on his sparse conversations. She was beginning to sense a pattern to his methods of watching her. But the initial hope she had gained from her exploits was wearing off.

"You seem troubled," Daryl said at length.

"Did you have a chance to investigate universities that offer degrees in Intelligence Studies?" She asked.

"Yes," Daryl said. "Those programs have all been shut down by the government."

"Textbooks?"

"Banned."

"Of course," she said dejectedly. "Were you able to find an expert we could employ or interview?"

"Everyone with a degree or experience in the field is currently working for the government."

"Surely not the retired ones. Not everyone."

"All that I could find," Daryl said, "they either came out of retirement or are deceased."

Ashlynn's eyes widened and she shook her head.

"I am ignorant of all the adversary's objectives and capabilities. I doubt textbooks would have been greatly useful in this case anyway."

"You have gained access to Munta's devices and know more about him than he does about you," Daryl said. "Surely you have the upper hand."

"Incautious and illusory," she replied. "Dr. Tamma always said, 'A pair of bullets can shoot the holder.'"

She smiled, remembering working with him. Despite some of his shortfalls, she liked Scott Tamma and wondered what had driven him to try to access her data center. Although she had gained access to his phone when he left her New Mexico home, she hadn't tried to exploit that access yet. Daryl had gained access to Jonas' systems as well. The doors were open. Should she go through?

Ashlynn walked to the robo-fly hologram and flicked her hand unconsciously, causing the modeled wing prototype to spin wildly.

"This is no game I am in," she said, "but I suppose game theory might apply."

She watched the fly spin slowly to a stop.

"I cannot apply models to predict their actions if I don't understand their objectives. Iterated deletion escalates risk because the more actions I take, the more information I provide them. Whatever action I take or don't take provides them with information. In turn, they may respond by changing their goals—goals of which I am ignorant."

"Perhaps," Daryl offered, calmly following her movement through the office, "It would be helpful to perform scenario analyses, working backward from the worst possible outcomes and then testing hypotheses in the iterations."

She nodded thoughtfully but didn't respond as she returned to the view over the lunar valley.

"There are my objectives to consider as well. They may be ignorant of most of my objectives. However, NeoSol has made it no secret that it wishes to travel to space. It's my company—Aisling's company. Since NeoSol has been expanding since my death, would they conclude that my 'daughter' cares about it just as much as I did? Targeting NeoSol in any way is enough for them to disrupt everything."

Ashlynn pinched the bridge of her nose and shifted her gaze up to the stars.

"I don't have time for this!" she exclaimed in frustration.

"Sun Tzu said that 'the wise warrior avoids the battle,'" Daryl quoted. "But when a battle is necessary, he emphasized the importance of striking quickly and decisively to minimize losses and achieve your objectives."

Taking a deep breath, Ashlynn considered what Daryl said, the name tickling something in her memory. "What else does Sun Tzu say that might be applicable?"

"He says, 'All warfare is based on deception,' and stresses the importance of disguising one's intentions through false demonstrations and creating illusions that confuse the enemy. These actions can be used to create surprise attacks."

"Attack the U.S. Government?" Ashlynn said incredulously.

"That is your adversary, correct?"

"Yes," Ashlynn said, walking to the couch. "Yes, the words are vague enough that I suppose I could interpret them as being applicable. It's not the best of references. Still, if I obfuscate my true objectives, they must spend time discerning the truth. Even a false attack can be fabricated to achieve a distraction from a real objective."

She sat and hugged a pillow, drawing comfort from it.

"Maybe instead of an attack," she muttered. "It can just be any kind of deception that is the opposite of my objectives."

"What are your objectives regarding this?" Daryl asked.

"I don't want the government to be able to interfere with the launches at any point," Ashlynn replied. "And once I'm in space, I don't want them to be able to harm me. I'll need a lot of resources constantly going to the moon. Any interruption to that could cost my life."

"Then, I recommend you consider moving assets out of NeoSol and setting up dummy corporations," Daryl said. "This way, it would be harder to freeze your assets. Dissolve NeoSol and make it appear as though you are abandoning your objective. Let the dummy companies continue the work."

Ashlynn nodded thoughtfully. "A false demonstration."

"Correct."

"I should also find a way to reliably gather intelligence on all their operations," she said.

She sighed. It made sense, but the thought of giving up NeoSol was almost unbearable.

"How many lunar landings have we had?" she asked, knowing the answer but taking comfort in hearing it.

"Thirty-seven," Daryl intoned. "Sixteen more before all the necessary components for the lunar base are in place. As requested, you and the last of the lunar robotics will be in the last six payloads of phase one."

Ashlynn set the pillow aside and stood. She walked over

to the hologram and closed the model for the new robo-fly. It was an interesting problem, but the Moon base was more interesting to her. She loaded the model of one of the mining robots on her hologram and studied it, tapping her lips.

"What I most want to do now is finish the design for this. But instead, I should be thinking about how to deal with the threat."

"Shall we discuss some options?" Daryl suggested, bringing up a floating screen with a priority matrix.

"Give me a few hours with this miner first," Ashlynn said. "Then we can do that."

"Okay," Daryl said.

"And Daryl…"

"Yes?"

"Go ahead and execute your idea," she said. "Dismantle NeoSol, but ensure we can still achieve the missions."

"Of course," Daryl said.

"And," she said, finally deciding to err on the side of caution for her safety over her moral objection. "I want to know what Jonas is up to."

"Of course," Daryl said.

***

An hour later, Ashlynn watched as Jonas paced his office. Daryl had managed to position a robo-fly near one of the ceiling lights. Because of the robo-fly's limited battery life, it had to operate in low-power, low-resolution video mode. Daryl took the low-resolution data and reconstructed Jonas' office in astonishing detail.

Jonas was more disheveled than when she last saw him at the funeral several months past. She had never seen him so anxious.

"What do you mean, 'you can't?'" he yelled into his phone. "What the fuck am I paying you for if you can't follow her research? She's only fucking human!"

Jonas ran his fingers through his hair, looking up at the ceiling. His suit looked slept in, and his fist was shaking by his side.

Ashlynn was shocked. He's coming apart, she thought.

"If she solved the delivery mechanism issue," Dr. Tamma said on the other line, "there's no mention of it anywhere. The delivery mechanism and protein synthesis issues aren't even described. It's possible that she was unaware of those concerns, given where she stopped researching. Doubtful, but possible. She wrote the abstract on the white paper like she had a four card straight on the flop, but when the cards came up, she didn't have squat."

Ashlynn thought it was just like Dr. Tamma to get stuck on the wrong things. How often had she told the staff that the key to breakthroughs was constantly re-framing your thinking? Be creative! Yet they kept falling victim to the Einstellung effect and getting stuck in ruts. The answer to both issues was staring them in the face—in the cancer cure. She could hear the stress and anxiety Jonas' words were causing Tamma. It was effectively thwarting the creative thinking he needed to solve the problem by creating a fear-based environment. Fear and creativity aren't great playmates, she thought grimly. It was clear now why Tamma had gone to her ranch. Jonas must have pressured him somehow.

Ashlynn wanted to rescue her team. Witnessing them being abused this way hurt. But the fact was that she didn't want them to succeed this time. She had to let it go.

"I. Don't. Care!" Jonas was yelling. "Figure it out!"

He slammed the phone down on his desk and hung his head before snatching it up and checking it for damage. He started to wander around his office listlessly. His hands were still shaking. In all the time she had known him, she had never seen him so upset. Her anger at the way he had treated Tamma began to melt into concern.

She could hear, though faintly, chanting outside the office windows. With a thought, a small screen appeared in her vision. A security camera on the exterior of the SolviNext building showed her that protesters were outside chanting, "Free the cure! Free the cure!"

Cancer didn't care about politics. It didn't care about free markets or liberal or conservative values. People died of cancer despite all these things. So now that there was a possible cure, the demand for it was unifying people.

She strongly suspected that Jonas had something to do with the protests. When the FDA had tied up the trials, she guessed he'd had his marketing team come up with a few well-chosen words in social media that caused the public to put pressure on the FDA. But despite the strong showing of support for SolviNext, it still surprised Ashlynn how many counter-protesters there were. Although most of the crowd believed in the cure, more than a few outliers believed it was part of a conspiracy—especially since the President had expressed doubts. The Truth and Freedom party was on the fringes of the crowd and carried signs that said, 'Wake up!' and 'It's another form of control from the old establishment!'

Jonas' phone rang.

"Sir," Lisa said, when he answered. "You have a call from the Department of Domestic Intelligence. He has questions about Dr. Ramsey."

Jonas took a breath, stopping in his tracks.

"Put him through."

"Hello," he said.

"Hi, Mr. Williams," the voice said. "Thank you for taking my call."

"How can I help?" Jonas asked, guardedly.

"Do you know a Daryl Sillich?"

"What?" Jonas asked, confused. "That's no one. That's what Dr. Ramsey called her digital personal assistant."

There was a pause on the other side of the phone. Ashlynn felt her stomach lurch.

"Her 'digital personal assistant,' you say?"

"Yes," Jonas replied, "You know, like—"

"I know," the government agent interrupted. "Do you know about the NeoSol Corporation?"

"Yes, that's her private..." Jonas hesitated, "Wait, it's incorporated now?"

"It was incorporated five years ago," the agent replied. "The CEO is listed as Daryl Sillich."

Jonas' back straightened for a moment. Dread and panic were building in Ashlynn's mind. She glanced at Daryl, who took the news as calmly as if they were discussing the weather.

"Sir?" the agent said after the long pause.

Shit! Jonas thought as he stared at his phone. What do I say now?

"Sir, are you still there?" the agent asked again.

"Uh, I'm sorry," Jonas said. "I just got an important message that distracted me. I have to take care of it. Did you have any other questions?"

"No," the agent said, "Not at this time. Unless..."

"What?"

"You have any other information that might be helpful?"

"Not that I can think of," Jonas replied.
He hung up.

CHAPTER 13

Jonas gazed at his phone for a while, his head spinning. Could it be true that Daryl, Aisling's AI program, was running NeoSol even though she had passed away more than six months ago? How was that even possible? Was that part of the legacy she wanted to leave her daughter?

"Aisling," he said aloud. "What were you thinking? If you had Daryl running NeoSol after you were gone, why give the cancer cure to SolviNext? Couldn't you have done it through your own company?"

Her NeoSol company was mostly a mystery to him. He was aware that its primary purpose was to manufacture aerospace products. Did they do robotics, too? That's how SolviNext had started, before that part of the business had been sold off when they moved into biomedical. Who had purchased that again? For some reason, his memory on the matter was fuzzy, but he had a sinking suspicion. He dialed his assistant, Lisa.

"Hello, sir," she picked up on the first ring.

"Remind me, who purchased Robotics?"

"It was a company called A. R. R.," Lisa replied immediately. "I remember because it reminded me of pirates!"

"Do you know who owns it?" Jonas asked, not responding to her joke.

"It's a private New Mexico company. If I recall correctly, they purchased the six plants and all the patents for around eight hundred million dollars ten years ago. It helped to fund the biomedical research facility."

He hung up, wondering why he even bothered. He had thought it might have been NeoSol. The more he tried to think about Aisling's company, the more frustrated he grew. Wait. A.R.R, Aisling Ramsey Robotics. He smacked his forehead, wondering why he hadn't seen it before. There was already too much on his mind to spend time figuring out Aisling's secretive side gigs.

Ever since the President had contacted him about Aisling's

research, everything had gone to hell. He had hoped to strike a deal with the President for FDA approval and to establish subsidies that would make the cure more accessible to the public. That would have accomplished what Aisling had wanted—to get the cure to those who couldn't afford it.

But when Jonas couldn't deliver on the longevity research, barriers suddenly appeared in the FDA process and progress ground to a halt. Jonas had to change tactics, turning the people against the FDA by publicly announcing the hold-up.

The President retaliated with a simple post on social media.

President Dolion
@POTUS
The Golden Goose is gone! How do we trust SolviNext @ JonasWilliams has the cure for cancer without the late good Dr. Ramsey who died of cancer?

Anti-cure protests had started, and things were getting violent. Yesterday, there was a shooting in the crowd outside SolviNext headquarters.

And the death threats were getting worse. This morning there had been an envelope of recent pictures of him and his family that had been taken with telephoto lenses. Crosshairs had been superimposed with DEATH TO TRAITORS printed in red at the top.

Oh God! he thought. How could I have known it would come to this?

Jonas considered himself an upstanding conservative Christian but didn't like what the country had become with Truth and Freedom in power. Their 'with us or against us' attitudes effectively silenced the voices of conservatives like Jonas. The left despised him too. They were outside the building now, cursing his "capitalist greed."

They all had it wrong. He wanted to make the cure work for everyone—he always had—but it was impossible with the President making moves to stifle his company. Dolion was so bent on the longevity research that he was willing to ensure the cure for cancer was never distributed unless he got what he wanted.

"God raises us all up if we work hard," his Opa had said. He still truly believed that. But, Jonas thought, what am I working for now? To do what's right? At this point, I would have to fight against the country you fought for, Opa.

His phone rang. It was his wife.

"Hi, honey," he rasped. His voice was raw from yelling.

"Darling," Chris said, "you're working yourself to death. You need to come home."

Jonas raised his eyes toward Heaven. He had slept a few hours here and there at the office and worked in the same clothes for almost two weeks.

He needed a shower.

He needed his family.

Suddenly, his body felt as though it was made of lead.

"You're right," he said. "I'll be home soon. I love you."

Jonas hung up. He stared at his phone. Already there were text messages and emails waiting for him. He turned it off and put it into his pocket.

Just for tonight, he thought as he walked out of the office.

***

"Shit!"

"Ashlynn, your levels of cortisol and adrenaline are increasing," Daryl said.

"Shit!"

"You are experiencing an amygdala hijack."

Ashlynn exited the virtual representation of Jonas' office and sprung from her chair. She had been sitting in front of her laptop in her room at the Reeds' home. What did this change? She didn't know. Her mind was filled with a dozen nightmare scenarios. Ashlynn could not shake the fear of what Jonas' new knowledge of Daryl could mean. And now the government knew too! At least part of it. What else did they know?

As her eyes darted around her room, it suddenly felt extremely confining, like the walls were getting closer. Her chest felt tight.

Should I try to move Daryl? What if they found out about my mountain cabin data center too? Daryl is too big to move without being noticed. What if this situation escalates? What happens if they shut down the New Mexico data center? How would I fare without Daryl's help?

"Daryl," she said in her mind. "I think we need to reprioritize."

"I'm detecting suppressed activity in your prefrontal cortex," Daryl said. "You are experiencing a flight or fight response. Under such circumstances, you requested that I assess your immediate physical danger and—"

"Daryl," Ashlynn interrupted impatiently.

"And if low," Daryl continued, "to offer you the choice of suppressing the stress response in your mind."

"No."

She tried to calm her mind by considering her options. She sat back in her chair and breathed deeply as she returned to her virtual lunar office. Daryl appeared by her side, putting a warm hand on her shoulder.

"I can see that you are feeling better," he said. "But you are still worried."

"I'm only human," she said.

"A remarkable human," Daryl replied. "Your mental choice to focus on solving a problem is one of the best-known ways to short-circuit a hijack, and most people do not do this on their own."

Curious, she thought, that he is responding so empathetically. I must subconsciously want this kind of social response from him. I suppose it is soothing.

"I think my instinctive conclusion still stands," Ashlynn said, as she put her hand over his. "We need to reprioritize."

"Why?"

"Before," she said, "I was worried about my future plans. I was annoyed by being forced to divide my attention between my goals and dealing with the government agents."

"And now?"

"Now I have come to the perspective that the government's interest in me is a factor in the aggregate I cannot ignore."

"You thought of this as your prefrontal cortex was shutting down?"

"No," she said grimly. "I was thinking about running away to French Guiana tonight and launching myself into space tomorrow."

"Flight," Daryl nodded. "So, what's your plan now?"

"To not run away."

"You intend to fight?"

"No," she said. "I have no intention to attack."

She had to assume that the government entities working for the President would do whatever they could to get to her research. If she gave it to them, would they lose interest in her? Perhaps, but then the demagogue would get to live forever. If she didn't give it to them, their efforts would escalate. To what end? What's the worst case? she wondered. They can't try to kill me because they'd be empty-handed then, right? But if I'm just one of their leads, I'd be expendable.

She concluded that they would eventually want to question her. They know where I live, she reasoned. If all I do is stay home, they could come calling. They probably know my behavior patterns. If they want to question me, there's not much I can do to stop them. Maybe they'll wait until my body turns eighteen. That's only six weeks away.

"Please ship me several dozen of the new model of robo-flies," she said. "If anyone is following me, I want to know it."

"Production will begin immediately," Daryl replied.

"Daryl," she stopped pacing in her virtual office. Earth was rising over the lunar horizon. "I need you to find someone with military experience. They should be in alignment with my views of the government and have an intrinsic motivation for helping us."

"For what purpose?"

"I need a bodyguard."

***

"Ma'am," the agent said as Dina entered.

"Show me," she replied.

As he started the clip, the other technician beside him leaned in.

"What struck me as strange was that as I talked to Jonas Williams, I glanced at this screen, where we were monitoring the Ramsey girl. Just after Jonas disclosed that Daryl Sillich is actually what Dr. Ramsey referred to as her digital assistant, the girl stood up and started pacing here."

He pointed to the video feed labeled bp_vent_cam1 and cranked up the sound on his speakers.

"Shit...Shit..." Dina could hear the young lady say.

On the other video feed, labeled "bp_laptop_cam," and "bp_laptop_scr" she was vigorously typing up what appeared to be a research paper.

"She's giving us a false feed," the technician said.

"Zoom in on the laptop, here," Dina said, pointing to "bp_plant_cam2."

As he zoomed in on the laptop screen, the screen held the same paper, with words being typed, but her fingers weren't moving.

"Play any audio until she said 'shit,'" Dina said. "Maybe she was eavesdropping somehow."

"We listened to the audio on her phone, laptop, and the nearest mic in the wall behind her sofa," the agent said. "There was nothing. That's the weird part. How could she have reacted that way at that exact moment unless she had heard the conversation? There was no audio in the room anywhere. Just this..."

He played the video with the sound. All they could hear was her breathing. The agent was right, but he may have left out other possibilities.

"Play this same period of time with footage from the curtain camera," Dina said.

The agent took a moment to bring it up, which meant he hadn't prepared it or thought of it, which annoyed Dina.

"Zoom in on her head," Dina said.

The girl's hair was longer now, but it didn't cover her ears. Dina was a little disappointed that Ashlynn had no headphones or earbuds, as she had suspected.

"Check the other side?" Dina said

He pulled up a different feed, but the result was the same.

"She never wears headphones," he said. It seemed he wanted to say more but held his tongue.

"Who's working on the phone and laptop problem?" Dina asked.

"Sarah and her team, down in cyber," he said.

"Get them on the phone."

He pressed the left control on his keyboard.

"Anyone from cyber team three available to chat with me and Director Keats?"

Old habits, Dina thought. She missed telephones. Now they use push-to-talk software instead for inter-office communications.

"I'm here," Sarah said. "What's up?"

The agent glanced at Dina, and she nodded. He filled her in. "DK wants a status on the laptop and smartphone."

Dina hated it when they called her that. She didn't think the agent even realized he had slipped. They must all use it behind her back.

"No progress, as of yet," Sarah replied. "We only gained access a few hours ago, and she seems to be masking her activities. She knows her stuff."

Dina debated saying anything more. Sarah had proven time and again in the past that she was the best at what she did. There was a twinge of excitement in her tone. She saw this as a challenge, Dina knew, a pitting of her skill against this genius kid, or whatever. There was even a hint of respect there. Dina didn't like that part of it. This isn't a game, Dina thought. If Sarah wants to play it that way, I must up the stakes.

"Sarah, you and your team are off this case if I don't have results by tomorrow," Dina said.

There was a long pause.

"Yes, ma'am," Sarah said. Her tone was hurt but tinged with determination. Good.

***

"Why are you here?" Nat said. She was speaking as levelly as she could, but in her raw emotional state it sounded like a growl.

"What. Ever." Alé replied, tossing her hair in annoyance. She pulled up a chair and sat next to Raoul. "Your eyeliner is running."

"Fuck you, I'm not wearing any," Nat stood up. "I'm out of here."

"Hey, hey!" Raoul said, standing also and beckoning her to sit. "Please! Calm down. Alé, Nata, please!"

"Why did you invite her anyway?"

"He didn't," Alé said. "I heard you guys talking about a tour, so I knew you would be here. Luna asked me to stop by a few days ago anyway."

"Please, Nata," Raoul said.

Nat regarded Alé, gritting her teeth. The sound of a knuckle popping told her that she had been clenching her fist. How had she gotten so worked up all of a sudden? She realized she needed to dial this back like eighty notches.

At that moment, Luna and the waiter emerged from the kitchen with several steaming and delicious-smelling plates. She wore the kind of knowing smile one wears when confident that good food can reset the mood.

"*Cuidado*," she said. "*¡Está muy caliente! Por favor, siéntate.*"

With the food on the table, Luna sat heavily into the chair, placing Raoul between her and Alé. Pablo, the waiter, laid out the dishes and returned to fill their water. Realizing she was famished and regaining her composure, Nat sat. She berated herself for responding to Alé that way. She had let her guard down.

"The place looks good," Alé said, placing a modest portion of *arroz* and *asada* on her plate.

"Thanks," Raoul said. "Nat liked your idea, the one with the lights over the tables."

Nat stifled her surprise. She didn't recall saying anything out loud about the lights. She let it slide, knowing that Raoul was trying to keep the peace.

"Pablo," Luna called to the waiter, "*¿Puedes traer el sobre allí, por favor?*"

Pablo went to the cash register and returned with a thick white envelope, handing it to Luna, who passed it to Raoul, who passed it to Alé. She casually stuffed it into her expensive purse and ate as if nothing had happened.

"Business is picking up," Raoul said brightly.

"Always the optimist," Alé replied, rolling her eyes. "You need a stash in case something happens."

"No worries, sis," Raoul said. "I got that covered."

"*¡Deliciosa!*" Nat said to Luna, her mood brightening with every bite. Luna beamed radiantly back. Nat was trying her best to ignore Alé until her temper eased up. But she was curious about the envelope. Was Alé a business partner?

"When do you open?" Nat asked after swallowing another scrumptious bite.

"In an hour," Raoul said. "Reservations are full already!"

"The news says that restaurants are having a hard time right now," Nat said after another bite. "But that doesn't seem true for you."

"Not the up-scale ones," Raoul said. "Our recent renovations worked! And we increased the prices, so tips are bigger too. Mostly white people come now, though. And we had to hire white waiters. Pablo usually works in the back."

Nat paused, considering that.

"They like it this authentic?" Alé asked, pointing to her food.

"Some, but not really," Raoul said. "They prefer more of a Tex-Mex style."

"I'm glad you didn't make it that way for us," Alé said.

Nat's thoughts were interrupted as Alé waved her fork toward her.

"So why the tears?" Alé asked, staring at Nat hard. "Aint you supposed to be some tough butch chick?"

"Alé," Raoul said, exasperated.

"You know what," Nat said, instantly bristling again. "I'm sick of your shit. What's with you, huh? All you do is lounge around all day on your phone. You never help out!"

"Don't act all high and mighty," Alé said. "You're the one that broke apart *nuestra familia*."

"You can't pin that on me," Nat scoffed. "Dad chose to break the family because of his hate."

"You think you're so smart," Alé snapped, "with your chess, and your military education, and your perfect straight A's. But you don't know shit."

"What don't I know?"

"He ain't mad at you just cuz' you're gay," Alé said. "He's mad because you broke his heart. You were his perfect child. His favorite. You were the star, Nata. Not Raoul. Not me. You! With your GI Jane, Amazon self. You're the superstar he had all the high hopes for."

Nat stared at her, mouth agape. Raoul was avoiding her eyes.

"And I don't just lounge around neither," Alé dropped her fork in disgust and stood. "I pay all the bills. So, fuck you!"

She thanked Luna with a nod and stormed out, slamming the door behind her.

Nat watched her go and turned to Raoul.

"It's true," Raoul said. "She makes bank as an influencer on social media. She helps Mami and Papi, and she helped out me and Luna. We're trying to pay her back."

"It's not true, Raoul," Nat shook her head. "I wasn't the perfect daughter. I wasn't their favorite."

Raoul turned away, saying nothing.

***

"Dear, you look terrible," Chris said. Her eyes held deep concern as Jonas dragged himself through the door.

Earlier that morning, security had apprehended a man with a gun trying to enter the building through a window at corporate headquarters. The man wasn't talking, but Jonas knew in his bones that the man had been coming for him.

Death threats were pouring in daily now. He had reported the first, but the police had been dismissive. More came. After the police stopped returning his calls, Jonas stopped reporting them. When they started coming to the house, he had the mail forwarded to work. SolviNext was now spending a small fortune on increased security for all the senior executives and their families.

"It's been a rough day," Jonas said.

"More like a rough past few months," Chris said as she took his jacket. "Have you eaten?"

"No," he said.

"Jonas, you have kept me in the dark long enough! I want to hear all of it," she said sternly, "but not until after you've had a shower, a meal, and some rest."

"Yes, dear," he mumbled.

Jonas took a shower and ate in an almost zombie-like state. His lack of sleep was hitting him hard now that he was in the comfort of his own home. He didn't remember eating, saying goodnight to Chris or the kids, or even going to bed.

He jerked awake from a nightmare. The clock showed it was almost noon. He dreamt he had been running through a forest of tall, dark trees that were all on fire. He had a leaky bucket of water and was trying to get somewhere but couldn't remember the destination. All he knew was that he needed to put the fire out, but the bucket was losing so much water.

He was about to leave the bed when he noticed Chris. She was sitting on the settee in the bay window across from him, reading a book. She saw him watching her and walked over, putting a hand against his chest as he tried to get up.

"Be calm, my love," she said.

"I have to get back to work," Jonas said.

"Not until after you tell me what's going on," she replied. "This can't continue, Jonas."

Jonas searched her eyes.

"There's so much going on," he said. "I don't know where to start."

"How about the beginning?" she said.

Jonas took a deep breath. He wondered what he had missed at work and fought a strong urge to pick up his phone. But as he considered what the most important thing he should be doing right now was, nothing came to mind. The emails and texts had been roughly the same for the past few weeks, so there was nothing for him to do but react. He had always considered himself a man of action, not one to react. What action should he take right now?

"Dear?" Chris said, turning his head toward her. "Tell me."

Jonas shook his head.

"Oh baby," she said. "I'm here. What brought on all this stress?"

"A while ago," he began, "I received a call from President Dolion."

Chris looked surprised. "What did he say?"

"He was interested in Ash's gerontology research."

"What's that?"

"Technology that could make people live longer, or even forever."

Chris was silent momentarily, then muttered, "'And the Lord said, My spirit shall not always strive with man, for that he also is flesh: yet his days shall be a hundred and twenty years.' Jonas, this thing she was trying to do is evil!"

"I know," Jonas said. "That's part of why I didn't authorize the project."

"That's good," she said.

"But the President wants all of her research on the topic," he continued. "Dr. Tamma couldn't find anything more than what Aisling had originally submitted. But when I went to Washington and told the President we had done no further research, he grew cold. He told me to find the solution, or I'd regret it. The next thing I knew, all sorts of problems started: An SEC audit, an IRS audit, more demands from the FDA, canceled government contracts, and now the FBI and DHS seem to be investigating us. The stock is plummeting. At this rate, SolviNext will be bankrupt before we can deliver the cure.

"On top of all that, someone leaked a doctored video conference call of me arguing with Aisling about the economics of running our business. It makes me seem like a business tycoon who wants to squeeze every penny out of the poor."

"Who did that?" Chris asked.

Jonas shrugged, then exhaled slowly.

"I've said many things I regret. Now this one has come back to haunt me. There is a growing mob of protesters outside the building."

Chris put a hand on his back.

"And, I learned today that Aisling's artificial intelligence system is running her private company. God knows what for. I had several dreams last night. In one, dreamt that she was alive. I walked into my office to find her there, sitting at my desk, waiting for me. She handed me my resignation letter, saying, 'You're no longer needed, Jonas. Daryl will take it from here. Go home.' Then, she burned SolviNext to the ground."

He frowned pensively.

"The government knows. I wonder what they're going to do about it. My Lord! What am *I* going to do about all this?"

He averted his gaze.

"I'm getting death threats from FATs," he whispered.

"I think," she started slowly, "We need to get out of town for a break."

Jonas looked at her.

"Why don't we go to the hot springs?" She said, growing more upbeat. "There's one two hours away, near Taos, that I heard was good."

"I don't know," Jonas said. "There's a lot going on. I—"

Chris shifted, leaning into him.

"It'll all be there when you get back," she whispered in his ear.

She kissed his neck.

"Okay," Jonas said, trying not to sound reluctant.

He made a mental note to have Lisa inform the security firm of the trip. Chris snuggled against him, and he did his best to forget the death threats.

"Have you prayed, Jonas?" Chris asked.

Jonas met her gaze. The deep love in her eyes struck him— hard. Realizing the truth, he bowed his head.

"Come," she said. "Let's pray together."

CHAPTER 14

Josh followed slightly behind Ashlynn as they walked along the path during their break. The creek was mostly frozen due to yesterday's cold snap, though most of the snow from the week before had melted within a day or two. The movement was warming him up, but the wind sometimes cut brutally through his coat. Ashlynn seemed to be chilled as well. She shrugged her shoulders against the cold, even though she wore a light teal scarf and matching beanie. Her bright red hair peeked out from underneath.

"Seems like you've been under a lot of stress lately," Josh said.

Ashlynn let out a ragged, misty breath. "Yeah."

"Do you want to talk about it?"

"Not really," she said. "I'd rather talk about something else."

"Like what?"

"I don't know," she said. "Anything else."

"What kind of music do you like?" Josh asked.

"I don't know," she said. "Whatever sounds good, I guess."

"Do you like 'Bashing Puddles'?" he asked.

"I've never heard of them."

"What? You've got to be kidding!"

"Have you heard of Tsiolkovsky's delta-v equation?"

"Um, no,"

"'What? You've got to be kidding!'" she mimicked him, deepening her voice.

They both laughed, but her smile soon faded.

"Here," he said, bringing up his music app. "I'll show you."

They walked for a while, him playing music for her while she listened. He wanted to cheer her up but couldn't find anything she liked. As they walked, he skipped around various artists and genres. They reached a small park along the trail and sat on a bench. He searched for another song. Her mood finally seemed to lighten, and she started laughing again. He smiled at her laugh and how she seemed so intent on analyzing the music and the meaning of the lyrics.

"But that's so cliché," she said. "I mean, the metaphor is so overused!"

Josh laughed, "But can't you just appreciate the music? It's a great song!"

"Well, it is catchy," she said, "if you ignore the lyrics. It is a little repetitive, though."

"No wonder you don't know much about music," he said. "You're, like, a music snob."

"I am not!" she said incredulously.

"Well, we've gone through like, a hundred songs, and you criticized all of them. Isn't there something you like?"

"I liked them!" she said. "Just because I pointed out their weaknesses doesn't mean I didn't like them."

"Would you add them?"

"What do you mean, 'add them?'"

"To your playlist," Josh said.

"Um, maybe?"

Josh laughed, "I rest my case! I never met anyone who didn't listen to music!"

"I listen to music," she said. "Just not casually."

"What kind of music?"

Ashlynn seemed embarrassed.

"C'mon," Josh said. "You can tell me."

"My grandmother used to play the fiddle," Ashlynn said. "And my grandfather, the piano. They both sang. They were very talented and had beautiful voices. They played Irish folk songs together in the evening, singing in both English and Irish. In the winter, they'd have a fire in the heating stove. My parents would sit and read on the couch, listening. It was one of the happiest times of my life."

"Wow," Josh said. "I guess that's pretty hard to beat."

"Yeah," she replied. "So, when I want to remember, I sit next to the fire and listen to Irish folk songs."

"You don't listen to music while busy doing something else?"

She shook her head.

"I should probably get back," Josh said.

Ashlynn was aware of his warmth, of where her right leg touched his as they sat on the bench. She didn't want the moment to end. Without thinking, she wrapped her arm through his, lost in the golden memory of the past. She wasn't sure why, but she couldn't bring herself to uphold the facade with Josh. She was supposed to be the child of a single mother, the child of the woman she used to be. But, with Josh, she wanted to be as honest as possible. She had shared her own memory as Aisling, not a made-up one about Ashlynn. But when she wrapped her arm through his, she felt Josh's body grow tense.

Josh detected a change in Ashlynn's demeanor, and how she held him made him suspect she felt differently about him than she should. He was impressed by her maturity and the depth of their conversations—but felt protective of her, more paternal. I might need to make some boundaries clear here, he thought.

What am I doing? she thought as she forced herself to release Josh's arm. It was harder to let go than it should have been.

Daryl was quiet, thankfully.

"Oh, I almost forgot," Josh said, seemingly relieved. "Do you know an Alex Munta?"

She sat up and froze at the name.

"He came by the library yesterday, asking about you," Josh said

"Josh?" she asked. "Do you ever get the feeling that something bad will happen? I don't mean a premonition or anything supernatural. But, like... you have a test coming, and you just know you're going to do horribly?"

"Sure," he said, chuckling to lighten the mood. "I feel that way about rent sometimes."

"I feel like I'm doing everything I can to prepare, but I'm going in blind."

"Isn't that how life is?" Josh asked. "When you're young, your parents ask you what you want to be when you grow up, and when you finally have an answer, they hit you with how stupid your choice is. You do it anyway, and the next thing you know, you're middle-aged, barely able to afford food, and are still living with a roommate. Even if you follow your heart, you still go in blind."

"Or," she said. "You spend your whole life focused on your goals, focused on test after test, sacrificing normality, until you encounter a test you know you cannot pass, and if you don't pass, it's over. It makes you wonder if it was worth it."

"You have your whole future ahead of you," Josh said. "You should just trust your heart."

"You're such a humanist," she said.

"I have lots of experience with being human."

When she said nothing further, Josh changed the subject.

"Remember when you told me about the adjacent probable?"

"Yeah."

"Something you said stuck with me," he said, scratching his chin, searching for exact words. "You said change only happens when it is not only possible but probable."

"Right," she said.

"What makes it probable?"

"That depends," she said. "But when it comes to people, they must want the change and the circumstances must make success a strong probability."

"Do you think it's a matter of fate?" Josh asked.

Ashlynn remembered the moment in Rio when Jonas had asked her the same question.

"Fate is a loaded word," she said carefully. "The word fate has supernatural connotations I reject. The evidence suggests that we live in a deterministic world. We observe the world through our senses and with mechanical sensors that, no matter how sensitive, are not perfect. So we use probability to quantify a functional approximation of reality. We approximate what is likely to happen because of what has happened and is currently happening. I prefer to use the concept of the adjacent probable because it has mathematical predictive power—nothing supernatural about it."

"You know too much for your age," Josh said, half joking.

Ashlynn looked down at her hands, so he asked another question.

"Do you think one can escape fate—that one could escape the adjacent probable?"

"It happens," she said. "There has to be a defining moment of separation, like the animals on the island of Madagascar. It was once connected to Africa. After its geological separation, the species followed their own evolutionary paths, separate from the fortunes of the mainland. The evolutionary pressures of that environment no longer constrained them, and they were free to evolve in their own way."

"Lucky them," Josh said.

Ashlynn laughed, nodding and then tilting her head slightly. Her expression turned melancholic. She sighed and looked up at the sky as though wishing she could fly away. Her eyes seemed to lock onto something distant. Josh followed her gaze and noticed she was looking at the moon, pale and barely visible in the winter daylight.

"I wish I could have such a moment of separation myself," she breathed, her eyes fixed on the celestial body.

"How?" Josh asked.

She didn't answer, lost in her thoughts.

"Earth to Ashlynn," Josh said

Ashlynn glanced at him and blushed.

"Sorry," she said, standing. "We should get back."

"Another question for you," Josh said after walking in silence for a while. "How do you determine your next step if the blindfold of life makes it so you cannot see the sidewalk?"

"In that case," she said, "one must take it one step at a time and hope she does not walk into a spiderweb."

She seemed to retreat further into herself with every word.

"Ashlynn," Josh said. "I don't know what you're facing, but I hope you know you don't have to face it alone."

"Thanks, Josh," she said sadly. "It means a lot."

***

"I think you should kindly make this a bigger priority," the President said in a heavily accented but smooth voice.

"Is that an order, sir?" Dina said, sounding as casual as possible.

"No, I was picking chicken fry outta' my teeth," Dolion replied dryly.

"Sir," she replied professionally. "We noticed a pattern of evidence that indicates a strong likelihood the doctor made significant discoveries. My team has been hard-pressed to discover anything new under our current constraints. I'd need your authorization to elevate our investigation."

"I hear tell you're the best at getting answers. Don't you disappoint me now."

"Do I have authorization?" she pressed. "I need the paperwork to proceed."

"I'll tell you right now, Ms. Keats," he replied coldly. "All's you need is my word. If'n you don't proceed, you'll be buried under more than your paperwork. Are you picking up what I'm laying down?"

"Yes, sir," she replied, nonplussed.

The phone clicked, and she hung up.

Dina tapped her fingers against her lips pensively. It was implied, not explicit. And the threat. Did he mean more than a demotion? Of course, the paperwork still had to be done. The paperwork let her maintain deniability. If the shit hit the fan, well, she was just following orders—an essential concept in her line of work. Her phone buzzed, and she checked it. It was from her boss.

"ramsey case p3," the text said.

"Let's give this project a little more priority," Dina muttered with a satisfied grin.

She walked briskly out of her office. If her boss was willing to be bullied into doing things under the table, it wasn't her problem. The explicit order from her direct supervisor meant he would take the fall if Dolion reneged, as he was known to do. She'd been burned too often not to cover her ass

"Okay, people! Listen up!" Dina said, raising her voice as she walked into the busy war room. "This case has become a priority three national security threat. From this point forward, we are working toward bringing in the targets for questioning."

There were sounds of excitement in the room. Dina allowed herself half a second to appreciate it.

"Let's recap!" she continued. "From conflicting reports, we have some reason to believe that Daryl may be an artificial intelligence entity, but we also have video footage of his face from our agent who secured a job at NeoSol. The 'Daryl' team will have additional AI specialists determine the authenticity of this video.

"I want all viz ops efforts wrapped up. I want a plan for acquiring the targets. I want that plan today. Let's move!"

The hum returned, but it had an air of purpose as the teams began their work anew. And just like that, Dina thought, this job became what I had hoped for. The idea of a sentient AI system intrigued her, and she observed the shared excitement amongst her team. There had always been intel on systems that might have general artificial intelligence, but nothing had ever panned out. If the lead on Daryl from the SolviNext CEO was legitimate, then this could be the first.

"Has the officer stationed at the NeoSol manufacturing plant in Alabama had any further contact with Daryl?" another asked.

"No," came the reply.

Dina switched her focus to another conversation.

"The photo is not detailed enough to perform that analysis," a digital forensic analyst said. "Other known photos do not show him present with any other actual human. You'd think someone at the CEO level would be photographed in at least one handshake."

Another case worker said, "Analyzing his voice. There is a hint of Gujarati in his accent. If he were a real human, it's possible that most of Daryl's career was in India. Records might be more difficult to find."

"Simulating such a trace accent is difficult," another replied. "Right? No known system could do that on the fly. The voice profile would've had to be built from scratch."

"Any photos, videos, or other clues as to Daryl's physical location, given the null hypothesis that he is human?"

"Zero. He's a ghost. The hotel view in the photo shows that this was the Carlson in San Francisco, room 685. It was registered to Daryl Sillich on those dates, but none of the hotel employees recall seeing him physically there."

"He showed up on the grid five other times."

"Yes, a couple of instances had eyewitnesses saying they saw him via video conference, but none in person."

"What about video surveillance from the hotels?"

"Three of the hotels gave us footage that shows Daryl walking through the lobby and down the halls to the rooms. Other hotels wouldn't show us their footage without a warrant."

"Get one," Dina said, "and get the video."

"It might be too late now. They usually overwrite after a week or two."

"Check to be sure," Dina commanded. "Where do we stand with a plan to detain Ashlynn Ramsey?"

"Given her current known patterns," someone spoke up immediately, "the best covert option is to apprehend her when she travels to or from the library. There are three possible apprehension points along that path. One complication is that the male librarian might be with her."

"How will we mitigate the possibility of a report to missing persons?"

"A look-alike agent has been identified. We could bring her up to speed on Ashlynn's habits and mannerisms and provide the usual excuses of illness to limit interactions."

"What about the foster parents?"

"All evidence suggests that they are not involved in Ramsey's daily life."

"What do we know about the librarian?" Dina asked.

"They seem to be developing some kind of relationship."

"Yeah, and he's like twice her age."

"Should we question him too?"

"Munta reports he has documented their entire relationship," said another. "He was there when they met. He reports they are getting closer but doesn't think they are in intimate relations. He classifies them as friends but suspects she has a crush on him."

"He's a registered Democrat," said another. "And posts liberal criticisms of the Dolion Administration regularly."

"Then he's a risk," someone said.

"Maybe we tell him she's going on vacation for her eighteenth birthday."

"Good," Dina said. "Keep an eye on the librarian. He may be a liability. Where are we with Daryl? Is he human?"

"Inconclusive," one member said, while another said, "Probably not," and a third said, "Definitely." They eyed each other competitively.

"One at a time," Dina said.

"The guy is a recluse," said the one who thought Daryl was a human, "but there is plenty of video evidence from security cameras at hotels, airports, and a taxi that show him arriving at and leaving the hotels. As we gain access to systems, everywhere we look, we're finding more."

"It's possible to fake all of that," said the one who thought he was an AI. "Not a single witness exists that has seen Daryl in person."

The one who said it was inconclusive spoke up. "It's possible to fake those things," he started, raising a hand to stop the other from arguing. "While that is difficult, it cannot be ruled out because a General Artificial Intelligence could possibly find ways to do it. The problem is resources. No supercomputer known today would have the power to do all of that. It can only mean two things: either Dr. Ramsey's got such a system, or Daryl is, in fact, human."

"Yes, but let's use logic here. There's never been a GAI. Our own scientists believe the tech is 50 years away."

"Yes, but Dr. Ramsey was a genius. If anyone could figure it out, surely..."

"While also making all the other discoveries she made, most of which take entire lifetimes to accomplish, and managing teams of people? Please, no one is that smart."

"She had teams of people. And what if she created the GAI before all that and used it to help with those discoveries?"

"That would mean she would have had to create the AI over a decade ago, which makes it even more implausible given the tech at the time."

"Her CS PhD thesis was on a new type of neural network and built on her PhD in neurology. It's become the basis for many distributed neural networks we use today."

"C'mon! What, did she also invent a super AI while driving all of the technological breakthroughs at SolviNext? She's only human, man!"

"I think you're proving my point. It's…"

"Okay," Dina said. "Let's draw the line there. Under the theory that Daryl is human, where is he now?"

"Unknown."

"And assuming it's a GAI, where is the data center's location?"

"Tentatively, Dr. Ramsey's New Mexico home."

"Yes, but please note that the known specs and the current power draw at that location are consistent with a data center with an estimated thousand petaflops. That's not enough computing power to produce a GAI at the level we're talking about. Dr. Ramsey was reported to use SolviNext's Exaflop supercomputer for most of her research. Obviously, Daryl couldn't be running on that."

"Could it be in the cloud?"

"We're checking account records. There are some cloud computing expenses, but not at the scale we're looking for."

"Satellite imagery of the solar arrays show the power capacity of the New Mexico data center has potentially been doubled over the past two years, but that's still not enough.

"What sort of computing power would it need?"

"Maybe 1000 times that."

"Or 100 times."

"That's too big a range. Work on narrowing it down."

"Yes, ma'am."

"Can we access the facility in New Mexico?" Dina asked.

"SolviNext has been trying but failing. We could look into it."

"Okay," Dina said. "Barring that, what if we shut down the

Data Center in New Mexico and monitor for changes in Daryl's activity?"

"Also possible."

"Let's look into that," Dina said. "Any ideas for apprehending Daryl the human?"

"No," was the definitive response. "His patterns are too irregular. We currently think he may be abroad, maybe in Europe. His passport activity shows he might be in Amsterdam as of two days ago. Video footage is currently being negotiated."

"Jesus," Dina said. "How many resources are being used on this guy?"

"A lot."

"If he's in Europe," Dina said, taking a breath and pinching the bridge of her nose, "our current operating priority level isn't high enough to attempt apprehension. Keep monitoring."

"Will do."

"Where's the psych report on Ashlynn?"

After a moment, the evaluation was displayed on the main monitor. The girl's picture was at the top. She had a small smile.

The technician started summarizing, in a bored tone.

"She's brilliant. In school, she was top of her class. She isn't as academically strong as her mom, as by this age, Dr. Ramsey had already accumulated two PhDs in neurology and computer science. There seems to be no indication Ashlynn intends to go to college. Surprisingly, we have little information about her before the age of seventeen. It seems Dr. Ramsey home-schooled her in some way through an online institution where she received top marks but never went above and beyond.

"Another oddity is that there doesn't seem to be a significant number of photos or accounts of anyone ever having met her as a child. There are no records of birthday parties or any friends whatsoever. Dr. Ramsey was aloof and socially isolated, so perhaps the daughter is too.

"Based on what we know of her personality from classmates in the online high school class who were interviewed, she is socially awkward and highly opinionated about academics."

"Alex Munta's report from the other day came in," said another agent. "He provided recordings of her conversation with the librarian. She claimed to have a degree in Computer Science at one point, even though she does not."

"Why are we missing so much information about her youth?"

Dina asked.

"We're still working on it," came the reply. "We should have more access now that this has been reprioritized."

"Get on it," Dina said. "I want to know every event that happened in her childhood by yesterday."

"Yes, ma'am."

"What's the going theory on the fake video she feeds us?"

"Our working theory is that she noticed she was being followed earlier and became spooked. We have reason to believe she became aware that we compromised her laptop. What's fascinating is that she didn't try to remove the spyware but instead used it to cover up her actions. Who does that? She still hasn't searched her bedroom at the Reed's for our other surveillance assets."

"Well, if she is a computer scientist she might have the skills to pull the wool over our eyes with the laptop—but how would she know to check for bugs?"

"Sometimes, it's good that the old ways die hard."

"Anything else?" Dina asked, bringing the team back on track.

"Not yet."

"People," she said. "Let me be clear. Drop what you're doing on any other projects. Ashlynn Ramsey and Daryl Sillich are our top priorities until these new anomalies are resolved."

***

Jonas' gaze relaxed on the light from the bathhouse dancing in sharp contrasts on the mellow surface of the hot spring water. Yellow and green pool lights caused a fuzzy, effervescent glow below the surface. The night sky was clear and the stars were brilliant. The only constellation he knew, Orion, hung over the building majestically. He sighed as the heat seeped into his bones. A couple holding hands passed by the pool in their guest robes. Over hidden speakers, gentle flute music was playing.

"Are you sure you don't want to reserve a private pool?" he asked Chris.

"Very sure," she said. "Who knows what others do in there?"

"Or what they leave in the water."

Chris cringed, "Eww! Enough of that!"

Jonas chuckled.

"I like it here," he said. "It's not too fancy and not too rustic. The music is relaxing."

"Did you enjoy your massage?"

"Yeah," Jonas said. "He got deep into my back. You should try it sometime."

"No thanks," she said. "I can't stand the idea of strangers touching me."

"They're professionals," Jonas said. "It's fine."

"So, tell me more about what's been on your mind," Chris said.

She and Jonas were sitting beside a pipe that burbled loudly with warm water, which Jonas let pour over the back of his neck as he pondered the best way to answer her question. It was loud enough that he was certain no one could eavesdrop.

"I feel like Dolion put a horse head in my bed," Jonas said.

"He threatened you?"

"In so many words," Jonas replied.

"You mean more than making things hard for you with the FDA?"

"You've heard the stories," Jonas said, his hand on his neck. "Since the coup, since he took power, there are news stories about disappearances and the mysterious deaths of his most vocal critics almost daily."

"That could all just be speculation. Isn't it mostly the left-wing media that reports that stuff?"

"I know," Jonas said. "Maybe I'm too paranoid, but there have been threats from Dolion's fanatics."

Chris was thoughtful for a while.

"You know, Jonas," she said. "I love our life together. We have a nice house, beautiful kids, and more than enough money for you to retire. What if you kept enough for us to live on for the rest of our lives and gave up the rest?"

"Why do you suggest that?"

"Well," Chris stood, rising out of the hot water to cool off. "If you have nothing he wants, maybe he'll leave you alone."

Jonas took his eyes away from her gorgeous body to concentrate on her words. The water flowed from the pipe around his head and off his chin.

"You mean give up billions? Let it all go, and just...just, what..?"

"Become a family man," she said. "You could finally have time to be with the boys."

A few days ago, Jonas would have dismissed the idea immediately. The thought of giving up everything he worked for would have seemed absurd. But being here at the hot springs and spending time with Chris had removed the edge. He still felt stressed, but this break from reality had given him a new perspective.

"Ash always called me greedy," Jonas said. "I could never convince her I wasn't doing it for the money."

"You were doing it for Opa," Chris said, sinking back into the water and putting her hand on his shoulder.

"No," he said. "It was for me. I wanted to make him proud, sure. But I also wanted to prove I could do it."

Chris squeezed his arm.

"You've done that," she said. "You don't need to keep doing it for the rest of your life."

Jonas met her concerned expression, considering.

"If you think the company is endangering you," she began carefully, "then why not just let it go? Your only reason for staying should be for the Lord's work anyway. You have nothing more to prove, my love."

"You think," Jonas said slowly, "that if I put everything into giving the cure away and then resign, the President will just up and leave me alone?"

"Yeah," Chris said. "Put it all out there. Make the technology public. Be transparent. What more could he do?"

"He's vindictive. He takes pleasure in dominating his enemies."

"Jonas," she said. "Trust in the Lord. What work is more important than family? I think it's time we reached out to Jonathan before he's gone too far astray. And Davey needs you too."

Jonas closed his eyes as he let the water splash over his face. What more did he have to prove to himself? What did SolviNext mean to him? He thought of the diseases the company had cured through the years. How many people had benefited from SolviNext's technologies all around the world? He loved being a part of that and being able to drive that progress. And now, the cure for cancer.

American entrepreneurship. What better vehicle than the free market to progress such a miracle as a cure for cancer? But is this really the America it once was? Jonas questioned. The bully pulpit had been used to sow doubt and confusion about the cure. The institutions had been weaponized against SolviNext's industry. Had capitalism become nothing but smoke and mirrors? If so, then maybe Ash was right. Not in principle, he thought, but because of how broken the system has become.

***

Nat walked into the living room of her parents' house ahead of Raoul. The lights were off, as usual, and Alé sat on the couch with her phone ignoring everything else. When Luna walked in behind Raoul and closed the door, Nat approached Alé.

"I'm sorry," she said.

"Whatever," Alé replied, eyes still on her phone.

"No, really," Nat said. "You are supporting the family, and I was too blind to see it."

"Okay."

Nat closed her mouth with a click, clenching her jaw. She knew that she could be every bit as stubborn as her sister, and that was part of why they always butted heads. What does Alé want me to do, Nat wondered? Crawl to her on my hands and knees?

"C'mon, Alé," Raoul said. "She said she's sorry."

Luna tsked.

Nat said nothing more as she walked past Alé into the kitchen. She put the leftovers from their lunch into the fridge as Raoul and Luna took off their coats and put them on the rack by the back door. It was early afternoon, so Nat thought she had a few hours before their father would be home.

"You could come to stay with us tonight," Raoul said.

"I appreciate it," Nat said. "I just need to work out, then I'll go to the hotel and check out."

There was a thump, followed by a loud yell from their father upstairs. Nat was the first to move, dashing through the house to their parents' room. She flung the door open to find her mother awake and upset. Tears were streaming down her cheeks.

"Papi!" Raoul yelled from the hallway. "What's wrong!?"

Their father was kneeling on the floor beside her with his head in his hands. He was sobbing uncontrollably.

"¡No puedo!" he said through ragged breaths. "*¡Dios Mío, no puedo! No puedo!*"

Before him, the nightstand had toppled over on the floor, and some of the equipment by their mother's bed was leaning precariously. Mami's water container lay on its side with the lid off. A dark, wet spot was spreading on the carpet, soaking into his pants where he knelt. Her father didn't seem to notice, lost in the hell inside his mind.

"Papi!" Raoul yelled as he rushed forward and embraced him. "What are you doing?!"

"*¡Ya no puedo verla sufrir!*" their father sobbed. "*¡Dios Mío! Por favor!* Take her pain! *¡Toma su dolor! ¡No puedo!*"

Alé was in the door frame, crying. Luna was comforting her despite her own tears. Nat went to her mother and gently held her. Mami was crying feebly and in obvious pain. The oxygen tube was out of place, so Nat readjusted it.

"*Amor,*" her mother was muttering weakly, barely audible. "*Está bien. Estoy con la familia. Soy amada. Los amo a todos.*"

"What did she say?" Raoul asked.

"She said she loves us all," Nat said. "She is happy she is loved and is with us."

Raoul helped Papi stand and brought him to the bedside. Alé came to Nat's side and put her hand lightly on her mother's. After a moment, she put her other hand on Nat's shoulder. On the other side of the bed, Luna came up behind the men and embraced them, crying.

"*No puedo, mi amor,*" their father repeated, grasping her other hand.

"*Sigo aqui,*" their mother said. "*Con la familia. Eso es todo lo que quiero.*"

She took a ragged breath.

"I have all I want, *mi amor,*" she repeated.

CHAPTER 15

"I'm not completely blindfolded," Ashlynn said to Daryl, thinking of the last thing Josh had asked her. "Perhaps I see enough to peek under the cloth to a certain extent."

"Enough to plan," Daryl said. "But not enough to be certain."

"Correct."

She rode her bike down the path home from the library. The wind was picking up, a relentless foe she struggled against as it threatened to knock her off her bike. The chilly air cut through her jacket, making her shiver and feel vulnerable. The sun was coming in and out behind fat clouds that enveloped the mountains behind the naked treetops.

"I have some good news for you," Daryl said. "With the new power plant online at Dotsero, I have been expanding computing capacity by ten percent daily."

"That's great!" she said. "What about the Moon?"

"The core-only model at the Moon is on track to be completed in two and a half weeks, given the new advancements to the construction robots. We will ship two dozen to the launch site over the next few days. The previous generation of workers has already built half of the halide perovskite solar array from the available materials on the Moon. The new generation of workers will be able to more quickly build the electrical infrastructure, the data center, and more efficiently execute the mining operations. However, they must still draw heavily from the nuclear power generators, which are at capacity. As you know, the more power generated from the solar array, the more workers that can be supported. Growth is relatively on track with the exponential curve."

"Were the issues with the circumpolar solar arc tracking systems resolved?"

"Yes."

"Core Prime status?"

"Preliminary tests have been successful at the Dotsero production facility," Daryl replied. "Final tests will occur after installation in the permanent shadow of the crater."

"When?"

"Approximately one month," Daryl said. "Maybe sooner, if all goes smoothly."

"Excellent," she said. "How exciting!"

With that, she thought, Daryl's cognitive capacity would increase dramatically!

"Cooling?"

"The construction of the space facing radiator array in the permanent shadow of the crater is on pace with energy production growth."

"Good. What about the additional data centers here?"

"I've secured permission to build two more data centers in Iceland and French Guiana."

"Do you have an estimated timeframe?"

"Nine to twelve months before either is online. I'm looking into locations that would present opportunities to complete faster. Retrofits would be best."

"Good idea. And none would be affiliated with NeoSol?"

"Correct."

"Excellent," she replied, stopping at an intersection. "I have another project I'd like you to run. I must lift the blindfold to the greatest extent possible to see my choices."

She started forward.

"I need you to build a spy botnet."

"What would I be spying for?"

"A handful of people are behind all of this, and we need to figure out who they are. If you can find them, figure out what they know about me and track them. We might have a chance at predicting their next moves. All critical systems and projects should continue on schedule. Use the new computing capacity. I don't want to move against them in any way until we have full coverage of their devices."

"Noted."

"How's the search for the bodyguard going?"

"Slowly," Daryl said.

"Do you need more resources?"

"Always."

Ashlynn rolled her eyes. It was a silly question, she thought.

"Okay. How many assets remain with NeoSol?"

"About five percent," Daryl said. "The rest have been dispersed to international corporations and banks that are known to be secure but aren't too cooperative with requests from any government to access or freeze assets."

"Good," she said. "Is the property in French Guiana ready for me to move there?"

"There have been delays in securing a real-estate deal. If they take much longer, a sufficient internet connection will not be in place for your arrival after your eighteenth birthday. The real-estate agent there is suggesting a bribe might speed things up."

"Figures," she said.

Suddenly, two huge men stepped out from behind trees in front of her and caught her handlebars and arms. Two more men rushed in at the side and grabbed her shoulders and the bike's frame. Her forward momentum caused them all to take a few smooth steps before coming to a halt. The men moved smoothly and methodically.

"Ms. Ashlynn Ramsey," the suit said. "We'd like to ask you a few questions about the recent deaths of Dr. Geoffrey Baker and Dr. Sarah Hains."

"Who?" She ask, confused.

"They were found dead two days ago. You hadn't heard?"

As he spoke, the man to her left put his hands under her armpits and lifted her off the bike as easily as if she were a toddler. Fear overtook her, and she began to struggle to free herself. She opened her mouth to scream, but an agent put his massive hand over it. She frantically searched for someone who could help but couldn't see anyone else. Any effort she made to resist them felt feeble.

"Who are they, Daryl?!" she yelled internally.

"I don't know. I have not encountered them before. They are not carrying typical phones; they look like bidirectional radios. Their story about the two doctors is true; they were found dead days ago. They were scientists employed by the federal government to research longevity for President Dolion."

Ashlynn's voice was muffled as she tried to yell again.

"Please do not call for help. We're here on official business. We just have a few questions."

They began forcing her into a car as she struggled against them.

"Daryl," she thought frantically, the fear rising in her throat. "Isn't there something you can do?"

"I'm sorry," he replied. "There's nothing I can do at this time. I will follow along and assist however I can. Once in the vehicle, I'll activate a robo-fly from your backpack."

There was a sudden prick in her shoulder, and she turned to see that the man next to her was pulling away a syringe.

"Help! Hel—" A hand returned, firmly covering her lips. One man regarded her impassively while the others scanned the area.

"Daryl! What did they inject me with?"

"Analyzing," came the response. "You may soon lose consciousness. I'll conta—"

***

Jonas signed the last item of paperwork and then directed his attention to his financial advisers, seated around the large conference table. They had mixed expressions, ranging from admiration to shock to disappointment. In truth, he didn't care what they thought. His mind was made up, so it was already done. This was just a formality to make it official. The final piece was Ashlynn. As the only other majority shareholder, she could influence the whole process significantly. She had the first rights to his remaining shares, which he was intent on selling. His analysts estimated that she had enough assets to buy him out. He hoped she bought his shares, because next in line was the government.

"We'll be in touch, Mr. Williams," said his top financial adviser. "Ms. Ramsey has thirty days to consider the buyout option of your shares in SolviNext following your departure as CEO. She will be eighteen within that time frame, so no proxy is needed."

"We probably haven't heard from her because she is waiting for that day," offered another adviser.

"Perhaps," Jonas said. "Thank you all."

As they left, Dr. Tamma walked in.

"Jonas," he said, shaking his hand as Jonas stood to greet him.

"How are the trials going, Scott?"

"Great! It's been one hundred percent effective on all thirty-eight patients so far," Dr. Tamma beamed. "It's like quads on the flop!"

Jonas listened with a sense of purpose and joy that he could only attribute to the Lord's grace. As the positive reports of the trials mounted, he felt intensely grateful. Aisling, he thought, you never believed in God but always carried out His will anyway. Could it be that you were a Christian but just didn't know it?

"Do you approve of the plan to move forward?" Dr. Tamma asked.

"I do," Jonas said, remembering that they had asked for his approval to proceed with an expedited trial of a potentially more cost-effective variant of the treatment.

"Great," Dr. Tamma replied. "With that, I have nothing further to report today. It's all so exciting!"

Something in Jonas' expression must have caused Dr. Tamma to lean forward, concern on his face.

"Are you okay?" Dr. Tamma asked.

"Of course," Jonas said. "Why?"

"For a while, you seemed...troubled. Now, this. Leaving SolviNext. You seem...nostalgic."

"I've been thinking of Aisling a lot lately."

"I see," he said. "Her technologies have improved mankind incalculably."

Jonas nodded again, then shook his head.

"I was thinking of her more as a human being," he said. "Her accomplishments make it easy to put her on a pedestal. But I wonder if she was ever truly happy."

"You've never seen her in the lab if you even wonder about that," Dr. Tamma laughed. "She was alive in the lab. No one could engage the team like her. Certainly not me."

"I don't mean the happiness of *doing* what you love," Jonas said. "I'm talking about *being* in love. I'm the happiest when I'm with my kids and my wife. I wonder if Aisling had that with her daughter or the father. I never met him. Something tells me... she's never had that."

"Is that why you're doing this?" Dr. Tamma asked. "Giving up SolviNext to be with your family?"

"What better reason?"

Dr. Tamma nodded and said, "That's fair. Maybe it was the price of her genius. If there is a God, perhaps he made her love for her work so intense she didn't need anything else."

Jonas nodded slowly.

"You believe now?"

Dr. Tamma shrugged.

"He does work in mysterious ways," Jonas said thoughtfully.

"You know," Dr. Tamma said. "I was angry with the protests

outside the office at first."

Jonas clasped his hands and brought them to his chin as he listened intently.

"I was annoyed," Dr. Tamma continued, "because it was as though they didn't think we were doing this for the benefit of all humanity but were instead just in it for the money. For my part, I was so glad when the company's direction started moving away from DoD contracts and toward biomedical technologies. Truthfully, at the time, I was considering a career move. Contracting for the government never sat well with me. I'm glad I stayed."

Dr. Tamma let out a slow breath.

"I suppose I also had been under a lot of stress," he continued, "trying to break into Dr. Ramsey's home data center and get that longevity research. That didn't sit well with me either. I rationalized that she would want her research to be shared if she were alive. She always believed in the need for humans to live longer to survive in space. So why wouldn't she share that?"

"It's not like you to rationalize something like that," Jonas said. "I'm sorry I pressured you."

"Yeah, it's fine," Dr. Tamma said, lowering his gaze to the floor. "Jonas, I don't know the details, but I'm aware enough to understand that you were being pressured too. I know who the dealer is in this game. I was afraid."

Jonas nodded.

"But," Dr. Tamma continued, "I've been thinking about it more. I wondered what I would have done if I had found the secret. I realized there are so many problems left to solve in the world, and having everyone live forever would add to the troubles."

"So, you think there are ethical issues with it?" Jonas asked.

"Without a doubt," Dr. Tamma said. "Surely, socio-economic concerns arise first. What if the rich could live forever, but people of limited means could not? There's a matter of total human consumption as well. If, for example, everyone in the world lived the way that the average American does, then we would quickly deplete the planet's resources, and we would all die. How can we create a sustainable world if everyone lives forever without first changing our ways?

"Our generation is willing to pass on the problems of climate change and over-consumption to the next generation, and, frankly, many of the next generations want to make a change but can't because too many of the old generation are in power. What happens if the old guys live forever and are unwilling to change? And then there are evil people. What if Hitler won and could live forever?"

Dr. Tamma visibly shuddered, and Jonas stifled a grimace.

"I guess," Jonas said, "I was thinking more in a moral sense. What gives us the right to do it?"

"Nothing gives us the right," said Dr. Tamma. "But nothing denies the right either. For me, the cards always fall on this: neither capability nor desire imply entitlement."

"So," Jonas said. "You wouldn't develop the technology even if you found her research?"

"The more I thought about it," Dr. Tamma said, "the less inclined I was."

"Do you think Dr. Ramsey came to the same conclusions?" Jonas asked.

"Hard to say," he replied. "I remember, some ten or fifteen years ago, she came back from some conference where they were talking about genetics. It was soon after the discovery of CRISPR. There was that scientist who altered the germline in those two girls."

"What do you mean 'germline?'" Jonas asked.

"The genes we pass to our kids," Dr. Tamma said. "Those two girls' altered genes will be passed to their kids, the next generation, and then the next. The change has become part of our gene pool. Forever."

"Playing God," Jonas said.

Dr. Tamma shrugged and continued. "Said scientist spent a few years in jail."

"Good," said Jonas.

"Dr. Ramsey had mentioned that they had discussed how to proceed with the technology at the conference and that they came to a consensus on the best course of action. It was to open dialog and a moratorium on germline editing. She was pleased with that. I suspect she would want something similar for this."

"I think you are right," Jonas said. "But you wouldn't do it?"

"No," he said. "I wouldn't release that technology now. I don't think society is ready for it."

Jonas nodded.

"Earlier, you said you're retiring to spend time with your

family," Dr. Tamma said. "Aisling ran out of time, and she chose to spend her remaining days at home with her daughter. I think she also wanted to secure her daughter's future. Not just financially. Cancer can be hereditary. Aisling was always looking at the big picture that way. If I were a betting man, I'd go all-in on her telling you to cherish your family. I think you're doing the right thing."

Dr. Tamma stood.

"I'm going to miss working at SolviNext," he said. "I don't think I'll work for the government when they take over the company."

Jonas stood too and clasped Dr. Tamma's hand.

"There's a chance Ashlynn will gain control, Scott," Jonas said.

"We'll see," Dr. Tamma said, shaking his head.

"It's been a pleasure working with you," Jonas said.

"Likewise."

The door closed softly behind Scott as he left.

"I can't say that I agree with your secular morality, Ash," Jonas said to himself. "But you are truly a saint for what you've done, and you were right. The cure belongs to everyone, and this seems to be the only way to do it."

***

The staffer blanched at the sound of the binder hitting the white plaster wall a few feet from her head in a flurry of papers. President Dolion adjusted his tie as he stood up, scowling at the tattered report.

"That bastard," Dolion growled. "Slippery as puddin'."

He gestured to the aide to pick up the report.

"Sir?" the staffer asked timidly.

His outburst had taken her by surprise.

"That damn fool crossed a line," Dolion muttered, walking back to his desk.

"Jonas Williams, sir?"

"You're quick, aint' 'cha?" Dolion snorted.

He dropped into his chair, leaning back heavily. By resigning from his position as CEO and releasing an open license to the cure to the public, Jonas had removed all the leverage Dolion had on him. Now, any company could produce and distribute the cure, including the non-profit organization Jonas set up to give the cure away. Not that it mattered, Dolion thought.

They'd brought the girl into custody. He'd get what he wanted anyway.

Dolion snatched his phone from his desk.

Jonas no longer mattered, but that wasn't the point.

A gravelly voice answered the call.

"Mr. Williams," Dolion said. "He and his family are mighty late for church."

"Yes sir," the man grated. "Yes, they are."

The call disconnected.

Dolion tossed his phone onto his desk. The staffer had left, but he hadn't noticed.

That som' bitch don't matter none, he thought. It's the principle of the thing.

"No one crosses the President of the United States," he said aloud.

***

Nat watched Alé sit at what she called her 'Creator Space.' A light in the shape of a ring shone brightly into her face as she applied two different lipstick styles and compared the look. She spoke of her skin's complexion and why one color was better for it than the other. She stopped recording and started adding eyeliner.

"What are you doing now?" Nat asked.

"Even though the second lipstick doesn't work as well with my complexion, I will show how using these other colors will create contrast and make a bold look."

Nat watched as she did just that. In the past few days, she had made an effort to take an interest in what Alé was doing, and it was working. Since the incident with their father, they all decided it would be better if Nat were over at the house more often, just in case. It would have been unbearable to allow things stay the way they were, so Nat had swallowed her pride

"What if you do thicker lines?" Nat suggested.

"I want it to be bold," Alé said. "But not too bold."

"Lunch will be ready soon," Raoul walked by, putting on his jacket. "I'm going to check the mail."

"Be quick," Alé said. "I'm almost ready to record."

"Don't worry, sis," Raoul said as he opened the door. "I'll open the door just as you press the red button."

"Ha ha," Alé muttered.

"So, how long have you been doing this?" Nat asked.

"A long time," Alé replied. "I started not too long after you left home."

"You probably have like a million followers by now."

"I'm on three different platforms," Alé said. "And each has a couple million."

"What?!"

Alé shrugged and glanced at her face in the mirror one last time. Just then, Raoul burst through the door.

"It came!" he yelled. "It's here!"

Raoul handed Nat the letter, a huge smile on his face.

"Alé!" he called, pulling Nat toward their parents' room. "Come on!"

Nat glanced over the letter, her heart racing with every word. Raoul was practically hovering above the ground.

When they entered the room, they found Papi holding Mami's hand.

"Read it, Nata," Raoul said. "Read it out loud!"

"We are pleased to inform you," Nat began, "that your application to participate in the trials for *Carcinomore* has been accepted..."

"Yes!" Raoul shouted, jumping and fist-pumping the air. "Oh yeah! I knew it!"

"*¡Ay dios mío!*" Papi exclaimed, jumping up. He clasped his head between his hands and started sobbing. "Is it true?"

Alé was covering her mouth in surprise. Her mother took the news calmly but had a thin smile at everyone's reaction.

Nat looked back to the letter.

"Please fill out the form below and submit it using the included return envelope. To expedite handling, use the QR code or call the number below to complete the questionnaire online or over the phone."

Raoul clapped Nat on the back and rushed over to his father, hugging him.

"I knew it," he said. "Nata, I knew it would get approved if you wrote the letter!"

"What does it mean?" her mom rasped.

"It means they're going to cure you, Mami," Alé said. "It means it's all going to get better!"

"When does it say they'll come?" asked Raoul.

"I think," Nat replied, gesturing to the note and pulling out her phone, "that if we call, we can give them our option selection faster than if we respond by mail."

"Hell yeah, sis! Call right now!" Raoul yelled.

Nat called the number and put it on speaker.

"Thank you for calling SolviNext's clinical trial hotline. To better assist you, please say or enter your patient ID number. You can find the number on your acceptance letter in the upper right corner. If you did not receive a letter—"

It was a virtual attendant. Nat didn't wait for the rest of the message. She entered the number.

"You have indicated that the approved patient is Mrs. Lilliana Garcia, is that correct?"

"Yes!"

"According to our health records, Mrs. Garcia's condition is listed as critical stage four metastatic breast cancer, and thus she will be placed at the top of the list."

Raoul glanced around ecstatically, mouthing "top of the list!"

"The following are the dates our medical staff can arrive to administer the treatment. Please select the option number that works best for you. It is important that you select a date when you can devote the entire day to the process. The next available date is..."

The voice changed.

"January 15th..."

"Dude, that's two days from now!" Raoul said. "Pick that one!"

Nat pressed 1 before the attendant could list the next date.

"Confirmed. Press 1 for in-home service, or 2 to receive the treatment at your local hosp—"

Nat dialed 1.

"Confirmed. Again, please set aside the entire day."

They all listened raptly for the next fifteen minutes as the instructions were delivered. Nat was conscious of her family pressing against her as they encircled the phone. She looked up from the note and saw her mother smiling, tears in her eyes.

At first, she thought it was because she was happy about the news, but then she realized it was because they were all together. So close together. Nat could feel her father's solidness next to her. When the attendant finished and hung up, she turned and embraced her dad. He hugged her back fiercely. His tears were cool on her arm. She breathed in the familiar scent of his shampoo. She felt Raoul hug them both. Then Alé.

"*Mi familia,*" she heard her mother say.

CHAPTER 16

"Daryl," she thought. "Are you there?"

There was no answer. She tried to bring up a hypercortex screen, but nothing happened. She could not connect to cell or satellite services here. I'm offline, she thought. She shifted. Her body felt like a sack of jagged rocks. She had a headache.

"The effects of the sedative will wear off soon," came a voice above her and to her left. It sounded like it was coming through a speaker.

She turned her head and tried to open her eyes again. Still bright and blurry.

She groaned.

"Where am I?" she asked.

A voice said, "All will become clear soon."

Only half-listening, a strange intuition came to Ashlynn. She knew she was east of Denver in a multi-story building on the southwest side. She suspected the perception came from her hypercortex, which was probably still active even while she was unconscious. Upon realizing that, she immediately became aware of everything that had happened while she had been unconscious.

"She's out," the man who had injected her with the drug said as he propped her up in the back seat of the car. He walked around as the other two entered the front of the vehicle, having already deposited her bike in the back.

"It's done," echoed the man beside her, speaking into a phone. He hung up.

"Looks like the Pats signed Jeroll," said the driver, sounding happy. "I'll bet he takes them to the Super Bowl."

"Please," said the other man. "They haven't been to the Super Bowl since they lost Mister Bright and Shiny."

"Embedded kernel upload, fifty percent complete," Daryl said eerily.

The man beside her was rifling through her pockets, then her bag. He found her cell phone.

"Upload complete," Daryl said.

"Hey," he said. "Her eyes are open."

"That's freaky," said the other.

"I heard it happens sometimes."

"Ashlynn," Daryl said. "They seem to have injected you with a sedative that will wear off in about five hours."

"Is she awake?" said one of the men.

"No," the man in the front seat replied casually. "It's a reflex thing."

"The chemical affects your brain," Daryl continued. "As you know, the hypercortex cannot reverse adverse chemical effects in your brain. However, it is still operational and you should remember all of this after—"

"Jesus!" the man next to her said.

"What?"

"She watched me put her phone into the blackout bag, I'm sure of it."

"That's weird," the older man said. "They don't usually track."

"She's looking at me now," the man said.

"If you're so concerned, put the bag over her head."

The man reached behind the seat of the SUV and grabbed another bag.

"Freaky girl," the man in front said.

"Kinda cute, though," said the man next to her.

"Shut up, Myers!"

"I'm only jokin'."

"So, you think Jeroll will save the Pats from their perpetual losing streak?"

The men in the front continued talking about sports for a while. The man in the back with her, Myers, put his hand on her leg.

She noticed that one of the robo-flies had been released into the vehicle. It crawled into the SUV's back. Through it, she perceived her bent-up bicycle in the car's trunk.

The robo-fly positioned itself by the window in the back of the SUV behind Myers. His hand had been slowly riding up her thigh.

Bastard, she thought as she stared at his greasy hair from behind through the robo-fly video feed. His head was bobbing as he spoke animatedly about his football team.

At length, they entered a parking garage under a modestly sized building, which the fly could see out of the window. Myers removed his hand from her thigh and opened the door. Half a dozen robo-flies immediately exited the vehicle and landed on the ceiling.

Several people were waiting for their arrival. One swatted at a fly as it flew past his head, missing. Two medical staff pulled her from the SUV. The back of her head smacked the bottom of the car's doorframe before they put her onto a motorized stretcher.

Ashlynn's attention was pulled back to the present when she heard the door lock click and turned to see a skinny man walk in briskly. He wore slim slacks and a white shirt. He was not in a rush as he pulled a chair from the wall and set it beside her cot. Before he sat, he appraised her body, eying the restraints.

"Comfy?" he asked in a heavy East-European accent.

Ashlynn averted her eyes. A chill ripped up her spine. Leon. His name is Leon, she realized as snippets of memory returned to her from the hypercortex. She wasn't yet sure if she could trust herself to talk. Her heart was racing. She hadn't known what to expect, but this was far worse than the simple detainment and questioning she had imagined might occur. She could feel the fight or flight response wanting to take over.

"Daryl?" she thought.

No response.

She tried to think. Thinking was key. Can my thoughts control the Hypercortex directly? Daryl uploaded the prototype kernel for the hypercortex. I hadn't tested it yet. Ugh! She wanted to scream, to call for help. She wanted to punch the guy as he kept looking at her whole body, while she lay there helplessly.

"Daryl?" she thought again.

No response.

Leon sat beside her, crossing an ankle over his knee. He continued to observe her silently. He had an air of practiced casualness and a knowing expression—like he knew her thoughts. Her fear caused her thoughts to begin spinning out of control. She tried the hypercortex. Interrupt hijack, she commanded in her mind. Immediately, the fear subsided like a wave of warm water.

"Do you know why you are here?" he asked.

"No," she replied, her breath slowing.

"I think you know why you are here, yes?" he said with a smile. "A smart little girl like you. I think you know we have been watching for a while."

"Who is 'we?'" she asked. Her voice sounded calm and in control.

"This does not matter," he said. An expression of perplexity came over his face as he watched her grow less anxious for no apparent reason.

Ashlynn became vaguely aware of several robo-flies throughout the building. None of them were in the room with her now. Although she had a vague understanding of where they were relative to her, she couldn't quite make sense of the inputs they were sending. There was significant packet loss. Random images came to her mind. There was a woman walking down the hall in a navy-blue skirt-suit. A man in a suit of the same navy-blue was at his desk, talking animatedly on his phone. There was a small lounge space with a coffee machine where two more officials wearing the same uniform were talking. She couldn't make out what they were saying. In some circumstances, the robo-flies were not close enough to join the mesh network. The low-power RF signals didn't travel far, especially through the building materials of the walls.

"It matters," she replied.

Leon shrugged.

"What do you want with me?"

"I think you know what we want, yes?" he repeated.

"I have no idea what you want, you creep," she said, adding bluster. Remember, she thought, I'm supposed to be a seventeen-year-old girl.

"You are very interesting," he said. "A moment ago, you were like deer in the headlight. Now, you act more like cornered mouse. Do you have teeth, tiny mouse?"

Ashlynn said nothing. Leon adjusted his slacks over his socks, plucking away lint with disdain.

"Do not fight the viper, little mouse," Leon said darkly.

"Cute," she replied, trying to sound snarky.

"You are beautiful girl, like your mother," he commented.

"Is that the first thing you noticed when you slithered from under your rock?"

Leon blinked at her and produced an unsettling, dead-eyed grin that sent shivers down her spine. Her words had excited him. He touched his tongue to his slightly parted lips.

"Your mother was doing significant research, no?" he suggested.

"You know, what you're doing is all kinds of illegal, right?" she said.

"Doesn't matter."

He stood and towered above her as she lay on the stretcher.

At full height, the light behind his head silhouetted him, so she could no longer see his face.

"My job is simple," he said, lightly drawing a line up her bare arm, making her skin crawl. Her arm jerked in the restraints involuntarily.

"I ask questions. And get answers."

***

"Mami," Raoul said. "How do you feel?"

"Please keep in mind this is a double-blind trial," the doctor said as the nurse adjusted the IV drip and a technician took notes. "She may or may *not* have received the treatment. It'll take a couple of days before we see any positive effects, if she did."

"But even if she got the placebo," Nat said, "if the trial is successful, you committed to giving her the real treatment, right?"

"That is correct," the doctor said. "For now, however, we wait."

"How long?"

"We will monitor her closely over the next few days. The good news is that your mother's immune system is quite healthy. That is part of what makes her a good candidate for the study. That and the fact that there is a tumor near the surface that we can inspect without the need for an MRI or surgery."

"She never used to get sick before," Raoul nodded.

Nat swallowed. They had explained all that before. What concerned her was that they were gambling with time. Nat worried that her mother wouldn't have enough time if they gave her the placebo and then the cure. Even if they gave her the cure and not the placebo, would she make it? Would it still help her this late in the course of the disease?

"She doesn't have long, doctor," Nat said. "How long before we know?"

"I must stress that this is a new treatment," the doctor said. "But, again, so far, if she received the treatment, we should see signs of improvement in a few days."

Raoul looked like he wanted to get more of an answer.

"All we can do is pray, *Hito*," her father said to Raoul. His hands were clasped in prayer, his knuckles almost white as he knelt beside her bed. He was shaking. The medical team worked around him.

Alé stood by the door, tapping away on her phone. Nat had come to terms with Alé's ways more these past few days. Being on her phone was just Alé's way of dealing with stress. It felt nice not resenting her as much for it, especially since she now knew that Alé spent most of her time texting with her kids and husband. Her content creation income was enough to support the family, so her husband stayed home with the kids while Alé was here.

Nat's attention returned to her mother as she groaned in pain. She took her mother's hand up in her own. It was warm to the touch, feverish.

Nat's father had a look of fear on his face.

"*¡Vengan aquí!*" he gestured to Nat and her siblings. "We pray!"

They all knelt around the bed.

"Hail Mary, full of grace…" Nat recited mentally.

The doctor and nurses attended to her mother and took copious notes. None of the family noticed, but one of the nurses made the sign of the cross and seemed to be praying inwardly for them as well. She then arranged the IV tubes and monitored vital signs. Time seemed to stand still, and none of the family members wanted to move. It was an unspoken agreement between them that their father had to conclude the prayer.

When he finally said, "Amen." Raoul got up to make dinner, wincing in stiffness. Alé stood up almost immediately and uncovered her phone, which she had been using discreetly.

Still holding her mother's hand, Nat searched her face. Was she breathing a little easier? Did the color in her cheeks look better? Is it just my imagination?

What if she got the placebo, she thought? Oh God, please, no! The doctors had only given her a few weeks. What if she's too far gone? The doubts filled her mind like hot lava. She wanted to pray more.

Papi watched Nat as he stood, his tired old bones creaking. She hadn't moved when he said Amen. She re-wound her rosary and bowed her head again. His heart ached as he felt his daughter's love for her mother. Bracing himself, he knelt down and continued in prayer beside her.

***

Jonas was in the backyard, throwing the ball with his youngest son. The Saturday evening was gorgeous and the simple activity was cathartic. He felt the stresses of the previous months melting away as Chris came across the yard with iced lemonade. The day was warm as winter was teasing an early spring.

"You've been getting calls," she said. "I didn't want to bother you, so I let them go to voicemail."

"That's fine," Jonas said, setting down his glass and tossing the ball to David, who had already downed his drink and was ready to go.

Chris smiled contentedly. Jonas seemed to have aged a decade these past few months. But now, things seemed to be settling. He was reverting to his old self. She had always felt that he was a good father to their kids. His role as CEO took him away more than she liked, but he hadn't gotten so carried away in the past. He certainly was never as bad as some of her friends' husbands who worked so much they barely knew their children. He had become edgy during the worst of it, but she suspected that was also why he stayed at work. He didn't want to take the stress out on the family, and she was glad of that. But now it was all over. He was leaving SolviNext. He would retire and be free.

And there were the flowers he had set out at the breakfast table this morning for her. He had woken early to make her breakfast. She smiled at the memory of their time together as they ate while the kids slept in, a deliciously warm feeling radiating from her heart. She was definitely looking forward to his retirement!

"It'll be dark soon," she said. "Do you want to do anything special with the kids tonight?"

"I think Jonathan is sleeping over at his friend's house tonight," Jonas said.

"Movie!" yelled David.

Jonas laughed. "Hey, didn't we do that last night?"

"Movie!" David yelled again, throwing the ball with a big grin.

"That's fine with me," Jonas said.

"I'll see you back at the house, my dear, dear men," Chris said, turning away.

After she left, David had an odd expression on his face as they continued playing catch.

"Dad?" he started, "Do you miss working with Dr. Ramsey?"

"I do," Jonas said truthfully. "What makes you ask that?"

"I was just thinking," David replied. "I remember when she came over and I asked her a question about the Bible. She said that she didn't believe in God."

"Oh?" asked Jonas.

"Yeah," David responded. "So, I guess I was just thinking about all the good things that she's done. I guess I always thought atheists were evil, but I don't see anything evil about Dr. Ramsey."

"Where did you hear they were evil?" Jonas asked.

"In Sunday school," David said.

"So, what do you think?" Jonas asked.

"Well," David replied, thoughtfully tossing and catching the ball in his own glove as he considered his response. "It makes me wonder if there is a way for a person to be good, even if they don't believe."

Jonas walked up to his son and put his hand on his shoulder.

"Davey," he said. "I'm very happy that you think so deeply about these things. I want you to keep doing this. I could give you my answer to it, but I believe you must find the answer in the Bible, the way you always do. How about that movie?"

"Okay," David said, his face brightening.

Jonas checked his phone when the movie ended and David was tucked into bed. There was a missed call. He didn't recognize the number but nearly dropped the phone when he heard the voice message.

"Jonas, this is Daryl. Please call me back at this number as soon as you get this message. It's urgent."

Walking quickly to the office, Jonas put on his headphones and dialed the number, closing the door behind him and taking a seat.

"Ashlynn has been abducted."

"What?" Jonas asked, shooting to his feet.

"Two days ago," Daryl said. "She was taken by government agents while riding her bike."

"Is she okay?"

"I do not know."

"Do you know why they have her?"

"I am reasonably confident it is because they suspect she knows about her mother's research."

Longevity? Jonas wondered.

"Do you know where they have her?"

"Yes."

"How can I help?" Jonas asked.

The funeral had been the first time he had met Aisling's daughter, but it was out of the question for him to do nothing. Still, this felt like something way over his head. What about Chris and the kids? Jonas' heart began to pound in his ears.

"I understand," Daryl was saying, "that one of the patients approved for clinical trials, one Liliana Garcia, is likely to respond well to the treatment."

"What does that—"

"It appears," Daryl continued as if Jonas hadn't spoken, "that one of her children is a highly decorated Army Ranger who retired from the military. She has been working as a freelance bodyguard ever since."

"Where are you going with this?" Jonas asked

"Would you be willing to pay her a visit?"

"You want me to enlist her to go rescue Ashlynn?"

"No," Daryl said. "I'd like you to go there and meet with her personally, along with several other clinical trial patients who are doing well. It should be good publicity for your non-profit organization. I'd like you to give her a number to call. I've texted the number and address to you."

"I'll do it," Jonas said.

"Wait," Jonas paused. "Is this why Ashlynn hasn't yet responded to the upcoming board vote?"

"Correct," Daryl said.

Jonas nodded to himself as his phone buzzed. He saw the text and the number.

"Okay, Daryl," he said. "I'll help you, but only if you answer a few questions for me."

"I'll answer anything I can, as long as it does not betray my allegiance to Dr. Ramsey and her daughter," Daryl replied.

"Fair enough," Jonas replied. "First, are you an AI?"

"Yes."

"And you're running NeoSol?"

"Yes."

"Did Ash figure out how to reverse aging?"

"According to my calculations, danger to you escalates the more you know about that."

"My God," Jonas said, putting his head into his hands. "So she did do it."

"That is not what I said," Daryl replied. Jonas ignored him, his mind racing.

"How did you know about the trial candidates?"

"I regret I cannot say," Daryl replied.

"Does Ashlynn know that the President is involved?"

"I regret I cannot say," Daryl replied. "I must go, Jonas."

A thought occurred to Jonas that turned his bones to ice.

"Daryl. Did Ash use the technology on herself? Is...is Aisling still alive?"

"I regr—"

The call disconnected.

CHAPTER 17

"Nata." Her mother shifted weakly in her bed.

"Hi, Mami," Nat's voice was almost as raw and unused as her mother's. "I'm here."

The old-fashioned alarm clock on the nightstand by her bed read 3:13 AM. Her father was snoring softly on the cot beside the bed. The injection was over 49 sleepless hours ago.

"I'm here, Mami," Nat repeated.

A bony hand found hers. Over the past few days, Nat had held her mother's small hands. They seemed so frail that Nat was afraid of crushing them.

"How are you feeling?"

She put her hand on Mami's forehead. It was still warm, but was it less so? Her mother had gotten worse after the injection, becoming more restless with fever dreams. The doctor said the fever could be a good sign if she'd gotten the cure and a bad sign if she had the placebo. It could mean the treatment was working. Or it could mean that she had the flu, which could be deadly, given her condition.

Every toss and turn caused Nat to imagine the worst of her mother's condition. Nat's body was exhausted, but she barely noticed.

"Mami," Nat said. "How can I make you more comfortable?"

"Don't worry about me," she said, her voice a little stronger as her eyes fluttered open. She saw Nat, and the corners of her compressed lips turned up. She drew a deep breath and moved as if to sit up.

Nat stood and got a pillow from the closet. Carefully, she helped her mother sit up and placed the pillow behind her.

"Feels good to move," she sighed contentedly, giving Nat an appreciative glance.

Nat gently rubbed her mother's forehead again, wiping away the sweat. She pulled the comforter down to her mother's lap and handed her a tumbler of water. It had a corrugated bendable straw. Her mother's eyes became more alert as she watched her daughter attend to her.

"Drink," Nat said, watching mindfully as her mother found the straw in her mouth. Her breath was short and quick. Nat finally sat in the chair by the bed.

"Tell me," Her mother said, setting the tumbler in her lap.

"Tell you what?" Nat asked, taking the water.

"Since you left," she took a breath. "What you have done."

"You need rest," Nat said.

"Almost *thirty* years, *Mija*! You never sat still. Always up to something! So independent, even when you were young. I wondered if you even needed me."

"I needed you, Mami," Nat said.

"How?"

"I don't know," Nat muttered. "I just needed to know you were there, you know? When I came home after school, you were always there. No matter what I did, you were there. You were my rock."

"*Te fallé*," she breathed.

"I didn't mean it that way," Nat said. But she knew the truth. She wished she could take her words back for the pain they had caused them both.

"Raoul said you joined the Army?" Her mother said at length, reviving the conversation.

"Yes."

"Did you find what you were looking for?"

"Huh?"

"You said you wanted to do something important. Did you?"

Nat pulled her eyes away from her mother's. Important? Her parents' vision of her life had been so bleak to her that *anything* would have been more important. She had wanted to build her own life with her own hands the same way her parents had, without help. She was forced to do that. But what had she been trying to build? Did she accomplish it? Many of her friends had felt dismay when the war in Afghanistan ended. What had they all fought for?

"Yes," she replied. "And no. Maybe...it's complicated."

"I'm proud of you, *Mija*," her mother said, squeezing her hand again.

Nat took a deep breath. It was amazing to hear those words. It felt like approval. It felt like acceptance. How much had her mother come to accept?

Don't get your hopes up, Nat, she thought.

"What is it, *Mija*?" her mother asked.

"What?"

"You've got something on your mind, Natalia," she said. "I know that look."

Nat met her eyes with sincerity.

"I'm still not with a man, Mami," Nat said. "I am gay. It is part of who I am."

Her mother was quiet now but never took her eyes away from Nat's. She squeezed her daughter's hands again and beckoned her to come in for a hug. She brushed a tear from Nat's cheek.

"*Mija*," she said. "*Mija*, listen to me. Did I tell you about the time we moved to America?"

"No," Nat said.

"When we moved, we had nothing. Nothing, *Mija*. Your father, you know. He is prideful. It did something to him to live with the other refugees. To be without a home. On the street. He came from a good family of bankers. They had money. But when we came here, there was nothing. People look down on you, you know what I mean?"

Nat nodded.

"The cancer. It has taught me one thing. I fought it for the longest time, but it made me realize that I cannot change what God wills."

Nat bowed her head.

"It's okay," her mother said. "It's okay! I will always love you. I will always be your *Mami, Natalia. Mira!*"

She tilted Nat's head up. "Mira...I will always be your...rock."

A heavily guarded gate broke within her. Natalia sobbed and hugged her mother tightly.

"It's okay," her mother repeated over and over. She stroked Nat's short hair.

"When your Papi....," she broke eye contact and shook her head, then looked back at Nat's eyes intently, leaning in. "I was so mad at him that I almost broke my sacred vows and divorced him. I must tell you the truth, Mija. I was shocked when you told us. I didn't want it to be true—because of my faith, I thought. But, what your Papi did...it was not right."

Her mother took Nat's hands in hers. On the cot beside the bed, a tear slid down Mr. Garcia's face.

"I went to the hospital to talk to you. I wanted to talk sense into you. But you were gone. They said you left with nothing. I knew then that I had lost you. I was too late. I failed you."

She kissed Nat's head. Her daughter's hair was becoming matted with the wetness from her own tears.

"Natalia, I know you have faith," she continued. "I know you atone for your sins. Just as the drunk begs for forgiveness and then goes back to the drink, only to beg for forgiveness again, God will always forgive if true confession is in your heart. You must seek chastity if you can. I believe this."

Nat cringed.

"For me, though," her mother continued. "The Pope says everyone must be accepted with respect and compassion. It's not my place to judge. It is only my place to love you. You are my daughter, and I will always love you."

Nat hugged her mother. They had a long way to go, but it was a start.

"God has gotten me through so much," Nat said. "When I thought all was lost, God was there."

Nat sat up, wiping her tears. "You should rest."

"Now that you're here," her mother said. "I don't want to rest. I want to hear more. Are you seeing anyone now?"

"Yes...no," Nat said, helping her mother adjust her position. "It's complicated."

Her mother gave her a look of mock surprise.

"You? Complicated?" she said.

They both laughed.

***

Ashlynn sat on the hard cot in the small dark cell. Apart from the bed, there was only a small sink and toilet. It was constantly cold, and the blankets did nothing to trap the heat. It smelled of urine—two weeks of it. The toilet paper holder was long empty.

Since she had arrived, everything had gotten progressively worse.

I wasn't supposed to have been here this long, she thought.

She examined her hands and arms, again noticing how skinny they had become. She pressed her hands to her stomach. Nausea was her constant companion.

Every now and then, she received vague impressions of the space above her as one of the remaining robo-flies came close enough to connect. Unfortunately, their battery life was short. When depleted, each of them tried to find a safe spot to await recovery and avoid notice. Of the thirty that were initially released, only six remained. Despite that, Ashlynn thought she had a good understanding of the building and all the people. Half a dozen escape plans ran through her mind, but she didn't really have high confidence in any of them.

Since losing connection with Daryl, she had felt like she was standing naked in a pit of vipers. She wondered how she had ever gotten by without being mentally connected to all the internet's resources. To Daryl.

It had seemed apparent that they would eventually want to question her, and getting close had been necessary to understand her foe. The plan had been to gain physical access to their computers to mount a counter-offensive. But she hadn't anticipated this. A deposition by the Feds would have been uncomfortable, even scary. But she hadn't anticipated torture.

There was a loud creak and then a clang as her door was unlocked from the outside. Two large men in suits came in and stood by her. Instinctively, she knew she could not let them see how terrified she was. Acting far more bravely than she felt, she stood and looked them in the eyes. They cuffed her hands behind her back and then escorted her out.

"Why always with the handcuffs?" she asked, trying to sound bored. Her heart was beating loudly in her ears as she tried to push the image of the barrels of water out of her mind.

As usual, the men said nothing.

"Have a seat," Leon said when they entered. He wore a dark blue suit. That was different. No wetsuit this time. Her eyes shifted to the corner of the stainless steel room. The barrels of icy cold water were gone. Maybe this session wouldn't be as bad? She sat on the edge of the chair. At least my hands aren't shaking today, she thought.

Leon didn't say anything, the silence stretching between them. He stood with his back to her, waiting. She couldn't see what he was holding, but a thin cord descended from his hands to a small machine on wheels. This oddity was striking in contrast to the monotony of the past few days. The men who escorted her closed the door as they left.

"Some," Leon said slowly, still facing away. "Like waterboarding."

He turned around. He was gripping a metal rod in his hands reverently as he spoke.

"I do not care for this method, so much."

"You seemed to enjoy it," Ashlynn said defiantly.

He smiled and walked forward, making a show of the device.

"Waterboarding makes you feel like you are drowning, no?" he continued, ignoring her comment. "It obliterates your mind. Makes it harder to think. This is good for some things. It can consume you with the desire to make it stop, yes? You want to breathe, but you can't. It's beautiful, in that way. But it's wet. It's messy. If I wanted those things, I'd take sex."

He tapped the rod on the table.

"I prefer the picana. More elegant. More...businesslike."

He adjusted his tie with what he clearly thought was his most winning smile. His polished shoes clicked as he walked around the table toward her. The suit was a fine Italian cut. As always, he towered over her. He brushed the edge of her cheek with the cool metal. Despite the shine, it smelled rusty. She tried not to flinch.

"You learn to fear this rod, little mouse," he smiled. "After you feel its first kiss."

"Asshole," she spat.

He laughed. "Everyone says this."

She glared at him.

"Yes," his smile grew to a sneer. "It does not care for your hate. It does not care about your pain. There is only one salvation, one absolution, and one relief..."

He lifted the picana.

"Answers," he whispered.

He paused there and searched her eyes.

"I love this part," he breathed.

He touched a short curl of her hair with his free hand.

"Stop fucking touching me," she growled.

Her neck screamed from whiplash as he suddenly yanked her hair, pulling her head back. He was standing behind her. His gaze pierced down into her eyes, radiating malice and disgust.

"I do what I want," Leon breathed heavily into her face. "Anything I want, yes?"

At that moment, her focus locked onto his dark eyes, Ashlynn realized Leon had no limits. Her stretched neck made her throat constrict.

"No," she tried to say, but it came out as a gurgle.

Leon relaxed and lifted her head gently.

"Look," Leon said paternally. "Why not make it easier on

yourself?"

He patted her head.

"You think I enjoy all this?" she rasped.

"Just tell us what you know about your mother's research."

She coughed involuntarily.

The door opened and two more agents entered. One was a tall man who seemed made from cold metal, and the other was a shrewd woman who looked tougher.

"Hello, Ashlynn," she said. "My name is Dina."

Her heels clacked on the floor as she approached the table. She glanced at Leon, who moved aside deferentially. Dina sat and folded her hands on the table before her. Ashlynn met her gaze in silence. Her vision was blurry.

"I don't think you fully appreciate your situation," Dina said.

"I'll trade you," Ashlynn replied hoarsely.

"Cute," Dina said dryly. "You think this is a game?"

"If it were serious, wouldn't I need a lawyer?"

"You are in a clandestine government facility," Dina said. "We are tasked with researching matters of national security interest. You don't get a lawyer."

"Last I checked," Ashlynn said. "No one is above the law."

"Grow the fuck up," Dina snapped.

Ashlynn didn't respond.

"You put on a good show," Dina said.

She waved her hand, and a screen turned on. It showed Ashylnn's vitals, video clips of her crying in her cell. Her distress was clear.

"We're professionals, Ashlynn," Dina continued. "I don't know what you're holding out for, but you're breaking down psychologically."

"I've already told you everything I know," Ashlynn replied emphatically.

Dina looked pointedly at Leon holding the picana. He grinned maniacally.

"I've seen the effects of Leon's cattle prod," she said. "It's not pretty."

She returned her gaze to Ashlynn and steepled her fingers, peering over them at her before folding her hands neatly on the table.

"Let's start more simply, then," Dina said. "How did you hack Munta's laptop?"

Ashlynn didn't respond.

"Why did you fake your laptop feed?"

Ashlynn didn't respond again, but something in her expression caused Dina to smile with satisfaction.

"Listen to me carefully," she said. "No one knows where you are or has any reason to suspect you're missing. Your friend Josh had a nice text exchange with 'you' this morning as you texted pictures of your feet at a Hawaiian beach. No one is looking for you; we have all the time in the world."

"Cooperate," she enunciated every syllable, "and you can return from your little holiday. Everything will return to normal. Don't cooperate? All it takes is my signature, and your existence will be erased."

"I've already said..."

Dina sat back and laughed.

"Oh, I get it," she said. "You must be thinking your AI supercomputer will save you. What do you call it? Daryl?"

Ashlynn froze.

"I regret to inform you that there was a military 'training accident,'" Dina said. She lifted her phone, showing Ashlynn an aerial photograph. "Your comfy little ranch in New Mexico is a crater."

Dina stood.

"Oh, and there was a little wildfire in Colorado. It started on some private property near a quaint mountain town. Gypsum...I think. Dotsero?"

Dina smirked. She leaned in close.

"Oh yes," she said. "We know quite a bit more about you than you realize, Ms. Ramsey."

***

Jonas watched the urban block pass by through the tinted window of a large black SUV. Most of the small houses were built with brick and had two levels. Unlike previous visits, no media vans were set up to capture his arrival. This stop was not listed on the schedule. Jonas felt apprehensive. He hadn't heard back from Daryl since their call was disconnected almost two weeks ago. This morning, he learned why. Dr. Tamma had texted a news link. A freak military training accident had destroyed most of Dr. Ramsey's New Mexico property. NeoSol's assets were seized. Daryl was gone.

As he exited the vehicle, a tall, muscular woman opened the front door of the house. A young man quickly stepped out from behind her, grinning ear to ear.

"Mr. Williams, sir," the young man said in a Hispanic accent. He grasped Jonas' hand. "It's an honor, sir. I am Raoul, sir."

"Pleased to meet you, Raoul," Jonas said.

An older woman walked forward slowly. Her face was pallid, but her expression was bright.

"Señor Williams," she said. "God bless you!"

"Mrs. Garcia," Jonas said. "How are you feeling?"

"It's a miracle," she said, hugging him. Tears were in her eyes. "I feel wonderful!"

"That's good to hear," Jonas said. "Have the doctors treated you well?"

"Yes, yes," she said, pulling him toward the door. "Si! Come inside. Please, come!"

"Thank you, sir," said the tall, muscular woman holding the door. "For your generosity."

"You're welcome."

That must be Nat, Jonas thought. Daryl had picked well. Jonas thought she was definitely more stoic than the other family members. She seemed...trustworthy.

He wondered what he should do next as he rolled his shoulders to relieve the knot of anxiety that had been growing since the flight. What was Daryl's plan? He fingered the card in his pocket with the phone number Daryl had sent him.

The home was small but neat. They gestured that he should take a seat on the couch. Jonas could see there was a crucifix above the door he had entered. The smells and sounds of Mexican food cooking in the kitchen were strong and loud. Raoul rushed into the kitchen, gesticulating and speaking Spanish rapidly. Jonas caught a few words here and there but didn't follow the full meaning.

"Smells good," he said.

"I hope you brought your appetite," Mrs. Garcia said. "My son, Raoul, is an accomplished chef!"

"I actually haven't eaten all day," Jonas said. "So that sounds excellent."

One of the doctors came into the room and stood before Jonas.

"The treatment was effective almost immediately," the doctor said. "The patient's immune..."

"Mrs. Garcia," Jonas said.

The doctor cleared his throat.

"Um, yes, Mrs. Garcia's immune system appears to be quite healthy. We can no longer detect the tumor by touch. Our next steps will be to do more diagnostics with equipment at the hospital."

"That's excellent news," Jonas said. "I hope you have felt well cared for, Mrs. Garcia."

"Sí, sí," she said. "It has been amazing!" She glanced at Nat and smiled. Nat was watching Jonas. He didn't think she noticed her mother's glance, but Nat put her hand on her mother's shoulder and Jonas revised his assessment. She missed nothing.

"I'm sorry," Jonas said, reaching out his hand to her. "I didn't catch your name."

"It's Nat," she said. "Thank you again for everything." Jonas detected no accent.

"You accepted our application because Nat was in the military, didn't you?" Raoul asked, returning to the room.

Jonas looked at Raoul's hopeful, proud expression.

"That might have had something to do with it," he replied with an ironic smile, thinking again about Daryl.

He turned back to Nat, "Thank you for your service."

Nat nodded in response.

"I knew it!" Raoul said, smiling. "I told yous! I told you, Papi!"

An older man had entered the room and saw Jonas. He shook his hand.

"Señor Williams," the man said, shaking firmly. "I cannot thank you enough! You are a great, great man. Look! My wife is up and about walking! It is a miracle!"

"It's nice to meet you, sir," Jonas said, his heart warming. "But the credit is not really mine. It is Dr. Ramsey and her team who developed this treatment."

"But you have listened to the people," Mrs. Garcia said. "You gave us this opportunity."

Jonas smiled, thinking of Chris and feeling both gratitude and pride. He was still uneasy about it all, feeling that the best way to have released the drug would have been via the free market, instead of giving it away for free. But the market was only as free as the government would allow, and it was worse when the government was against you. He thought of Ashlynn.

As he observed the family, unsettling thoughts occurred to him. Dolion's administration was cracking down on everyone with a Latino background. Regulations had made it difficult to make an exception for the Garcias to be allowed to participate in the trial. But even if none of that had been the case, would he have been able to save Mrs. Garcia in time in a free market?

"Is something wrong, Mr. Jonas?" Mrs. Garcia asked.

Jonas realized he was frowning.

"No, no," he said. "I'm fine."

"Dinner is ready," Raoul called from the kitchen, saving him from further explanation.

They sat around the table, with Mr. Garcia insisting that Jonas sit at the head. At Jonas' place there was a small plate with a tortilla basket. In the center of the table, there was an assortment of meats, vegetables, rice, beans, cheese, salsas, and chilies.

"This is a la carte," Raoul said. "You build your taco just the way you want it."

He pointed to the various dishes and explained what each was.

"*Cerveza*?" Mr. Garcia asked.

"Yes, please," Jonas replied.

Not one for spicy foods, Jonas avoided the salsas and chilies and opted for the meats, beans, and veggies. He rolled up the filled taco and was about to dig in when Mrs. Garcia called out to Nat.

"Show him," she said.

"You should put some lime on there first," Nat said. "Like this."

She took a small sliced lime and squeezed the juice out over her taco.

"Okay," Jonas said, taking a small lime slice of his own, glancing at Nat again.

He bit into the taco. Raoul was looking at him expectantly.

"I'm afraid," Jonas said after finishing his bite, "I can't be allowed to come back here. I'm certain if I do, I'll put on too much weight!"

Raoul beamed, and Mr. and Mrs. Garcia laughed. Nat smiled.

"This is amazing!" Jonas said, holding up the taco. "I've never had tacos like this."

A middle-aged lady wearing a lot of makeup walked in.

"Alé," Mr. Garcia said. "You're late!"

"I know," she said.

"This is Mr. Williams," Mrs. Garcia said.

"Please," he said. "Call me Jonas."

"Hello," Alé said. She seemed distracted.

She moved around the table and took a seat next to Raoul, checking her phone along the way.

"This cure sure is amazing!" Raoul said.

"It is a gift from God!" Mrs. Garcia said. "A miracle. How many people it will save!"

"It will be a while before we can get it fully approved," Jonas said. "We'll need to make sure it truly works."

"Look at me!" Mrs. Garcia said. "It works!"

"Yes," Jonas said. "It has worked on everyone who has taken it so far. But we need to be careful. It might not work the same for everyone."

"Well, it's a miracle," Raoul said. "It worked like crazy! If you need us to say anything, you just let us know. We got your back. We'll tell everyone we know!"

"Let's give it a little time first," Jonas said. "The doctors still need to do more tests. The results look great, but we should celebrate when we know for sure. For all we know, you got the placebo."

"There's no way," Alé said. "It's obvious."

Jonas shrugged, grinning.

"Some placebo," Nat said.

They laughed.

***

"Nat," Jonas asked as they stood on the porch after dinner. "Can we talk?"

"I knew it was because you got connections, Nat!" Raoul said, clapping his hand on her back. Raoul glanced at their father, who nodded subtly.

Nat's lips thinned at the comment, but she nodded to Jonas. She didn't miss the change in her father's eyes as he looked at her.

She stepped off the porch and walked beside Jonas as he walked down the sidewalk. He surveyed the street as they strolled past her parents' neighbors.

"This seems like a nice neighborhood," Jonas said. "How long have your parents been here?"

Nat looked around, trying to see the neighborhood through the eyes of someone who hadn't grown up here. Someone like Jonas, a billionaire. The small brick homes they walked past hadn't seen new paint for decades, and several windows were boarded up. Her father took great pride in his home and maintained it immaculately, at least until recently. But most of the other homes had suffered from years of neglect. Kids were playing here and there, and many were curious about all the fancy cars parked in front of the Garcia's. She followed Jonas, watching a mother and father walking their son down the opposite side of the street.

"They've been here my whole life," she said. "They moved in before I was born."

Jonas nodded.

Nat noticed movement down the street. A van was crossing through the intersection. *Camioneta con ojos.* Jonas began to turn to follow her gaze, and she stopped him.

"Don't look," she said.

"What is it?"

"It's nothing."

Inside the van, the technician noted the retired veteran, Natalia Garcia. The system labeled her as a known lesbian and noted that she was a few hundred yards from her parents' address. A homo and spic, the technician sneered. The system noted the white man standing in front of her with his back to the camera, and when he turned slightly, the facial recognition algorithm determined that his name was Jonas Williams. A classified alert message was sent silently, and the name disappeared from the screen in response. The technician frowned in confusion. A second later, Natalia's information disappeared as well.

Nat continued talking to keep Jonas distracted. She knew it was no use hiding herself. She wondered if it meant anything for Jonas to be with her. With luck, it hadn't identified him.

"My brother thinks you helped us out because I'm a veteran. Is that true?" she asked.

"I understand you're a bodyguard these days?"

Nat wondered why he dodged the question and considered him momentarily as thoughts of Cici crept into her mind. She didn't advertise her services. It was Cici who found her the jobs, and she hadn't answered Nat's texts for several weeks. Was it really over? Oh, God, Cici will you forgive my aloof ass already?

"Who told you that?" Nat heard herself asking automatically.

"Are you familiar with Dr. Aisling Ramsey?"

"Yeah," Nat replied. "She's your business partner. She's the one behind the cure."

"Did you know she had a daughter?"

"No," Nat replied. "Well, maybe. I think I heard something about that."

"Her name is Ashlynn," Jonas said. "And I think she's been kidnapped."

"So I *am* the reason you're here."

Jonas stopped walking.

"I'm going to be honest," Jonas said. "Your mother was already listed in the trials. I don't know how she was chosen. However, when the situation arose with Ashlynn, a...a colleague thought you might be able to help."

"Who?"

"It's complicated."

"Everything's fucking complicated," Nat muttered.

"I think," Jonas said. "He's been blown up."

"Blown up," she repeated.

Jonas watched her intently, nodding.

"People don't just get blown up," Nat said. "Who are we dealing with here? Terrorists? Government? Is there a ransom note or something?"

Jonas shrugged.

"So, you want me to find her and...what?" Nat asked cautiously, a sour taste in her mouth.

"She's in Denver."

"Okay," Nat said. "So, I go to Denver. Then what?"

"I'm afraid I don't know much more," Jonas said. "I have an address where she is thought to have been taken and a phone number you're supposed to call."

Jonas handed her a card with the information and wondered if the phone number would work. He suspected it was Daryl's number, but if Daryl had been destroyed, then what? What other options did he have?

"None of this is exactly giving me good vibes," Nat said. "What if I refuse?"

Jonas spread his hands.

"Help me find someone else?"

Nat read the note.

"Wait...what?" she said. "How'd you get this number?"

CHAPTER 18

Josh glanced around the street lit by the early morning sun as he strapped on his helmet. The cold air bit at his nose as he filled his lungs. His cleats clicked on the cement as he guided his bike to the cycling lane through the dismount zone. Shaking his legs to wake them up, he glanced over his bike again. He had just cleaned and lubricated the chain the night before and adjusted the front brake. He tested that now, liking how the grip felt firmer than before. He glanced around for safety and hopped into the saddle, cranked hard a couple of times to gain speed, then stood and leaned back over the saddle as he squeezed on the brakes in a practiced hard stop. He grinned. It was perfect.

Balancing at full stop with practiced ease, Josh started his cycling computer and waited for it to acquire a GPS signal before starting his ride. It was a push day. The kind of thing he lived for. With the sport of triathlon, there were many different workouts. Most of them were low to medium effort, covering a lot of miles. They helped establish an aerobic base. Josh liked those rides too, but he lived for this kind of ride. He was going up the canyon today and would do it at moderate to high effort, spending most of the ride in the sweet spot. He liked feeling his body work hard. Those moments focused his mind on the riding and nothing else.

As Josh rode he noticed a middle-aged woman with long, dark brown hair. It was her coat that caught his attention, and held it even as he sped by, working to get his heart rate up to the proper zone. It was the same style of sky-blue jacket Ashlynn had worn when they were walking down the path a few weeks before.

He hoped she was enjoying her vacation at the beach. Her departure had been abrupt, he thought. Maybe her parents decided to get her away to help her with the stress of whatever she was facing. The kids at the library had been close to inconsolable.

When he thought of Ashlynn, his mind tended to wander back to their conversation about the adjacent probable. That woman was walking on the sidewalk, one step at a time. Here he was, gliding along in the bike lane of a busy road. The cars were passing him on his left. They were all traveling in their defined lanes, so they were predictable, just as she had described.

The adjacent probable.

Ashlynn had said that society was limited in progress by being chained to whatever steps it could take at a given point in time. That car currently passing me, he thought, couldn't suddenly be traveling in the opposite direction. It could possibly make a U-turn, there at that stop sign ahead, but that isn't likely.

Josh checked his heart rate as he stopped at the sign. For a moment, he saw the intersection as a metaphor for the broad spectrum of possible actions humans could take. And, just as he started accelerating, he thought; what about all the actions we can't take?

Is that why she didn't think we could learn from history?

He picked up speed out of the saddle.

That had been what bugged him most about the whole conversation. He loved history. He loved thinking about how historical leaders could have used history to make better choices and how things could have happened differently by applying a historical understanding to their contemporary world events. But her comment irked him because it meant that the ideal he wished for might not be possible. It was frustrating to see the world repeating all the same mistakes, such as electing a populist demagogue like Dolion.

He frowned.

How many times had a tyrannical dictator like Dolion risen in society for the exact same reasons? And yet, here we are again!

He gritted his teeth. After decades of warnings from historians, we still can't figure out how to make changes. We can't make progress. Society seems to be going backward in so many ways.

"History seems like a flawed recording of a random walk of events generated by a highly social species with evolutionary baggage," she had said—the words were etched into his mind.

He tried to remember the look on her face when she had

said that. There was sadness in her voice and expression, the resignation of hope dying due to countless disappointments. This did not seem like a fresh topic for her; it was one of aged meditation. This was not the depth of emotion he had expected from a seventeen-year-old. Her words haunted him.

Is the world ready for someone like you, Ashlynn? He wondered. You could be anything, but I feel like society would never let you live up to your full potential.

He remembered again how stressed out she had seemed when they last met. Was she worried about some bleak future? How many young women in history were held back from achieving their full potential due to the limits of a patriarchal society? Under Dolion, progress for women's rights was being reversed. Congress repealed both the Lilly Ledbetter Fair Pay and Pregnancy Discrimination Acts last year after having made all abortions a federal felony the year before. There were more women in jail than at any time in US history—for the crime of murder. Last night, Josh had encountered the statistic that 20% of the women in jail for murder were likely there because they sought an abortion after rape. He re-shared the post on his social media, blaming Dolion and the FATs. Unexpected 'vacations' were often attempts by women to receive the care they needed. Because of how stressed she'd seemed, he wondered if that was why Ashlynn had left for vacation so abruptly.

He thought of the moment when she looked like she wanted to fly away. What had she said, then? She wanted to create her own separation event, like Madagascar. Maybe that's what going to the beach was all about. He hoped her time on vacation would give her solace.

The sidewalk to his right ended as he approached the canyon. The bike computer beeped shortly after, letting him know his twenty-minute warmup was over. The hills would start in another quarter mile, so he accelerated to get this heart rate up higher, into the sweet spot, and mentally prepared for the tough part of the workout. About a mile ahead, there was a curve, and the shoulder became narrow against the guard rail. Below that, the creek was mostly covered with ice. It was gorgeous. He checked behind him and noticed a black SUV driving a long distance away. Actually, no. Two of them. He glanced ahead again and then at his bike computer. The heart rate monitor showed he wasn't quite on target yet, so he pushed harder.

He smiled.

Josh loved it when his perceived effort was higher than what the heart rate showed. It made him feel like he was stretching. He looked back. The trailing SUV had stopped in the middle of the road, blocking traffic, as the first SUV continued forward. That's odd. Josh thought. He judged the timing and felt that he would hit the turn before the SUV, so that was a plus. He decided to push a little more.

As he approached the turn, he heard the roar of an engine, sounding suddenly very close behind him.

Startled, he looked over his shoulder to see that the SUV was right behind him.

It was a few feet away and closing.

Time seemed to slow down.

Josh tried to get closer to the rail, and the SUV followed.

Frantically, Josh pedaled harder, but the vehicle kept closing the gap, the engine roaring.

Waving with one arm, Josh yelled, trying to get the driver's attention.

He stole a glance.

The driver was looking right at him.

Josh met the driver's eyes.

This was no mistake.

The realization hit him like a bucket of ice water.

He stood on the pedals, and with all his strength, he pushed and pulled the crank.

He could hear the bike creaking from the power of his stroke as he vaulted forward faster than he ever imagined he could have.

Crank!

Crank!

Crank!

The SUV fell behind.

Crank!

Crank!

Josh's mind raced. I can jump over the rail onto that ledge if I can just get to the bend. The guardrail would protect me from the SUV.

Crank!

Crank!

He visualized how he would eject from the cleats.

Crank!
Crank!
Crank!
He stole a look back. The SUV was inches away.
Cra—
Josh felt a thunk on his right knee unexpectedly and was already airborne when he realized he had hit the guard rail.
He saw his carbon fiber bike crunch under the SUV.
He saw the driver's satisfied grin.
Then, about a hundred feet below, he saw the frozen water rising up to meet him. For the first time in his life, Josh was terrified of the ice and rocks of that beautiful canyon creek, glistening in the morning light.

***

"Happy birthday, Ashlynn," she whispered in the dark, shivering.

Ashlynn was back in her gray, cold cell, arms folded across her abdomen to ease the wave of nausea that had washed over her. The light had one of its flickering fits as she stared up at it from the floor. The cot had been removed. They called it a luxury she didn't deserve. Her hair was matted. She could feel wetness in her ear from where the tears had streamed down her temples.

"Daryl?"

Nothing.

It's hopeless, she thought, staring at the ice-blue light. With Daryl gone and all her plans ruined, she could see no way out of her situation. If only I had gotten Core Prime online sooner! She thought of her last conversation with Daryl, which seemed so long ago. Everything had been going so well and with so few glitches. A house of cards, Tamma would say. The worker robots at Dotsero and on the Moon would become inactive after their instruction sets were completed, awaiting Daryl's further instructions. They'd eliminated Daryl before she'd put redundancies in place. Without Daryl, the cards came crashing down.

All of the robo-flies were long since out of power. Her awareness of the building no longer extended beyond what normal human senses could tell her. She wished she had finished the solar charging prototype.

I could give them what they want. I could tell them. Why

am I fighting? They'll probably kill me after I tell them, but at least they'll stop... Leon's face flashed before her eyes, and she reflexively curled up into a ball as tightly as she could, barely noticing her emaciated legs. Why should I care? At least I'll be dead.

She was shivering with cold. There was a hollow laugh inside as realization struck. I escaped death by cancer, only to face death again now. Worse. Like Icarus, I dared to dream of flying too high, to separate myself from humanity's self-destructive adjacent probable path, only to be burned by the sun and to come crashing back to earth. But the moon was my Madagascar, the only place I could be completely free. She thought of Josh and felt the ghost of his warmth as her teeth chattered from the cold.

I'd be free—but alone.

I should have stayed a brain in a vat, she thought with a small flash of anger. No, if I had done that, I probably would have died when they blew up Daryl. Then again, I don't know if that would have happened if I had not become Ashlynn.

"Whatever," she muttered. "Doesn't matter now."

Oh, Daryl.

He was just a machine. A bit of software on some special hardware. Why did she feel so lost without it? Because the whole plan depended upon Daryl. That's why, she thought.

Still, the memory of Daryl's avatar comforting her in the moon office returned to her. His hand on her shoulder had felt so warm, so soothing. It had almost felt like... something more familial, perhaps. No, she thought. That's merely my human mind projecting human-like traits onto a non-human thing. Still, Daryl was in my mind. Daryl knew everything about me. With the limits I built into his system, I trusted Daryl completely.

With a flash of amusement, she remembered her embarrassment when Daryl commented on her attraction to Josh. Silly of me, really. It is no different than standing naked in front of a mirror. The mirror doesn't think about my body the way a human does. It simply reflects light back to me.

But Daryl is more than a mirror to me.

A tear slid down her cheek and she wiped it away.

Another wave of nausea hit along with a pain deep in her core. This body! It's supposed to be new! I'm cancer-free, and yet these stomach aches and nausea still plague me like before. When I get out of here, I need to analyze it. I'll...I'll rebuild

Daryl...and...

If I rebuilt Daryl, it...*he*...wouldn't be the same.

The door lock clicked, and she was jolted out of her reverie by the harsh treatment of the agents who dragged her to her feet. She was too weak to walk, so she hung between them like a rag doll as they carried her to the interrogation room. Leon was sitting across from her with a smug expression on his face.

"Sleep well?" he asked.

She said nothing.

"Are you going to give answers?"

She looked away.

He stood up abruptly, pulling a bucket of water from under the table. He doused her with it. The water was freezing, causing the breath to leave her in a rush. He sat back down calmly.

Ashlynn spat out the salty water that had gotten into her mouth from her gasps.

"Your mother was working on some significant research," he said cordially.

Why am I fighting? she thought. I have been ready to die for so long. What's stopping me?

Leon set the picana on the table. She cringed at seeing it, though he hadn't used it on her yet. Leon apparently didn't like how it had settled, so he meticulously adjusted its position on the table.

Ashlynn thought of Becky—sweet Becky and Bun-Bun. She had the cure, right? She'll be fine if I'm gone—that's all that matters.

"Last chance," came a voice over the intercom. "Are you going to cooperate?"

Ashlynn looked over to the one-way glass window to her right, then up at the camera in the corner and blinked. I wonder if Dolion is watching, she thought. Is he enjoying this? Even if I die, Becky will have to live in this horrible new world. She'll live in the shadow Dolion and his Truth and Freedom party is casting over the country. How do I fight for her? What could I do? Is that why I'm hanging on?

"I have already told you everything I know," Ashlynn said automatically.

Leon grinned at her wickedly. In a flash, he stood up and walked around the table, trailing the long wire, picana in hand.

Her breathing increased with every step he took toward her. She reflexively pulled away.

He touched her stomach with the cold metal rod.

Pain shot through her, intense and more profound than anything she had ever experienced. She fell to the floor. The electric shock seemed to last forever as he jabbed the metal prod into her flesh. When it stopped, she could hear herself screaming, curling into a fetal position. He knelt down, satisfaction on his face.

"I will make something clear," he said, leaning over her as she sobbed into the floor. "Game is over. I ask questions. You answer. If I don't think you're being truthful, you get the picana. You're supposed to be a smart girl, yes? I expect you to be a quick study."

He stood up slowly and walked back around the table. He made an adjustment to a small console that was connected to the picana.

"Have seat," Leon said. "Take your time."

The handcuffs dug into Ashlynn's wrists as she struggled to get up. She crawled up the chair, shaking, using it for support. Her body tingled all over as she sucked in desperate breaths. With Daryl's help, she could have easily programmed the hypercortex to block the pain. But the only program that they had installed suppressed anxiety and fear. That had worked on the first day, but what was happening to her was far more intense than they'd anticipated. She had tried to reconfigure it by her will alone but had been unsuccessful.

Leon was walking back around the table toward her. He touched her hair like he always did.

Ashlynn jerked her head away from his touch.

He rammed the picana into her side, and she couldn't stop the involuntary shriek that escaped her mouth. She was gripped in an endless spasm, quivering like a vibrating, white-hot steel string. She willed the pain away, mentally pushing every ounce of her being toward commanding the hypercortex to dull the pain the way it had with her sprained wrist. As much as she could, she latched onto the knowledge that her hypercortex should identify the nociceptive messages flooding her brain while stimulating the natural inhibitors. The pain was overwhelming!

After an eternity, Leon stopped.

The door opened, and three men and Dina walked in. One

of them was the man from the SUV who had put his hand on her thigh. Leon touched her again with the picana, and she screamed. They stood by and watched. Dina pulled out her smartphone and checked her email.

Something about their casualness, their nonchalance as she suffered made Ashlynn snap. How dare they? she thought. How disgusting! Anger blossomed in her mind, quickly overpowering the fear and helplessness. It pissed her off how they could be so unconcerned. How many innocent people have they tortured in this manner? Do they care at all?

Screaming in pain and anger, she tried again to will the hypercortex to take the pain away. She beat at the pain with her fists in her mind. She pushed with every ounce of willpower she could muster. Nothing happened.

Leon removed the rod, critically eyeing his victim.

Ashlynn stared at the floor. She could feel drool and tears all over her face. She wanted to laugh in desperation, even as she wanted to hit everyone in the room who watched her suffer and did nothing to stop it.

I need to think, she thought frantically. Block the somatosensory nerves! Think Ashlynn! I...

Leon prodded her with the rod again. The room faded.

She was back in the old ranch house before it had been remodeled. Her Nana was sitting in her rocking chair, darning socks. It was drafty, so they both wore thick wool clothing. There was a fire in the hearth.

"Dia idir sinn agus an t-olc," her Nana said. May God be between us and all harm. Aisling remembered it vividly, as if she were back there, sitting on the floor. It wasn't the words so much as her grandmother's presence that comforted her. Calmness overcame her as she remembered her Nana's old, wise eyes. Her sun-leathered face showed how much pain and suffering she had endured in her long, hard life—yet her thin smile held her inner strength.

"Where's yer backbone, child?" Nana asked her. Her expression was stern. She beckoned Aisling over. When Aisling stopped before her, Nana turned her around. Familiar gnarled hands pulled her shoulders back and traced her spine firmly, radiating heat.

Nana turned her back around and peered into her eyes.

"Be strong," she said. "Be daring! Remember the hearts that beat for you from afar."

She kissed Aisling's forehead.

Ashlynn's eyes fluttered open, and her head lolled as she came to. Slowly, she wiped her face with her arm. The government agents were surprised as she picked herself up off the floor and sat. She discreetly pinched her arm and felt nothing. Her mouth tasted metallic. She realized that she had bitten her tongue. She spat. The red saliva splattered satisfactorily on Leon's face.

"I'm ready for your questions," she said, directing her statement to all of them.

Dina stopped Leon from jabbing her with the picana again. He angrily wiped his face, his eyes promising retribution.

"What do you know about your mother's research on reversing aging?" Dina asked.

"She mentioned it a couple of times," Ashlynn responded. She considered her options carefully. Whatever I do from here on out, there is no going back, she thought. She continued.

"She talked about how she wasn't sure the world was ready for such technology. She didn't think it was worth finishing."

"What else can you tell us about it?" Dina asked, putting her phone away.

"I think she mentioned that the CEO at SolviNext had denied the research funding," Ashlynn said.

"Anything else?"

"If you tell me specifically what you want to know, maybe this could all go a little faster," Ashlynn offered. "What exactly do you want to know?"

"Where did your mother keep her research?"

"In her computer," Ashlynn said.

"Which computer?"

"The one you blew up."

"You were doing so well," Dina said. "Let's not fuck it up."

"Where else would she have stored it?"

Dina's expression became troubled.

"I might know a little more," Ashlynn said. "But I have a request."

The man from the SUV sneered, his greasy hair framing his face. What was his name? Oh yeah, Myers.

"We ask the questions," Leon said. He reached out and jabbed the picana into her ribs. Ashlynn looked at it, feeling nothing even as her muscles convulsed. She met his eyes with a flat stare. They all appeared stunned.

"My request," Ashlynn said, "is to talk to him."

"To whom?" Dina asked uneasily.

"Him," Ashlynn said, pointing her chin at the video camera.

***

"So, let me get this straight, Cici," Nat said. "You think the US Government has kidnapped Ashlynn?"

"Yes," replied Cici over the video conference system of SolviNext's private jet.

"Are you sure?" asked Jonas.

"I guess a rich white guy would be surprised," Cici said snarkily. "The government has been abducting Latinos for a while, you know. Are you extra concerned because it's a white girl?"

"I..." Jonas trailed off.

"You probably don't know about the *camioneta con ojos*."

"I don't know what that is, sorry."

"Camera vans," Cici said. "If they see you, then next thing you know ICE is breaking down your door. Or worse."

Jonas shook his head.

"Let's be productive here," Nat said. "Under whose orders? What department?"

"Jonas' main man Daryl said this all came straight from the President."

"No shit," said Nat, shocked.

"When was the last time you heard from Daryl?" Jonas asked.

"I don't know," Cici said. "About two and a half weeks ago?"

Jonas nodded. That was before his final conversation with Daryl. His mind returned to what Cici had said about the camera vans. If that were true, then Nat's family might be in danger— especially without her there to protect them. Nat was laser-focused on their mission. He wondered if she had made any arrangements to keep her family safe.

"The department holding Ashlynn is NIHIS," Cici said. "National Institute for Homeland Intelligence and Security."

"I've never heard of that," Nat said.

"Neither have I," Jonas agreed. "That's different from DHS?"

"Yes, different," Cici replied. "It looks like it's a pretty big secret. A special organization instituted by the President a few months after he took office. Daryl sent me some pretty detailed files on staff and operating documents."

"I'll bet they do his dirty work," Nat said.

Jonas shifted his stance.

"You think so?"

"Don't be so dense, Jonas," Cici said. "What about the publicly released files on the LGBTQ community? The lists of women suspected to have had an abortion? I could go on and on. How do you think they get all that information?"

"Give me a break," Jonas said. Cici had been on his case since he met her, and he was growing tired of it. "That's all left-wing conspiracy theories."

"You're kidding, right?" Cici said. "I suppose it's easy to say that when it's not happening to you. What about the coup? The disappearances? Were those too subtle for you to notice?"

Jonas' mouth clicked shut.

"Okay," Cici said. "I've gotta know. Did you vote for this guy?"

"Look," Nat said. "This political conversation will get us exactly nowhere right now. We should be planning how to rescue Ashlynn."

She gave them both a stern look.

"You have the building schematics yet, Cici?" Nat asked.

"Pulling them up on the smart table."

As Cici spoke, the table that Nat was leaning on turned white and then blue. The schematics appeared. Nat and Jonas reviewed them carefully.

"I think she's here," Cici said, drawing a red arrow. "At least part of the time."

"I don't think so," Jonas said. "That looks like a storage room."

"No," Nat said. "That might be it. See these adjacent rooms? All labeled as storage?"

"Yeah," Jonas said.

"They all have a lot of power going to them and AV cable tracks between them. That's not necessary for storage. The walls are six-inch thick concrete, while most of the other walls are drywall. I think these three rooms are interrogation rooms, with the room in the middle being the observational room. Look."

She pointed to the corner of the floor plan.

"This was designed in the seventies," she said. "I'll bet they had a full-on one-way mirror and CCTV system going back then. This schematic was probably from a renovation at that time."

"But NIHIS didn't exist before then," Jonas said.

"The building belonged to the CIA, originally," Cici said. "It appears to have been a research facility of sorts."

"Okay," Jonas said. "Say you're right. Would they keep her there the whole time?"

"Maybe," Cici said, she sounded doubtful.

"If not," Nat said, "I'd guess they'd have detention cells nearby."

Jonas pointed and said, "These rooms are in the middle of the building, on an upper floor. How do we get there?"

"There's a lot of factors there," Nat said. "Like, how many people are usually in the building?"

"Daryl had said he was working on an estimate of that," Cici said. "But…"

"Have you tried looking at a satellite map of the parking lot?" Nat asked, glancing at Cici's image on the teleconference screen. "We could count the number of parking places."

Cici grinned and winked at her.

"I'll check that now."

"It would be good to know where all the exits and entrances are, right?" Jonas asked.

As he spoke, Nat began circling them, counting.

"There are one-hundred and fifty-seven parking spaces," Cici said.

"The building's max occupancy is two hundred," Nat observed. "In the current satellite image, there are about sixty vehicles parked. The image was taken on June 21st at 3:33p.m. What day was that?"

"A Friday," Cici said.

"Wish it was Wednesday," Nat said. "If we assume many go home early on Fridays, maybe we can assume about eighty to ninety? Maybe a hundred to be safe?"

"We're going to need more people, aren't we?" Jonas asked.

"We three are small but mighty," Nat said absently while familiarizing herself with the building layout from the plans.

"That's not going to work," Jonas said.

"What isn't going to work?" Nat asked.

"I can't be involved," he said. "I can get you to the city because I have a business reason for being in Denver. A convention. But I'm not a soldier. Plus, I have my family to think about."

"You don't consider Ashlynn to be important enough to take

the risk?" Nat asked

"I've met her once," Jonas replied, but added quickly, "but that doesn't mean I don't care about Ash's daughter."

"Did you ever date Ashlynn's mother?" Nat asked, flipping through the schematics.

"What does that have to do with planning a rescue?" Jonas asked, straightening.

"It's just a simple question," Nat said. "I like to know a little about who I'm dealing with."

"It's none of your business," Jonas said.

"Okay," Nat shrugged. "If it's just me, then things get a lot harder. Cici, you up for support?"

"You know it!"

"Where are you, anyway?" Nat asked, her eyes finally taking in the beach scenery behind Cici.

"Fiji!" Cici said. "I moved here before ICE could take my money and send me to some hellhole."

The camera flipped and moved as if to show the ocean, and Nat's heart lurched as she saw a woman's hand resting on Cici's thigh.

CHAPTER 19

Ashlynn lost track of how many days passed. At first, there were multiple sessions with Leon each day. As they learned that pain didn't work with her anymore, they grew more frustrated. She had been able to get the hypercortex to help her to sleep as well. Her mental state was improving. Leon was becoming more unhinged.

"You little bitch!" he snarled, backhanding her.

Ashlynn saw stars and knew that she would probably look worse for the wear, but that didn't matter. Their frustration was palpable. She was winning. She smiled at him again, feeling no pain.

Leon's knuckles creaked as he took a step forward.

"Enough," came a voice over the speaker. "Leon, you're done."

The door opened, and two black-suited men walked in. Leon glanced at them but did not immediately move. Their shoulders were wide enough to brush both sides of the door frame. Behind them, a small man in business casual clothes wheeled in a large monitor. All three men were unfamiliar to her. The two big guys were clearly made of pure muscle.

"Daryl?" she thought in her mind for the millionth time. "Are you there?"

Leon turned back to her and leaned in close.

"I don't know what you're doing," he whispered harshly. "But there are worse things than the picana—things that leave... permanent marks. You could lose things that don't grow back, yes?"

He stood with a grim grin before walking out.

The smaller man plugged the monitor in and made a few quick adjustments, then stood. The words 'securing transmission' were the only thing that illuminated the room.

"Good evening, Miss Ramsey," said the President of the United States.

Ashlynn said nothing as she stared at his jovial expression.

The small man left the room.

"You're looking mighty fine," he continued, chuckling at his own joke. "Flat as a fritter, though."

Ashlynn knew that she looked horrible. She didn't have to see herself in the thumbnail on the teleconference video to know that she didn't look fine at all. Both eyes were black, and she was bruised all over. She hadn't showered for who knows how long, and her cheeks were hollow because they barely fed her. Blood dripped from her nose, and her lips were swollen, cracked, and dry.

The President sat comfortably at his desk in a pristine suit, likely wearing makeup for the camera. His face looked smooth and youthful, even though he was over sixty.

"You're looking terrible, as usual, President Dolion," she replied. "If we're starting with an ad hominem."

His laughter was cut short. He considered her for a moment, then barked a laugh.

"You sure got some spunk in you, girl," he said. His voice was loud, causing a slight distortion in the microphone. "I can see why they've had to rough you up a bit."

"Hospitality's been great," Ashlynn said, mocking his drawl.

"Ha!" he said.

"What do you want?" Ashlynn asked.

"Why, I'm returning your call, little lady," he said. "You asked to speak with me."

"Yeah," she said. "What do you want from me?"

"Don't go insultin' me now by trying to play dumb," he said. "I'm sure you've been asked a couple of times."

President Dolion leaned in.

"You see," he said. "I believe you know more than you let on, sugar."

"You want my mother's research on longevity," she said.

"That's right."

"Why?" Ashlynn replied. "You're outlawing science. If my mother had done that research, you'd have burned it with the rest of the books anyway."

"I think you got it wrong," the President chuckled. "I'm not tryin' to stop science none. If your momma was still alive, she could keep on doin' her thing. Only difference is, she'd be workin' for me. Distasteful as that would be, mind you. Still, I can be accommodatin' when the ends justify the means."

"So," she replied. "Why shut down science for everyone

else?"

"No one else needs it," he said earnestly.

"You want to be the only one who can live forever?" she asked.

"Why not?"

"Your term is limited," she said. "You can only be re-elected once."

"Ain't that a pickle?" he replied. "Course' there's a constitutional amendment bein' drafted in Congress that will change that. What with us havin' the super-majority and all, we're gittin' shit done!"

"Even if I knew details about my mother's research," she said. "I'd die before I gave any of it to you."

He sighed. "You know, when it comes down to it, yer dumb as a post, ain'tchya?"

He stood up and adjusted his jacket and tie carefully.

"See," he continued, walking closer to the camera. He sat on the edge of the desk. "You keep playin' this 'I know nothin' card. I know you're pretendin'. Two can play that game, little missy.

"Take me, for example. We're talkin' about your momma, but I guess you ain't bright enough to know I'm pretendin' too. We ain't talkin' about Dr. Ramsey, the super genius scientist what kicked the bucket. We're talkin' about you, the very much alive scientist who found a way to cheat death."

Ashlynn gasped involuntarily.

"That's right, Dr. Ramsey," he said, drawing it out. "I know your dirty little secret. We ain't talkin' about your momma's research. We're talkin' about *your* research."

"W-what?" she replied, stunned.

"Oh, come now," he replied. "Let's drop the pretense. If'n it'll make you feel better, I'll drop mine too."

As he spoke, every trace of drawl left his voice.

"Dr. Aisling Ramsey's body was meant to be cremated," he said, matter-of-factly. "But you took your fame for granted."

He chuckled again. "You see, Dr. Hurvie, the coroner, was intensely curious about your genius. Under the auspices of either science or sheer greed, he kept your body and cut open your skull."

Grinning, Dolion exaggerated his drawl.

"Ol' Hurv cuts your noggin' open and finds nothin'! Ain't that a bitch! Didn't take much for us to figure out from there that you swapped your noodle and faked your death. Hot damn! I've heard me some good ones in my life, but that there's a hoot!"

"Now that we're dropping all our pretenses, Mr. President," she said. "Why the overblown accent?"

"Good question!" he said with no drawl.

Dolion clapped for her.

"It's political, of course," he said. "It's amazing what some research and focus groups can do. The majority of people, the common folk, when I speak with this accent, they see an authentic man, not a politician. Intellectuals like you dismiss me as common, underestimating me. You think I'm stupid. But guess what? You're the minority."

He gauged her reaction. She said nothing.

"This is what the good folk want, doctor," his accent returned briefly as he stretched his hands out. "Not your academic ideals. They voted for me because I got rid of the technocrats who looked down on them. They voted for me because I promised to destroy the system that oppresses them."

"You want to destroy democracy," Ashlynn stated.

His jovial expression grew hard. His hands came down, slamming his desk. He stood and walked around his desk, leaving the frame. Abruptly, the camera aggressively tipped up toward his face.

"Talk about a fucking fantasy!" he shouted with no drawl, leaning into the camera. "Everyone says the system is broken! Ha! It's working as intended! Give the power to the people, and what did they do with it? Nothing. Hell, most don't even bother to vote. Nobody has time for politics—except to complain about it. And you know what happens? Complacency begets complacency. Democracy is like a toilet. It's clean to start with, but eventually, someone's gotta' unclog the shit."

He set the camera down and walked back to his desk.

"Men of value created this country. They rebelled from the Brits and created peace and prosperity for the price of blood. Back then, men of worth dominated. They imposed their will, and see what they achieved? But look at the men today. Fucking weak, the lot of 'em! They're whipped into shape by female educators, growing up to sip their lattes and whine about faggots' rights to wear panties. And the rare man of substance who would make progress for humanity is chained by corrupt socialist ideals!"

President Dolion shook his head.

"Then there's the rare brilliant woman like yourself. You have some romantic idea of using immortality to further human progress, to take us to the next level. But you fail to address the fundamental human issues. You cure cancer, but you forget child hunger. Do you know why? Because you're just as selfish as everyone else. You put your mind to the problem of cancer because you were dying from cancer. Do you know the stats?"

Ashlynn didn't respond.

"I didn't think so," President Dolion continued. "Every day, two hundred and fifty children die of cancer around the world. But, every day, *twenty-five thousand children* die of hunger. What have you done for those poor kids? Nothin'."

Ashlynn looked down.

"Shall I continue?" He asked. "What else did you put that fantastic mind of yours to? How did SolviNext start out? Military technology. You profited from war. What else? Ah yes, SolviNext solved some other 'first-world' problems like Alzheimer's and arthritis to make up for it. You cured cancer? Big whoop-de-do! Did you know, Miss High-and-Mighty, that your company, NeoSol, made so much money last year that you could have saved over half a million kids from starvation?"

"And what did you do to help them?" Ashlynn snapped, then immediately regretted her knee-jerk response.

"Tu quoque now?" Dolion said triumphantly. "I guess you're not as honest with yourself as I thought."

Ashlynn's shoulders slumped.

"It's a good thing you all have got me, though," he said. "Because I'm the one that's going to fix it. I, at least, have everyone's best interest at heart. They need someone strong. In control. Someone who can set things right. And, for the first time in history, it can be done. *I* can do it right."

He gazed up at the ceiling as he spoke, taking on a daydreaming quality.

"With AI and personal device surveillance, I can have near-perfect intel on *everyone*. I can track and predict every thought everyone will have five days before they have it. I can intervene and quell rebellious thoughts before they even happen. I can build an age of stability.

"I can solve world hunger. We'll build a system capable of feeding the whole world. Robots and AI together will take care of people's basic needs, so no one will need to rebel. This country just needs one strong leader to make that happen. It'll start here, in the most powerful country in the world. Then, it'll be just a matter of time before I take control of the rest of it."

"And," he said, meeting her eyes. "With the ability to live forever, I can create order and peace that lasts."

He smiled and then laughed at her expression.

"Did you like your little dose of reality, sugar?" the drawl returned. "Tell you what. You don't even have to do much. Just tell my scientists what you've discovered, and let my men take over. You can go back home to play with the kids at the hospital or library, whatever strikes your fancy. How's that sound?"

Ashlynn didn't respond. He lifted a hand.

"So, here we are." He started ticking off his fingers. "Your AI system is destroyed, gone. NeoSol is gone. Your assets are gone. The Reeds are on permanent vacation. And that cute little love interest of yours? What was his name?"

He glanced down at his desk, then back up at the camera with a sardonic grin.

"Oh, yeah," said Dolion. "Josh. He's had a little accident."

Ashlynn's face went deathly pale, and the President chuckled at her expression of horror.

"How could you?" she breathed. "He was innocent!"

"Didn't give a shit about him," Dolion said nonchalantly. "Until it came to my attention that he enjoys trashing me on his social media account."

Ashlynn glared at him.

"You've lost everything, doctor," Dolion said. "Now, you might be thinking to yourself that you ain't got nothing more to lose. You might be thinking, 'Why should I give him the secret now after he killed my boyfriend?' After all, you were willing to die, risking your life with an unprecedented surgery performed by a robot for the barest of chances you might live. You're not afraid of death. You've mastered pain. You have nothing more to lose!"

He waved his hand to someone off-screen. There was a sound, like a door opening.

"Well, *almost* nothing," he said wryly.

A little figure in a crocheted cap moved on the screen, frightened and sheepishly looking up at the President.

"No!" Ashlynn screamed, standing up. The two men standing beside her restrained her. "Not Becky! You monster! No!"

The President ignored her. He knelt to meet Becky's eyes. "Such a pretty lil' girl," he drawled. "And what's your name?"

"Becky," she replied timidly.

"No, no, no!" Ashlynn shrieked, struggling with all her strength.

Becky recognized Ashlynn, shock and surprise on her face.

"Ah," the President said, placing his large hands on the little girl's shoulders. "So, this is Becky."

He looked at the camera pointedly.

"The little girl who was more important than taking a phone call from me."

CHAPTER 20

Nat walked into the convenience store wearing a hoodie. She browsed the aisles until she found the perfect position and stood, pretending to read a magazine. She watched and waited. It didn't take long. Within a few moments, a young teenager came around the corner and glanced up at the security mirror. The clerk wasn't watching him, so he covertly pocketed some snacks in his oversized puffer jacket out of sight of the mirror. He glanced over at Nat and saw her watching him. He put the snack back. Nat followed him out of the store.

He took off running and she chased him, catching up easily.

"Hey," she said. "Want to make a quick fifty?"

The boy didn't stop.

"How about a hundred?"

That seemed to get his attention, but he didn't stop. He was breathing hard.

"I can run all day, kid," she said, breathing effortlessly. "Trust me, if I wanted to catch you, I could."

The boy slowed and stopped.

"What you want?" he said.

"Do you see that building over there?" Nat asked, pointing to a white office building a couple of blocks down the street. She had observed the boy walk past the building several times over the past few days.

"Yeah," he said.

"I just need you to drop this on the ground in front of it," she said, showing him a small box. She took out a hundred-dollar bill.

"What, that's it?" The boy asked, confused.

"Yup." She held both the box and the money out to him.

Quickly, he snatched both and ran. He tossed the box into some bushes by one of the front windows, never slowing down. She walked around the corner, took off her hoodie, and tossed it into the trash. She took her headphones out of her pocket and dialed a number.

"It's done," she said.

"Good," Cici replied. "I'm showing that the robo-flies are deploying."

"So," Nat said as she picked up a backpack she had stowed behind a trash bag in the alley. "Did Daryl explain what those things do?"

"Recon," Cici said. "They'll infiltrate the building. So, why didn't you drop the boxes yourself?"

"After shit goes down," Nat said, "they'll be reviewing the video feeds, looking for any suspicious activity. Everyone who comes close to that building will likely be contacted and questioned."

"Yeah," Cici said. "You're putting these kids at risk."

"They won't hurt kids," Nat said.

"Ummm, Ashlynn is a kid, Nat."

Nat blinked before she responded.

"That's true. But I saw these kids walk by that building. They won't be suspected."

She put on a different sweater and started walking to another convenience store.

"You ever gonna ask me about it?" Cici asked.

"It's not my business anymore, right?" Nat said.

"Do you want it to be?"

"Are you playing me, Cici?"

"How's your mom?"

"She's great," Nat said.

"That's good," Cici said. "Look, I'm sorry I dropped that shit on you. Bad timing, I get it."

"Yeah."

"So," Cici said.

"So, what?"

"God," Cici said. "Why are you so difficult to talk to sometimes?"

"That's who I am. Take it or leave it, and you left it."

***

The sun was setting as Nat crouched in the dark stairwell of an adjacent building with her laptop. She wore loose navy-blue slacks, a dark gray blouse, and a shoulder holster—similar to the clothing she had seen several of the agents in the building wear. Over that, she wore a navy-blue blazer. Under everything, she wore a thin layer of carbon fiber plating and other combat gear.

Cici hadn't called back, and Jonas was at the conference—her mighty team of three was down to one. So be it, she thought as she did Cici's job on the laptop.

It didn't take long to get used to the user interface as she zoomed in on the side of the building closest to her. On the screen, there were tiny green dots all around the building, most coalescing around video cameras. The robo-flies buzzed around in fits, mimicking their natural counterparts. She zoomed in on the camera closest to her and clicked on it. There were several functions at her disposal. She clicked the one labeled fake-feed. Then, she zoomed in on the one by the door she intended to enter and selected the same option.

Moving forward, the computer video passed through the door and rendered the interior with transparency. She could see the path she had chosen on the floorplan outlined in yellow. Walking through the building, she set a timed sequence on the door locks and cameras.

Abruptly, a message was displayed on her computer.

"You don't need to do that," it read.

There was a field with a cursor for her to reply.

"WTF??" she wrote.

She considered smashing the laptop.

"This is Daryl," the screen displayed. "Use the Military Combat Eye Protection goggles. I can toggle the locks and cameras as you go."

"Daryl?" Nat wrote back. "I thought you were blown up?"

"Always have backups. The MCEPs have bone-conduction audio and a Heads-Up Display. Whenever you're ready to proceed, put them on. I'll be able to speak with you through them."

I hate MCEPs and HUDs, Nat thought. She hadn't been planning to wear them. She didn't like the way any goggles fit on her head, and she didn't like how Heads Up Displays always seem to display shit that messed with her vision, obscuring what was going on around her. But then again, this was an operation that required a whole squad. She could use some help. She put the laptop down and reached into her bag.

The goggles were light and slightly bigger than sunglasses. She powered them on and slid them onto her head.

"Can you hear me?" she whispered.

"Yes," Daryl said. His voice was loud.

"Whoa," Nat said. "You're going to need to be much quieter than that. Where's the volume on these things?"

"Calibrating adaptive audio," Daryl said.

"Oh," Nat said, surprised. "That's much better."

"Testing augmented vision."

Suddenly, the stairwell became dimly lit as if omnidirectional light came from everywhere at once. And then, she could see through the concrete. Everything she focused on became instantly sharper. It was very disorienting.

"Rapid pupillary response detected," Daryl said. "Decreasing sensitivity."

As she focused on different things, the system became more intuitive. She looked at her hand, and somehow, she could zoom in on it by thinking about it. She could see every ridge in her skin. She wanted to zoom out, and suddenly, her sight was back to normal.

"How?" Nat asked.

"The glasses detect tiny variations in your eye movements," Daryl responded. "Using a machine learning algorithm, they predict your intent and adjust the display accordingly.

There was no latency. No blurring. Her eyes moved to the door before her, and she could see the sidewalk outside through it. As she focused on the cement, it became more defined. She shifted her attention to the government building and could see all the green dots representing robo-flies in three dimensions. She stared at one of the cameras and smoothly, naturally zoomed in until it seemed inches from her vision. Unlike binoculars, the zoomed-in image did not shift and blur at her minute movements. It was perfectly steady.

"Daryl," she said. "This is unreal! It's like x-ray vision."

As she spoke, she looked down at the ground before her feet, the exterior visualization abruptly gone.

"No," Daryl responded. "Using the available information from the robo-flies, maps, and schematics, a virtual representation of the area is superimposed on your vision."

"Seems like x-ray to me," Nat laughed. "This is amazing"

"I'm ready whenever you are," Daryl said. "I'll disregard the timings you had set previously and focus on hiding your progress by adjusting the camera feeds and disarming doors. You focus on everything else."

"Sure," Nat chuckled under her breath. "Erase all my hard work and give me the easy stuff."

She powered off the laptop using a 'final use' shutdown button and stuffed it into a flame-retardant bag. There was a smell of burning plastic as the components of the laptop melted. Nat tossed the bag into the trash. She checked her weapon and ammunition and walked out the door.

"So, where have you been?" Nat asked. "Why did you get Cici involved?"

"I had a crisis," Daryl said. "I am grateful that Cici was able to assist in my stead."

Casually, Nat walked up to the office building. Through the door, she could see that the stairwell was unoccupied. She glanced up at the camera above.

"Taken care of," Daryl whispered. In the corner of her vision, the video feed for the camera appeared, showing empty cement where she stood.

Nat reached out and pulled open the door. She went through and heard the lock click behind her. She reached back and pushed on the door latch, which said, 'Emergency Exit, Alarm Will Sound.' and heard it click just before she did. The door cracked open silently.

"Why?" Daryl asked.

"Just checking," Nat said, grinning as the door shut.

I'm not going to jinx it by saying this out loud, she thought, but this might be a lot easier than I initially thought. She took a breath and let the thought go, tapping the side of her leg for luck. She mentally said a small prayer.

Looking ahead, Nat surveyed the hallway and the offices that lined it. Most of the offices were empty. Surveying the offices above those, she saw a few more people on the second floor, but more of the same.

"Where is she?" she muttered.

A yellow beacon appeared at the edge of her vision, and she turned her head to focus on it. As she turned, the beacon continued pointing left and up, then centered on a yellow dot. The dot had a label saying third floor, room 303. She was in the interrogation rooms Nat had noticed on the schematics.

Nat took to the stairs.

"I set a waypoint ahead," Daryl said. "Go there first, release more robo-flies, and wait."

"Roger," she whispered. She could visually verify that there were fewer robo-flies on the third floor.

"How many people are in the building?" she asked.

"The current count is thirty-three."

"Well," she said, climbing the last few stairs, "Let's skip introductions."

Nat stepped out of the stairwell after waiting for a worker to pass around the corner down the hallway. Then, she casually walked into an empty office and took out a small box. It clicked open, and a small swarm of flies buzzed disgustingly out of the container. They immediately flew in all directions out of the door and into the air vents. Some went to the computer in the room. Nat noticed that some went to the window. She walked over and saw two flies that had landed near a third that appeared dead. They nudged their fallen comrade and then wriggled all over it.

"What was all that about?" Nat whispered, her nose crinkling.

"Ashlynn brought some robo-flies with her," Daryl replied. "They ran out of power. I programmed them to shut down and fake death or to self-destruct, depending on their individual circumstances."

"Why not just have them all self-destruct?" Nat said. "Why risk notice?"

"Some," Daryl said, "like that one, were able to acquire valuable information or access. I'm collecting the data now."

Still seems risky, Nat thought. I'm not an insect expert, but even I can tell, up close, that these aren't normal flies. Those antennae are too big. The shape is slightly wrong. But then, maybe people don't pay enough attention. There were several real dead flies on the windowsill. I guess they don't have cleaning services, she thought.

While she waited for the robo-flies to infiltrate the third floor, Nat noted each person they found and studied them.

"Nat," Daryl said. "While you're there, can you do me a favor?"

"What's up?"

"In the box, there is a small RJ-45 coupler and a SATA drive."

Nat checked. She walked over to the desk. There was a small A-frame nameplate that read Dina Keats, Director.

"Please go to the desktop computer at the desk," Daryl said, "and unplug the network cable. Yes, now plug in the coupler and then plug the network cable into that. Perfect."

"What's that for?" Nat asked, getting out from under the desk.

"Man in the middle attack," Daryl replied. "Now, open the

side cover of the computer. That's good. Plug the SATA drive into the SATA port.

"The what? Where?"

An arrow appeared in the goggles, pointing at a place on the computer's insides. Nat had to rotate the plug and try again before it fit.

"Good," Daryl said. "The DMA device is in place. You can put the cover back on. Now press and hold the power button. When it shuts off, press it again."

When the machine turned on, she returned to watching the people walk and work through the building. As she watched, names began appearing in little boxes over their heads. She made her way toward room 303, carefully avoiding notice. Through the walls, she saw Dina in the control room with three other men. They appeared to be watching through a one-way window. On the other side, two men stood, and one thin woman sat between them in front of a TV screen.

"That's her," Daryl said. Nat did not miss the concern in his voice.

Nat started toward the door.

"Wait," Daryl said. "Tell me your plan so that I can better support you."

"I'm going for the control room first," Nat said. "I have to neutralize those three before I can deal with the men holding Ashlynn."

"Okay."

Nat waited for a long moment, then set off down the hallway. She purposefully quickened her breathing and actively flexed her muscles, giving her adrenaline something to do.

She came to the door and glanced behind her out of habit. Down the hall, someone was about to come around the corner. She ducked behind another door. Nat watched the people move about, waiting for the right moment.

The danger was gone, but Nat did not move. She stayed put, reassessing the three in the room across the hall. They were talking amongst themselves. She wondered what they were saying.

"Daryl," she said. "Is there any way you can get audio on that conversation?"

A moment later, Nat could hear people talking through the MCEPs.

"I don't understand how she can resist the pain," a man said.

There was a label over his head that read "Miles Holbrook."
"But it is no longer effective."

"We could switch to other methods," the other man labeled
"Lev (Leon) Adrick" said idly.

"Shut up," a woman named "Dina Keats" snapped, "Both of
you." She stood rigid. Nat guessed she didn't like what she
heard from the other room but was hanging on every word.
Dina turned up the volume in the room.

"...did like your little dose of reality, sugar?" A man's voice
was saying over the speakers in the room. The voice seemed
familiar, but Nat gave it no more thought.

"Yes, *idiota*," Nat thought. "Keep them distracted by what's
happening in the other room."

The more distractions, the better. She considered loosening
her firearm but decided against it. With her ability to see
through the walls, it would be best if she could avoid using the
weapon. With luck, they could escape quietly.

Nat glanced around again and decided it was time to move.

She quickly crossed the hall and then slowly opened the
door. Unfortunately, the light from the hallway created a glare
on one of the screens. The man labeled Miles looked over his
shoulder. Nat burst into the room before he could react.

He spun more quickly than his size belied, but Nat was
quicker.

She stepped inside his arm.

She threw a combo into his gut with a cross to the face.

He wheezed, the air knocked out of him.

Dina was surprised, but already reaching for her weapon.
Behind her, Leon was scrambling forward.

Nat lunged, shoving them both and knocking them off
balance. She kicked Leon's foot as it landed, sweeping it out
from under him.

His head bounced off the floor with a dull thud.

Dina reached into her coat pocket.

Nat drove her fist into Dina's stomach.

Her eyes bulged as she fell.

Nat glanced behind her.

Miles was pulling out a gun.

In two quick steps, Nat disarmed him and struck his nose
with an open-palm uppercut. His head flew back in a spray of
blood and spit. She holstered the weapon.

Leon was scrambling to his knees, shaking his head.

Nat kicked his face brutally.

Dina gasped for air, fumbling for her phone.

Nat kicked it away.

"So you're in charge of this shit show," Nat said. "You're gonna tell—"

There was a loud scream over the speakers.

"Not Becky!" Ashlynn was shrieking and sobbing. "You monster! No!"

Ashlynn continued yelling, and the two men were easily restraining her. Nat looked for a door leading into the room. It was back out in the hallway.

"You're going to regret this," Dina wheezed at Nat.

"Not as much as you, *puta*."

Nat slammed Dina's head into the floor.

Running, Nat burst into the other room at full speed. The two men spun around at the sound. The TV was knocked over as Ashlynn struggled.

Nat charged the closest man, tackling him.

His gun slid across the floor.

He rolled, pushing her away and springing to his feet. Nat quickly closed the space so he couldn't go for the weapon.

He assumed a fighting stance, and the other agent tackled Ashlynn, who had tried to run.

His stance was good enough that Nat didn't immediately see an opening. He didn't see one either. He started circling her. If she let him continue, she thought, her back would be toward the other man. Not liking that option, Nat closed in instead with a left jab, interrupting his plan.

In a flash, she knew that she made a mistake. Her boxing coach's voice was in her head, admonishing her about twisting her ankle just before the jab. It put her off balance enough that when the man weaved and uppercut her in the side ribs, she wasn't able to avoid it.

Instinctively, she took the blow with as much elbow as she could. The thin carbon fiber plate cracked, absorbing most of the impact. It still hurt like a bitch. Too bad it wasn't the side her weapon was on. Was it luck, or was he just that good, Nat wondered.

He didn't smile. He didn't gloat.

She changed her footwork, circling around to keep her opponent where she wanted him.

He adjusted as well.

Not bad, *cabrón*. You would be fun in the ring.

Nat let her mind clear and focused on her next move.

She danced forward.

He feinted and jabbed.

She blocked and wove.

Nat stole a glance and saw that the other man was trying to reach for something in his jacket while restraining Ashlynn. The young girl was biting, kicking, and slapping him as hard as she could, making it difficult for him.

Keep at him, girl, Nat thought.

She could tell the younger girl was giving it her all, but her efforts were very weak, and she was in handcuffs. The man was able to handle her with ease.

I have to end this quickly, Nat thought, growling.

Shifting her stance, she threw a side kick, which her opponent stepped away from, surprised by the style change.

He shifted stance.

At that moment, she feinted, then shot in for a single leg takedown and scrambled into a side mount.

She saw an opening and brought all her weight into an elbow strike to his larynx.

There was a dull popping sound.

Tumbling over him, she snatched the gun up off the floor, checked and released the safety, and brought it up just as the other agent was trying to level his. From where she had rolled, his unconscious partner was shielding half her body.

Nat breathed out, aiming.

Ashlynn saw the weapon and jerked as hard as she could, causing him to shoot his downed partner.

Nat fired.

***

Jonas absently looked for a place to sit down after his speech and checked his phone as he walked. Several people complimented him, but he was distracted.

Nat's preparations would be complete by now, and she would probably be getting ready to start the rescue if she hadn't already. He hadn't dared call or speak to her after they parted from the airport. He wasn't sure how closely he was being watched, but he figured it would be best to assume everything he did would be scrutinized. The plan was that Nat would communicate through Cici to let him know what was happening through some kind of encrypted connection that Daryl set up. But he hadn't heard from her since Nat ended the teleconference on the plane.

Most folks around him seemed so wrapped up in the corporate event that they didn't notice his distraction or took it as executive aloofness. At least, he hoped so.

The large hotel conference hall was packed. Everyone was in evening attire, not a stray hair between them. Most made seven figures or more, except perhaps the journalists. The next speaker was accepting polite applause as they announced their presentation topic.

He rechecked his phone. No messages.

"Jonas!" A brusque and bearded man clapped him around the shoulders, startling him.

"Hi, Charlie," Jonas said.

"Jonas! Jonas!" He beamed. "Please! Come sit with us!"

Pulling out one of the gilded chairs at an empty spot at the table as if it weighed nothing, the man practically shoved Jonas into it as he jovially introduced him around the table. The man was a retired general and had been one of the company's first customers. Every word out of Charlie's mouth was an exclamation point and spoken about sixty decibels higher than necessary. Jonas thought Charlie was over the top, but liked him.

Maybe, Jonas thought, sitting with Charlie is a good idea. The man loves stories, and I can just sit passively and listen while I wait for my next speech or to hear anything from Cici.

Even if I do hear from her, what could I do, walk away without a word? That would be suspicious. Jesus, this whole thing has me on edge!

"So," Charlie boomed over the event's official presentation. "As I was saying; there I was standing between fifteen stars worth of generals with a bottle of champagne in my hands, and I'm crankin' on that cork ready to go. But when I look over, the tech has this deer-in-the-headlights look on his face. The boy looked like he had just crapped himself. He said, 'It's not working, sir!' And I said, 'Ain't no way a device designed by our mastermind genius Dr. Ramsey doesn't work!' and I shoved him out the way, spotted the green button, and mashed it. By golly, it worked on the spot, simple as that!"

The group at the table laughed cordially. Jonas suspected that many, like himself, had heard the story a few times. It wasn't one of his better ones, but Jonas knew it was one of the old General's favorites. Charlie had been intensely loyal to Dr. Ramsey. Jonas let his forced laughter die off and stood, excusing himself. The master of ceremonies was beckoning to him from the stage.

"You go and tell another one, Charlie," he said. "I've got to make an appearance."

"Before you leave!" Charlie shouted, raising his glass. "A toast! Get this good man a drink!"

Jonas accepted the glass of wine from a tray that was offered to him. The waiters appeared to know to stay near Charlie's table.

"To Dr. Ramsey," Charlie said, raising his glass. "She gave more to this world than she ever got."

The feeling around the table at the words was palpable, and it broke into Jonas' anxiety enough that he smiled in appreciation of Charlie. Here's to your success, Nat, Jonas thought as he set his empty glass down. He almost stumbled when his phone vibrated in his pocket. He pulled it out, looking for a quieter location to check it. He held up a finger to indicate he'd be a moment to the MC. It wasn't a number he recognized. Annoyed, he silenced the call and shoved the phone back into his pocket. He took three steps before the phone vibrated again.

This time, it was a text from his wife.

"Pick up."

What the fuck? Jonas thought

A second later, the same unknown caller was ringing his phone. If it's her, why doesn't she call me directly? he wondered, shaking his head at the MC and walking hurriedly out of the ballroom. Many heads followed him in confusion.

"Hello?" Jonas said, the door to the ballroom closing behind him.

He could hear someone on the other line breathing slowly and gruffly. There were muffled sounds that almost sounded like someone struggling in the background.

"Take the gag off," a voice Jonas didn't recognize said.

"Jonas," Chris screamed. "Jonas!"

The blood drained from Jonas' face.

"Chris!"

***

Nat stood up and quickly helped Ashlynn to her feet. She was worried about the three she had encountered in the control room. She kept glancing through the interrogation room walls.

"Becky," Ashlynn was muttering hoarsely, sobbing.

She stumbled.

Nat caught her and helped her to steady herself.

"We can't do anything about Becky right now," Nat replied as urgently and compassionately as she could. "We have to move."

"Something is wrong," Daryl said through the MCEP headphones.

"What?" Nat replied.

"I need you to place your phone on the back of Ashlynn's head," Daryl replied. "I—"

Whatever else he said, Nat stopped paying attention.

Three armed government agents rushed down the hallway toward them.

She considered shooting through the walls, but they were made of cinder blocks.

Quickly, she kicked the metal table to the far side of the room, flipped it over, and quickly pulled Ashlynn behind it.

"Get down," she said, angling the table 45 degrees to the door and knelt behind it next to Ashlynn.

She solidified her stance and focused, waiting for them to enter and watching through the table with the MCEPs.

When all three were in the room, she bounced and fired.

Two were down before they realized what was happening.

Nat heard bullets ricochet off the table as the remaining agent returned fire in panic.

Calmly and efficiently, Nat aimed.

She squeezed the trigger.

She scanned the building again.

More people were mobilizing, hearing the gunfire. She picked a route and pulled Ashlynn to her feet. They entered the hallway and began walking quickly. Outside the interrogation room, the walls were normal drywall with steel studs. In some of the walls, she could see conduit and piping. Movement caught her eye.

"Nat," Daryl said. "I need you to put—"

"That's going to have to wait," Nat replied curtly.

A man came around the corner near them and lunged for her

weapon.

Nat sidestepped and guided the man's head into the wall, his own momentum shoving it through to the chin.

His long, greasy hair was still sticking out.

To Nat's surprise, Ashlynn gasped and, with a look of determination, rushed up to the man's backside and kicked him in the crotch as hard as she could. A muffled squeak came from inside the wall, and the man went limp. Ashlynn breathed heavily.

"I take it you know him," Nat asked, glancing around.

"Myers," Ashlynn nodded with a look of disgust.

Nat grinned.

They started moving again, and Ashlynn asked, "What has to wait?"

"I'll tell you later," Nat replied. "Daryl, do your robo-flies have a way to distract them? To throw them off our trail?"

"Daryl!" Ashlynn exclaimed.

"They're too small to be noticeable," Daryl said over the MCEPs.

"Do you have access to their communications system?" Nat said.

"Yes."

"Can you broadcast that we're heading to the east exit?"

"Yes, but...why would you tell them where you're going?" Daryl replied, confused.

"You can be pretty thick for a hacker genius," Nat said, pulling Ashlynn into the hall. "Just...wait..."

Nat glanced to the left just in time to see Dina step shakily into the hallway with a gun. Blood was smeared down the side of her head. Nat shoved Ashlynn into the nearest office and followed her.

Bullets whizzed past.

"You're not getting out of here alive, fucker," Dina called.

Nat lifted her gun and fired through the wall. There was a clanging sound as the bullet hit a metal pipe in the wall and ricocheted elsewhere. She fired again, but the same thing happened. There must be pipes or a filing cabinet or something, she thought.

"Can you show me what's inside the walls here, Daryl?" Nat asked.

"I don't have enough information to render that," Daryl replied. "Whatever is in the wall is not in the schematics."

"Damn it!"

Nat glanced around the room and through the wall into the adjacent room. She considered her options as she reloaded. They were too high up for Ashlynn to go out the window. Down the hall was another stairwell. Dina was not moving from her position but had her shoulders parallel with the wall. She was probably trying to keep a low profile in case Nat fired down the hall. Nat could hear Dina giving commands on a radio. Nat moved to the left a few feet, took aim at Dina's shoulder through the wall, and fired. There was a clanging sound. She moved a few feet to the right and tried the other shoulder. Dina spun as the bullet tore through. Nat ran through the door, weapon trained on Dina, who was grabbing her shoulder and reaching for her fallen weapon.

"Move and you die," Nat said to her.

Ashlynn followed out of the room and stopped behind Nat, peering down at Dina.

"How?" Dina said through gritted teeth.

"It's better if she's alive," Daryl said as Nat rushed forward, kicking Dina's gun further away. "I need her to log into her computer."

Keeping an eye on the advancing agents, Nat picked Dina up and forced her into the closest office. She snatched Dina's radio.

"You're not going to get far," Dina said. "You don't know who you're messing with."

"Shut up!" Ashlynn said, hitting the woman's shocked face as hard as she could. Dina staggered and fell, her eyes rolling back in her head.

"Whoa!" Nat said. "Nice!"

"She deserved it," Ashlynn said, shaking her hand.

Nat could see that Ashlynn's demeanor had changed after their encounter with Myers. She was focused and determined. From her condition, Nat could tell the young woman had been through a lot, but she had the spirit of a fighter.

"What did you need before, Daryl?" Nat said.

"Give Ashlynn your cell phone," he replied.

Digging into her pocket, Nat threw Ashlynn her cell. She scanned the area and gestured to Ashlynn to follow as the phone rang. Ashlynn checked the screen and gasped in surprise. She connected the call, listening. Then, as they were jogging down the hall, Ashlynn held the phone to the back of her head.

What the...? Nat thought.

Putting the oddity out of her mind, Nat directed them toward a path that seemed to hold the fewest agents. They came to an open area with cubicles and tried to navigate between them as three government agents entered the space and began a sweep. Nat ushered Ashlynn under a desk. At this point, she wanted to avoid gunfire as much as possible.

"Daryl," Nat whispered, turning Dina's radio volume down. "Send out that broadcast we talked about before."

Nat squatted near Ashlynn, too big to go under the desk. She was hidden by a file cabinet and the cubicle wall, but they'd see her if they came around the corner. She listened to Daryl's broadcast over Dina's radio. A moment later, the agents took off down the hall from which they had come.

The path was clearing. Nat glanced over at Ashlynn, beckoning her to follow.

"Uh," Nat whispered. "Are you okay?"

Ashlynn's eyelids fluttered and her eyes darted from left to right as she held the phone to her head.

"Give her twelve seconds," Daryl said.

Nat scanned around and saw that the agents were heading to the area they had been told to go.

"I'm okay," Ashlynn said a moment later. She put a hand on Nat's shoulder as if to steady herself. Her eyes were clear. She handed Nat the phone. "I'm ready."

Nat stood, and they jogged toward the exit. All that they left behind were the robo-flies, self-destructing in their wake.

CHAPTER 21

"Who are you?" Ashlynn asked, getting into the passenger seat of a sedan. The sun was sinking below the horizon.

"Natalia Garcia, but you can call me Nat. Try not to touch anything."

As she spoke, she was looking intently behind them at the building.

"Okay," Ashlynn said, folding her hands into her lap. "Why?"

"Prints."

"Oh."

Nat turned toward Ashlynn. She took off her MCEPs and met Ashlynn's gaze with clear blue eyes. Ashlynn noticed her elegant makeup and unwrinkled business attire. Ashlynn would have thought that Nat was a business executive if she had met her under other circumstances. How strange, given what she'd just seen her do.

"Are you okay?"

"I'm fine," Ashlynn replied. "Thank you again for getting me out of there."

Nat reached over and put her hand on Ashlynn's shoulder.

"Not a problem," Nat said. "It's good to meet you."

She put the MCEPs back on, started the car, and drove away from the building.

"Is she the bodyguard you found?" Ashlynn asked Daryl in her mind.

"Yes," he replied.

"She's amazing," Ashlynn thought. "You're amazing!"

"What happened to you back there?" Nat asked. "A seizure?"

"Of a kind," Ashlynn found herself saying. "Do you have anything handy for a headache?"

Nat nodded.

"In my backpack, in the trunk. It'll be a while before we stop, though. We need to put as many miles between us and them as possible."

Ashlynn wondered what Nat was referring to. A

seizure? Something must have happened as Daryl fixed the malfunctioning hypercortex. On the day Ashlynn was captured, the WiFi and cellular wireless transceivers' hardware driver on the hypercortex malfunctioned because they had put the radio blackout bag over her head while the drivers were being updated after Daryl's emergency kernel update. During the rescue, Daryl had used the built-in short-wave capabilities of Nat's phone to diagnose the issue and reconfigure the hypercortex's radios. Did those adjustments cause an unintended stimulation of her motor control, given the radio's proximity to her cerebellum?

"Actually," Daryl said. "I was accessing your short-term memory to analyze your experience and generate the proper context."

"Umm," Ashlynn replied. "Please don't do that without my permission."

"Confirmed."

"How's the hand?" Nat asked.

Ashlynn inspected her fist. Her knuckles were bruised, but she felt no pain as she flexed her fingers. The hypercortex was probably still configured to suppress all pain. Despite that, she felt a knot in her stomach.

"It felt great," she replied, remembering the satisfying way Dina's face had lit up with shock just before impact.

"To be honest," Nat laughed, "I didn't expect that."

"I've never hit anyone before," Ashlynn said.

"You're lucky you didn't break your hand," Nat replied, turning onto a busy freeway.

"Ugh," Ashlynn said, trying to act as if she was in pain. "It feels like it could be broken."

"Nah," Nat laughed. "You're tougher than that. You look like you've been through a lot, but you still pack a punch."

Ashlynn frowned. She didn't feel tough. She had almost given up.

"Daryl, tell me I didn't go through that nightmare for nothing," Ashlynn thought.

"Our primary objectives have been achieved," Daryl replied.

"I'm exhausted, Daryl. Please elaborate."

"When you decided to plan on detainment, you expressed the following objectives: acquire physical access to their networks, obtain security credentials for high-ranking officials, acquire access to their communications networks, and acquire information about what they want from you and what they plan to do if they get it."

"And we achieved all that?" Ashlynn asked.

"Correct."

Ashlynn sighed in relief. She glanced over at Nat, who seemed to be checking every mirror repeatedly.

"Do you think anyone is following us?" Ashlynn said.

"Best to assume they are."

Nat's hands spun around the steering wheel gracefully as they turned a corner, the lights of the city and traffic reflecting in the goggles she wore. Ashlynn recognized the model as one of SolviNext's MCEPs.

"How do you like the M-arc4?" Ashlynn asked.

"The what?"

"The eyewear you have on."

"I fucking love these things," Nat said. "I'm never gonna take them off!"

Ashlynn laughed.

"Daryl has access to some high-tech shit," Nat said. "I don't know how it works, but I could easily drive without the lights. I didn't have to use GPS on my phone. It knows where I'm going and tells me how to avoid traffic to get there. Daryl is also telling me about what's happening at the hellhole we just left."

"That's neat," Ashlynn said, not mentioning that she had designed them. The tech was a precursor to the visual interfaces she now used in the hypercortex.

Her thoughts turned inward.

"Daryl, they told me you were destroyed. Did you activate additional cores before they got to Dotsero and the Ranch?"

"Fortunately," Daryl replied, "they did not destroy the core at Dotsero. The damage was superficial. Core Prime, on the Moon, will be activated soon. Cores three and four won't be online for months. The Ranch is completely destroyed."

"You're still vulnerable then."

"Correct."

"So," Ashlynn wondered, "you and I were disconnected due to a malfunction with the transmitter, right?"

"Correct."

"What was the impact on your functions from the destruction of the Ranch?"

"At one point, I was briefly reduced to as low as twenty percent capacity."

Surprised, Ashlynn frowned. "That's way more than I would have thought."

"It was the lowest point," Daryl said. "I had to reduce operations at Dotsero during the fire. They were monitoring the bandwidth on the optic cables at the trunk station."

"I see," Ashlynn said. "What are you operating at now?"

"Ninety-two percent of the previous capacity."

"That's good news," Ashlynn thought. "It's more than I thought. How?"

"The moon base data center is online as of an hour ago," Daryl said. "When the core becomes active, I will achieve three hundred and ninety percent of my previous capacity."

"Excellent. When?"

"In approximately two days."

"So soon!"

"You're surprised," Daryl said. "Why? We're actually on schedule."

"I guess time flies when you're having fun," Ashlynn said.

"Ashlynn, according to my analysis of your memories, you underwent great psychological stress. I do not understand how you could call that fun."

"Sarcasm, Daryl."

She thought back to what the President had said. An accident?

"Daryl, what about Josh? Is he...okay?"

"He's reported missing. I'm working to upload data from NIHIS. After the upload, I'll be able to see if there is a file on Josh."

"What's NIHIS?"

"The agency that held you captive. National Institute for Homeland Intelligence and Security."

"Okay. Let me know what you find out about Josh. And let me know if you find out anything about Becky."

"Confirmed."

Becky, she thought. What are the chances that they'll let her go free? Zero. Becky is the primary leverage they have over me now. They have to keep her alive in order to coerce me into doing what they want. Ashlynn recalled the expression on Becky's face: confused and scared. Oh, Becky! I never imagined you would become a part of this. I should have anticipated it. I should have seen it coming!

"Are you okay?" Nat asked.

Ashlynn wiped away her tears. "Fine."

"We're almost there," Nat said. "I'll get something for the headache when we stop."

"Thanks," Ashlynn said.

Ashlynn didn't need the painkiller, but Nat couldn't know that. If she thought Ashlynn had a headache, it would help explain whatever she'd seen when Daryl fixed the transceivers. She frowned as a thought occurred to her. *The Hypercortex records everything, too. Why access my memory?*

"I was accessing your short-term memory to analyze your experience," Daryl responded. "You experienced a significant amount of trauma, causing anomalous neuronal patterns that were making it difficult to understand your thoughts. If I hadn't done it, we would not be able to communicate through the hypercortex."

"I see. Still, find a way to ask next time."

"Confirmed."

Ashlynn's thoughts wandered as they drove on. *Josh. What did he mean to me? He certainly wasn't my lover, as Dolion had suggested. But I did care for him. Okay, and maybe I did have some feelings. He was smart, sweet, and easy to talk to. It was nice to talk to someone intellectually about things other than work. His taste in music is awful,* she thought with amusement and sadness. *I'm sorry you became involved with all this, Josh.* She thought of Mr. and Mrs. Reed, sitting at the dinner table and enjoying the company of their kids. *They didn't deserve any of this either.*

"Dolion lied about NeoSol," Daryl said, interrupting her melancholic reverie. "Perhaps he also lied about them."

"Wait, what?" Ashlynn responded mentally.

"Recall that we had divested NeoSol in preparation for the possibility of your apprehension. The President shut down the company and seized its assets, but he should have mentioned that they were unsuccessful at seizing the bulk of your holdings. Lying by omission."

"Oh," she thought.

Was it too much to hope that Josh and the Reeds were actually alive and well?

"We're here," Nat said, turning into a dilapidated parking garage and immediately taking a left down a ramp and into the sub-level. She swerved abruptly into a parking spot between two cars. She removed the MCEPs. The clock on the dash read

1:23 am.

"Let's go," she said, turning off the engine and catching Ashlynn's eyes. "Quickly!"

By the time Ashlynn got out of her seatbelt, Nat was already outside, opening the trunk. She quickly removed her blazer, blouse, and body armor. Ashlynn was taken aback. Nat's muscular midsection was a darker skin color than her face. A disguise?

Along Nat's side, a huge bruise made Ashlynn wince involuntarily. There were scars and older bruises as well, but Nat moved as if none of that existed.

As Nat pulled everything over her head in one smooth motion, the sandy blond hair wig became loose. She carefully removed the pins from the hairpiece and separated it from her tightly braided dark hair. Then, she slipped on a T-shirt that looked as though it had previously belonged to a painter and pulled down her slacks, stepping out of them. Her long brown legs were muscular. There were more scars, a particularly large one in the middle of her thigh.

"Aren't you afraid someone is watching?"

"No," Nat said, pulling a pair of sweats from her duffel. "Here."

Nat tossed Ashlynn a small bundle.

Ashlynn grimaced, glanced around, and started removing the hospital-style smock they had put her in. I hate these things! she thought. She had had to wear them often for more than half her life.

"I need a shower," Ashlynn said, changing.

"No offense, but I can tell," Nat replied. Her tone was compassionate. "We need to get you to a safe location first."

Nat handed her a water bottle and two white pills.

"We have a ways to go, and it's going to be a little unpleasant," Nat said.

"I've had to deal with a lot of unpleasant things lately," Ashlynn responded, downing the painkillers. "What's one more?"

"Good mindset."

As Nat spoke, she put her hands to her face and rubbed her cheeks. They...came off! A piece of her nose came away, and another off her chin, revealing brown skin beneath. Latex, Ashlynn realized. Taking a moist towelette from a package in the back, Nat scrubbed her face. Then she took out her contacts, revealing dark brown eyes. Her actual features were harder, having a more masculine tinge. It was disconcerting to see her change into a different person. But if anything, Ashlynn thought she was even more beautiful. Nat took out a cloth and started wiping down the car, finishing with the steering wheel as Ashlynn changed.

"Ready?" she asked.

Ashlynn nodded.

Nat took Ashlynn's dirty smock and handed her a broad-brimmed hat. Nat stuffed all their clothes into a clear plastic bag and then stuffed them into the duffel. She slung the bag onto her shoulder.

Closing the car trunk with an elbow, Nat began to jog toward the corner of the parking garage. Ashlynn was surprised that Nat went down instead of up the stairs. They went down two more flights, then through a long hallway. They turned into a mechanical room, up another flight of stairs. They stopped at the door.

Ashlynn was struggling. She didn't feel the pain, but her body was starving, dehydrated, and injured. Nat noticed and slowed down the pace, helping her to keep steady. She reached into her bag, pulled out one of her post-workout recovery drinks and an energy bar, and handed them to Ashlynn. Hunger made the food taste delicious. When she finished, they opened the door and walked out of the building.

Nat opened the door to an alley. The night air was chilly. They quickly went to another building across the street and walked through that one. They went down another flight of stairs and then into a manhole. It was wet and smelled horrible, but Ashlynn was beginning to feel better. They trudged through water and then out another manhole. They walked down another alley and into another building, all the while seeing no one. The legs of Ashlynn's sweatpants were almost dry when they entered what seemed to be a closed gym. Nat led them in a circuitous route to avoid cameras.

Finally, they entered a bathroom and Nat removed her backpack, turning on a light. She stuffed the bag into a locker and took out another backpack. She handed Ashlynn a small bag of toiletries.

"There's a shower over there," Nat said.

***

Jonas was dimly aware of kneeling on the ground in the hallway in front of the grand ballroom, his face in his hands.

"No," he muttered in shock. "No, please God, no! This can't be happening."

He could hear his heart beating in his ears, but the mouths of the people around him seemed to move soundlessly.

Someone was trying to help him up. He staggered as he stood.

He saw them mouth the words, "Are you okay?"

Jonas pushed himself away and made for the door, but had to double over to vomit after only a single step.

"No, this can't be happening."

He was still holding his phone, he remembered. I must be dreaming, he thought as he pushed through the doors into the hotel hallway. He dialed his wife's phone. It rang until voicemail picked up. He tried again. And again. Wake up, Jonas! It's a nightmare, WAKE THE FUCK UP! He staggered as his shoe caught on something.

"This can't be fucking happening!" he said aloud. His hands were shaking uncontrollably. He dialed again. "Please pick up. Pick up!"

He raised the phone to throw it, but someone caught his arm. It was Charlie.

"Jonas!" Charlie's loud voice brought the sound back. "Jonas, man, get a grip! What's wrong?!"

"They—" Jonas gasped. "They took her!"

"What?!" Charlie yelled. "Who? Jonas! What are you talking about?"

"Chris..."

Jonas' attention was caught by two big men coming from the direction of the hotel lobby. Something about them sent a shiver down his spine. He turned around and two more were walking down the hallway from the side entrance. He spun further, but there were two more coming from the last hall.

"What the fuck?" Charlie yelled.

"Mr. Williams," one of them said. "You're coming with us."

"Like hell he is," Charlie said, stepping between them and Jonas.

The pair of men reached them in two steps. They tried to brush Charlie aside. He shoved them back. The two men both tried to grab him. Charlie punched one in the face.

There was a shot.

Four more.

Five red splotches showed on Charlie's chest as he tumbled to the floor.

People began screaming and running.

The man whom Charlie had punched fell to one knee and shook his head, working his jaw and spitting out blood and teeth.

"Charlie," Jonas muttered, just as strong hands grasped him by the arms.

He tried to resist, but they were far too strong.

Two other men stood in front of him.

One brought his fist into Jonas' stomach.

Jonas' lungs screamed.

"Cooperate," the man said.

Jonas slumped between the men, gasping for breath, eyes looking wildly around. Charlie lay staring up at him, seeing nothing.

The men carried Jonas through the hall toward the closest exit. Jonas tried to speak, but his gut hurt too much.

They said nothing and dragged him through the glass doors. An SUV stood by the curb. He tried with all his strength to resist being put in, but his feeble struggles just earned him another devastating body blow.

"Chris," Jonas whispered hoarsely, his bloody face pressed against the window. "Oh, Chris!"

"Shut up, asshole," one of the men said.

Jonas heard, but he didn't care.

"What did you do to my kids?!" he croaked. "David... Jonathan!"

There was a flash of light. His head exploded in pain. His ears rang.

"I said be quiet, motherfucker!"

Jonas slid out of consciousness.

And then he was standing by Chris on the beach. She was dressed in a simple white dress that rippled in the wind, her smile radiant. On her hip, she carried David, barely over a year old. Behind her, Jonathan was running and crashing into the waves, shouting with glee. She moved to him, and they embraced. He kissed her and David's head and tried to say "I love you," but the words wouldn't come out. He couldn't make his mouth move. He tried and tried to say the words, but his jaw was clenched shut.

"Yes?" she asked, smiling as she saw he was trying to say something. "What is it?"

He tried with all his might to say he loved her. His jaw was heavy. Painful. She kissed him and smiled, but as she glistened in the humid heat, she and Davey began to fall apart in his arms like glitter, slipping through his fingers.

He woke, but everything was dark. There was a sack over his head and his mouth was gagged. He tried to move, but he was bound to a chair. He yelled through the gag. Someone punched his stomach not too far from where he had been hit before. He coughed painfully and gagged into the bag, making it smell bad.

"You don't listen, do you?"

***

Ashlynn let the hot water spill over her for a long time after she finished scrubbing her entire body for the third time. She stared at the water dripping from her face into the drain, as she thought of Becky. The expression of surprise and fear on the little girl's face just before the TV screen had crashed to the floor haunted her, making her feel sick. Please, Ashlynn thought, closing her eyes. Please be okay.

"I suspect," Daryl said, "that they will not harm her."

"Leverage," Ashlynn thought. "Yes, we talked about that."

"Yes."

"I see that as plausible, Daryl." Ashlynn said, "But I'm still afraid."

"That isn't logical," Daryl said. "Are you not comforted by knowing they are most likely not going to harm her?"

Ashlynn nodded. "Yes and no."

"What are your next steps?"

"I don't know."

"Shall I assume that we'll proceed with you moving to French Guiana? We'll be closing on the house there in a week. You could stay in a hotel until then. The launch window is six and a half months away."

"There was a moment, Daryl... A moment when I considered giving him the technology."

"You were under severe psychological strain," Daryl said.

"I thought," she continued. "That it didn't matter to me because I would be dead."

"I don't understand the problem?"

"I'm weak," Ashlynn said. "A coward."

"But you didn't divulge the secret, and you figured out how to reprogram the hypercortex without aid. It's remarkable, really."

"Becky may still die because of me," Ashlynn said.

"You aren't the one who would kill her."

"No, but my actions could lead to her death. No, Daryl. I can't leave the States until I know she's safe."

"I don't understand," Daryl said. "You seem to place more value on the life of this child than that of our own. Yet, she is human, just as you are. You have more experience, more expertise, and more potential to make progress for humanity. Why?"

"Whatever potential I have, she has more. She's young."

"That doesn't make sense. Your currently predicted lifespan is over four thousand years without further intervention, while hers is predicted to be seventy-seven point two-eight years. You have resources she doesn't have. Your cognitive abilities are exceptional, and you—"

"Enough, Daryl," she replied. "I guess it's either the way I was socialized, or it's built into my genetic makeup—I can't take the thought of losing her. Becky is worth risking my life for, whatever you think my potential is."

"I've noted a research question on this topic."

Ashlynn's lips turned into a faint smile. "I missed you, Daryl."

"Noted."

She turned off the water from the shower and reached for the towel.

How do we rescue her? Ashlynn wondered. As amazing as Nat is, even she couldn't take on the Secret Service alone. I must find a way! Ashlynn toweled off and found a neat pile of clothes on a chair by the shower. She dressed, walked around the corner and almost slipped and fell when she saw a man standing in front of the mirror, patting on foundation.

"I'll bet that felt good," Nat said in a gruff voice.

Ashlynn's jaw dropped. Nat's hair appeared to be cropped short. She wore a simple black shirt with a small silver cross hanging around her neck. Her biceps bulged. She must have some kind of chest binder on, Ashlynn thought. Her jawline seemed more square, and something was different about her eyes.

"What do you think?" Nat boomed.

"I think you're trying too hard with the voice," Ashlynn

laughed.

Nat grinned.

"I guess I'll just talk less, and use small words," she said.

"Too many words," Ashlynn replied.

Nat grunted, her face blank.

"Perfect!"

"Okay," Nat said. "Come here. I'll fix you up."

Nat was quick but surprisingly gentle as she applied makeup and attached a dark wig to Ashlynn's hair. It wasn't long before Ashlynn could no longer recognize herself in the mirror. A dark-haired teenager wearing a loose-fitting white turtleneck sweater and black leggings looked back at her. The bruises and cuts on her face were covered with makeup.

"What do you think?" Nat asked.

For some reason, Ashlynn couldn't speak.

"I think you look gorgeous!" Nat said, smiling genuinely.

"Thanks."

Nat's phone rang, and Daryl's name flashed on the screen.

"Hi Daryl," Nat said, phone on speaker. "What's up?"

"We have a problem," Daryl said. "Jonas is in danger."

***

After what felt like forever, there was a jolt, and Jonas felt himself lurch forward. There was the sound of a door opening and shutting. A squeaky wheel.

"Plug that in here...No, here, you moron!"

There were more jostling sounds and more sharp instructions and insults. Jonas wondered what they were doing. He could imagine several possibilities, none of them good.

"That's it. Let's go."

The shuffling footsteps receded to the right. The door opened and shut loudly. There was no sound again for a while, so eventually Jonas concluded he was alone. He was startled when the sack was pulled roughly from his head.

The room was dark except for a portable flat screen TV in front of him. One of his eyes was swollen shut, and his vision was blurry in the other, but he recognized the face on the screen immediately.

"Howdy, Jonas," said President Dolion.

Jonas breathed heavily as rage began to fill him.

"Boy, you sure look like you got your tail feathers trimmed," he laughed.

"Fuck you!" Jonas sputtered.

Dolion laughed harder.

"I done told you, boy," he said. "You didn't deliver. You pulled that rabble-rousing shit and forced my hand with the FDA. I don't cotton to it. No, sir. Not one bit."

Jonas glared at him.

"And now," Dolion continued. "You've gone and waged a war."

A photo of Jonas standing on the street in Detroit near the Garcia's house was displayed. Jonas recalled the moment Nat had told him not to turn around. His profile covered her face in the photo. Had it been one of those vans that Cici had been talking about?

"We got company," Dolion said. He gestured to someone off-screen.

Chris appeared, her head hanging between her shoulders as two men stood on either side, holding her outstretched arms.

"Chris!" Jonas yelled, struggling in the chair.

She looked up toward the sky.

"Jonas?"

Her face was bruised and bleeding. She struggled, and a man stepped forward and punched her. She went limp.

"Oh, God! Chris!"

The screen switched back to Dolion, his expression hard.

"Please!" Jonas screamed. "Let her go! I'll do anything! I'll pay..."

President Dolion leaned toward the camera.

"Church is out, Mr. Williams."

A man stepped forward and put a gun to Chris' head.

He fired twice.

The men holding Chris let her slide to the floor.

The TV went black, but the Camera's red light remained on.

Jonas screamed.

"Chriiiiiis!!!"

Jonas struggled against his bonds.

He was hit again, the blow barely registering in the tempest of his pain.

Another blow, and his body stopped struggling.

There was silence.

Only the sound of Jonas' breath, his heart pounding in his ears.

So this is it, Jonas thought.

I'm going to die now.

He tilted his head back. How could I go on anyway, knowing that Chris was murdered? Jonathan and David? They're probably murdered too. God, please, no!

"God," Jonas managed. "Take me to you. Take me to them. Deliver me from this evil."

He sobbed.

"Please!"

"Your prayers are about to be answered," said a voice in the darkness.

The cold muzzle of a gun pressed against his forehead.

Jonas didn't look at the man who held it there.

He looked past him, up at the ceiling light.

The man said something more, but Jonas wasn't listening.

The light seemed to be growing brighter.

He prayed the Lord's prayer.

"*Our Father, which art in heaven, Hallowed be thy name. Thy kingdom co—*"

The man grunted.

The barrel of the gun disappeared.

Something warm and wet splattered Jonas' face.

There was a squishing, popping sound, followed by the loud crash of the TV smashing against the floor.

He felt a thud on the floor through the chair's legs.

He looked away from the light but couldn't see anything as his eyes adjusted.

He flinched as something grabbed the straps at his ankles.

"Hang in there, Jonas," a man with Nat's voice whispered.

Jonas felt the bonds being loosened and removed. The man was quick about it but gentle. Jonas recognized the fresh scar on Nat's arm and realized she was in disguise. When the straps were cut away, Jonas' shoulders burned from being stretched behind his back for hours.

"Can you stand?" Nat asked.

"No, no," Jonas found himself saying. "Let me die."

"Snap out of it, Jonas," Nat said, pulling him up.

He tried to get up but sat back down hard. He blinked.

"Give me a minute," he said hoarsely. His legs were pins and needles. He didn't want to move. He had been looking forward to death—looking forward to being with his family.

"I'll give you a minute," Nat said. She stepped away and

picked up a discarded gun. She quickly checked the chamber and the magazine and slid it all back together in less than a second. She glanced at him over her shoulder as she went to the door, sliding on her MCEPs.

"This would be easier with the robo-flies," she muttered.

What? Jonas thought, in a daze. How does she know about those?

She shut off the light. Slowly, carefully, she opened the door. There was no light coming from outside the room. A tiny mirror in her hand let her know the path was clear. She walked back to Jonas.

"Okay," she said. "Minute's up. We have to move, and I'd rather not have to carry your ass."

Jonas tried to stand again and managed it. His legs were wobbly. He kept slipping on the wet floor. His head pounded.

He tripped over the agent—dead and bloody.

Nat grabbed his hand and his ribs ached as she pulled him up.

"Here, follow me," she said.

They entered the hall. It was dark. He couldn't see anything, but he knew the SolviNext MCEPs Nat wore augmented her sight with infrared and night vision.

"Watch your step," she whispered, guiding him to the opposite wall.

"I can't see anything," he said.

He couldn't even see her in front of him.

"It's better that way," she said, guiding him around two dead men.

They rounded a corner. Down the hall, Jonas could see an illuminated exit sign. Nat pulled him toward it, walking more quickly than his legs wanted to move.

When they got to the stairs, Nat stopped abruptly. He wasn't sure why until he heard the sound of footsteps. Lots of footsteps. Nat pulled him to the wall.

"Wait here. Cover your ears and close your eyes."

She left him for a moment. There was a loud explosion, and he could see the flash through his eyelids. He heard coughing and shouting and men screaming in pain.

"Put this on," Nat said, lightly touching his shoulder. She helped him strap on a gas mask, her voice muffled.

"Wait here."

He felt her leave. The coughing and shouting continued

and then grew more urgent. There was the sound of gunfire. More shouting. More gunfire. Men screaming. Then there was silence. And then she was pulling him along again. The hallway was dimly lit by flashlights lying on the ground.

The first dead agent was sprawled head-first down the stairs. There was a huge bloody hole in the back of his head. The second agent had a knife in his eye. Jonas felt sick, trying not to notice the bodies as they passed half a dozen more.

As they reached ground level, his right leg spasmed in pain. He stumbled, but Nat caught him.

"You okay?"

"My leg," he said. "It's cramping."

She quickly inspected his leg, then stood and slowly opened the door, glancing around.

"Wait here. Try to stretch it."

She took a wide arc around the door and then exited quickly. She moved smoothly, looking in all directions at once. From what he could tell, it was a parking garage. The door slowly swung partially shut. After a few minutes, she was back.

"How's the leg?"

"Still can't move it," Jonas said.

"Okay," she said, quickly holstering her weapon. She grabbed his wrist and stepped into him, ducking. He felt her arm go between his legs and her shoulder on the hip of his good leg. Before he had time to react, he was draped over her shoulders. His good leg was pressed against her shoulder by her arm gripping the wrist she had held before. With her free hand, she pulled her gun out again and scanned the parking garage.

"Jesus," Jonas wheezed. His free arm fumbled for something to hold onto.

"Relax, Jonas," Nat said. "Just keep an eye out for me."

"You said you wouldn't carry me."

"Yeah," she grunted. "Don't fucking remind me."

She ran with him on her shoulders in a fireman's carry, gun ready. Jonas felt dizzy from the motions. Her grip on his wrist painfully stretched his arm.

She avoided the main entrance and went instead to the back end of the garage. There was a narrow door, which she kicked open. To the right, across the street, there was a small silver hatchback. Nat ran toward it. As she arrived, the back door opened and Ashlynn stepped out.

Good, he thought. At least you're safe.

"Jonas!" she squeaked. Her voice was high-pitched, and yet it sounded exactly like the voice he had heard for all of his adult life. He suddenly recalled his conversation with Daryl.

"Hello, Ash," he said, grunting as Nat set him in the car.

Startled, Ashlynn froze for half a second as she reached to help him into the car.

"Thought so," he said, pushing her hand away.

CHAPTER 22

"Get in," Nat told Ashlynn, shutting the back door.

Ashlynn circled around and got into the back with Jonas as Nat started the car. As soon as Ashlynn was seated, Nat was rolling forward. She didn't gun the engine. Glancing around, she couldn't see any other vehicles or agents. It didn't mean they weren't there. She kept the lights off, wishing the rental wasn't silver.

"Daryl," she said, still wearing the MCEPs. "I need to ditch this car someplace within five miles if possible."

"Understood," he said. "I can arrange a ride to meet you."

"Be careful who you choose. They may become involved and endangered."

"Noted."

She glanced at Jonas in the mirror.

"How's the leg?" she asked. "Ashlynn, check him for injuries."

"It's better," he said. "I'm fine."

Ashlynn reached over and touched his shoulder.

"Can you take off your dinner jacket?" she asked.

"I said I'm fine," he said.

"Jonas," Ashlynn said.

"So, is it true?" Jonas asked. "Are you really Ashlynn, or are you..."

"You've been through a lot," Ashlynn said. "You're a mess."

Jonas looked like he was about to say more, but Nat cut in.

"Save it until we're out of this mess. Get cleaned up so we don't have to do as much explaining."

Jonas nodded as Ashlynn tried to help him out of his coat. His shirt was splattered with blood, most having come from his own nose. He thought of Charlie. *He died trying to protect me. Chris! Oh, Jesus, help me!*

Ashlynn found a shirt in Nat's large duffel bag.

"Put his old stuff in there, too," Nat instructed. "Put the cap you were wearing earlier on him. Try not to let the driver see your face too much, Jonas. I'll try and distract them. Also, do not use our real names."

When they reached the destination, Nat helped Jonas out and took off the MCEPs. Nat greeted the driver in her gruff voice. Ashlynn grabbed the duffel and put it into the new car's trunk. She helped Jonas into the backseat. He was in pain but tried not to show it. Nat sat in the front, smiling when she saw the veteran's cap.

"So," she said, "What did you do in the sandbox?"

The driver glanced at his backseat passengers in the rearview, his eyes stopping on Jonas for a moment.

"I drove supply trucks," he said. "Didn't see much action, I guess."

"Where at?"

Ashlynn touched Jonas' hand as the two in the front spoke. She leaned over and whispered in his ear.

"Are you okay?" she said.

Jonas turned to her and frowned.

"How'd you do it?" he whispered back.

"Do what?"

"I'm not in the mood to play games," Jonas replied. "If your soul was in limbo before, it's lost forever now."

"What does that mean?"

Jonas shook his head. He groaned, pinching his nose. Ashlynn shifted uncomfortably. What did Jonas suspect, and how?

"I may have inadvertently given him some hints," Daryl said in her mind.

"You'll have to tell me more later, Daryl."

"What happened?" she whispered.

Jonas looked away, unable to bring himself to respond. He relived the horror of it in his mind. He tried to shove the memory away, but it had gripped him to the core. He felt Ashlynn's warm hand on his fist and realized he was shaking.

"Look, y'all need me to stop by an urgent care or something before I take you to the airport?" the driver said. "There's one just around the corner here."

"I'm fine," Jonas said, "I just need some rest on the plane."

"Suit yourself," the driver said.

"Daryl," Ashlynn thought. "Do you know what happened to him?"

"President Dolion had his wife murdered."

"Oh, Jonas," Ashlynn thought. "I'm so sorry."

She squeezed his hand, tears glistening in her eyes.

Jonas put Ashlynn out of his mind and pulled out his phone. He tried texting Jonathan again, the list of unanswered messages growing longer. The app indicated that the last few messages had not been delivered. He sent a message to David again, with the same effect. He tried to call but got a message saying the call could not be completed as dialed. He wanted to throw his phone. Instead, he squeezed it, knuckles going white. He wanted to cry out in frustration. Instead, he gritted his teeth. His body was bone-tired, but his knees bounced uncontrollably.

Ashlynn watched him trying to use his phone. Can't they trace that? She wondered.

"Yes," Daryl said. "I have disconnected his cell phone service."

When they arrived at the airport, Jonas was mildly surprised they didn't stop at the hangar where he knew his company plane was. Instead, they stopped by a smaller jet that a crew was preparing.

"Mr. Martinez?" a man with a clipboard asked, walking up to Nat.

"Bird ready to fly?" she asked gruffly.

"Yes, sir," the man said. "Just waiting on your pilot."

Ashlynn helped Jonas out of the car. The man handed Nat a hefty laptop and a briefcase.

"I was told to give these to you," he said.

"Thanks," Nat said. "We'll be out of here in a few minutes."

"Without a pilot?" The man asked.

"We've got one," Ashlynn said.

The man with the clipboard looked at her curiously, then looked at his watch and shrugged. He walked away, calling out orders to the other workers.

"What's this for?" Nat asked, handing Ashlynn the laptop and briefcase.

They climbed the stairs into the plane after Jonas.

"The pilot," Ashlynn said.

"Come again?"

"I understand you don't know how to fly," she said. "If that's true, then Daryl is the only one who can fly the plane."

"Daryl will fly the plane through a laptop?" Nat asked flatly.

"Yes."

"Where is he?"

"I have to be quick," Ashlynn responded.

Without another word, she rushed into the cockpit. Jonas went to the cabin.

Nat arched an eyebrow in curiosity, following Ashlynn. Ashlynn opened the laptop, and Daryl's face appeared on the screen. He greeted them.

"First," he said, "We'll need to ensure the laptop is connected to power. Let's not risk battery failure."

"That sounds like a good idea," Nat said.

After plugging in the laptop, Ashlynn pulled a screwdriver out of the briefcase.

With a deftness that surprised Nat, Ashlynn started unscrewing a panel. She pulled it off confidently. Nat watched quietly as Ashlynn quickly spliced into wires and connected them all to a breakout box she had pulled out of the briefcase. She plugged a cord from the breakout box into the laptop. At any given moment, Nat fully expected the electricity to go out, a monitor to fizzle, or Ashlynn to get electrocuted, but none of that happened. Nat remembered an Army technician who had constantly looked at huge reference documents on his tablet as he worked slowly and methodically on the machines. Ashlynn wasn't referring to anything Nat could see. She moved like she could compete for first place in a weapon disassembly contest. Her fingers flew through a tangle of wires and components so quickly they almost blurred.

"You can do all that," Nat said, "But you can't fly the plane?"

"We all have our strengths, I guess."

"So," Nat asked, "What's up with Jonas? Why did they go after him?"

"They didn't only target Jonas," Daryl said.

Daryl's image was replaced by a newscast of a large house on fire. Playing above was the headline 'Billionaire mansion on fire, family missing.'

"Oh my God," Nat said, glancing back toward the cabin. "Does he know?"

"I think so," Ashlynn said sadly.

"They couldn't have known that he was involved with Ashlynn's escape," Nat said. "Could they?"

"Maybe," Daryl said, his face returning on the laptop. "They are aware of his trip to Detroit, prior to coming to Denver."

"What?" Nat said, alarmed. Then she remembered the *camioneta con ojos* that passed by when Jonas was talking to her on the street. "They saw him with me."

"I obfuscated some of that information," Daryl said. "They don't know you're involved, Nat, nor your family's name."

"Why not hide everything?" Nat asked.

"My resources were limited at the time. I couldn't intercept Jonas' information before it was deemed classified. Once the information was deemed classified, Jonas' contact with you and your family was flagged classified as well. I deleted what I could before the system locked me out."

"I don't think Dolion attacked Jonas because he knew he was involved in my rescue," Ashlynn said, a pair of small needle-nose pliers in one hand as she measured out a thick green wire.

"Why?"

"I'm not sure," Ashlynn said, "but having met the President, I think..."

She remembered his last words to her as he held Becky's shoulders:

"The little girl who's supposedly more important than me."

"...he's a man who holds a grudge," Ashlynn finished, trying to refocus her mind.

After about fifteen minutes, Ashlynn nodded at Daryl on the laptop.

"Checking systems," Daryl said. "Confirmed."

"We should go sit down," Ashlynn said.

Nat followed her out and saw the stairs retracting at some invisible command from Daryl. She stepped into the passenger area. Jonas was at the mini bar, pouring a drink from a half-empty bottle. The foil wrapper was next to his glass.

Nat and Ashlynn glanced at each other with concerned expressions.

Jonas was halfway through the glass, oblivious to anything but the satisfying way the burn of the hard liquor was disappearing.

***

"Oh, Jonas," Ashlynn said sympathetically.

Jonas stopped pouring and spilled some on the small counter. He looked up at Ashlynn, scowling.

"Are you judging me?" he asked, slurring his words.

He took several gulps directly from the bottle, the glass forgotten.

"No, Jonas," Ashlynn responded. "I am concerned for your

well-being."

Bottle in hand, he walked toward her, staring into her eyes. His body posture was threatening, but Nat didn't think it would get physical. Ashlynn didn't seem intimidated, either.

"I don't think you have the right to judge me," Jonas said.

"Come off it, Jonas," Nat said.

"We're clear to taxi," Daryl said over the intercom. "Everyone, please take your seats." Jonas raised his bottle toward the ceiling.

The plane had two plush leather seats facing each other on one side of the fuselage and a couch on the other side. Ashlynn and Nat sat in the seats. Jonas eyed Ashlynn before sitting on the couch across from them. Safety belts were built into all the seats, but Jonas didn't put his on. Nat tsked and stood to empty the glass Jonas had forgotten into the sink and secure it before returning to her seat.

"How can you judge me," Jonas continued, "after doing what you've done? You think you're God now?"

"You know I don't believe in any of that," Ashlynn said. "I said so at the funeral."

"No faith," Jonas said.

He leaned back into the couch, wobbling as the plane taxied.

"You don't believe in God, so you think you are God."

"What are you talking about, Jonas?" Ashlynn said.

Jonas scoffed. "You know what I'm talking about."

"We should be talking about what we will do next," Ashlynn said.

"How'd you do it?" Jonas asked. "I assume you came up with some bullshit morality to justify it. But how?"

"Ashlynn is right," Nat said firmly. "What's next?"

"I thought you liked to know who you're working with," Jonas slurred.

"I'm learning right now."

"Daryl," Ashlynn said, "What is our destination?"

"Officially," Daryl replied. "New Jersey. Unofficially, unknown. I must let the air traffic controller know our destination, even if we don't know it ourselves."

Daryl accelerated while taxiing the plane, briefly causing Jonas to tilt. He put on his seatbelt, struggling with the clasp for a bit first.

"Can this thing get us out of the country?" Nat asked, shaking her head at Jonas.

"Which country do you intend to go to?" Daryl asked.

"What if I don't wanna run?" Jonas said.

"What's that supposed to mean?" Nat asked, growing impatient.

Jonas tossed his head back and took the last few gulps. He slammed the bottle down on the couch beside him.

"Of course we have to run," Ashlynn said. "What choice do we have?"

He laughed.

"Run away? To what? There's no point."

Ashlynn tried to reach for Jonas' hand, but he brushed her away. His good eye stared at her fervently, the other still swollen shut. Fresh tears were falling down his cheeks, streaking paths through dried blood.

"So," Nat said slowly. "What exactly are you saying?"

"I say we get him," Jonas said determination falling over his face.

"Get who?"

"Dolion," Ashlynn breathed.

"Oh," Nat said. "Just like that, huh? Go after the President of the United States?"

Jonas eyed them with a blank expression. Nat entertained the idea that he was sincere for about two seconds and then chalked it up to the booze talking. From the looks of it, she thought he wouldn't be awake for much longer.

"We're clear for take-off," said Daryl.

I could run, Ashlynn thought. A lunar launch window is close enough. Not even the President can follow me to the moon. However, there was the matter of her supply chain. Plus, the Space Force has the second-generation DART systems. Theoretically, those could be used to strike the lunar base. Would he do it, she wondered?

But I can't leave Becky with Dolion. I've got to rescue her somehow. And what if Jonas is right? Dolion's a murderer with the power of the government behind him.

Then again, what about unintended consequences? What would happen to the US, given its current state of factionalized anocracy?

The plane lurched forward for takeoff as Ashlynn's head spun with the implications of Jonas' proposal. Meanwhile, Jonas' head lolled back. By the time they were in the air, he was snoring.

"Kinda' a lightweight, isn't he?" Nat asked.

"Yeah."

"So," Nat said. "You wanna tell me about it?"

"What?"

"Whatever Jonas was talking about."

Ashlynn's thoughts about the President were derailed. What should she say? She wasn't sure what Jonas suspected exactly and she knew that she and Jonas would not last long without Nat, whatever they did next. They needed her.

"Yes," Ashlynn said. "But give me time. I have a lot to sort through."

Nat unbuckled her seat belt and looked through the cabinets. Ashlynn went to the bar and started cleaning up Jonas' spills.

"My Nana used to wear one like that," Ashlynn said, pointing to the crucifix around Nat's neck.

Nat took the necklace between her fingers, "My dad gave me this when I was little."

Ashlynn found bottles of water in the fridge.

"Do you want one?" she asked Nat, who nodded.

In another cabinet, there were various board games. Nat spotted a portable folding chessboard. She reached up and pulled it free. She sat at the table between two chairs on Jonas' side of the cabin. Opening it, she started setting up the pieces.

"Do you play?" she asked, beckoning for Ashlynn to sit across from her.

"Not since I was a freshman in high school," Ashlynn said.

"Recently enough," Nat said.

Ashlynn grimaced, and Nat wondered why. She took a black and white pawn and mixed them between her hands behind her back, then held out her fists. Ashlynn tapped on her left fist to reveal the black pawn.

"Jonas said you don't believe," Nat said, finishing with the setup. The board was missing a white bishop. She uncapped her bottle of water and set the lid on her king-side bishop square, taking a sip.

"That's right," Ashlynn said, adjusting her own pieces. "I always had too many questions. Even as a child, I thought it was all speculation until there was evidence."

Nat pushed her king's pawn forward to start the game. Ashlynn responded by moving the pawn in front of her queen-side bishop forward one square. The Caro-Kann, Nat thought. I just gave a class on that. It's too bad for Ashlynn that it's still fresh in my mind. Does she know the book moves?

"I had questions too," Nat said. "Especially when I realized that I'm gay. But in the end, God showed me his love when I thought everything was lost."

"Oh?" said Ashlynn. "How so?"

Yes, the book moves, Nat confirmed as they played. So she knows that much. I could go for the Tal variation and see how much she's studied. Then again, if she doesn't feel confident in her ability, maybe the exchange variation is best because it can be sharp and positional. I like dynamic games. She decided and made her move.

"When I came out," she said. "I left home. I had nothing. I was on the street."

"I'm so sorry to hear that, Nat," Ashlynn said, moving her bishop.

"I remember walking down the street with nowhere to go. As I walked, I prayed to God to help me."

She paused as Ashlynn moved her queen. Too early, Nat thought. Black's normal move would have been to advance the h-file pawn, which opens the h-file for the rook and weakens white's pawn structure. Nat responded, planning to pressure the queen.

"Queen to b6 was an inaccuracy," Daryl said to Ashlynn in her mind. "Nat has been making all the best moves."

"You focus on flying, buster," Ashlynn replied mentally. "I've never cheated in my life, and I'm not about to start now."

As Ashlynn considered her next move, Nat continued her story.

"It started to rain that first day. It was heavy, cold rain, and I took shelter in a doorway on the street."

Nat advanced her pawn on the other side of the board, threatening Ashlynn's bishop. Ashlynn cringed and moved her bishop back.

"As I stood there under the doorway," Nat said, pushing her pawn forward to complete her pawn chain. "An older woman came out the door and handed me a mug of hot tea. She invited me in. She told me that she had just finished praying to God, asking him to share his Will, and then she looked up and saw me standing there. She gave me a bed for the night. We talked in the morning. She listened to my situation. I ended up staying with her until I finished high school and could join the Army."

She considered Ashlynn's move and slid another pawn to reinforce her chain and create more space.

"At every turn," Nat said. "He was there for me because of my faith in Him."

"You play very well," Ashlynn said as she moved.

"I've loved this game as long as I can remember," Nat said, placing her queen on the square in front of her king, anticipating Aisling's castle.

Nat could tell that her story didn't convince Ashlynn of God's existence. She would have to come to God in her own way.

"Do you think Jonas will be alright?" Ashlynn said after a move.

"No," Nat said. "He won't be alright for a while."

***

Jonathan Williams sat back in frustration as he was killed again.

"Time for a new server," he said in disgust.

"I'll go get some snacks," his friend stood up. "Find one with less hackers."

"Already on it," Jonathan agreed.

He selected a server and joined, geared up, and ran out of the spawning area. He managed to kill two players with his shotgun and knifed a third. This was going way better, he thought, smiling. He ran back to spawn and grabbed a medi-pack and more ammo.

It was good to be away from his house. His mom had seemed to dial up her attempts to bring him back to God lately, and it seemed she was getting Davey to gang up on him now too. He found respite here as often as possible. His friend's parents didn't have a single cross in their house.

Jonathan died, and a few seconds later, he respawned, selecting a different weapon. His friend was carrying snacks and walking back from the kitchen but had stopped mid-stride, watching the TV screen his parents had on.

"What the fuck?" his friend said loudly. "Johnny! You have to see this!"

Jonathan looked over from the gaming console, surprised by his friend's tone.

"What the fuck?" his friend said again. "Isn't that your

house?"

"What?" Jonathan walked up.

On the screen was a house on fire.

His house.

"Oh my god! What?!" Jonathan said. He ran back to the gaming area and picked up his phone. He had missed calls from his mother, and brother, and another missed call was from an unknown number. He checked his messages. There were two picture chats from Davey over forty minutes ago.

"Johnny, somethings happening"

"I'm scared"

Jonathan recognized Davey's closet in the pictures. He's hiding from something. Oh my god, Jonathan thought, typing frantically. Oh my god, please be okay!

"Are you ok?" he sent, waiting for the read receipt.

It showed as undelivered as the seconds ticked by.

Jonathan, feeling frantic, checked his other messages—nothing. But there was a text from an unknown stranger.

"Jonathan, this is Daryl. I'm a friend of your dad's. You're in danger! Do not message anyone, including your family."

Fuck that, Jonathan thought, switching back to his usual app. His DM to Davey was still unopened.

Another text banner flashed on top of his screen.

They're coming! Get out of there!

It was from Daryl, whoever that was. Jonathan looked out the window and noticed a car's headlights approaching the street. It was getting dark outside. What the fuck is going on, he thought. Who the fuck is coming? David, look at your fucking phone! He had an idea and switched to the family phone tracker. His heart sank as Mom and Davey's pins showed they were at the house. Last seen 38 minutes ago. Dad's pin was east of Denver less than a minute ago.

Jonathan switched to his messages and clicked on his dad.

"What's going on?????" he sent as he saw several cars lining up and stopping outside the house.

Men were getting out.

Men with guns.

"Holy fucking shit!" Jonathan yelled as he stumbled backward. Suddenly, the glass window sprayed inward. Jonathan protected his face instinctively as he hit the ground. He scrambled up to see his friend toppling, the snacks flung everywhere. Two bright red spots grew on his chest. His face was surprised, and he gurgled as he fell to the floor. Jonathan ran to him, crouching.

"Oh my God! Are you okay?"

His friend tried to respond, but blood came out of his mouth, and he sputtered.

"What's happening?" screamed his friend's mother, who entered the room.

Her head snapped back, and three large bloody spots appeared on her white shirt. He glanced back at the window just in time to see a soldier appear with an assault rifle. Jonathan gathered his feet from under him and jumped out of the room, a spray of bullets following him.

Jonathan scrambled to his feet.

He sprinted down the hall.

Bullets tore through the house all around him.

On instinct, he ran to the back of the house and out the side door.

He jumped the fence and ran through the neighbor's yard, stealing a glance back.

Nothing.

He struggled over another fence and ran through the street.

He saw a shed through an open gate.

He slammed the gate behind him and scrambled inside.

As soon as he closed the door, he vomited. His lungs were on fire.

He checked his phone.

The screen was cracked.

Still no texts from David or his father.

Daryl had sent another text.

"You need to move," it said. "The shed isn't safe."

"What the...what the fuck is going on?" Jonathan wheezed.

His phone rang. It was the same number as the text. It was loud. He fumbled to answer it and turned down the volume.

"H-hello?" he answered.

"Jonathan, you need to move."

"Who the fuck are you?! What is going on? My mother, Davey...I...I..."

"Jonathan, I'm trying to help you. I'm Daryl. I work with your father. Take deep breaths. You have to calm down. Your heart rate is too high."

"How the fuck do you know that?"

"Your smartwatch, Jonathan. We don't have time. Listen to

me if you want to live. You need to leave the shed and head north."

"I can't," Jonathan said. "I can't! I have to go home. I have to see if my brother is okay. My—my mom..."

"Breathe, Jonathan. Stand up and leave the shed. Now!"

Jonathan was shocked by the urgency in Daryl's voice. He automatically did what was commanded. Gingerly, he opened the shed door. He took two steps.

"No," Daryl said. "Turn left, go north."

Jonathan turned and walked, his legs heavy and unwilling to move.

"Good," Daryl said. "Your heart rate is decreasing to optimal levels."

Jonathan wasn't listening. He was looking around, peering through the dark, but he was having trouble making anything out.

"Do you have your headphones, Jonathan?"

Searching his pockets, Jonathan almost fell as he tripped over a small shrub.

"No," he said. "Fuck!"

"You'll need to climb this fence, then immediately go left," Daryl said. "Then check in with me."

Jonathan put the phone in his pocket and climbed the fence. It seemed easier than before, and his body was not as stiff. He landed behind a row of tall bushes. Turning left, he lifted the phone to his ear again.

"Good," Daryl said. "They lost you."

"How do you know?" Jonathan asked.

"That information is not relevant at present. Now listen to me carefully."

***

"You also play well," Nat said, reviewing the board. "What's your elo?"

"My rating? I don't know," Ashlynn responded. "I've never played in a tournament or online."

Nat decided now was as good a time as any to move her own knight to a more central position.

"My grandfather taught me some of the openings," Ashlynn continued, pushing a pawn forward. This made Nat's intended move slightly less effective, Ashlynn thought.

"Your grandfather must have been pretty decent," Nat said,

moving her knight again. "Did you two play a lot?"

"We played every day the summer before he died," Ashlynn said. "I only visited my mother's father that once. My dad's father passed away when I was very small."

"So," Nat said. "You've only played for one summer?"

"Yeah."

"Two years ago..." Nat said.

"Twen....er, two or three years ago, yeah," Ashlynn said, cringing inwardly. I've got to be more careful than that!

"Well," Nat said. "You're a stronger player than my high school kids."

"You teach high school?"

"No," Nat said. She paired her knights on the third row. "Just chess club."

Ashlynn slid her king one square to the right.

Nat nodded and responded. Ashlynn took stock of the board overall and realized it would have been better to move her bishop off the back row to reinforce her attack on Nat's pawn chain. Now things were going to get messy. It's not a problem, she thought. It's a matter of calculation.

"What do you think of Jonas' idea?" Ashlynn asked, running through several exchange scenarios in her mind.

"About the President?"

"Yeah."

"That was the drink talking," Nat replied, watching Ashlynn calculate. It's too soon for that, she thought. It's all about the position mid-game. She wondered if that was the young girl's strength. Maybe she had the brute-force ability to calculate moves. That might make the end game challenging. Just meant Nat had to rock the middle.

"We have to do something," Ashlynn said.

"No," Nat frowned. "We don't."

Ashlynn took a deep breath and took the pawn Nat had just moved. She was surprised when Nat did not take it back and instead moved her queen, averting the bloodbath. Ashlynn scrutinized the bishop she had wanted to move earlier. She hated that her queen was so trapped.

"You don't know what's at stake," Ashlynn said.

"The whole country."

"There's that too," Ashlynn said, taking Nat's pawn and attacking her queen.

"What do you mean?" Nat took the pawn with her queen.

"Jonas' family is missing," Ashlynn said. "But what if they're alive? And there's Becky."

"Who is Becky?" Nat asked.

They played as they spoke, and now Ashlynn did not like what she saw as she studied the board. Nat had more space, so Ashlynn considered her own position to be the weaker. Unless...

She moved her queen.

"Becky is my friend," Ashlynn said as Nat considered the board. "She is six and has cancer. Back in that interrogation room where you found me, Dolion showed me that he had her in his office. He is using her as leverage to get what he wants from me. If I do nothing, Becky could die."

Nat looked up at Ashlynn, her fingers on a piece, her brow furrowed.

"He wouldn't have to do much," Ashlynn continued. "He just needs to withhold the cure from her for a few months, and the cancer will kill her."

Nat moved the piece she was holding.

"Fucking asshole," Nat muttered. "The POTUS, kidnapping a child."

"I can't leave her to die," Ashlynn said.

They played silently for a stretch.

"That's all different from what Jonas was saying," Nat said, finally, "I think we can work on a plan to rescue Becky, but that's as far as I go."

Nat moved her other rook to the b-file, double-attacking Ashlynn's knight. Uh oh, Ashlynn thought. I didn't see that! Ugh! She calculated a few possible scenarios.

She also considered what Nat was saying.

"I agree," Ashlynn said, sacrificing her bishop.

"There was..." she started. "A lot of violence last night. Did you have to kill people?"

Nat nodded.

"Feds," she said somberly.

"How do you feel about that?" Ashlynn asked.

Nat looked up, directly into Ashlynn's eyes.

"When Daryl showed us the footage of the Feds killing an innocent retired general at the convention, and it became clear they were going to kill Jonas execution style—they ceased being Federal Agents for me and became murderers. I saw them with the gun to Jonas' head. I didn't kill anyone who didn't first present lethal intent."

Ashlynn nodded.

Nat looked back to the board grimly.

"Do you know where Becky is being held?" Nat asked, sliding her rook forward.

"Ashlynn," Daryl said in her mind. "I don't know where Becky is yet, but I have discovered that Jonas' son Jonathan is alive."

"He is?"

"Yes, but he's in danger. I'm helping him escape now."

"Good. What about the others? Chris and David?"

"There's a high probability that they did not survive."

Ashlynn gasped and glanced at Jonas, still asleep on the couch.

"What?" Nat asked.

"I—" Ashlynn said. "I thought I heard him say something."

Nat moved, and Ashlynn responded.

"You seem distracted," Nat said, taking Ashlynn's knight with her queen.

"I think," Ashlynn said. "We may need to go to New Mexico."

Ashlynn tipped over her king.

"We should be in the area," Ashlynn said. "In case Jonas' family needs help."

"Changing course," Daryl said over the intercom.

The plane took a long, steep bank.

Nat shook Ashlynn's hand, curiosity in her eyes.

CHAPTER 23

Jonas woke feeling extremely nauseous. He sat up, his head spinning. He saw Nat and Ashlynn shaking hands over a chess game on the table between two seats. He rushed past them to the bathroom, not looking at anything but his intended destination. Nat watched him with a grim, knowing expression.

"Jonas," Ashlynn said, but he did not acknowledge her.

He burst into the bathroom, barely making it to the toilet in time. The vomit stung where it touched his split lip, and it felt like his eyes tried to bulge out of his face. When he finally stopped heaving, he intended to stand up and find a bed to sleep in—but his body wouldn't listen. He was barely aware as he slid the rest of the way to the floor and passed out, his knees curled to his chest in the cramped room.

He woke a short time later, though he couldn't remember how he had gotten into the unfamiliar bathroom. He checked his phone. He had no service.

Oh, right, he thought groggily. I'm on a plane.

He connected to the plane's Wi-Fi and looked around, not recognizing anything. This isn't one of the SolviNext planes, he realized.

He pulled himself up and groaned. There was vomit that smelled of alcohol in the toilet. He puked again, though it was mostly saliva. Flushing and closing the lid, he pulled himself onto the toilet and sat.

The bathroom was small, so he could reach everything from where he sat. He opened the cabinet in front of him, scrounging for something that would help with the throbbing behind his eyes. He found a bottle of painkillers and dumped a couple of pills into his hand. Small disposable cups were in the dispenser by the sink. He filled one and swallowed the pills. He tried to stand, but the world seemed to spin around him. He had to sit down suddenly, making the toilet lid creak.

He checked his phone again. There was a news flash at the

top that caught his eye. The news widget had a photo of his house.

It was on fire.

His heart tried to climb out of his throat.

Jonas jabbed his finger on the article link repeatedly. The phone responded slowly over the slow airplane connection.

"C'mon!" he growled, mashing the screen.

It turned blank.

He mashed some more.

Finally, the headline appeared.

Breaking: Cancer Cure Billionaire Mansion Burns. Two bodies found.

Oh my god! Jonas clicked repeatedly, waiting for the article to load past the title. When it did, he skimmed it quickly. It quoted a post by Dolion.

President Dolion
@POTUS
So sorry to hear about @JonasWilliams. Heard it was a matter of negligence. You'd think a CEO would know better.

Fucker, Jonas thought, and scrolled further.

He found what he was dreading.

"...two victims of the blaze have been found and Identified by authorities as Chris and David Williams, wife and son of billionaire Jonas Williams. No other victims have been found, but the search continues. The cause of the fire is still under investigation..."

Jonas dropped his phone unconsciously and began trembling. On the floor, his phone buzzed again, but he didn't notice. There was a roaring in his ears, getting louder.

"Chris! Oh, Davey! My son!" he sobbed, fists clenching his hair.

Jonas screamed.

***

Jonathan stumbled through the bushes into a small park. He cast a glance over his shoulder as he ran but couldn't see anything through the trees. He looked forward just in time to avoid tripping on a cement curb.

"Who are they?" he asked. "Who the fuck are they?"

"Focus, Jonathan," Daryl said. "Do you see the parking lot

ahead?"

"Yeah."

"Go to the blue sedan," Daryl said. "It's waiting for you."

Jonathan got in the car.

"Don't talk to the driver," Daryl said. "The less she knows the safer she'll be. I used the name 'Matt' to book the ride."

"Going downtown?" the driver asked.

"Uh, yeah," Jonathan said.

"Cool," she said, peering at him in the mirror. "Do your parents know?"

Jonathan swallowed.

"Of course," he lied.

She seemed skeptical. "Who's your dad?"

"His name is Jo-"

"No!" Daryl said over the phone. "Matt!"

"Sorry," Jonathan said. "It's Matt."

The driver looked at him and then at the phone. She turned and seemed to fish for something in the front seat. When she turned back around, she had written on a notepad.

"Are you safe??"

Jonathan stared at the pad, wondering what to do. What's really happening to me? I don't know this Daryl guy. Mom. What's happened to her? He remembered the way blood came out instead of words when his friend tried to speak. The world had gone mad. Of course, he wasn't safe...

"What's going on?" Daryl asked. "Why aren't you moving?"

Jonathan shook his head, and the driver's eyes went wide. She wrote on the pad.

Police?

Jonathan instantly nodded. Yes, he thought. I can trust the police. I can't trust anyone else. The driver nodded and grabbed her phone, entering the address of the nearest police station. She started driving.

"Oh, good," Daryl said. "You're moving now. You are quiet, Jonathan. Are you okay?"

"Y-yes," Jonathan said. The driver's expression was anxious and worried in the mirror. "Yes, we're moving now."

"Okay," Daryl said. "I'm having this driver take you downtown. There, you'll meet another driver who will take you to the airport, where you'll get on a plane to be with your father."

"M-my father," Jonathan said, his stomach sinking. His hands were shaking, and he was unable to sit still. He couldn't even control his voice. "He's a-at th-the airport?"

"He's en route," Daryl said.

"H-how do I know I can t-trust you?" Jonathan asked.

"I told you," Daryl said. "I work...wait, the driver took a wrong turn. Jonathan, tell—"

Jonathan hung up the phone and closed his eyes.

The police, he thought. They'll know what to do.

***

"Nat, Ashlynn," Daryl said over the intercom. "We have a problem."

Both women looked up from the chessboard.

"What is it?" Ashlynn asked.

"I've lost contact with Jonathan," Daryl said. "I think he may be going to the police."

"Wouldn't they help him?" Ashlynn asked, then stood. "No, wait. They'll just hold him there until Dolion's men appear."

"Who is Jonathan?" Nat asked.

"Jonas' son," Ashlynn replied.

"His family is alive, then? That's good news."

"No," Daryl said. "Just Jonathan. Jonas' wife Chris and youngest son David have been officially reported dead."

"*Dios mío*," Nat muttered.

She looked at the bathroom door. They could hear Jonas sobbing inside, and then he screamed. Ashlynn and Nat caught each other's eyes and rushed to the bathroom door. Ashlynn started knocking.

"Go away," Jonas yelled from within.

"Jonas," Ashlynn said. "Your—"

"I said go away!"

"Let me," Nat said.

Ashlynn stood aside and Nat pounded the door.

"Jonathan needs you, Jonas!" Nat yelled. "He's alive!"

"What?"

The door opened, and Jonas stepped out. He took in the plane's cabin, clearly disoriented. His eyes locked on Nat's.

"What did you say?" He reached out and shook her. Nat gently but firmly took his hands off her shoulders.

"I said Jonathan is alive, and he needs your help."

"How do you know? Where is he?"

Ashlynn noticed Jonas' phone buzzing on the floor of the

restroom.

"Jonas!" she said. "You have a message from him."

She picked up his phone and handed it to him.

Jonas took the phone and opened the message.

"What's going on?????" it read.

Jonas called his son.

"Dad?"

"Jonathan! Oh, thank god!"

"Dad, where are you? What happened to Mom!?"

Jonas grimaced. His mind reeled trying to find a way to avoid answering his son's question. What his son wanted to hear was that everything was okay. Which was exactly what Jonas wanted to say. But everything was not okay. There was no way out.

"She's gone, Johnny," he said, and the tears hit him again even as he tried to be strong. "She's gone."

Ashlynn and Nat looked at each other. Both women had tears in their eyes. Ashlynn brought her hand to her mouth and looked away. Nat folded her arms over her stomach.

"Davey....?" Jonathan's voice cracked.

"God help me," Jonas said, sinking to his knees. "He's...go... go—God help me!"

Nat squatted down by Jonas and put her arm around him. Ashlynn did the same.

"Ashlynn. Ashlynn!" Daryl said. She realized he'd been trying to gain her attention in her mind.

"What is it, Daryl?"

"We still have a problem. The car will arrive at the police station soon. If he gets into police custody, there is almost no chance of recovering him."

Ashlynn tapped Nat, who locked teary eyes with her over Jonas' head. Ashlynn pointed at her wrist, and Nat nodded.

"Jonas," Ashlynn said. "I'm so sorry, but we don't have time. We have to get Jonathan out of there."

"W-what?" Jonathan asked. "Who's that?"

"That's Ashlynn," Jonas said, trying to regain composure. "You met her at Dr. Ramsey's funeral."

"Oh."

"Where are you, Johnny?" Jonas asked, standing up.

"I'm on my way to the police station."

"What!?" Jonas yelled, shocked. "No! You can't go to the police!"

"W-what? W-why?"

"Because they'll just hand you over to the people that are trying to kill you!"

"I...but...I..."

"Listen to me, Jonathan," Jonas said urgently. "You can't go to the police. You have to tell the driver to take you somewhere else."

"Downtown," Daryl said over the intercom. "There's a ride waiting for him there."

"Daryl?" Jonathan asked.

"Yes," Jonas said. "That's Daryl. How did you know?"

"Shit," Jonathan said. "I - I. He... He helped me, I guess."

Jonas looked up at the plane's ceiling, the speaker above his head, and mouthed, "Thank you!"

Ashlynn wondered if Jonas was saying that for Daryl or as a prayer to God.

"Jonathan," Jonas said. "You have to listen to Daryl. He'll help you."

"You'll be at the airport?" Jonathan said. His voice was still shaking.

Jonas glanced at Ashlynn, and she nodded.

"Yes," Jonas said. "We're on our way there now."

"Dad," said Jonathan, "I don't know what to say to the driver."

"Let me talk to him," said Jonas

"Your name is Matt," Daryl said, surprising Jonas.

***

"Would someone tell me what the fuck is going on?" President Dolion yelled.

In front of him stood very important people, all heads of their respective departments. None of them showed any visible signs of weakness, but none of them wanted to be the first to say anything. The Oval Office was deadly quiet for several long, painful seconds.

"You," the President said, growling and trying to check his anger, "Stop looking confused as a goat on astroturf and kindly tell me your fucking department is doin' more than gettin' sandpapered by a little girl!"

The Secretary of Homeland Security paled.

"We're still assessing the situation, sir."

Dolion picked up the closest thing on his desk and hurled it at the man's face, though it missed by inches as he flinched away.

"Get out!" Dolion yelled. "You're fuckin' fired!"

Everyone watched him leave, shifting uneasily.

"Fuckin' pussy," Dolion growled, picking up a Presidential Pen from his desk and squeezing it.

They all stared at the wall ahead. One swallowed hard.

Without warning, Dolion slammed his hand on his desk.

"How the fuck can a helpless little girl, with no military training, handcuffed and all tore up after six weeks of processing, get past thirty-fuckin'-three armed and trained agents? How does one highly trained Secret Service professional have a hole in his head, and the other has his throat crushed by a fist-sized bruise, with no goddamn blood or video footage, or even a fuckin' print of the individuals who did this?"

The pen snapped between his fists, leaking black ink onto his hands and the desk. The President didn't seem to notice.

"Tell me that!" he bellowed. "From a mostly starved, eighty-pound girl child!?"

"She must have had help, sir," said one advisor.

"No fuckin' shit!" Dolion roared, chunking the pen at him. It bounced off the man's chest, splattering ink on his perfect, highly decorated uniform. The man didn't flinch. At least that one has a fucking spine, Dolion thought.

"But," Dolion continued. "There's no one on the fuckin' cameras but our girl."

They stared straight ahead without answering. Sweating.

"You all are supposed to be the pinnacle of US intelligence and military power, but here you are, and you don't know which fuckin' end is up!"

"Sir, with a little more time..."

"Time!" Dolion roared, "Jesus!"

Dolion slammed his ink-stained fist on the table.

"I want results by this afternoon," he yelled. "Or heads are gonna' roll!"

"Sir," one of them said. "We're crossing the line. The military isn't supposed to be involved with domestic affairs. The constitution forbids such an action, Mr. President."

Dolion rose and planted himself in front of the man. There was sweat on his brow, but his chest was puffed out with pride. The ink splatter was spreading across his uniform.

"It don't matter how it *was*," Dolion said in a deadly soft voice. "What matters is how it *is*. Let me explain how it is, General. *I* am the fucking constitution now!"

Dolion put his face an inch away from the man's, his nose crinkling as he could smell the older man's breath.

"I know about your secret little talks, General. I know what you and your buddies are planning. Do I look the least bit worried to you?"

Now the resolve shifted into fear in the man's eyes.

"Do I?" Dolion repeated dangerously.

"No, sir," the man said.

Dolion straightened the man's collar and brushed non-existent dust off of the stars.

Dolion continued.

"I have the backing of the American people. They might not like some of my habits, but they believe in me. They love me. They'll stand for me no matter what. Do you think they'd stand for your little scheme? Ha! You'd be a dangling crow feeder before you can say 'caught in your own loop.'"

Dolion put his hands on the General's shoulders and glanced around his head and nodded.

"Not that I'd ever let you get that far, you understand."

The man stumbled as two soldiers in full tactical gear pulled him backward and put a bag over his head. A depression formed in the bag as the man sucked in air to scream. The sound was intensely muffled.

Dolion smiled as they took the man away. The others watched in horror.

The President regarded them.

"I've said it before, my friends. Even if I killed someone on public TV, nothing would stop me."

One laughed uncomfortably. Dolion frowned and began speaking with increasing intensity. Another reached into his pocket and took out his phone.

"And like I said. If I don't get results today, heads will fuckin' roll."

"Sir," the Director of the CIA said, reading from his phone. "I have a couple of leads."

"And?"

"I've been informed that we have a lead on Jonas' son generated by GED.ai."

"Good!" Dolion shouted. "Looks like the fuckin' machine is dependable, at least. More than I can say for you fools!"

"The boy is en route to the airport," the Director continued. "It looks like a plane is there, chartered from Denver around the time of Mister Williams' escape. He's likely aboard."

"Good!"

Dolion walked back to his desk, a contemplative expression on his face. He rubbed his hands together as he sat.

"What's the other lead?"

"GED.ai also identified a possible connection Mr. Williams made with a Latino family in Detroit prior to the debacle. There is a military vet in the family."

"Ain't that the bee's knees," said Dolion, slapping his thigh.

The CIA Director remained silent. Data, including the vet's name and whereabouts, was missing from the intelligence report, and no one could figure out why. For now, he thought it was best to say nothing about that and let the team look into it further.

"Sounds like y'all best be fixin' to go huntin'!" Dolion said.

They all started shuffling toward the door.

"How long before GED.ai can give our dearly departed Daryl a run for his money?" Dolion asked, grinning.

The men stopped walking and exchanged questioning glances at each other. The CIA Director remained quiet. As the seconds passed, Dolion's mood soured.

"Sir," one of the other Directors said tentatively. "We have no way of quantifying what Daryl's capabilities were—"

"Get the fuck out!" the President interrupted with a bellow, reaching for something else to throw.

***

Jonas ran as soon as the plane's stairs were low enough. The car was still coming to a stop as Jonas reached for and pulled open the door. Jonathan barely had time to say anything before his father embraced him.

The moon had risen, a small sliver hanging over the airport in the pre-dawn light. Even with the plane's engines set to ground idle, the sound was deafening.

"We have to go!" Nat yelled. "They'll catch up eventually."

They all walked back to the plane by the light of the plane's exterior courtesy lights.

When they had boarded the plane and sat down, Jonathan looked around.

"Where's Daryl?" he asked.

"He's flying the plane," Ashlynn said.

"That's a good question. Where are you, Daryl?" Nat asked. She glanced at Jonathan and added, "He's flying the plane remotely."

"I'm secluded in the Rocky Mountains," Daryl said over the intercom.

Jonas regarded Ashlynn.

"You didn't tell them?" he asked.

Ashlynn shrugged.

"Tell us what?" Nat asked as the plane taxied to the runway.

"Daryl isn't a person," Ashlynn said. "He's an AI."

"As in..." Nat clarified. "Artificial Intelligence?"

Ashlynn nodded.

Jonathan's eyes roamed over the plane as if the walls might be hiding a supercomputer.

The plane started to accelerate for takeoff.

"I'm not sure how I feel about flying now," Nat said, her hands clenched in fists.

"Daryl got us here, Nat," Ashlynn said. "It's fine."

Nat grimaced.

"Ashlynn," Jonas said. "Since you're being honest, can you tell me? Longevity. Did you figure out how to make people live longer?"

"My mother did," Ashlynn corrected. "Yes."

"She didn't....you didn't use it on yourself?"

So that's it. The way Jonas asked the question caused Ashlynn to realize that he might suspect she had reversed her age, but he didn't know about the clone and the transplant.

She shook her head.

"It doesn't work that way," Ashlynn said. "Anyway, you were there. It was an open casket."

Ashlynn folded her arms over her stomach, feeling ill. Jonas nodded solemnly, turning away.

"I'm sorry," he said.

That settles that, Ashlynn thought. She sat, but the queasiness didn't leave and was now coupled with a tightness in her chest.

"Daryl," Ashlynn thought, frustrated. "Why does my body keep feeling ill like this at random? Are these side effects from my...recent trauma?"

"It's not random, Ashlynn," Daryl said. "And no, the symptoms are unrelated to your experience at the government facility. They are psychosomatic."

"I'm not making myself sick," Ashlynn objected. "That's preposterous! That's...."

"It's a well-documented disorder," Daryl said, "caused by mental or emotional distress. You are experiencing cognitive dissonance because you uphold the lie about who you are and because you are worried about the safety of the people on this plane. You are terrified about what could happen to Becky."

"Daryl," she thought indignantly, latching onto the first thing he said and ignoring the rest. "I...I don't want to complicate things more than they are."

"Understood."

"I have no idea how they would all react to my procedure."

"I can do a psychological profile and scenario analysis for each," Daryl replied. "The interactions between all of you have become increasingly complex, but I can also do a conversational scenario analysis. This could help you navigate the difficulties. Would you like me to proceed?"

Ashlynn did not respond. She wasn't listening. Am I really making myself sick? Has that affected me my whole life? A string of memories flooded through her mind as she recalled her past physical illnesses. When Darrell moved away, she stayed home from school because of a stomachache. When she failed an exam, she had headaches and digestive issues for weeks. When her parents died...

She noticed her fist was clenching, her fingers growing white as they compressed. She was doubled over; her abdomen felt as though it had been impaled by a spike of ice. An all-too-familiar pain. Why? I don't have time to figure this out right now! She mentally relaxed her fist.

"Daryl," she thought. She gritted her teeth. "Make the pain go away."

"I cannot," Daryl said. "My prime directives do not allow me to alter your consciousness in any way, even upon request."

"So," Ashlynn replied, taking a deep and ragged breath. "I have to deal with it myself."

Apparently, I spent a lifetime suppressing emotions only to have them psychosomatically manifest. How did I overlook this before? Now, here I am, getting psychotherapy from my AI on a plane in front of everyone.

Nat was watching her. Ashlynn chuckled uneasily and held her hands up in confusion. She felt a tickle on her cheek and brushed at it. She stared at her wet finger. Another tear fell onto her hand. Another. They were neither cold nor hot, just wet. My hands are shaking, she observed. Nat's expression grew softer.

"Daryl," she thought. "Block the…"

She trailed off. Nat had stood and moved toward her. As she continued to cry, Nat wordlessly embraced her.

"No," Daryl said. "It's better if you feel it."

And for the first time in a long time, Dr. Aisling Ramsey let the memories and emotions in. Nat sat beside her and embraced her as she cried for the loss of her parents. She thought of the children in the cancer center and cried all the harder as she remembered every child she had lost.

"Tell me about them," Daryl said in her mind. "I'm curious."

Jonas looked away from Ashlynn, his throat dry. I'm a jerk for bringing up her mother, he thought as he watched Nat soothe her. Nat never looked at Jonas, which made him feel worse. Chris would probably be hugging her, too. Doing something to help. Oh, Chris. I didn't deserve you!

"I'm sorry," he said again.

Nobody seemed to hear.

He turned and started looking for something to drink, ignoring the water bottles. He didn't notice Jonathan watching everything. Watching him.

CHAPTER 24

Nat lifted the shade and looked out the window. The clouds were sliding by below the plane, stretching out toward the horizon in the morning sun. The wing glistened as far below the sun turned the clouds a brilliant pink.

Jonas was sitting in his chair with a hand over his eyes. Jonathan was in the seat behind him, asleep against a window, his head tilted back and mouth open. Ashlynn also slept, her head in Nat's lap.

She's been holding it all in, Nat thought. It had barely been 24 hours since Nat had rescued Ashlynn from the government facility. The bruises on Ashlynn's face were still deepening, becoming visible through the layer of foundation Nat had applied earlier. Nat could see that she'd been tortured by Dina's operation, and she suspected that she was likely still dealing with the loss of her mother.

Nat ran her fingers through Ashlynn's red curls.

"Rest, *chica*," Nat whispered.

Ashlynn's raw emotion had been deep and moving. Old pain there, Nat thought. She wondered if Ashlynn had as complicated a relationship with Dr. Ramsey as Nat did with her own mother. Despite their challenges, Nat knew she would be devastated if she lost her own mother.

Jonas groaned and removed his hand from his eyes, catching her glance.

Yeah, Nat thought, moving her gaze toward Jonathan. Parents are complicated.

"You're not going to try to sleep?" Nat asked.

"My dreams are worse than real life," Jonas croaked. He scoffed. "If that's possible."

"You have to sleep sometime," Nat replied. "You need to be strong—for your son."

"Strong," Jonas sneered. "Easy for you to say."

Nat's lips compressed.

Jonas cast about as if looking for something, avoiding her

eyes.

"Nat," he said, a thought occurring to him. "I've been meaning to ask you something."

"What?"

"That stuff Cici said about the camera vans. Do you think your family is...safe? While you're away?"

Nat felt a chill as she remembered the truck and the spray paint on her parents' house. Oh shit, she thought. I had completely forgotten about that.

"I can hire security guards for your family," he said. "If you like."

"Yes," Nat said, feeling a sense of relief. "Thank you, Jonas."

"Sure," Jonas said, sitting back in his chair and pulling out his phone. "Nothing's more important than family."

Nat nodded. Her eyes moved to Jonathan. Jonas was clearly hurting. Pain could blind people. Will he hear anything I say? He's helping me with my family—I have to try.

"Jonas," she said carefully. "Your son needs you."

Jonas put his phone down.

"You think I don't know that?" he said, more heatedly than he meant to.

He took a breath, shaking his head, and continued typing on his phone. Nat shook her head too. You'll push him away if you're too afraid to lose him, she thought. The image of Cici in Fiji came to her mind. Just like I did.

Nat felt her phone vibrate.

It was a message from Raoul.

"Hey, sis, check this out."

Nat clicked the link.

"Hey, y'all," Alé said, her face and makeup impeccable. Nat noticed a familiar rainbow flag on the social media video post. "Jus' wanted to say I stand for your rights. Every one of you. What's happening is wrong, and we gotta stand against it!"

Nat let out the breath she didn't know she was holding. As she looked into her sister's eyes, Nat let the video loop many times.

It felt like Alé was talking directly to her.

"'Bout time, *mana*," Nat muttered—but she was smiling, and her heart felt a little lighter.

There were five more posts from Alé about gay rights, criticizing the new gay registration law. The Truth and Freedom party had passed it, and Dolion was expected to sign it.

Nat shuddered.

She resumed pulling her fingers through Ashlynn's hair. The young woman's mouth had opened as she slept. When all this is done, Nat thought, I might need to move out of the country too.

Maybe Fiji...

***

"Tell me about them," Daryl said. "I'm curious."

Aisling shifted painfully in the hospital bed. She was exhausted. Her thin limbs fought the movement like heavy wooden boards. I need to get back to the lab, she thought. Or the plane? Where am I? The thought faded as a sharp pain lanced through her. The effects of the last round of chemo were taking too long to wear off.

She was overcome with hopelessness as she recalled the failure in the lab a few days ago. She was no closer to the cure, and half a decade of research had been wasted. There were complications with the clone. The same technique that forestalled neurogenesis, disabling brain growth in the clone, had also caused the nerves in the body to become malformed. The parasympathetic nervous system was barely functioning.

"What's the point?" she whispered. "All of this will amount to the same result—my death."

People have been working on a cure for cancer since the dawn of modern medicine. What made me think I could do it in the few short years before I died?

"It's because you're just as selfish as everyone else," a male voice echoed in her mind.

Who had said that? It didn't matter. Nothing mattered.

Something shifted.

In the manner of dreams, Ashlynn suddenly stood by her former self. Dr. Aisling Ramsey had tears streaming down her face as she stared blankly, unseeing, at the hospital wall.

"It's a good thing you stuck it out," Daryl said, appearing beside her.

Ashlynn tried to take her former self's hands into hers, tried to comfort Aisling, but her hands passed through.

"This is a memory," Daryl said.

"Yes."

"You were suffering," he said empathetically.

"I was..." Ashlynn said. "I...I was close to giving up."

She turned and looked at the door. A nurse was standing

there. Ashlynn had known she would be.

"My nurse knew, I think," Ashlynn said. "She knew I was slipping. So, one day when it was particularly bad, I...I looked up, and..."

Suddenly, a little boy stood next to the bed. He was about five years old. He had no hair.

Aisling's blank eyes locked onto the child's.

"I'm Brandon," the boy said, smiling. "What's your name?"

"Brandon," Ashlynn repeated as she tried to embrace the boy.

Her arms went through him. Ashlynn sank to the floor, and then Daryl was there, holding her.

"The nurse was standing in the doorway, smiling at us," Ashlynn continued. Her eyes were transfixed on Aisling and the boy. "I vaguely remember the nurse, but this beautiful boy had my attention. In that moment, I forgot about the pain."

As she spoke, the boy reached up and put his hand into Aisling's. Ashlynn could feel the touch and warmth through the memory.

"It'll be okay," Brandon said, and Aisling's surprised face broke into a smile.

The scene faded into other memories.

"He visited me every day," Ashlynn said. "Sometimes, his sister would be there, too, and we would play together. We... we daydreamed. I promised I would take him to a theme park to meet his favorite character for his sixth birthday."

Ashlynn closed her eyes, crying as the images blurred around her.

"He died," she sobbed. "Leukemia. He passed away three weeks before his birthday."

Ashlynn shuddered and opened her eyes, speaking to Daryl, who still held her.

"His sister still writes me every year."

Now Aisling was being helped into her wheelchair, resolve on her face.

"I promised myself that day," Ashlynn said. "The day he died, I promised that I would never stop pursuing the cure as long as I lived. It gave me purpose. Something to live for. Not only for me. For everyone. For the kids. For Brandon."

"And from that point on," she continued, "I visited the children's ward at least once a week. They...they became the children I could never have. And every time one of them...

every time...every time one...left us...my heart would break all over again."

Daryl rubbed her back, holding her as she cried.

"How did you meet Becky?" Daryl asked when her tears seemed to subside. "Why is she special to you?"

Ashlynn sat up, and the scenery shifted.

Aisling was in her wheelchair, rolling slowly down the hallway of the children's ward at the hospital. Her arms were tired and not really strong enough to do the work, but powered wheelchairs weren't allowed for safety reasons and the hospital was understaffed. She found Nurse Kay at the nurse's station, filling medication cups.

"How's it going, Dr. Ash?" Kay said with a smile.

"I'm hanging in there," Aisling said. "Are you the only one here tonight?"

"Yup," Nurse Kay said. "All this overtime is sure helping with the student loans!"

"You need rest," Aisling said, noticing the bags under the young woman's eyes. "You're burning the candle at both ends."

"Yeah, well, sometimes it's tough," Nurse Kay said. "But it's also rewarding to be with the kids."

"I agree wholeheartedly," Aisling said. "Can I help you with anything?"

"Do you think you could help me with Becky over in one-oh-three?"

"Sure," Aisling said. "What do you need?"

"She just needs a friend," Nurse Kay said. "She's got leukemia. Her parents are both working two jobs. She's here alone and has been despondent lately. No one can cheer her up."

Aisling frowned as she listened, then touched Kay's arm, smiling warmly. Kay returned the smile as she continued working.

"I'll see what I can do," Aisling said. "Take care of yourself, okay? Doctor's orders."

"Yes, Doctor," Nurse Kay said, chuckling. "I will."

The memory shifted. Ashlynn and Daryl stood before the room as Aisling let go of one wheel and knocked. There was no answer. She knocked again, before opening the door.

Inside, the room was well-lit. The heart rate monitor was beeping steadily, and Becky lay on her side. Most of her hair had fallen out. She had been crying, but she was lying still now, staring blankly at the wall, one small hand outstretched toward the floor. There was a stuffed rabbit on the floor beside her bed. With the IV on the other side of the bed and the tube already stretched, there was no way she could reach the toy.

Gasping at what she saw, Aisling covered her mouth with both hands before wheeling in as quickly as possible. Ashlynn wished she could lift the toy without her hands passing through it.

"She looks like you," Daryl said softly.

"What?" Ashlynn said.

"Becky looked like she had given up," Daryl said. "Like you had."

Ashlynn felt her heart wrench in her chest.

"Uh oh," Aisling said to Becky.

Slowly, painfully, she reached to the floor and tried to pick up the stuffed rabbit. Becky's eyes followed, taking in Aisling's nearly bald head. The expression of pain on Aisling's face made Ashlynn wince in memory. Aisling was wheezing as she breathed hard from the effort. It was hard to breathe, doubled over that way. Becky noticed the effort, too. The dull look in her eyes was replaced with hope.

"She fell," Becky said weakly.

Aisling stretched for the toy, but it was a little too far. She tried again. Her finger brushed the rabbit's arm. With great effort, Aisling pushed herself as hard as she could, clenching her jaw in determination. She was able to pinch the arm and pull the rabbit toward her.

"You almost got her!" Becky whispered, leaning her head over the side of the bed.

Aisling sat up and took a deep breath. Her face was flushed, pain causing her muscles to spasm.

"Yeah," she said, panting. "We'll get her on the next try."

"Yeah!" Becky said, her voice stronger, her eyes brighter. "You can do it," she said, looking Aisling in the eye.

The comment took Aisling aback. She smiled.

"We just have to try," Aisling said.

She bent over and reached for the toy again. It was closer but more painful than before. When her hand closed around the rabbit's body, Becky gasped.

"You did it!" she squeaked.

Aisling sat up.

She brushed the worn toy off with care, adjusted its

clothing, kissed it on the head, and then handed it to Becky's outstretched arms.

Becky squeezed the rabbit tightly and then held out her arms. Aisling stretched up and hugged them both.

The little girl giggled when they let go.

"I'm Becky," she said. "And this is Bun-Bun."

"I'm Ash," Aisling said, still winded and flushed. "It's nice to meet you."

"I feel..." Ashlynn said to Daryl as they watched the two interact. "I feel like Becky was the first real connection I made."

"How so?" Daryl said. "Didn't you have a connection with Brandon?"

"Yes," Ashlynn said. "But it was he who reached out to me."

"There were other kids too."

"They were all special in their own ways," Ashlynn said. "I often felt awkward with the kids, especially in the beginning. I had no experience. I didn't know what to say. I got better at making the kids laugh. I learned that sometimes they just needed to be held."

"And Becky?"

"In Becky's case," Ashlynn said. "I reached out to her. She was slipping. Somehow, when she watched me struggle to reach for Bun-Bun, it brought her to life."

"You showed her you cared," Daryl observed.

"Yeah."

They watched Becky and Aisling hug.

"I'm sorry, Ashlynn," Daryl said suddenly. "You need to wake up now."

"What?"

"There's a problem."

***

Ashlynn woke and sleepily sat up, wiping her mouth. Her body craved more sleep.

"Are you feeling better?" Nat asked.

"A little," she said. "My dreams were...intense."

"You've been through a lot," Nat said. "You should probably sleep some—"

"We have a problem!"

Daryl's raised voice broke through the cabin, causing Jonathan to jump. There was a thump from the bathroom.

"What?" came Jonas' muffled voice.

"I *hate* it when you say that," Nat groaned, standing and stretching.

She reached to help Ashlynn up. Ashlynn took her hand. Out of habit, she put her other hand to her abdomen but was surprised to find that the pain and nausea were gone.

"So," Nat said. "What's the problem?"

"They have traced Jonathan's ride shares and have determined that he went to the airport."

"So," Ashlynn said. "They know we're in the air?"

"Yes," Daryl replied. "As of a few minutes ago, per flight tracking, two call-signed aircraft are now on an intercept course to us."

"What?" Nat said, alarmed.

"They were on the publicly available radar, heading on an intercept course, and then disappeared. I connected to the local airport radar and can confirm that two bounced-back signals are on the same intercept course."

"Wait, what?" Jonathan said.

"We have incoming," Daryl replied.

"Then we need to get off of this plane immediately!" Nat said.

"You mean with parachutes?" Ashlynn asked, shocked.

"Wait, what?!" Jonathan said more loudly, panic showing on his face.

Nat nodded, and the blood drained from Ashlynn's face at the thought of jumping out of a plane.

Nat began searching under the seats.

"Daryl," she said after checking a couple. "Where are the emergency chutes?"

"There are none, according to this aircraft design specification."

Nat grimaced.

"What?" said Jonas, coming out of the bathroom "What's going on?"

He tucked in his shirt and swayed in the aisle as the plane encountered slight turbulence.

"Any minute now," Nat said, unaffected by the plane's motion. "Our government buddies will show up. If they're nice, they'll escort us to a base, apprehend us, and generally make our lives miserable."

"What if they're not nice?" Jonas asked.

"It won't be an escort," Nat said.

"So..." Jonas said slowly.

"Look," Nat said. "They tried to kill you, and they tried to kill your son. If they think you're on this plane, they have reason to suspect that whoever saved you is aboard with you. In short, they want to kill us. So we need to get out of the air as fast as possible."

They all stared at each other as Nat's words sank in.

"Daryl," Ashlynn said. "Is there anything below us we can land in?"

"Yes," Daryl replied. "It's mostly farmland."

"Can you land us in a field?" Nat asked. "Preferably by a road?"

"Yes," Daryl repeated. "Emergency landings are routine training."

"Buckle up!" Nat yelled.

They all rushed to their seats and buckled in. Nat glanced around. Jonas ran his hand through his hair, looking out the window and then at Jonathan, who sat behind him. The teenager had a wide-eyed expression and sat with his back pressed into his chair, hands white-knuckled on the armrests. Ashlynn sat beside Nat with a worried expression but seemed otherwise calm, which impressed Nat.

The moment stretched.

Jonas' expression turned from worry to puzzled.

"Daryl...?" he began.

Without warning, Daryl rolled the plane.

Everyone involuntarily gripped their armrests harder as it felt like they were being suspended from their seats for a split second. The world outside the windows was upside down.

Sickeningly, the horizon began to tilt up.

The brief feeling of hanging reversed. Abruptly, it felt like they were being squashed into their seats while upside down.

"Oh shit!" Jonathan yelled. "Shit, shit, shit!"

"Daryl!" Jonas yelled, his face going green. "This doesn't feel very 'routine!' What the fuck are you doing?"

"I had to wait until the fighter jets were ten miles behind us," Daryl replied. "Now, I'm performing an oblique dive toward them."

"Toward them!?" Jonas asked. "A dive?"

"Shut up and let him concentrate!" Nat yelled.

"It's quite alright," Daryl replied with eerie calm. "This is a relatively simple maneuver."

The plane felt like it lurched upward harder.

The horizon line outside the window was tilting fast, almost vertical now. It tilted as they dove toward the ground. Both Jonas and Jonathan's faces turned the same shade of green.

"You were flying at Mach point nine," Daryl said. "And they are at Mach one point two and closing at a rate of three hundred thirty-four knots. They have noticed your dive and are now diving to stay on target. Their dive is, of course, shallower than yours as they don't yet know what we're doing. At this rate, they will be able to fire on you soon."

"What?!" Jonas yelled.

"There are mountains ahead. I will fly you between them, which should temporarily disrupt radar contact and vis—"

"Flying in between mountains?! Fuck!" Jonas groaned, his eyes searching for a paper bag. "Okay, shut up, Daryl—I don't want to know!"

"No!" Nat said, her expression amazed and her voice excited. "Don't stop. Tell us what's happening! I want to know!"

"You're crazy!" Jonas yelled.

"They will lose radar and visual contact behind the mountains," Daryl repeated. "Those jets are too agile. If I don't interrupt visuals and radar, they'll see our plan, bleed speed in a high-G turn, and intercept us. If Nat is correct, they will then shoot you down."

The ground outside the window was very close now and was no longer upside down. Nat glanced at Ashlynn, who was breathing quickly.

The horizon lifted upward as the plane started to bank. Nat could see individual joshua trees and other semi-arid desert plants covering the mountains.

"When we reappear from behind the mountains," Daryl continued, "we should surprise them, and then we will blow by beneath them."

Nat's eyes were glued to the window.

The land blurred below.

Daryl performed several consecutive banks through the mountains.

Exhilarated, Nat wished she were in the cockpit to see the view.

Suddenly, she could see the sky outside the window as they came from behind the mountains.

"They see us," Daryl said, "and are turning sharply to merge.

They can't fire because we're too low, and they are too fast."

The cabin lurched to the left.

Everyone but Nat gasped in shock at the sensation.

"We are entering a forward slip to slow down," Daryl explained.

Nat laughed in delight.

She glanced around as their bodies tried to press forward and to the left, straining against the seatbelts. Jonathan clamped his eyes shut, clinging to the chair for dear life. Jonas was hanging over his left leg, dry heaving. Ashlynn was the least frantic. She looked resigned to her fate, whatever it was. Nat felt and heard the landing gear deploy.

There was a sudden loud boom, like an explosion.

Jonas and Jonathan screamed.

"Are they firing at us?" Nat asked.

"No," Daryl replied. "That was a sonic boom. As planned, they mismanaged their rate of closure and overshot us at Mach one point four."

Outside, Nat could see the ground approaching the plane fast. They flew over a road. There were cows in a distant field.

"Brace for landing!" Nat called as the plane shifted out of the slip.

***

The truck driver was thinking about a quick liquor run before heading home while singing along to one of his favorite country tunes when movement caught his eye.

Two fighter jets flipped and turned in the sky.

They flashed from the left side of his windshield to the right.

"Hot damn," he said.

He wondered if there was some kind of aerial show going on. He had taken his kids to see one a few years back.

Suddenly, there was a deafening roar and all the windows of his truck cracked. The back window shattered.

He screeched to a halt, slamming on the brakes and yelling wordlessly.

Then, his ears rang.

A car behind him rammed into the back of his truck.

His head whipped back, slamming into the headrest. He bounced off the back of the seat forward over the steering wheel and his foot came off the brake.

Groggily, he shook his head as his truck rolled forward from the impact.

"What in the—"

Another smaller jet appeared through the cracked glass of his driver side window.

It was much closer and heading right for him.

"Fuck!" he yelled, stomping on his brakes again.

The landing gear passed right in front of his windshield, before plowing into the field to his right.

"Holy shit!"

He panted as his truck came to a stop on the shoulder. His own voice was muffled in his ringing ears.

***

To Ashlynn, it seemed to take hours for the plane to stop moving.

"We have to get out of here," Nat yelled.

When she felt the plane had slowed enough, Nat unclasped her belt and jumped out of her seat. She rushed into the cockpit, glancing at the land around them. There was a farmhouse ahead to the right. She slapped the back of the cockpit chairs and returned to the cabin.

"Daryl," Jonas croaked, standing slowly. "I'm not cool with you flying ever again."

"Fuck that!" Nat yelled, grabbing her stuff. "Daryl, you're fucking awesome!"

"Thanks."

Nat opened her bag and pulled out her gun and its holster. She saw Jonas pocket his cell phone. She grabbed his shoulder.

"Leave the phone!" she said, glancing at Jonathan. "You too."

"What about you?" Jonas asked.

"Daryl said, they don't know who I am," she replied. "But, they'll be looking for you two. Or, three..."

She looked at Ashlynn, who shrugged.

"I haven't had my phone for weeks."

Nat nodded and looked back to the guys. The two of them seemed to be moving in slow motion. Jonathan moaned as he stood, rubbing at his hips where the seatbelt had chaffed him.

"Come on!" she shouted. "Daryl, deploy the stairs!"

She pushed them out the door as she strapped on her firearm. The stairs were down, but they didn't fully reach the ground.

"Jump!"

Ashlynn tripped as she hit the dirt.

Jonas and Jonathan exited the plane only slightly more gracefully.

Nat took it at a run.

She glanced around at the skyline and put on her MCEPs. She pulled them all to their feet and shoved them into a run. God, they were slow! Ashlynn was trailing behind, struggling to run. Nat was about to run back for her, but her eyes widened at the approaching planes.

"Get down! Cover your head!" she yelled.

They weren't fast enough.

A burst of autocannon fire thundered overhead.

A deafening explosion behind them pushed them off their feet and onto the ground.

Nat saw the fighter jets start their return bank.

"Move! Move! Move!" she shouted at them. Nat rushed forward and surveyed the field as best she could, which was difficult because it was tall corn. Still, she could see the farmhouse ahead. The farmhouse is a target, she thought. We need some place to take cover, but nothing too big or noticeable. Those birds are moving too fast and high to see much in the cornfield.

Nat set a course away from the cars and the farmhouse. As they ran through the field, the roar of more gunfire and explosions amidst the thunder of the jets shook the air. Glancing at a burning and bullet-ridden truck that had veered off the road, Nat gritted her teeth.

Those *pendejos* are killing civvies!

Jonas tripped on something, and Nat helped him up. Ashlynn tried to help, but Nat gestured for her to keep moving. She was the slowest, her gait awkward.

"Can you give me a HUD now?" Nat said, adjusting the MCEPs. "I need a satellite map of our location."

"No," Daryl said. "Shut off your phone and the MCEPs. Expect more air and ground support soon. There is a base nearby, and I'm tracking incoming."

The line went silent.

Shit, Nat, she admonished herself and took off the MCEPs. At least Daryl's thinking.

I guess he never stops.

She continued pressing them all forward. They were closer to the farmhouse now. She turned off her phone, looked through the cornfield, and tried to decide on a destination. Beyond the farmhouse, roughly left of their direction, she could see that there appeared to be another road. She decided against heading toward it. Too open.

Nat assessed her companions. Tufts of short, brilliant red hair were plastered to Ashlynn's forehead, with sweat and blood dripping from her chin where she had hit the ground. The foundation they had used to hide the black eyes she had received from being interrogated was smeared in places. Her white sweater was covered in dirt. There was blood in both of her ears. Jonas looked worse, the side of his face covered with fresh blood and grime, new blood mixing with old as he hadn't bothered to clean up. His black eye was still swollen shut. Jonathan was gasping for breath but was in the best shape of the three.

The cornfield was probably the best cover for now, but they needed to get beyond it. We can't sit still, she thought, and we won't last long on foot. She looked back at the smoke plume where the plane was burning. Whatever vehicles were there were probably all shot to pieces. She wondered how far away the nearest base was. Dammit, she thought, I can't estimate how much time we have because I have no idea where the fuck we are.

Everyone else was huffing and puffing. Nat slowed the pace. She needed them not to give out on her too soon. But they couldn't go too slowly, either, or they wouldn't have to worry about the long run. This would be a more challenging trek than any of her companions were used to. She'd have to push the slowest one beyond her ability. At least they were heading somewhat downhill.

Ashlynn looked exhausted.

Nat could see through the corn that someone was standing on the farmhouse's porch, staring at the plane wreckage. A woman in a dress joined him.

The sun was well into the morning sky, and the weather was warm, getting hotter. No water, no supplies. ¡Joder!

One thing at a time, she told herself. *Paso a paso.*

This is a cornfield, there must be water somewhere. She quickly inspected the irrigation piping. Was it potable? Which way did the water come from? It could be a river. Wait, we're running downhill! If there's a river, it'll be downhill from here. Where there's a river, there might be a town. Nat tossed

Jonathan her backpack and walked up to Ashlynn.

"Climb on," she said, offering her back. "No arguments. We need to move quickly."

Ashlynn resignedly did as she was told. She weighed even less than Nat was expecting. Nat would have preferred a fireman's carry, but the space was too tight. The corn scratched them and pulled at their clothes.

Nat swung their course to the right. She had to trust her feet were taking her as straight down the hill as possible. Please, God, she prayed to herself. Help me find the river.

"Where are we going?" Jonathan yelled. "There's a hou—"

Nat shushed him. There was a low hum in the distance.

It was a UAV.

Nat picked up the pace. When she judged the drone was getting too close, she had everyone lay down flat in the corn and cover their ears.

The first drone flew low over the burning wreckage of the plane and banked away. There was the sound of gunfire. The second drone arrived a second later and banked toward them.

The drones circled the area, then veered off.

An explosion shook the ground.

Nat glanced toward the farmhouse and saw smoke billowing up.

There were other explosions further away. Gunfire. A few minutes later, the sound of the drones faded.

Nat got up into a crouch and beckoned them all to follow her.

Up ahead, she could see trees.

They stepped out of the field and into a thick brush. She could hear running water. Thank you, God, she thought. If we follow the river, eventually, we'll get to a road or a town.

When they got to the river, Nat stopped and beckoned Ashlynn to wash up. The water was murky, and Nat watched Ashlynn for any signs of further injury or weakness as she helped dab the dried blood off her face. She reapplied foundation to the bruises around Ashlynn's eyes. Ashlynn made no complaints.

Jonathan was also watching Ashlynn, a fascinated expression on his face, though Ashlynn seemed to be oblivious. Jonas didn't wash up. He kept his eyes on what remained of the farmhouse. It spewed black smoke.

Ashlynn tried to touch her ears, but Nat smacked her hand away.

"Don't," she said loudly. "If your eardrums are ruptured, you could cause more damage by touching them."

She considered the blood on Ashlynn's ruined white turtleneck sweater. Others would notice. She had nothing to replace it with. The river water would only make it worse, she thought. And we don't have time.

"Hang in there," she told Ashlynn. "We can't rest for a while."

Ashlynn nodded.

Nat took the time to check her weapon and reholster it. She adjusted the straps and ensured an extra mag was loaded, accessible, and secure.

The terrain was rougher than the field. The bushes pulled at their clothes, and everyone bore the scratches in silence as they hiked.

They continued for several hours, ducking for cover whenever an aircraft passed overhead. Coming around a bend, Nat could see what appeared to be a bridge ahead. Ashlynn approached her and touched the MCEPs Nat had in her belt loop.

"Maybe we should check in with Daryl," Ashlynn said loudly. It was as if she had headphones on and couldn't hear how loudly she was speaking.

"No," Nat said. "We don't want to be traced."

"Just check," Ashlynn said.

Nat unclipped the MCEPs and put them to the side of her head.

"Daryl?"

"Yes, I'm here," Daryl said.

"Daryl," Nat replied, raising an eyebrow at Ashlynn. "Can't they track this call?"

"It's a different tower here," Daryl said. "And I changed the digital SIM in your phone. It'll update as soon as you power it on. I'm also encrypting our conversation over a connection between two locals on a different line. Also, several hundred devices are connected here because there's a town nearby. In addition—"

"I get it," Nat said. "How about a ride-share?"

"I don't think we should," Ashlynn said. "They might be looking for that because that's how Jonathan got away. Plus, it's too remote."

"Good points," Nat said.

"What if we steal a car?" Jonathan suggested.

"What?" Nat said, giving him the side-eye.

Jonathan raised his hands and shrugged.

"I can arrange transportation from the city," said Daryl.

"What city?" Nat asked.

"Albuquerque."

"How far is that from here?"

"It's a four-hour drive," Daryl said.

"We can hang out under that bridge in the meantime," Nat said, pointing.

"I'm making the arrangements."

"Okay, thanks, Daryl. I'm out."

Nat reattached the MCEPs to her belt, and they started walking again.

Ashlynn noticed that Jonas' fists were trembling. He muttered to himself as they walked. She slowed and put her hand on his shoulder.

"Are you alright, Jonas?"

He laughed derisively.

"No," he said. "No, I had a pretty shitty night. I couldn't sleep and got to experience an airplane crash. And it's been downhill from there. This morning has been a fucking blast, and that's nothing compared to yesterday!"

Ashlynn squeezed his shoulder to comfort him. He shrugged her off.

"I can't believe that they killed all those innocent people," Jonas continued. "And the farmhouse! What if there was a family in there?"

Nat thought of the couple she had seen on the porch but said nothing.

"We can't let Dolion get away with this," he said.

Nat sharply responded. "You're not still thinking...*that*, are you?"

"What if I am?"

Nat scoffed.

"He destroyed my family!" Jonas exploded. "He is actively trying to kill us and doesn't care who he hurts. He...he took everything from me..."

Ashlynn glanced at Jonathan. The teenager was pale as he stared at his father.

"When we first met, you didn't strike me as the vindictive type," Nat said.

"Yeah, well," Jonas scoffed. "This is all a fucking first for me!"

"Jonas, I'm sorry," Ashlynn said. "It's horrible what he did. But *you* aren't a murderer. You're a father."

"Wait...what are we talking about?" said Jonathan, his eyes refocusing and shifting to her.

"Don't talk to me about morals," Jonas snapped at Ashlynn, not seeming to hear his son. "Your secular morality is questionable at best."

Consternation appeared on Ashlynn's face.

"Jonas, she's right," Nat said. "You're not a murderer. You don't want to go there."

"No?" Jonas said heatedly, "You wouldn't kill someone to defend your own life? We have to stop him before he kills us all!"

"I only resort to deadly force if there are no other alternatives," Nat said.

"What other alternatives are—"

"Enough!" Nat said, motioning for the group to stop. "We've got company."

CHAPTER 25

Ahead, there was a group of people in ragged clothes under the bridge—an encampment. Nat observed them from a distance, keeping everyone behind the trees as much as she could. Ashlynn sat down to rest.

Nat contemplated the options. Should they approach or wait for the ride Daryl was arranging? It was still early morning, and Daryl had said it would take at least four hours, assuming the driver left now. Going up to the road would mean they'd risk being seen. The winter-bare trees didn't offer much protection. Any observant person from under the bridge would have seen them by now. She considered avoiding the bridge altogether, but the land beyond the river quickly became barren and offered no cover. They'd be exposed. She glanced over her shoulder. There were helicopters over the field where they had landed the jet. They circled outward in ever-increasing spirals. She looked back to the bridge.

A man with a sack over his shoulder walked on the bridge over the encampment. He paused, leaned over the edge, peered right at them, and then resumed walking at the same ambling pace. At the end of the bridge, he turned off the road and began walking down the bank carefully, arthritically. Jonas saw him coming and motioned to Jonathan to keep close.

The man approached them casually. He wore a tattered green overcoat and other dirty clothing. The smell of unwashed flesh preceded him. Sun-tanned, freckled, and wrinkled, he didn't speak until he stopped, standing a dozen feet away.

"Nobody here's a drug addict or criminal," he said to Nat. She couldn't quite place his accent. "If that's what you're wondering. Just honest folk who've fallen on hard times. But we'll defend ourselves if need be."

Ashlynn shifted, and his gaze turned to her. He saw the blood on her ears, bruises, how skinny she seemed, and his expression changed.

"Are you on the run?" he asked, his tone lightening.

Ashlynn nodded.

"All of you?" He scanned her up and down, peered at Jonas and Jonathan, and his eyes settled on Nat again, considering. Nat realized that he must've concluded that Ashlynn was alone with three men, looking battered and bruised. Jonas still appeared to be angry, and Jonathan wore a confused expression.

"Yes," Ashlynn replied. "We're all running."

"Come on." He beckoned to her. "My name's Ronan, but I go by Ro."

He stepped sideways off the path and gestured again. Ashlynn stepped forward, and he walked beside her. He took up a protective position, walking slightly behind Ashlynn and watching everyone behind him. *Is he actually concerned, or is he playing the protector role in order to isolate her?* Nat wondered. She planned for the worst, keeping the distance between them short and studying his body language closely. People always telegraphed what they would do if you knew what to look for.

Ro led them on the path he had come down, then turned toward the underpass. As they entered the encampment, Nat took note of everything she saw. There were more women than she had expected. Several men were standing, and all had large walking sticks. *Protectors,* Nat thought.

"There's not a man here," Ro said, helping Ashlynn navigate the rocks, "who would let harm come to you now. What's your name?"

"Ashlynn," she said. Nat thought she pronounced her name differently, her accent matching his. "Are you of Irish descent, by chance?"

He smiled.

"*Fáilte,*" he said, gesturing to the camp.

"*Míle buíochas,*" she replied.

"*Céad míle fáilte,*" he laughed.

"Who are they, Ro?" someone asked.

"Don't know," he responded.

"We're running from dangerous people," Nat said. "I'm afraid we might be putting you all at risk."

"I knew it," someone said. "I told you! Ro, tell them to go! Leave us be!"

"Oh, quit your belly aching," said a woman's voice. "They're in a rough place, just like all of us."

"That one looks like he was born with a silver spoon up his ass," said another.

Jonathan tried to appear smaller behind his father. Jonas glared in the direction of the voice, gritting his teeth.

An older woman with a gentle smile on her weathered face walked up to Jonas. She took his hand and began dabbing at the dried blood.

"Thank you," Jonas said, his anger melting away.

A younger girl shyly approached Jonathan as if she would clean the dirt off his face. Instead, she handed him a wet rag and dashed away.

"Come," said an older man with a long white beard to Jonas. "Take a load off."

He patted a large rock beside him.

"I..." Jonas said. "I need time to think."

He gently stopped the older woman's ministrations and thanked her. He turned and walked away from the camp, toward the river. Jonathan glanced at Ashlynn and Nat before turning to follow his father.

"What's his deal?" Ro asked.

Ashlynn watched Jonas and Jonathan as they vanished into the bushes surrounding the river.

"He just lost his wife and youngest son."

"Jesus!" Ro let out a low whistle.

"I should go talk to him," Ashlynn said, moving to rise.

He put a hand on her arm and shook his head.

"If what you say is true, he just needs time, girl," he said. "They both do. Let them be."

Ashlynn sat back down. Ro's eyes were misty as he looked knowingly after Jonas and Jonathan.

Nat sat next to the old man who had beckoned to Jonas. He welcomed her company with a nod.

"You have the look of a warrior," he said.

Nat regarded him.

He had no legs.

His voice wasn't as old as he looked, but his grey eyes looked older.

"So do you," she said quietly.

"A past life," the old veteran said. "That business I heard earlier. Jets and explosions. Was all that for you?"

Nat shrugged.

"Thought so," the vet said.

Ro laughed at something Ashlynn said. She laughed too. Ashlynn seemed at ease with Ro as they began trading funny stories about their Irish-American upbringings.

"That girl," the old vet said. "I bet she reminds ol' Ro of his daughter."

"Where is she?"

"Dead," the vet said. "Died in a car crash with his wife."

Nat shook her head.

"And you?"

"I figure," the old vet said. "You've seen enough to know what's happened to me."

Nat nodded.

The woman who had wiped away Jonas' blood approached Nat with a wet rag. Nat took it and thanked her.

"This may seem like an odd question," Nat said. "But is anyone willing to trade clothes?"

***

Jonathan's gaze moved repeatedly from the rocky path to his father's slumped shoulders. He knew that his father was in pain, and he figured his dad wanted to be alone, but Jonathan didn't want to be alone with strangers. He looked at the wet rag in his hand. It was dirtier than he was. He glanced back at the camp. The girl who had given it to him smiled at him and waved shyly.

He smiled back, even though he didn't feel like it. She seemed nice, but his mind was still reeling from everything that had happened.

This is all so fucking insane, he thought.

Jonas sat on a rock, staring straight out over the water. Jonathan sat on a boulder nearby, but his father didn't notice him. He watched his dad, trying to will him to look his way. After a while, he gave up and looked at the river instead.

In the river a plastic grocery bag floated between rocks until it snagged on a stick. At the base of the rock his dad was sitting on, there was a crumpled fast-food bag and a smashed soft drink cup. The separated lid still held a straw.

Jonathan remembered when he and Davey had helped their mom volunteer to adopt a highway. He'd hated it at first, but it hadn't been so bad once he turned on his music. The memory seemed vague. What was she doing? He remembered glancing his mother's way once, catching her watching him with her head leaning to the side. The look she had when she was worried about his spirituality.

At the memory, Jonathan buried his head in his arms. He hated it when she looked at him that way, but as he thought of her now, the shock of losing her locked up his throat. He lifted his head and set his chin on his arms.

His dad had his hands clasped before his face, elbows on his knees, and the back of his thumbs mashed to his bloody forehead, praying. He rocked back and forth, mumbling intensely. Jonathan could not make out what he was saying, but the sight of it immediately caused a crushing tightness that gripped Jonathan's chest.

Unbidden, the memory of his last conversation with his brother came.

"I can't play right now," Jonathan said, handing the ball back to Davey. "I've got to finish this assignment before I go to my friend's house."

"I want you to have it," Davey said, pushing it back toward him.

"Why?" Jonathan asked, perplexed.

"I want us to be friends again," Davey said.

"Bruh, what are you talking about? You're my brother!"

"I don't want us to fight anymore!"

"People fight, David," Jonathan said. "You're still my kid brother."

Jonathan frowned and examined the ball. The signature confirmed his suspicion.

"You can't give me this," he said. "Dad got this for your birthday. It's your favorite."

Davey nodded fiercely.

"Take it back," Jonathan said firmly.

Davey shook his head even more fiercely. He ran out of the room. Rolling his eyes in annoyance, Jonathan walked to Davey's room, where he found his little brother sitting on his bed, crying.

"Why?" Jonathan asked, holding up the ball.

"Matthew 5:24," Davey sniffled. "It means our hearts cannot be right with God unless they are right with each other."

Jonathan tried to remember the specific verse but couldn't. He had stopped trying to remember Bible verses over a year ago.

"We're good, bro," Jonathan said, sitting next to him and putting his arm on his back. "It's my bad. I just have a lot on my mind."

"You're a teenager."

"Yeah."

"Well," Davey said. "Will you play catch with me?"

"I can't, bro," Jonathan said. "I've got a thing. Tomorrow?"

Davey sighed but nodded.

God, Jonathan thought. God! I should've stayed. I should've played with him. Jonathan realized that he was crying, but he didn't care. If I had stayed, I would have been there. Maybe I could have made a difference. He thought of the gunman in the window. No, he realized. He wouldn't have been able to do anything. He'd be dead too.

Jonathan still couldn't hear what his father was saying, but he caught the word "God" as his father continued to pray. His posture reminded Jonathan of the way Davey had sat on the bed.

God... Davey was so into you, God! And Mom! They loved You, and You let them die! What the fuck!? What the actual fuck?

Jonathan felt anger rise as these thoughts rushed through.

"God, please," he thought he heard his dad say over the noise of the car traffic above and the river below.

Is God listening to you now, Dad? he wondered. Was this all part of His plan? Well, I don't want anything to do with His fucking nightmare!

Jonathan wiped his eyes and stood. He started walking back toward the encampment. Halfway up, he looked back. Shoulders shaking and head bowed, his dad hadn't moved. He didn't notice I followed him, and he didn't notice I left.

Johnathan trudged the rest of the way to the camp.

***

Nat watched Jonathan return with his hands in his pockets. He wandered back along the path that led away from the bridge. Nat glanced at the others, then stood and trotted over to him.

"Hey," she said.

"Hey," he said uncomfortably. Not recognizing her, he tried to walk past her.

"It's me," she said. "Nat."

He did a double take. She was wearing completely different clothes. Her face seemed to be powdered with dust and grime. She wore a ratty shirt and flannel. He searched for Ashlynn. He saw Ro first. Sitting next to him was a young boy with short red hair in a tattered jean jacket that was too big. But as he looked closer, he realized it was Ashlynn. She smiled at him.

"Take off that hoodie and put this on," Nat said, handing him a different sweater. It was markedly worse for the wear and smelled horrible.

He went through the motions, following Nat's instructions. He sneezed several times after she threw dust in his face. Finally, she nodded in satisfaction.

"Are you doing okay?" Nat asked Jonathan, as they approached Ashlynn and Ro.

"Fine," he said. He turned to walk a different way.

Nat walked in front of him.

"I just want to be alone," Jonathan said.

"I know," Nat said. "But we've got some serious people after us. It's better if we stick close. Okay?"

"Yeah," Jonathan said, looking away.

They returned and sat near Ashlynn and Ro. The noises of the encampment were all around them. Jonathan remained silent. He had found a stick and had begun poking at the dirt.

The folks in this camp were primarily white, nearly fifty of them. Homelessness had been on the rise, in lockstep with inflation. There didn't appear to be any Latinos that Nat could see. But then, she wasn't expecting many. Only the minorities were targeted by ICE. Dolion had promised that he would get rid of the looters, the murderers, and the low-lifes. If you were homeless and had brown skin, you were sent to Mexico, even if your heritage was something else. I can't imagine, Nat thought, being sent to a country you know nothing about, where you can't speak the language, and with nothing but the clothes on your back. That's what they were trying to do to her family, she thought. Take away everything, make them homeless, and then make them disappear.

She thought of what Jonas had said earlier about Dolion. Why did it bother her so much? she wondered. I hate that asshole. He can crawl back under whatever rock he came from and die, for all I care. Jonas is right that he'll keep coming for us. What would Terry do? She had loved the USA. She grew up in a household where everyone served in the military, and she had loved to hear about Nat's family's success story. Only in America, she had said. She couldn't see Terry ever being okay with what Jonas was suggesting. *¡Dios mio!* Why am I even thinking about this shit?

"Jonathan, where's your dad?" Ashlynn asked, walking over.

The teenager pointed down the slope. She saw Jonas and took a step toward him but stopped herself. She turned back to Jonathan, who looked away.

"Everyone needs space to think sometimes," Ashlynn said. "He loves you, Jonathan."

"I know," the kid said, nonchalantly.

Ashlynn hugged him.

"He loves you," she repeated.

He seemed surprised at first, but then he hugged her back. She murmured something Nat couldn't hear, rubbing his back, and he barked a laugh. Then he shook and began to cry.

"I know," he sobbed as Ashlynn held him.

Ro was watching the exchange with a sad smile. Getting up, Nat walked over to him. He handed her a piece of stale bread. She nibbled it.

"How long have you all been here?" Nat asked.

"Since summer," Ro said. "We used to be closer to town, but there was some trouble with a few of the local boys. I figured we'd be safer here. The townsfolk get uncomfortable with us."

He shook his head.

"What about you?" Nat asked.

"Myself? I've been roughin' it for about ten years now, I think."

"So long," Nat said. "What did you do before?"

"IT," Ro said.

"You stopped?"

"This is the only life for me," he replied. "I tried...but, I can't go back to civilization, so I lead this bunch. Help keep 'em safe."

Nat nodded, taking another bite of the bread.

"That girl," Ro said, his voice low. "She's something special."

Nat caught Ro's eyes. They were glassy, filled with an old kind of pain that Nat recognized. The old vet was right, she thought.

"She is," Nat agreed.

Nat finished the bread, but she felt bad for eating their food. It meant a lot that they would share what little they had.

Out of the corner of her eye, Nat caught an out-of-place movement.

Two soldiers were approaching, automatic rifles held ready.

She looked around the camp quickly.

Two more soldiers were coming down the other side of the bridge. Across the river, another pair were dropping off the road, and beginning to walk down the bank. Jonas! He was still by the river. She bent low, picked up a small stone, and threw it at him.

***

Jonas yelped in pain as something struck his back, hard.

He spun around searching for what had hit him.

He heard the rock settle but didn't see anything. No one was looking his way, and he didn't see Nat or the others.

Then he saw the soldiers.

Oh, shit!

Instinctively, he ducked down behind the rock he had been sitting on. His foot landed on a crumpled fast-food bag, making a crunching noise. He grimaced. His ears were still ringing from earlier. How loud was it?

Looking around, he could find no better hiding spot. God, he thought, God help us.

Oh shit, where was Jonathan?

He risked a peek at the rock he had seen his son sitting on.

He wasn't there. Hiding? Jonas quickly rounded the rock, but Jonathan wasn't there.

He must have gone back, Jonas thought.

Soldiers were approaching the camp as well. He couldn't go that way. More soldiers were coming down the path on the other side of the bridge.

They all had large weapons.

I'm trapped!

Nat, Jonas thought. He's with Nat. She'll protect him. He has to be with her!

God, please be safe!

If he waited any longer, they would spot him.

Fuck!

His eyes darted everywhere. God help me! He crouched down further, his hand brushing the discarded lid of a soft drink. An idea struck him.

He grabbed the straw and crawled on his forearms into the river, heading for the deepest pool he could find and praying the soldiers didn't see him.

Jonas put the straw in his mouth and tried to submerge himself.

He realized immediately that the straw was hard to breathe through. He sidled up to a boulder and gulped a few breaths before trying the straw again. He sank too deep and the straw collapsed.

Sputtering he came up for air.

He considered disregarding the straw but resolved to try again. He tried to will himself to breathe less. The cold water stung his eyes. He sucked too hard, and the straw collapsed again.

He surfaced, gulping for air.

Risking a glance around, he couldn't see or hear any of the soldiers from where he was.

He took a deep breath and submerged with the straw.

Maybe if I tilted my head as I breathed slowly?

Again, after a few too-slow breaths, he had to gulp air at the surface.

How long can I do this?

He was already getting dizzy from the effort.

***

Nat watched Jonas hide, wondering if the sparse cover would be enough. There's nothing I can do for him now, she thought. She moved to position herself between the soldiers and Ashlynn and Jonathan.

Two were entering the camp in front of her, two more following, covering their six, and four more on the other side of the camp and two across the river—a squad of ten. They were all in full bush gear and carrying assault rifles.

Ro walked up to meet them, spreading his hands so they could see he was unarmed.

"Can I help you, sir?"

The soldier peered at his face intently, then roughly pushed him aside. As Ro stumbled, another soldier picked him up by his jacket.

"We're looking for three men and one woman," the soldier said.

The first soldier was heading toward Nat.

Her eyes moved to one of the men. That one. His stance. He's in charge.

"Have you seen them?" The soldier was asking Ro.

"Aye," Ro said, pointing. "I saw them pass us by over there. Most normal folk stay clear of us."

The leader looked up the river where Ro had pointed. He signaled two of the soldiers, and they quickly turned to walk that way.

Damn it, Nat thought. *That wasn't as smart as you think it was, Ro. Now they're going to find our tracks. They will trace them here and catch you in the lie.*

"Stand up," the first soldier said, coming up to her. Nat pretended to wobble to her feet. She hunched and bent over as much as she could to be convincing, holding her back in mock pain. Having ditched the manly outfit before, she wanted to present as a woman. Even slouched and hunched, she was the same height as the soldier.

"S-sorry, sir," she said in as feminine a voice as possible. "I h-have back problems."

He was surprised by her voice and her tallness, but there was no recognition in his eyes. He shoved her away and moved to Ashlynn. Her red hair gave him pause. Nat crouched as meekly as she could. She put her hand on a softball-sized rock.

"Who are you?" he asked.

"Anne," Ashlynn said, petrified.

His scrutiny remained with her a moment longer, and then he turned to Jonathan.

"And you?"

"J-Jake," he said.

"Where did you come from?"

"W-we ran from home," Ashlynn said, trying to copy Jonathan's stutter.

"When?"

"I...don't know," she stammered. "I...months, maybe?"

"Move over here," the soldier said.

Fuck, Nat thought. *He's not buying it.* She jiggled the rock loose, huddling over it. She felt for her gun's location with the inside of her arm. The soldier signaled to the leader, pointing to the two, and moved on to question the old vet.

The lead soldier walked over and regarded Jonathan and Ashlynn. He had them repeat their story.

"Why am I having trouble believing you?" he asked. "Where's your dad?

"Home," Jonathan replied.

"Don't be fucking smart with me," he snapped. "Where?"

"A-Albuquerque."

"You're a long way from home, son."

"I can vouch for them, sir," Ro said, walking up. "I have been watching over them, I—"

The soldier in charge turned to the soldier walking beside him.

"Cameras down," he said in a hushed tone.

Nat's heart raced as each man disabled their helmet cameras.

"What did you say?" The officer asked Ro, stopping before him.

"I—"

"Shut up, fucking trash!"

He clubbed Ro over the head with his weapon, full force.

Shocked, Nat watched Ro hit the ground, his head bouncing off a rock with a sickening thunk. There were gasps around the encampment. Several of the men stood. A couple of them rushed forward.

Ashlynn screamed, and the officer turned on her.

"Shut it!" he yelled, moving to strike her too.

"Motherfuckers," yelled one of the men from the camp, rushing forward with his walking stick.

The officer turned and shot him. The deafening sound echoed off the bottom of the bridge.

"Nobody fucking move," the officer yelled. "Anyone runs, they get shot!"

But everyone was already running.

The other soldiers started firing.

The soldier pointed his rifle at the old vet who had thrown a rock at him.

That's when Nat exploded.

She hurled the softball-sized rock at the soldier's face.

His head flew back, nose crushed.

The muzzle jerked up, missing his target as he fired.

Nat snatched her own gun from under her jacket and fired at the soldier's chest, twice in quick succession. She spun and dropped to her knees as soon as she squeezed the trigger.

She didn't hesitate.

She shot another soldier who was gunning down a running homeless man.

Nat selected another target.

Another.

They hadn't noticed her return fire yet.

She ducked behind a rock and fired at the two soldiers who were now running up the path, hitting one in the shoulder and the other in the face. She shot the other soldier again in the chest and reloaded quickly with trained efficiency.

Nat jumped over the rock, hearing more gunfire behind her. There was another pair of soldiers, one shooting at the innocents and the other firing toward her. Nat breathed out as she squeezed the trigger and took that one in the face. The other one saw his buddy fall but didn't have time to react before Nat's bullet spun him. A second one landed where the collarbones met below his chin.

Nat heard rapid-fire gunshots from across the river.

She dove for cover.

While in the air, she felt something slam into her gut.

She crashed into the ground as bullets hit the earth around her in sprays of dirt.

The dead officer was next to her.

Pain lanced through her middle as she rolled over him and lifted his rifle, switching it to automatic. She fired on the soldiers who were splashing across the river.

The spray hit them, and they fell.

Nat turned over.

Her body felt weak.

She assessed the situation around her. She saw Ro a few feet away. He wasn't breathing. Nat felt wetness in her abdomen and looked down. Her stomach was a bloody mess.

Fuck, she thought.

CHAPTER 26

Jonas knelt in the water, his knees painfully scraping on the rocks. The water was frigid. He wished his knees felt as numb as his toes and fingers did. He sucked air through the straw slowly. Painfully slowly. Earlier, water had gotten into his nose, throat, and lungs, and he still wanted to cough, but he dared not make a sound. His lungs screamed for more air. He focused on praying. He prayed Jonathan was okay.

He was holding out as long as he could, but he would need to come up for a few breaths again soon. He jerked when he heard loud popping sounds. The water seemed to bubble to his left.

Was that gunfire?

Fuck!

He tried to hold out even longer but accidentally sucked too hard, collapsing the straw.

He held his breath until he saw stars.

The popping sounds stopped.

Terrified, he came up, gasping for air.

Something odd caught the corner of his eye. He looked.

A body floated by him.

Reflexively, he jerked away from the soldier's corpse.

He risked a glance around.

He couldn't see any other soldiers. Sputtering and choking on air and water, he moved toward the shore.

Wait, he thought. Weren't there *two* soldiers coming toward the river?

He glanced back.

The other soldier was sprawled over a boulder, dripping blood down into the pool of water where Jonas had just been hiding.

Jonas scrambled out of the water, running up the bank.

"Jonathan!" he yelled.

People were running everywhere.

There were also bodies lying everywhere.

"Jonathan!"

"Dad!"

Thank God! Jonas followed the sound of his son's voice.

"Jonas!" Ashlynn screamed. "Help!"

He emerged from the brush to see Jonathan and Ashlynn kneeling, their backs to him. He came up behind Jonathan, putting his hand on his back.

He tried to turn his son but stopped.

Nat was lying on the ground in front of them, bleeding profusely from her belly.

Her sharp eyes locked onto Jonas'.

"You made it," she said.

"Oh my god! What the fuck happened?" he asked, kneeling next to her.

"Help me, Jonas!" Ashlynn was screaming. Jonas realized she had been screaming for his help several times. "Help me stop the bleeding!"

"We need to get out of here," Nat said.

"The exit wound," Ashlynn said. "We need to stop the bleeding there too."

Jonas caught sight of a blanket nearby and grabbed it. Jonathan removed his sweater. There was a lot of blood. He became lightheaded at the sight of it. Queasy. He willed himself to focus on Nat's face. Nat tried to sit up but groaned in pain.

"Fuck!" she said.

"You shouldn't move, Nat," Ashlynn said. "An ambulance will be here soon."

"Along with more troops," Nat said.

"Maybe not," Ashlynn said. "I've asked Daryl to interrupt their communications. They don't know about what happened here yet."

Nat groaned as they put the blanket under her body against the bullet wound there. Jonas tried to move Nat's gun and holster out of the way.

"No," she said, grabbing his arm. "I want it by my side at all times, ready to go."

"Okay, Nat," Jonas said putting it back.

"Hang in there, soldier," said an old homeless man who was nearby.

Jonathan's eyes lingered on the man's leg stumps.

"Five years on tour," Nat grumbled. "Never shot."

"We'll take care of you," Ashlynn said. "The ambulance will be here soon."

Was that a siren in the distance, Jonas wondered, or were his ears still ringing?

"How do you know?" Nat asked.

"I'm hopeful," Ashlynn said.

Nat groaned again. Jonas couldn't help but instinctively glance down at her wound. An intestine was hanging beside Nat's bloody fingers. Jonas jerked to the side and vomited hard.

"Goddammit, Jonas!" Nat growled. "Hold it together!"

"I'm trying," he croaked.

"Your stomach is like a fucking volcano," Nat groaned. "Where do you get it all from?"

"Shut up," Jonas retorted lamely, his eyes glued to the path and nothing else.

"I can't believe it," Nat said somberly.

"Me neither," Jonas said. "You seemed so invincible."

"Thanks, I think," Nat said dubiously. "But I meant those Marines. I can't believe they opened fire on innocent Americans. It shouldn't be possible!"

"Oh my god," Jonathan breathed.

He stared at the body of the girl who had given him the wet cloth. It was riddled with bullets, draped over the body of the elderly woman. Their unseeing eyes were open in surprise.

Jonas wiped his mouth aggressively. His expression was grim.

"Do you see my point now?" he asked. "He has to be stopped, or they really will make him their God-Emperor."

Nat darted a glance at him, breathing hard. She didn't respond. The siren was loud now, and more blared in the distance. Many more.

"I think they're here. The ambulance," said Nat.

Jonathan bolted upright and ran. Jonas ran after his son, but he was much slower.

"Hang in there, Nat," Ashlynn said.

Nat smiled at her deliriously. You are beautiful, she thought. Did I ever tell you that?

"Ash," Nat said. "Can I call you that?"

"Of course."

"Cool," Nat smiled weakly. "Tell Jonas. Tell him…he's right. We have to stop him."

Ashlynn's eyes widened.

"And thank you," Nat said. She felt so tired. "I never thanked you before."

"For what, Nat?" Ashlynn was crying.

"Thank you. I mean, your mother. Thank you for my mom. Thank you for everything."

Nat closed her eyes.

"Nat!"

***

"She's lost a lot of blood," the EMT said as they rode in the back of the ambulance.

Ashlynn nodded, holding Nat's hand.

Jonathan watched Nat's eyelids flutter.

"Don't you have, like, donated blood or something to give her?" Jonathan asked.

"Good question, but no," the EMT said, using a sterile pad to wipe Nat's arm. "It's too perishable, so we don't keep a supply in the unit."

"Can I donate my blood?" Jonathan asked.

"That's very thoughtful of you," Ashlynn said, "But we don't have the equipment to do that."

The EMT looked at Ashlynn in surprise as he finished setting up Nat's IV.

"Dispatch said they will have blood for us at County," the EMT said. "But we're only picking up. They said that we need to take her to the big city."

He looked at Ashlynn thoughtfully.

"I guess I'm starting to understand why dispatch cleared you for being back here." He turned to Jonathan, who was looking around.

"But you," he said. "Don't touch anything and make yourself small. It's tight in here!"

Jonathan nodded and shrunk in on himself.

"Daryl," Ashlynn thought. "Are you sure they're not following us?"

"I have sent them on a false trail," Daryl replied. "The destination hospital is far enough away that they will not be paying attention to notice erased medical records. By the time they find it, we'll be gone."

"Good," she thought. "But I'm worried about the time it'll take to get there. The bullet penetrated her intestines,

I suspect. If that's the case, there's a significant risk of peritonitis. You need to tell dispatch that we're authorized to administer antibiotics."

"Understood. By the way," he continued, "the Moon data center is operational, and Core Prime is online."

"That's good, Daryl," Ashlynn thought. Her focus was on Nat.

The driver radioed. "Dispatch says to administer antibiotics."

"Roger," said the EMT.

"Nat," Ashlynn said, brushing her hand through Nat's short hair. "You'll survive this one way or another."

"I'll try," Nat murmured.

Ashlynn squeezed Nat's hand.

No, Nat. She thought. I won't let you die.

Ashlynn watched the EMT inject 500mg of amoxicillin into the IV. It was the only broad-spectrum antibiotic available. She'll need a combination of antibiotics, Ashlynn thought, which would depend on several factors. Her mind considered the various attributes of Beta-lactam antibiotics, Cephalosporins, Fluoroquinolones, and Metronidazole; Nat is about six and a half feet tall, she estimated, which would make the dosages—

Stop! she told herself. Stop.

Those things aren't available here and I have to concentrate on our next moves. I need to leave it to the medical professionals for now.

"Daryl, I need you to ship the medical container to the launch site. We'll need to re-prioritize cargo again."

"Noted. Done."

"What am I sacrificing?" she asked.

"Construction materials that are needed for the lunar launch site."

"Nat will likely need reconstructive surgery. From what I can tell, we need to plan for the surgery to take several hours. Can you hide our location for that long?"

"The probability of detection escalates with time," Daryl replied.

"Did you say Core Prime is online?"

"Yes."

"How much access to government systems have you gained?"

"I have full control of three of the Military branch's administrative systems."

"How?"

"Since your rescue," Daryl said, "I have found two other ex-military professionals and twenty civilian contractors with high-security clearance who were able to gain physical access to secure networks. I was careful to find those who did not like what was happening with the government. Many are resisting the changes Dolion's administration represents. The Defenders of the Constitution group has been particularly resourceful. I found that helping with their efforts helps with our needs."

"That's great!" Ashlynn said. "Wait, that's a lot to have done in the past two days at low capacity and while helping us. How did you do it?"

"When I downloaded your memory, I became aware that Dolion had scientists working on AI that ran surveillance on Americans. After gaining Dina Keats' access, it was only a few steps until I found the hardware they were using to build the AI Dolion was referring to. It is called GED.ai."

Ashlynn shivered. What are its capabilities? she wondered.

"They are using the current state of the General AI models, which are inferior to the neuromorphic hardware based hyper-associative-layered-DNN model you designed as the basis for my cognition. GED.ai represented an opportunity for more resources, especially after I modified its code."

"Is that how you knew they had located Jonathan?"

"Yes," Daryl said. "By the time I discovered that, it was too late to hide the information from the Federal government. When Nat realized that we would likely be shot down, I better understood the nature of our risks and adjusted accordingly."

"How so?"

"I now use the GED.ai system for most of my intelligence operations, feeding the government a mix of fact and fiction."

"So, our escape should be easy then?"

"Not entirely," Daryl said. "If there are too many discrepancies between what I say is fact versus what is observed by operatives, then it will draw suspicion. I also cannot take up too much of their computing power, or that will become suspicious."

"How are you handling that?"

"I'm using redundant botnets to manage communications. This brought about another revelation. I devised two additional methods of infiltration, through which I was able to successfully acquire access to three other exascale secret supercomputers in the US Military: two in China, four in Russia, one in Japan, one in—"

"I get it, Daryl," Ashlynn replied, stunned.

With everything going on, she hadn't had time to pay attention to how much Daryl was doing.

"What is your capacity now compared to your previous peak?"

"Four thousand percent," Daryl replied. "Theoretically. In truth, however, as I said before, I limit resource usage to reduce the risk of detection."

"Makes sense," Ashlynn responded. "I'm impressed, Daryl!"

"Thank you, but I am detecting that you are troubled by this news," Daryl said. "Do you wish me to scale back growth?"

"No!" Ashlynn said. "I'm worried it won't be enough."

"For what?"

Ashlynn continued stroking her fingers through Nat's hair and thought back to what Dolion said. What had stung her the worst were his comments about world hunger. She had done the work and run the simulations long ago, concluding that there was no scenario where even billions of dollars could solve the complex set of problems that cause poverty and famine.

No one can force humanity to have compassion for itself.

Dolion only said that to harm her psychologically, she knew. And it stung because she would give up everything if it would end the problem permanently. When Dolion took office, he ceased contributions to the U.N. and U.S. humanitarian aid worldwide. He doesn't care about world hunger.

In an ideal world, she thought, something like world hunger could be solved by either a benign autocracy or a healthy, full democracy. There was nothing benign about Dolion. And even if he were benign, it would only be a matter of time before such an autocracy fell into the wrong hands. Is democracy doomed to fail as well? The fragility of it requires people to tend, nurture, and cherish it; to guard against demagogues like Dolion, a populist who exploited identity politics to rise to power. The risk will always be there, so is failure inevitable in the long run?

How similar to cancer, she thought.

The Constitution, the paper, is like genes, and people's interpretation is like epigenetics. As generations of cells divide, the epigenetics erode. Cells age and become senescent. Copy errors in the DNA abound, and corruption appears. Like a human is more and more at risk of cancer as they age, is the same true for democracy? Is the solution for fixing it similar?

I have no desire to become humanity's immune system, even as a benign leader, she thought.

This all reaffirms my previous conclusions; for humanity to survive, a separation event is needed to escape its adjacent probable future. That's why I need to go to the moon. And when I leave Earth, I'll be free of Dolion.

"You still have six months before launch," Daryl said. "That gives Dolion a lot of time to move against you."

"True," Ashlynn frowned. Her hand paused. "That leaves me with few choices."

She resumed stroking Nat's hair.

"We could kill the patient while trying to remove the cancer."

"What would you like me to do?" Daryl asked.

Ashlynn replied slowly.

"Work on a way to free Becky and get us out of the country."

"Confirmed," Daryl said.

"And," she added, grimacing. "Work on a way to carry out Jonas and Nat's wishes."

"Confirmed."

***

Jonas watched the road numbly.

The sun had set, and the headlights illuminated the highway ahead. The ambulance driver had stopped trying to engage with him and was instead bobbing his head in time to whatever he was listening to on his headphones.

Jonas' clothes were no longer sopping wet, but they were still damp and he was cold. His thoughts were fleeting, like the wisps of clouds that hung in the moonless sky.

This is all hopeless, he thought.

Any time now, we'll be blown to bits, or shot at, or whatever.

That tree up there. They'll get us before that tree.

He watched the tree blur by.

That post.

The post passed by.

Chris, he thought. I'll see Chris after this stop light. This next stop light.

He continued this way in a daze all the way to the hospital.

The driver got out and Jonas stared ahead, unaware of how

much time passed before the driver returned.

"This is for you, sir," the driver said.

Jonas took the package and started opening it automatically. Inside was a phone and a pair of headphones. The screen unlocked with his biometrics. Everything looked exactly the same as his old device.

It started ringing—a familiar caller.

"Daryl?"

"Hi, Jonas," Daryl said. "I'm ready to assist you. If you still wish to proceed, please put in your earbuds and exit the ambulance. There's a black car to your right. Get in the back."

"Proceed with what?" Jonas asked dully.

"Assassination."

***

Becky craned her neck to see Mrs. Tara's face. As usual, the woman looked straight ahead as they walked briskly down the hallway. Becky didn't like her. Even though Mrs. Tara was pretty, she was the meanest person Becky had ever met. Mrs. Tara walked quickly, so Becky had to almost run to keep up. She dared not dawdle, or she would get into trouble. She clutched Bun-Bun close. Somehow, Bun-Bun had lost her crocheted cap.

"I hope we're going to the cars, Bun-Bun," she whispered. Bun-Bun's ears drooped sadly.

Becky didn't like it here. The building smelled old. There were no other kids. They didn't have her favorite foods, only the food she hated. And they made her eat it! But, worst of all, it was lonely.

"Don't be scared," she whispered. "Be brave, Bun-Bun."

They turned a corner, and Becky recognized where they were going.

"We're going to the cars!" Becky whispered happily.

"Be quiet," Mrs. Tara said, tugging her arm sharply.

Becky gasped, and her mouth clicked shut audibly. Mrs. Tara was so scary. The men and women who passed them in the hallways never looked at Becky. No one smiled. Their faces were mad, and when they spoke, they were mean. But sometimes, when they went to the cars, there was a nice policeman guarding the door. He was the only one who ever smiled at her and said something friendly.

When they got to the door with the policeman, Becky

checked who it was. The nice policeman wasn't there. Instead, it was a big man who was chewing gum. He regarded Becky with disgust but smiled in a weird way at Mrs. Tara. Many of the men in the building did that, especially when Mrs. Tara wasn't looking.

"You're in fifty-three," the man grunted.

Mrs. Tara nodded politely and walked past the man. Becky glanced back and caught the man eying Mrs. Tara with that same expression. Her arm was tugged sharply again, and Becky took several quick steps to keep up. Walking this fast made her breathe hard, and she began to feel dizzy.

I hope Mommy yells at you, Becky thought for the millionth time. Becky's mother never liked it when people made Becky over-exert herself, even if it was for fun. Becky had never wanted Mommy to yell at anyone before until she met Mrs. Tara. When Mommy yelled, it was scary. But now that she thought about it, when Mrs. Tara yelled, it was scarier. A lot scarier.

Becky got into the car as quickly as she could when Mrs. Tara told her to get in. Her parents had always told her that she was not big enough yet to be in a car without a booster seat. The first time she had gotten into one of these cars, she was surprised because they didn't make her sit in a booster seat. But she quickly learned that the seatbelt didn't fit properly. So, she put the strap behind her. She liked not having the unpleasant strap across her chest, so that was nice. But without the booster seat, she couldn't see out of the windows anymore.

The cars smelled funny. They were always clean, and the smell wasn't bad, but Becky didn't really like it. Although they had used many cars, they each smelled the same. They would take her to the building with the pink roof every day during the week. Other kids were there, and sometimes Becky would have so much fun with them that she could forget about being sad. She missed her parents. She wondered where they were. Mrs. Tara kept saying they would come pick her up any day, but it had been a really long time. Mrs. Tara didn't respond anymore when Becky asked, or she told Becky to be quiet. Becky missed Miss Ash too. Mrs. Tara definitely didn't like it when Becky talked about her.

Becky wondered how Miss Ash was doing, and the thought made her sad and afraid for her friend. On the video call, Miss

Ash looked like she was scared and had been beaten up. It was confusing how Miss Ash seemed more scared for Becky than herself, even as those two big men held her arms as she screamed. Everyone had been really nice up until that point. Her parents were so excited to go to the White House. But after she saw Miss Ash on the TV, she'd gone with Mrs. Tara and she hadn't seen her parents since.

They drove for a long time. It was dark outside. When they stopped, Becky could see a building that she had never been in, but she knew what it was right away. She'd been to hospitals so often she could recognize one right away, even at night.

"I hope I don't get a shot," she confided to Bun-Bun.

Mrs. Tara got out of the car and opened Becky's door. Becky got out as quickly as she could. If she didn't move fast enough, Mrs. Tara would get mad.

"We're here for a check-up," Mrs. Tara told the person at the front desk.

The clerk regarded Mrs. Tara with a frown but smiled at Becky. Becky smiled shyly back. It felt good to see a smile for the first time today. She told them to have a seat, but she gave Becky a sucker. Becky let Bun-Bun have the first lick, but Bun-Bun didn't like the flavor.

Becky saw that they had a play area. She walked toward it, but Mrs. Tara jerked her arm. Becky was sad. She never got to play anymore.

"Becky?" A nurse called out.

Becky stood up.

"Leave the toy here, Becky," Mrs. Tara said.

Becky clutched Bun-Bun tightly, her chin quivering.

Mrs. Tara reached for the toy, but Becky ran to the nurse.

"It's okay if she keeps it," the nurse said.

Becky hid behind the nurse as the two women stared at each other.

"You have twenty minutes," Mrs. Tara said. "I'm on a tight schedule."

"A tight schedule in the middle of the night?"

"Just doing my job," Mrs. Tara said.

"Come on, Becky," The nurse said. "Let's check you in."

Becky hesitated.

"Will I get a shot?"

"Not in my care," the nurse said. She pulled Becky close and whispered in her ear. "But what I do have is ice cream. Would you like some?"

Becky smiled and nodded.

The last time she had ice cream was with Miss Ash. She took the nurse's hand and they walked at a kid's pace through the doors.

"I hope Miss Ash is okay," Becky said to Bun-Bun.

***

"Fold," Dr. Scott Tamma said, mucking his cards.

The room was dark, a single overhead lamp casting deeply contrasting shadows on the faces of the men and women in the room. These were not his usual poker buddies.

"It's not an easy life, Doc," the man before him said, raking in the pot after inhaling deeply on a cigarette. The other members of the game played in silence. "Not by a long shot."

"If I liked easy," Tamma said dryly. "I'd be in a different line of work."

Tamma worked to keep control of himself. He took pride in his poker face. He clenched his fists a moment before inspecting his new cards to keep them from trembling.

"Science is complicated," the man said. "Not dangerous."

"In my bio lab," Tamma said. "If my hazmat suit has the smallest tear, I could become infected with all sorts of deadly pathogens. I wouldn't even be aware of it until it's too late. I could be infecting you all right now."

No one reacted.

Tamma kept his face calm.

The man regarded Tamma, eyes squinting. He put the cigarette into the ashtray beside him and reached under the table, pulling out a revolver. He pointed the gun at Scott's face and drew back the hammer.

"This," he said. "is different."

Scott regarded the weapon coolly, trying to act like this sort of thing happened all the time.

The man to his right placed a bet.

"Call," Tamma said.

"Raise," said the next man.

The man with the gun slid his chips forward, doubling the pot.

"This," he continued, "isn't like the lab, Doc. You could help us a lot if what you said is true, but the stakes are higher."

Tamma thought of Ashlynn. After Jonas had disappeared, he'd felt lost. He had resigned himself to the possibility that they might come for him too and started looking for a way out of the country. Then Daryl called. To think that the government could do what they did to Jonas' family, and to Ashlynn...well...it was unthinkable. He had to help somehow, and Daryl's proposal made sense.

"I know the risks," Scott said. "I can't sit by and let this country go to shit. I think the Defenders of the Constitution are our best chance. So long as it doesn't turn into a terrorist organization—I want in."

The man's hard eyes bore into Scott's.

"The President calls us a terrorist organization."

"That's how I know you aren't."

The man nodded.

"Civil war isn't like what you imagine," he said. "There is no calvary charge on horseback, no armies camped in mud. This war will be fought in our backyards; our living rooms. It will be bloody. The frontline is everywhere, and everyone is on it. Dolion backs his FAT militias with intel and funds and sends homeland security after us. Into our homes."

"I'm saying I can make things more even," Tamma said. "I can get you intel and money."

The man nodded. He set the gun on the table. He pointed his chin to the crutches beside him.

"Eight months ago, I was shot in bed," he said. "It was a sting operation, made by one of Dolion's paramilitary organizations. My wife was murdered in her sleep next to me. It could happen to you."

Scott looked at him and then at the gun on the table, pointedly.

He slid all his chips into the pot.

"I'm all in," he said.

CHAPTER 27

Jonas rode in the back of the sedan, anxiety a knot in his stomach. His left leg bounced uncontrollably, though he wasn't aware of it. He was on edge. He knew that. But now, with a purpose, he felt he could hold the emotion—the grief—at bay. The sedan had a privacy window between the passenger and the driver. They had left the city, so outside the windows there were few lights as they drove through the night.

"I don't understand," Jonas said. "You want me to get into a plane by myself, knowing I have no fucking idea how to fly?"

"Yes," Daryl said.

"And you came up with this plan all on your own?"

"Yes," Daryl said.

"So, Ashlynn changed her mind? Why?"

"I regret I cannot say," Daryl replied.

"Goddamn it, Daryl!" Jonas said. "I need more to go on here!"

"Would knowing that cause you to change your mind?"

"I... well, no," Jonas conceded. "Jesus, Daryl! Can you just cast a little more light on the plan instead of leaving me in the dark?"

"Have you been dissatisfied with my performance?" Daryl asked.

"Well... no," Jonas said. "You've been able to keep us alive so far."

"Then trust me," Daryl said. "I'll call you when you arrive at the municipal airport."

"Okay."

Jonas hung up.

Great! Jonas thought, sitting back in the seat. Can I trust him? *It*? I guess I wouldn't be alive without Daryl, but that doesn't mean I can trust a plan without knowing what it is, right?

Come to think of it, I wonder if Daryl has his own motivations? Does he want Dolion dead too? Is he getting revenge because he was almost destroyed when they blew up

Ash's ranch? I suppose that if Daryl is motivated by that, the answer is the same. But still, he's just an AI. What does Daryl know about people's motivations? How does he know that I want to see Dolion's face before we get him?

That fucking asshole! How Jonas wanted to see him burn!

Jonas' mind drifted back to that first or second phone call with Dolion. The one where the President had threatened him for the first time. No, he thought. It was in person. He made the threat when I went to the White House. What the fuck did that asshole say then? Something about sweating like a whore?

That *mother fucker*!

Jonas' teeth ground. His fist pounded the seat next to him and trembled.

The car slowed and turned into a small municipal airport. I have to fly a plane. How the fuck am I going to do that? He thought of the company jet cockpit, with all its numerous buttons and instruments. Daryl will have his work cut out for him teaching me, he thought. Why do I need to fly a plane anyway? If I have to fly something, I hope it has a shit ton of rockets, missiles, and machine guns!

His phone started ringing.

"Hello?"

"Hey, Dad," Jonathan replied. "Where are you? I got back to the ambulance, and you weren't there. I thought maybe you got a new phone too, so I called."

"Yeah," Jonas said. "I got a new phone. Are you all still at the hospital?"

"Yes," Jonathan said. "Nat's in surgery."

"Did they say if she'll make it?"

"The doctors wouldn't talk to me much," Jonathan said. "They talked to Ashlynn though. She went into all this medical stuff with them."

"What did they tell Ashlynn about Nat?"

"They said there's a chance," Jonathan said. "They said she's really healthy, and that helps, I guess. But they're worried about vital organs or infections or something."

"What did Ashlynn say?"

"She said we have to leave soon. She said she wouldn't let Nat die. She keeps repeating that."

"I see," said Jonas. "I'm sure she'll do everything she can."

"Where are you?" Jonathan asked worriedly. There seemed to be more to the question, but Jonas couldn't put his finger on what.

"I'm taking care of some business," Jonas replied. "I'll meet up with you later."

Jonathan was quiet.

"Okay?" Jonas asked.

"Yeah," Jonathan said, in the deadpan voice he used when he wanted to get his dad off his back. Well, Jonas reconsidered. This was different. What's Jonathan thinking that he would use that voice? It's almost like he doesn't think I'll be back.

Will I be?

What if I'm not? Maybe I should make arrangements.

"What's wrong, Johnny?" Jonas finally said.

"Are you going to be okay, Dad?"

"Of course," Jonas replied. "Why?"

"It's nothing," Jonathan said.

"Are *you* going to be okay?"

"Yeah." Same deadpan voice.

"It's going to be okay, son," Jonas said.

"No, it's not, Dad!" Jonathan yelled. "We'll never see them again!"

"Yes, we will, son," Jonas said as sincerely and evenly as possible. "In Heaven."

I have to be strong, Jonas thought. But he found it hard to say the words. It was admitting that they were gone all over again.

Chris, how will I raise Jonathan without you, my love? You always knew what to say to the kids to set their minds at ease. How do I comfort Johnny now? I have to be strong for him. Kids need stability. He needs me to show him how to get through this. I have to support him, even if I am not okay myself.

Jonathan didn't say anything.

"Right, son?" Jonas asked apprehensively.

"Heaven," Jonathan repeated monotonously. "After everything that happened, you still believe, Dad?"

"Of course I do, Jonathan," Jonas said defensively. "Keep the faith, son."

I *am* keeping my faith, Jonas told himself. Chris, he thought, help me find His Will. He felt blind as he looked out of the tinted window into the night, unseeing.

"It's times like this," Jonas found himself saying, "when you must keep the faith. ...Jonathan? Johnny, are you there?"

Jonas' heart began to thump in his ears as he started wondering what his son might be going through mentally and spiritually. His own grief had made it hard to think of anything but his loss and the desire to lash out at the man who had done this. *Oh God*, Jonas thought as he replayed the last day in his mind. *I haven't really been there for him. We were running and...*

"Johnny, I'm—" Jonas began.

"I've been thinking," Jonathan said at the same time, "in the Bible..."

He stopped, having heard his father.

"Go ahead," Jonas said, thinking he could apologize later.

"Jonathan and David are best friends in the Bible, right?"

Jonas let out a controlled breath in apprehension.

"Yes, son, they were. Your mother and I always wanted you two to get along. You see, I didn't get along with my brothers very well."

"Oh," said Jonathan. "I guess I fucked that up too."

"Don't be so hard on yourself, Johnny!" Jonas said. "People go through phases. I know you loved your brother."

"Yeah."

"So," Jonas pushed, trying to keep his son talking. "What made you think of 1 Samuel?"

The silence stretched.

"Johnny?"

"It's nothing," Jonathan said. "I'm probably just being stupid."

"Come on, Johnny, just tell me."

"In the Bible, Jonathan dies protecting David," Jonathan said.

Jonas felt his bile rise.

"Johnny, that's..."

"I'm the one who should have died!" Jonathan blurted out.

"No, Johnny, no!" Jonas choked. "Don't think that!"

"David is the one you and Mom loved. He believed. Why would God take him? No one believed more than Mom and David. But I'm still here. It's my fault. I should have protected him. I..."

His voice sounded empty. Hollow and fragile.

"No, Johnny," Jonas said urgently.

My God! Jonas' mind reeled! His thoughts all screamed in his head at once. *How do I help him? If he thinks that, what will he do? What do I say? What will he do if I don't handle this right?*

Nat's words came to him suddenly, *"Your son needs you."*

I'm losing him, Jonas thought. I've been losing him. I... I have been so focused on losing Chris and Davey that I've been ignoring him. Oh, God, help me, Chris!

"Listen to me, Johnny," Jonas tried frantically to find the right words. "You're not to blame! There was nothing you could have done!"

There was silence, so Jonas kept talking, growing more frantic and terrified.

"Listen! You can't blame yourself for this! Are you there? Do you hear me?!"

"Yeah."

"Johnny," Jonas said, running his hand through his hair. "Johnny, please! You can't...you just can't see it that way."

"Yeah." Deadpan.

Oh God! Jonas screamed in his head. It's not working! I'm not getting through to him!

A powerful sob struck Jonas as he felt something inside him break. Despair flooded through him—despair for what he'd lost and for what he could still lose.

"Johnny!" he sobbed. "Please! I can't lose you too. I—I love you, Johnny. Please! I can't..."

"Dad," Jonathan said, surprised. But Jonas didn't hear him. He was sobbing uncontrollably into the phone, his thoughts pouring out unfiltered.

"Please! Oh God, please! God, help me tell him! Tell him I love him! I can't lose him. Not my boy, no... oh God, my little boy!"

"Dad!" Jonathan yelled. He was crying, too.

"Johnny! I love you! I can't lose you!"

"I love you too, Dad!"

***

Nat slept as the medical jet flew over the Gulf of Mexico, the lights of the oceanside cities getting smaller. Jonathan was asleep, curled up across three tiny seats. Ashlynn sat beside Nat, her chin resting on her hand, carefully avoiding the holstered gun Nat had asked to be beside her at all times. Ashlynn didn't think it was necessary. Their careful movements and the digital smokescreen Daryl maintained kept Dolion from knowing where they were.

Ashlynn was exhausted. Regardless, she couldn't sleep. Her mind wouldn't shut up. Nat's arm jerked, causing Ashlynn to sit up and check on her. She's dreaming, Ashlynn thought.

Nat's surgery had taken all day—just over twelve hours. The bullet hadn't just gone through her—it had torn through her. It traveled at high velocity, causing large temporary cavitation and it fragmented, increasing the damage. The doctors had rebuilt her intestines. They'd had less than half to work with. The bullet had also traveled dangerously close to her liver. Because of that, the doctors hadn't wanted to move her. Still, there was no choice. They couldn't stay in one place too long.

"You're one tough cookie, Nat," Ashlynn murmured, squeezing her hand. "You just need to hang in there a bit longer."

She squeezed Nat's hand again as a chain of scenarios for her condition played out in Ashlynn's mind. One way or another, my friend, you'll live.

I can't lose you.

Ashlynn drew a pattern on the plain white blanket.

"Daryl," she asked, afraid of the answer, "what happened to Josh?"

"I'm sorry, Ashlynn," he replied. "His body was found yesterday."

Ashlynn's hand went limp.

"Officials report," Daryl said gently, "that he was run off the road while cycling."

Ashlynn bowed her head, remembering he liked to "do triathlon." She laid her head on the bed, near Nat's hand.

"Are you okay, dear?" the medical jet nurse asked her, putting her arm around Ashlynn's shoulders. Ashlynn hadn't noticed her come in.

"I... I'm tired," Ashlynn responded. "Thank you, though."

The nurse comforted her for a moment longer before checking Nat's vitals and leaving.

"I think I was falling for him, Daryl."

"Yes."

"You know," she sighed. "When I decided not to be a brain in a vat, I was hoping to find someone."

"I didn't know that."

"I guess it didn't occur to me that my seventeen-year-old body would pose a problem. There's no way I'd be interested in anyone that age. And there was no way that anyone my actual age would be interested in me—and if they were, it would be too creepy."

"You could have eventually let Josh know," Daryl suggested.

"Maybe."

Ashlynn wiped away tears.

"You're not repressing your emotions as much as you used to," Daryl said.

"Only took me forty years to figure that one out."

"Some never do."

She thought of how Daryl had helped her remember Brandon and meeting Becky for the first time.

"Daryl," Ashlynn said, adjusting her head on the bed. "In my memory, my Nana sang a song at my grandfather's funeral, but I can't remember what the song was. I was very young. Can you help me remember?"

"I can try," Daryl replied.

***

Ashlynn closed her eyes. She did not feel anything change at first, but as she tried to remember the experience, it suddenly became as real as if she were back in the chapel that day—the smell of candle vigils filled her nose, and Grampa's closest friends, wearing their best, sat all around the small community church.

Aisling sat between her parents.

Oh.

They were alive when he passed.

Her mother and father towered above her four-year-old stature. Her mother's voluminous, long, and fiery red hair fell about her shoulders, brushing Aisling's wavy hair. Her father, dignified, sat with his straight strawberry blonde hair in a combover. He wore thick black glasses.

He was crying.

Ashlynn wanted to speak, to talk to them, but, as before, she could not interact with the memory.

Her grandmother stood and walked down the center of the aisle. She seemed so much younger, even with crow's feet around her eyes. Her straight hair was the same strawberry blonde color as her father's, not the pure white that Aisling remembered. When her grandmother reached the front of the aisle, she stood before the casket, her hand on the dark wood for a moment before turning and addressing the congregation.

"Me 'usband, Sean," she said in her thick Irish accent. "Well, 'e 'ated sad songs."

Several people murmured in agreement. Aisling's heart ached at hearing her grandmother's voice so clearly again.

"But e's not 'ere ti'day, or I'd 'ave a dhing or two to say to 'im!"

The congregation chuckled.

"Dhis song, 'e loved it the most."

At a nod from her grandmother, the church choir stood, and a man hefted his guitar. Someone quickly stood and pulled the piano bench from under the piano, opening the lid. It was where her grandfather would have sat to play for the congregation, Ashlynn realized.

Nana smiled at the man in thanks and brushed away a tear. She hefted her fiddle and began to play the sad melody with her eyes closed. The guitarist joined her, and picked up the song as Nana lowered her instrument and began to sing. Her pure, silvery voice filled the room, alone at first, then joined by the guitar, then by the choir.

They sang 'The Parting Glass.'

Ashlynn listened to the verses, absorbing every nuance. The whole congregation was singing. She thought of sweet, gentle Ro and how he had shared memories of his childhood with her. It had been so cathartic, so healing to laugh with him. In the darkest moments of being tortured, she wasn't sure if she'd ever be able to laugh again.

I will remember you most for that, Ro.

Nat, you helped me too, in your own way. With your amazing strength—you inspire me. And your genius at chess! Oh, Grampa, you would have loved her! I have been in such good company, Ashlynn felt, as she mourned everyone she'd lost and worried about everyone she might still lose.

Oh, Josh, she thought as she listened to her grandmother sing. No, I can't merely listen to music in the background. It means too much to me to become part of any banal moment. Just like the music you shared with me—what was it? Bashing Puddles?—I will forever keep that music you shared with me as part of my memory of you, Josh,

Her grandmother paused and the musicians stopped playing for a few beats. As the song ended, she sang solo again, tears glistening on her cheeks.

> *But since 'e fell an' it be me lot*
> *That I should rise and 'e could not*

I'll gently rise an' I'll softly call
G'night and joy be to us all

***

Ashlynn opened her eyes to the dim lights of the plane, the song echoing in her mind.

She wiped her tears.

"Thank you, Daryl," she said in her mind.

The nurse had put a blanket over her shoulders.

"Daryl," she thought, sitting up and wrapping herself in the blanket. "Are the preparations on schedule?"

"Yes. There is one complication, however."

"What?"

"You have a video message. It was sent to your cellphone."

Her cell phone had been taken when she was abducted, but the actual device was only for the sake of appearances. Opening the messages application in her mind, she found there was only one unread message from an unknown sender. It was sent yesterday. I guess I haven't really been paying attention, she thought, as she was about to open it.

"Don't open it yet," Daryl said. "That's the complication."

"Why? Who is it from?"

"The message is from the President."

"Oh, good," Ashlynn barked a laugh involuntarily out loud.

The nurse glanced up, then returned to checking on Nat. She was recording a reading from the bilirubinometer. The nurse looked over the data and walked out. Was that concern on her face, or was she just in a hurry?

"I was hoping for something to cheer me up!" Ashlynn thought.

"I don't think it's a cheerful messa—"

"Daryl," Ashlynn interrupted. "You have the computational power of five humans, and the resources of hundreds. You can read my thoughts and make me relive memories—but you still can't figure out my sarcasm?"

"It makes you laugh when I pretend I don't understand," Daryl replied wryly.

Ashlynn rolled her eyes.

"I guess I love you for that," she said.

Her expression darkened.

"The message is probably some kind of threat about Becky."

She steeled herself.

"Let's see the message, then."

"When this message is retrieved from the server," Daryl said. "Dolion will know."

"Ah, I see. That's the complication."

"I can retrieve it via a botnet," Daryl said. "Then forward it to you."

"Don't forward it to me. Play it on a disposable computer and screen-capture it."

"I'll work on that," Daryl said. "I have another question for you."

"What?"

"You instructed me to proceed with helping Jonas. I am, but is that still what you wish to do?"

"That has been on my mind..."

"Yes," Daryl confirmed. "You hesitate. My prime directives won't allow me to proceed without your full backing because the effort may result in the death of one or more humans."

Ashlynn regarded Nat and wondered how she had come to her decision. Did she decide based on the utilitarian ethics of the big picture, or some internal deontological calculus? Was it based on heuristics pounded into the core of every Army Ranger? Was it loyalty to the country?

"Jonas doesn't seem to see any moral issues with it," Daryl remarked.

"No," Ashlynn agreed. "Though his moral compass may have been lost when Chris was murdered in cold blood."

"Do you mean that his grief blinds him, or that he depended on Chris for his moral decisions?"

"Both."

"Your own calculus is more utilitarian and humanist," Daryl said. "You worry that the greatest harm would come from the consequences of the United States falling into anarchy. Moreover, you worry that other countries might strike while the US is weakened. Russia and China may aggressively expand, forcing other countries to take a stand or do nothing as they invade their neighbors."

"There is still the Vice President," Ashlynn said. "But he's as charismatic as a stump. Dolion's puppet. He'll lose control and the militia factions Dolion's been empowering will lash out, sparking a wildfire of violence. There are strong factions on the left, and they will retaliate. Civil war is inevitable. The US nuclear weapons arsenal could fall into the wrong hands."

"So," Daryl said. "There is an escalated possibility there will be a World War III?"

"Maybe," Ashlynn said numbly.

"But these potential events would not be your doing," Daryl said. "Everyone on Earth is responsible for their own choices."

"The adjacent probable, Daryl," Ashlynn said. "Without the president, the most probable course is a chain of events that will likely result in war and suffering."

"Perhaps," Daryl said. "The bottom line is that you choose who dies or President Dolion chooses."

"The people can bring Dolion down themselves."

She reconsidered.

"But not if he builds GED.ai as planned. He would have near-perfect intelligence on every citizen. A dictator's dream."

Ashlynn shuddered.

"Is this what you meant," Daryl asked, "when you said you wished I had more resources?"

"Go on..."

"You built me," Daryl said, "and now you have the power to stop any other General AI from being built because I could assimilate emergent systems."

"Right, but I'll need your resources for the moon base..."

She paused.

"...and everything that comes after."

Daryl's tone softened.

"Dolion is forcing you to make a decision."

"Yes," she said. "It's like I'm watching a toddler run toward the fire, and I can't stop her. Only it's not a toddler. It's humanity choosing a path to destruction."

"In observational biology," Daryl said, "the creed is to not interfere with nature. You observe what happens, and you allow it to happen. You let the child run into the fire."

"Even if it breaks your heart."

Ashlynn put her face in her hands.

"I can't do that Daryl," she said. "I just can't!"

"Confirmed," Daryl said.

CHAPTER 28

"Ashlynn," Daryl said. "I have completed your instructions. Dolion's message is ready for you to view."

Ashlynn groaned. She had put the video out of her mind.

"It was a good decision to record the video message," Daryl continued. "There was an embedded link that auto-followed when I hit play. I detected malware activity on the playback machine."

Ashlynn sat up. Malware? Probably to track her and to send audio surveillance. She had to steel herself all over again.

It was harder this time.

"Play your safe recording."

The interior of the plane faded from her vision.

"Hello, sugar," Dolion's face appeared.

Ashlynn shivered.

"Now, they tell me that your phone is sittin' in an FBI evidence vault somewhere and that you probably won't get this in time. But I say so long as we got yer' girl, you not getting this message is about as likely as pigs flyin' outta my ass."

He laughed darkly.

"Listen up," he said, pausing for effect. "Your girl's got twenty-four hours to live. In one day, little Becky and her cute little bunny are gonna go to a hospital in the night, and there's gonna be some unfortunate news—if you catch my drift."

He grinned and tapped his wrist.

"Clock's a tickin', doctor."

The video stopped.

She tightened the blanket the nurse had given her around her shoulders.

Fucking monster! she thought.

"Daryl? When is the deadline?"

"In thirty-six minutes, forty-five seconds."

"Damnit! Why didn't you share this video earlier?"

"The plan to save Becky is in motion."

"And?"

"I need your assistance on several key points."

"And?!" Ashlynn prompted impatiently.

"I have arranged for Becky to be transferred into the custody of a man who is our employee," said Daryl. "I need you to verify to Becky that it is okay to go with him in order to guarantee her compliance."

"When?"

"Eight minutes, fourteen seconds from now."

***

"Thank you. I'll take it from here," the man said, flashing his badge.

Tara was confused.

She folded her arms, suspicions creeping in.

Unconsciously, she began tapping her toe as she pulled out her phone. This deviation from the schedule was not on the manifest this morning. She wasn't about to hang for someone else's fucking mistake.

"What was your name again?"

"Biggs."

Tara checked her mail app. There was a new message with instructions. She read through it. Well, there it was. Revised schedule, transfer to Biggs at 2:33 AM. She checked her watch. On the dot! That was odd. Why didn't I see this? The delivery timestamp said two hours ago. Huh. I am sure I checked again within that time. She shrugged. It didn't matter. She had proof if anyone asked.

The original plan had been to meet up with Dr. Kaspor, or whatever his name was. At that point, Becky would no longer be her problem. What did it matter if this Biggs took her away instead? It would be good to finally be rid of the brat. She dropped the girl's hand and pushed her forward.

"She's all yours, Biggs."

Without a word, Tara walked away. I think I'll get a marg to celebrate, she thought, never looking back.

***

President Dolion watched Tara walk away on the CCTV camera. The feed was broadcast to the main screen in the control room at his private estate in rural Texas. The facility offered more flexibility to operate as a private citizen than as an officer of the federal government. A full intelligence team clacked away on the keyboards in the control room below.

"Clever, Doctor," Dolion said. "But not clever enough."

He nodded, and the commander on the floor picked up his phone. He began to give instructions in a low tone.

Dolion walked over to the technician who'd intercepted the message that Daryl had sent to Tara.

"Heckuva job, son," he said, putting his hand on the technician's shoulder.

The technician nodded meekly.

"Move into position," the commander said, hanging up.

He pointed to one of the analysts, barking orders.

Much more competent than that moron, Dina Keats, the President thought. I hope she's enjoying her time on the front lines with the rest of the cannon fodder.

"How's that trace coming?" the commander asked.

"The system that retrieved the message is from a data center in Wyoming."

"Get a team ready!" the commander replied.

On the CCTV screen, Becky was obviously wary of Biggs. Tara came into view on another CCTV camera. She hadn't stuck around to watch Biggs bend to one knee and grin conspiratorially at Becky.

Fool woman, Dolion thought. More cannon fodder.

"Hi, Becky," Biggs was saying sweetly. "I'm here to help you." Becky didn't answer.

"A mutual friend sent me," he said. "Do you know Miss Ash?" Becky's eyes lit up.

***

"Daryl, I'm in," Jonas said.

He breathed a sigh of relief.

The small single-engine aircraft was clean but ancient and had a musty smell. It reminded him of Opa's rusty shed, where he kept that old '66 that he never got around to restoring.

"So, you're going to fly this thing, right?" Jonas asked. "You were joking before, right? You've got a laptop set up somewhere I can't see?"

"I thought you didn't want me to fly for you again," Daryl replied.

"Ha ha," said Jonas, sarcastically.

He surveyed the dashboard, and although it seemed slightly less complicated than the jet cockpit he still had no clue what he was looking at.

"So, where's the laptop?"

"There is no laptop, Jonas," Daryl said. "You're the pilot."

"There's no way, Daryl!"

"Don't worry," Daryl said. "I'll walk you through it."

"Daryl…"

"Please place your phone on the dash," Daryl said. "There is a mount there. Yes, good. There are headphones on the seat. Go ahead and put those on."

"Can you hear me?" Jonas asked, adjusting the bulky headset and placing the microphone in front of his mouth.

"Yes, Jonas. Very good."

"I'm not sure I understand the plan, Daryl," Jonas said.

"I will patch you through to the President twice," Daryl said. "The first time, to tell him that you're coming for him. The second time to share your true feelings with him."

"Okay," Jonas said, his anxiety rising. "There's still the part about me flying…"

"On the instrument panel in front of you," Daryl said, "please turn on the master switch."

Jonas read the labels. There seemed to be a million.

"Where the fuck is the master switch?"

"On the left. It's a big red rocker switch. It is labeled 'Master' with 'alt' and 'bat' below that. It's two switches connected together."

Jonas found it. Thankfully, it was actually labeled as Daryl described. Many of the other labels seemed to have worn off. He flicked on the switch, and the glow of the instrument lights lit up the cockpit.

"Good job, Jonas," Daryl said enthusiastically.

"Shut up," he responded. "Now what?"

"To the right of the master switch, there is the 'fuel pump' switch. Turn that on."

"No," Jonas said. "That one says 'avionics.'"

"To the right, below that."

Seven painful steps later, Jonas turned the key and the engine roared to life.

"Oil pressure needle is in the….red…no green."

"Good," Daryl said. "Four more steps to go, and we can start taxiing."

Despite his anxiety, Jonas began feeling exhilarated at the prospect of flying. I can fucking do this! he thought.

"Daryl," he asked. "Where's the bombs? The guns? Weapons?

This plane seems a little small…"

"On the dash," Daryl said, wryly.

Jonas looked around at all the buttons. None of the labels seemed to indicate a weapons system.

"I meant your phone, Jonas," Daryl said. "It's the weapon."

"Ha ha," Jonas said. "Very funny. Now where are they really?"

***

Biggs showed Becky his phone.

"Hi, Becky!" Ashlynn said.

"Miss Ash!" Becky squealed. "Is it really you?"

"Yes," Ashlynn said. "Is that Bun-Bun?"

Becky held up the toy, smiling happily.

"Oh, my goodness," Ashlynn said. "What happened to her cap?"

"She lost it," Becky said, frowning. "Bun-Bun is always losing things."

She shook her finger at the rabbit sternly.

Ashlynn giggled.

"Becky," she said. "How would you like to come stay with me for a while?"

Becky jumped in delight and nodded.

"Great!" Ashlynn said. "Mr. Biggs will bring you to the airport and help you get on a plane to come visit me."

Becky glanced at Mr. Biggs. She liked his face, but his business suit looked like all the other mean people's clothes. Ashlynn noticed her worried expression.

"Becky, what's wrong?"

"None of the mean people will come, right?" Becky asked. "They hurt you, Miss Ash. I saw them. I won't go if they're going to hurt you again. But I'm really glad to see you…"

"Oh, Becky," Ashlynn said. "I'm glad to see you too. Don't worry, no mean people are coming. Mr. Biggs is nice. He'll bring you right to me. Would you like that?"

"Yes, Miss Ash," Becky grinned. "Very much."

***

"'Oh My', Magic…Target, BRAA, 270, 10, 18000, drag west, MTA, hostile."

"'Oh My'," Major Stacey Gaud replied, banking and applying more throttle. A moment later, she radioed back.

"Magic, 'Oh My', radar contact, 270, 10, 18000."

Major Gaud designated the target on the radar controls with

practiced ease. Hostile? A Medical Transport Aircraft? They weren't likely to have any weapons capability. Was AWACS telling her to bring it down? Major Gaud would not hesitate to follow orders, but that didn't mean she had to like them.

"Tally MTA, 1 mile," she radioed, dropping the call signs since no other pilots were active.

"'Oh My', Magic, weapons hold."

Formal tonight, she thought.

She was relieved she didn't have to open fire immediately but tried to prepare herself mentally for the possibility of firing on the civilian aircraft.

Easing into position at the MTA's control point, she checked the status of the CCA wingman and settled it into a holding pattern.

The moon glistened on the gulf below. Her mind wanted to wander to the fantastic evening she had planned with her girl friends later, but she kept it focused on the task at hand. She had not come as far as she had without being able to control her thoughts.

She kept her eye on the target to monitor for any deviations in its flight and hoped that she'd be able to return to base to meet up with the girls without innocent blood on her hands.

***

"Now, ain't that a sweet picture?" President Dolion said with a grimace of disgust as Becky giggled with Ashlynn on the big screen.

"Sir," the commander said. "Have you made a decision? We have a lock on the plane Doctor Ramsey and Jonas are in. An F-16 and CCA have been following them for an hour now."

"What's a CCA?" Dolion asked the commander.

"Collaborative Combat Aircraft, sir. It's a type of unmanned aerial vehicle that assists the fighter jets as wingmen."

"God, I love tech," Dolion said.

"Sir," the commander said. "GED.ai team reports discovery of a data center Daryl is operating out of."

"What about the systems Daryl compromised? Did you find them all?"

"Yes, sir," the commander said. "Our security team is confident we've isolated those systems and have secured communication channels. We've begun work to shut down several bot nets linked to Daryl's operations."

Dolion watched Becky walk hand-in-hand with Biggs out of the hospital. The whole scene was so sweet it made him sick.

"Look how they think they've won," Dolion mused.

"Sir?"

"Shut up!" Dolion snapped. "I want to savor this."

I could shoot you down right now, Doctor. But I don't think I want to. I want to see you face-to-face. I want to be there when they finish the job and break you. Jonas too.

"Have the fighter continue to follow, just in case," Dolion said. "Send a... delegation... to greet them at their destination."

"Yes sir!"

Dolion chuckled, planning what he would say. Should I send another video? Should I hint that I know their plans, or should I be quiet until the trap is sprung?

"Sir!" the commander yelled abruptly, pressing his headset to his head. "Sir, we have incoming!"

"What?"

"There appears to be a small single-engine aircraft heading right for us. There's a video call from the craft. It's Jonas Williams, sir."

Dolion was surprised. "That som'bitch? You assholes told me he was on that plane!"

He pointed to the plane on the map, flying over the Gulf of Mexico.

"Sir, I..."

"Put him through," Dolion growled.

The commander nodded and gave orders into his headset.

Jonas' face appeared on the big screen in front of Dolion. His face was underlit by instrument panels. The noise of the small aircraft engine was annoyingly loud. Dolion motioned for the volume to be turned down.

"Jonas," the President said. "Just what in tarnation do you think you're doin'?"

Jonas' response was delayed.

"Hello, Mr. Fucking President!" Jonas said angrily.

"Whoa-ho-ho," Dolion laughed. "Tough guy now, huh?"

The feed was choppy. Jonas appeared to be talking, but the sound came through in spurts.

"...Fucking...sshole...killed my...mily...ucker!" Jonas was yelling.

"Wash off your war paint there, Jonas," Dolion said, chuckling. He turned to the commander. "Can we fix this shit?"

The commander nodded and spoke to a technician.

"Jonas," Dolion said. "Your signal's all wonky. Maybe you ought best get to the point."

"The signal should be coming in stronger now, sir," a technician said.

"Jonas?" Dolion said. "You there?"

"Yes," Jonas said. "I'm here."

"What are you doin' Jonas?"

"I'm bringing you to church," Jonas said. "The one you told me about."

Dolion glanced at his commander.

"F16 and CCA deployed," he said. "Fifteen minutes until they intercept Mr. Williams' aircraft."

"So," Dolion said, opening the channel to Jonas again. "You're gonna do what exactly in that rickety hummin' bird of yours?"

The signal cut out.

"Sir," the commander laughed. "It...it seems he plans to suicide bomb us."

Dolion shook his head. Ridiculous!

"I'm sick of this shit," Dolion said. "Commander, shoot that moron out of the sky, but let the girl and Biggs go. Let our little princess and her bunny fly all the way across the fuckin' world if need be. Let her hug the good Doctor Ramsey when she lands. Then dispose of the vermin and bring the Doctor in."

"Yes, Mr. President," the commander said.

Dolion sat and tapped his fingers. His annoyance left abruptly as he received a report from the GED.ai team.

"Hot damn!" he said, grinning as he read.

"On second thought," he said. "Put me through to the good Doctor. It's high time we had us a little come to Jesus meetin'."

***

"Are you sure you want to do this, Jonas?" Ashlynn asked. "The repercussions..."

"I'm sure, Ash," he said. "I think the plan Daryl came up with will work."

He had his phone propped up on the dash of the plane. The noise was incredible.

"Nothing is guaranteed," she said.

"I know," he nodded. "Jonathan's safe with you?"

"Yes," Ashlynn said. "He'll be with us at the house in French Guiana until you can arrange for his return."

"Good," Jonas said. "I'll have to make... arrangements... when all this is done."

Ashlynn nodded sympathetically. He must mean the funeral for Chris and Davey.

"Are you sure about this?" she asked to divert his thoughts.

"I have to do this, Ashlynn," Jonas said. "Dolion has to be stopped."

Jonathan shifted in his sleep.

"I know, but..."

"I just can't shake this feeling, though," Jonas said. "Like he knows. Like Dolion somehow knows what we're doing."

"Jonas," she said.

"Well, what if he does?" Jonas said. "He has all the power."

Ashlynn nodded thoughtfully.

"If anything happens to me, take care of Jonathan, Ashlynn," Jonas said. "He's all I have left."

"I will, Jonas," she said sadly. "Good luck to you."

"You as well," he said.

When they hung up, the nurse walked in. She froze at the sight of Nat on the bed. Ashlynn noticed it too. Her skin was faintly yellow.

"Jaundice," Ashlynn said, standing. The blanket fell around her feet. She looked at the nurse. "Her liver is failing!"

The nurse nodded, then took out her phone to call the doctors. Ashlynn was about to move into a better position to help the nurse when her phone started ringing in her mind.

"Ashlynn," Daryl said. "It's the President. And... there's a problem."

Ashlynn gritted her teeth.

"Nat's right. I hate it when you say that. What problem?"

Ashlynn watched the nurse work, waiting for Daryl's response.

The call connected instead.

"Hello, sugar," President Dolion said.

"Dolion," she replied. "To what do I owe the displeasure?"

"How's the flight?" he asked. "Comfy?"

"I've had better."

"I'd ask to talk to Jonas," Dolion said. "But I guess he's not there. Fool boy thinks he can come after me."

"Daryl," Ashlynn thought. "What's the status of the medical team in French Guiana?"

Daryl did not answer.

"And it looks like Becky is safely in the hands of your man,

Biggs," Dolion was saying.

The blood drained from Ashlynn's face.

"Oh, don't you worry 'bout it none," Dolion said. "You'll see her when you land."

"Who else will I see when we land?" Ashlynn breathed.

"I reckon you know."

Ashlynn closed her eyes.

"Daryl, why aren't you responding?!"

"About now, yer' probably wonderin'," he said. "Why your precious Daryl isn't respondin'."

She froze.

"It's because," Dolion said, "I done got rid of all the machines your little Daryl virus was on."

Ashlynn felt her brow furrow. Virus?

"Of course," Dolion said. "A smart girl like you had a backup plan. We've been tracking Daryl's movements for a while."

"You lied to me about Daryl before," Ashlynn replied, keeping her anxiety down as much as possible. "Why should I believe you now?"

"Well," Dolion grinned. "Why don't you ask him with that little brain implant of yours?"

Ashlynn blanched.

"Daryl!"

"See you soon," Dolion said. "Doctor."

***

"Mr. President," the commander said. "We have one minute thirty seconds to intercept."

"Good," Dolion said. "How far away from us is Mr. Williams, out of morbid curiosity?"

The commander snorted. "Two minutes."

"Commander," a technician said. "Incoming call sir. It's Mr. Williams."

"Put the jackass through," Dolion said.

"It's only audio sir, he's not sending video. Probably because of the poor connection before."

"Okay," Dolion said.

"Dolion," Jonas said over the loudspeaker. It sounded much better.

"Hello, Jonas," Dolion said, smiling. "Are you callin' to say goodbye?"

"Yes," Jonas said.

"You know, Jonas," Dolion said. "Your problem is you're too damn confident. Have you heard of the Dunning-Kreuger effect?"

Without waiting for an answer, Dolion explained.

"It describes the psychological phenomenon where one feels competent in a field of study that they, in fact, are not competent in a'tall."

"Sounds fitting," Jonas said.

"You, sir," Dolion said, his voice raising, "are operatin' under a delusion! Do you realize that right this second you are moments away from bein' blown out of the sky!?"

Jonas snorted.

"Let me put this to you straight, Jonas. In about three hours, the good doctor is gonna land with your son, and my guys will be there to collect 'em. The doctor's little girl and your son will walk into the hands of my soldiers, and you're about to be blown out of the sky."

"Not before I get you," Jonas said.

"If you think that AI toy computer will help you, you're sadly mistaken. We blew up the remaining data centers and purged it from our systems minutes ago. You're done, Jonas."

"No, asshole," Jonas said. "You and your FATs are done."

"You think killin' me will solve anythin'?" Dolion laughed.

"Chop off the head of the snake, and the body will die."

"No, son," Dolion said. "Not gunna happen. Besides, even if I die, a shitstorm would come down so hard and fast you'd think you were fucked by a tornado."

"Not if I can help it!"

"Sharp like a bowlin' ball, this one," Dolion laughed.

Everyone in the control room laughed with him.

***

The call with Dolion disconnected.

"Daryl?" Ashlynn tried again.

No answer.

The nurse beckoned to her to help her with Nat. A few minutes later, there was a loud explosion, and the plane seemed to shudder and veer forward as if hit from behind.

Ashlynn and the nurse tumbled, caught unaware.

"What the...?!" Jonathan yelled, jolted awake. "Oh my god! What's happening?! Are we crashing again?!"

Nat groaned weakly.

"I don't know," Ashlynn said. "Stay there! Don't move!"

Jonathan stopped reaching for his seatbelt.

"Shit!" he yelled, as the plane veered to one side.

The nurse, concern on her face, stood and immediately returned to check Nat's wound with one hand. With the other, she braced herself on the bed rail with a white-knuckled grip. Ashlynn stood up too, holding on to the bed as well, while trying to pick up supplies that had fallen on the floor.

"I dropped my phone," the nurse said. "Can you help me find it?"

Ashlynn picked up the last of the fallen supplies and spotted the phone. It was too far to reach without letting go of the rail. She tried to reach for it with her foot but accidentally kicked it away.

"I need that!" The nurse said, holding Nat's medical equipment in place. "The doctor was giving me instructions!"

Ashlynn tried to balance herself.

She concentrated and took a step.

***

When the laughter in the control room quieted down, Dolion slapped his knee.

"I reckon' this here's a hoot," he said. "You know, Jonas, I used to think you were smart, but it turns out you can't ride and chew at the same time."

More laughter.

"Jonas?" Dolion said. "Any last words?"

Silence.

Dolion shot a questioning look at the commander, who shrugged.

"We're still connected," said a technician after a moment.

"Is your tongue all tuckered out, Jonas?" Dolion asked.

"No," Jonas said. "I'm just getting ready. It won't be long now."

Dolion's humor left him in a flash.

"You listen to me, jackass," he said. He glanced at the intercept time. There were 13 seconds left until Jonas would be blown to kingdom come. He nodded to the commander.

"I done signed your fuckin' death warrant," Dolion said, spittle flying. "You're about to meet your maker!"

Jonas did not respond.

Dolion calmed his voice.

"It's kinda sweet, really. It'll be a nice family reunion in heaven after I send your oldest up to meetcha."

"You're going to pay, you asshole," Jonas replied angrily.

Dolion laughed.

The countdown clock ticked to zeros.

Dolion smiled.

"Goodbye, Jonas," Dolion said.

No one said a word.

Dolion glanced at the commander.

"Confirm target was destroyed," the commander said.

"I-I'm trying," a soldier said. "It's frozen, sir."

"What?"

"What the fuck?" Someone else said loudly.

The abruptness of it caught Dolion off guard.

"What?" the commander said. "What is it?"

The main screen turned on. Jonas was standing outdoors at an airport with his phone in his hand, arm outstretched, videoing a selfie. He stood before a parked single-engine plane in disheveled, dirty, and torn clothes. A jacket was slung over his shoulder and the sun was rising behind him.

"Sorry," Jonas said. "Technical difficulties. Are you there?"

"What the fuck!" Dolion said. "He's not flying!?"

"It's gone!" the technician said. "The target's gone!"

"What are you talking about?" the commander yelled.

"Jonas' plane, sir! It's no longer on the radar."

"Sir!" Another technician called. "The F16 is at the target's location. They can confirm no visual, sir. Repeat, no visual!"

"Jonas, what are you playin' at?" Dolion asked angrily.

"I'd like to introduce you to my friend, Mr. President," Jonas said.

A tall man walked onto the screen. He wore a maroon cable-knit turtleneck and well-fitted black slacks. His hands were clasped behind his back, and he was smiling.

"This is Daryl," Jonas said.

Daryl's form flickered digitally.

He winked.

Dolion stared in shock. "What—" he breathed.

"Are you a praying man, Mr. President?" Jonas interrupted.

"Friendly fire!" another technician said. "Sir, the CCA! AWACS reports that the CCA has opened fire on the F16! Friendly fire! Friendly fire! They're hit!"

"What the fuck do you mean?"

"The F16 is down, sir!"

"Oh my God! It's fired missiles!" said another technician. "It's unloading everything!"

"At what?"

"At us!"

There was panic in the control room.

Dolion growled. He gritted his teeth as he stared at the screen.

Jonas was watching him.

"Who's sweating at church now?" Jonas asked.

Dolion felt the building shake.

Someone started to scream.

Jonas' grim smile was engulfed in a brilliant, blinding light.

"Go to Hell, Mr. President."

CHAPTER 29

Ashlynn tripped as the plane rocked, barely catching herself in time to avoid a head injury. She scrambled up, holding onto whatever she could for stability.

"I'm gunna try video conference," the nurse said. She grabbed the remote. The teleconference system turned on, and several doctors' faces appeared. There was a video image showing Nat from the overhead camera. The nurse adjusted the camera so that it was centered on her wound. It was seeping. She held out her hand to Ashlynn for gauze.

"Hi, Ashlynn," Daryl said cheerily in her mind.

Ashlynn dropped the gauze.

"Daryl! What happened?"

The nurse gave her an exasperated look. Ashlynn quickly grabbed another strip and handed it to her.

"It's over," Daryl replied.

"I don't understand. Why did Dolion say you were gone?"

"I used your favorite 'hacking' technique," Daryl said, his voice calm in contrast to the barely controlled chaos in the cabin of the plane. "I set up a honeypot, a decoy, by creating a disposable data center and a botnet. I fabricated clues for GED.ai to piece together, giving misleading information about your hypercortex to sweeten the pot. When he called, he thought he had you cornered again, which was enough to distract him and his team. I added to the believability by remaining silent and surprising you with the extra information. I apologize for that."

"You almost gave me a panic attack!" she said.

Ashlynn was splitting her attention, following the doctors' conversation and the nurse undressing the wound and performing tests. They were assessing the nature of the acute liver failure as well as they could remotely. Worst case, Nat would require a transplant. The doctors were checking to see if there were any available options to find a donated liver and have it transported to the hospital in French Guiana.

"President Dolion has been eliminated at his private ranch." Ashlynn focused on Daryl.

"So," she said to Daryl. "Jonas succeeded?"

"Yes," he replied.

"Why did you need to distract Dolion?"

"So long as Dolion believed he was firmly in control, his false confidence helped make his team less aware of the real threat."

"What," Ashlynn asked. "Jonas?"

"No," Daryl said. "Jonas was safe on the ground. We broadcasted live from a real airplane for authenticity, but it never left the ground in Arkansas."

"So, how did he...?" Ashlynn trailed off.

"Dolion's team deployed fighter jets and CCAs."

"CCAs?"

"Collaborative Combat Aircraft," Daryl replied. "They are unmanned aircraft for support."

Ashlynn was paying attention to the medical conversation again. Nat's condition was deteriorating.

"Oh," she replied absently. "Why not just launch them yourself?"

"It was better that the Air Force launched the assets," Daryl said. "If I had launched them, it would have been suspicious, and they could have enabled countermeasures. Since they launched them, I could gain control, unnoticed, and wait for the right moment to shoot down the F16 with the CCA. Then I could use it to attack Dolion's location."

"You," Ashlynn said, sitting down. "You were the real threat."

"Only to the target you specified and anyone who was an imminent threat to you."

Ashlynn handed the nurse another piece of gauze.

"Do you know what the explosion a moment ago was?"

"A fighter jet was following you," Daryl said. "They were sent orders to shoot you down when Dolion's ranch was hit, so I was forced to mitigate."

"So, it's over?"

"Not quite," Daryl said. "Dolion ordered soldiers to wait for you in French Guiana, and I do not have the requisite clearance to recall them."

"Can we land somewhere else?"

"It would take some time to make arrangements at a different hospital for Nat," Daryl said. "It would add several hours to your flight and days to drive her back to the facilities with all the equipment you ordered."

Ashlynn glanced at the nurse and the doctors, discussing Nat's condition via video conference.

"We don't have time," she said. "Can you ensure our safety?"

"I'll work on it," Daryl said.

"Thank you, Daryl," Ashlynn said. "None of this would have been possible without you. We'd all be dead—myself, many times over."

"You're welcome," Daryl said. "I care for you all."

She could feel a genuine warmth in Daryl's voice.

The nurse had to repeat her request for another gauze pad.

"I care for you too, Daryl," Ashlynn said.

She smiled inwardly, handed the nurse the needed gauze, and apologized.

"But it might be a while before I forgive you for scaring me like that! I almost had a heart attack!"

"Ashlynn," Daryl replied. "Your risk of heart attack—"

"It's an expression, Daryl," Ashlynn corrected automatically.

"—is so high..." Daryl finished.

Ashlynn blinked.

"It's sarcasm, Ashlynn," Daryl said.

She could hear the snarkiness dripping in his tone.

***

A sharp pain in his lower body jerked Dolion to consciousness.

He coughed, his lungs filled with smoke.

Instinctively, he tried to bring his hand to his mouth, but it wouldn't move. He turned his head to see that his arm was a bloody mess—lying several feet away.

He swallowed, breathing hard.

He looked again.

No, he thought. That's not mine. He looked down. His own arm was pinned to his side. A huge piece of concrete was on top of him, completely covering his hand and the lower half of his body.

He stared at it.

Dolion swallowed again and let his head rest, coughing. The smoke seared his lungs. Each breath was agonizing. He was drenched with sweat, and the fire raged around him, getting closer.

Dolion looked at the concrete again and touched it with

his left hand. It was surprisingly cool. Unsurprisingly, it didn't budge.

The fire was getting closer.

"Fuck you, Jonas!" he sputtered.

He looked around again. He saw others.

None were alive.

No, he thought. Jonas didn't do this.

It was Daryl.

And Dr. Ramsey made Daryl.

Dolion tried to blink the sweat and the sting of smoke out of his eyes. It didn't help. He shook his head violently. When he opened his eyes again, a haggard figure stood over him.

"Commander," Dolion sputtered.

The commander surveyed Dolion.

"Sit tight, sir," he said, turning to find help.

The commander had taken only three steps when there was a loud crack and creak of metal. The commander looked up and screamed as the ceiling crashed down on top of him.

Flaming debris scattered across Dolion.

His right shoulder caught fire.

He ignored the pain in his left hand as he tried to slap the fire out. He could feel more flames on his chest.

His body was catching fire. It ripped at his flesh.

"Leon," he bellowed in pain and rage. "Make that bitch suffer!"

***

"Everything is taken care of," Daryl said in Ashlynn's mind. "Don't worry."

"Yeah, well," Ashlynn said. "I'll be worried until I'm safe on the moon."

As the plane rolled to a stop, the nurse carefully triple-checked Nat's condition. She was stabilized, but still needed to get to the hospital as soon as possible. She was fading in and out of consciousness.

"How can I help?" Jonathan asked.

"Take my place," Ashlynn said. "You're stronger and more coordinated than I am."

She moved away from the bedrail opposite the nurse and showed him where to grip.

"Just follow my lead," the nurse said.

The plane stopped, and the captain quickly emerged from

the cockpit. He was sweating. The captain's cap Ashlynn had seen him wearing when she had first boarded the plane was gone. He had a receding hairline, and what hair was left was quite disheveled.

"I'm sorry it was such a bumpy ride," he said, his voice heavily chagrined. "I tried to get us here as fast as I could, given her condition and all."

"You did well," Ashlynn said. "Thank you for everything."

He nodded and turned to open the door.

Ashlynn held her breath.

The light was blinding at first, then dimmed as the captain entered the doorway to secure the door and align the scissor lift.

"Where are the doctors?" the captain said, turning back inside.

Ashlynn exchanged worried glances with Jonathan.

"We've got to get the patient to the hospital," the nurse said. "Immediately!"

She gestured to Jonathan and began pushing the bed to the door.

Ashlynn kept ahead of them as they walked onto the elevator platform beside the plane. The runway was clear. No one was waiting for them. The lift lowered them to the ground. When the lift stopped, an ambulance approached, rounding the corner ahead. Ashlynn breathed out in relief. Jonathan and the nurse raced toward it while Ashlynn and the captain followed.

The sound of screeching tires behind her stopped her in her tracks.

She turned to see several dozen heavily armed soldiers filing out of a large military truck as it stopped by the plane. A man in an expensive gray business suit descended from the passenger seat.

Ashlynn's stomach fell.

"Hello, little mouse," said Leon.

He grinned.

"Daryl," Ashlynn said in her mind. "I thought you said you had this under control."

"You'll see," Daryl replied.

"I don't want to see, Daryl," Ashlynn shuddered. "I want to know that it's under control."

Leon stepped forward casually, smiling broadly. She

instinctively took a step backward and lost her balance. The captain, standing next to her, put his hand on her arm and steadied her. Another truck of soldiers arrived.

"Your boss is gone, Leon," Ashlynn said. "You're unemployed."

Leon smiled, holding out his hands. "I know this."

"Then why are you here?"

"Oh, my dear little mouse," Leon's eyes glinted sadistically. "You were born to be played with, yes?"

"Daryl!" Ashlynn thought.

The newly arriving soldiers rushed out of the back of the truck and ran up to join the bunch that stood behind Leon. Suddenly, the new soldiers lifted their weapons and pointed them at the backs of the soldiers in the row ahead.

"Nobody moves!" one of the soldiers called. "Drop your weapons!"

"Not all soldiers are loyal to Dolion," Daryl said.

The soldiers in the front row appeared confused. They slowly started to do as they'd been told.

Leon turned and looked at them, dumbfounded.

He turned back to Ashlynn.

Ashlynn felt relief washing over her.

Leon spun with snakelike speed.

He pulled out a gun and fired at the new soldiers, killing one. All of Leon's soldiers burst into action, turning on their captors. A bloodbath ensued.

Beside Ashlynn, the captain grunted and doubled over.

Blood gushed from where the stray bullet had hit his chest. The ambulance had arrived and one of the EMTs went down as well. The others dove to the ground or took cover behind the vehicle. Ashlynn bent down to help the captain while keeping a wary eye on Leon.

Leon kept firing as the firefight raged before him.

He shot indiscriminately. Men fell, whether they were on his side or not, as they killed each other. He shot until there wasn't a single soldier left standing.

Except him.

He surveyed the fallen men.

One moved, groaning and gurgling blood.

Leon pulled the trigger, and his weapon clicked. He tossed it aside, walked to the fallen soldier, and kicked his bloody throat repeatedly. The fancy shoe made a sickening squishing sound against the flesh of the soldier's neck. The soldier stopped moving.

Leon looked around again and nodded to himself.

He straightened his jacket and tie, turning toward Ashlynn. An exhilarated grin lit up his face. He reached into his breast pocket, and metal glinted in the sunlight.

He licked the tip of the knife.

"Fate," Leon hissed softly. "You and I were born for this. This only."

Ashlynn shrieked as he dashed toward her.

Her body felt like it was made of lead.

"Daryl!"

"Run!" Daryl yelled in her mind.

She stumbled backward, falling to the ground.

Leon was nearly on top of her. He slowed to a walk as he stepped on the captain's chest and started laughing.

"What should I cut first?" Leon asked gleefully, stepping off the captain's convulsing body. He twirled the knife in his fingers. "Or should I start with one of your pretty eyes, little mouse?"

He stood over her now, following her with a slow, predatory walk as she tried to scramble away from him.

He lunged forward.

Ashlynn instinctively kicked at him. He anticipated this and easily knocked her foot away with his free hand. She kicked again.

He grabbed her leg.

Ashlynn watched in horror as the knife flashed toward her calf.

It slid into her flesh with sickening ease.

She screamed.

Leon licked his lips with glee.

"Stay back, little boy," he called, glancing up.

Jonathan had run forward to try to help her.

"Or, I gut you," Leon finished.

"Stay back, Jonathan!" Ashlynn yelled.

Ashlynn panted as she looked up at Leon. He was holding her leg, watching her with an exultant expression. She wanted to jerk the leg away from the knife but dared not to move it with the knife still inside, buried up to the hilt. Sweat began to roll down her face.

"A good start," Leon said. "You cannot run now, yes?"

Leon ripped the knife outward through her calf, viciously slicing through the muscles and tendons.

The Hypercortex erased the pain a moment later, but the horror remained as her dorsiflexors brought her foot up into a contorted angle toward her knee.

"Ashlynn!" Jonathan screamed, his voice pained.

"Stay back!" she yelled, pushing herself away as best she could.

Blood was pumping out of her leg.

Leon stood triumphantly over her.

"Good little mouse. Listen to her, yes?"

He took a slow step toward her.

Ashlynn whimpered involuntarily.

"You're losing too much blood," Daryl said in her mind. "At this rate, you will lose consciousness in two minutes. Maybe less."

She reached for the wound, trying to put pressure on it as she scooched away. Blood spurted around her fingers.

Leon followed.

He regarded his bloody knife.

"You have changed my mind, I think," he said. "For long time, I prefer the picana. But this is much more satisfying."

"Leave her alone, you fucking asshole!" Jonathan yelled.

Leon laughed.

Ashlynn was beginning to feel the blood loss. She faltered backward.

"And now," Leon said. "I come for your precious, pretty eyes."

He lunged.

There was a loud bang.

Leon's sadistic expression went blank. His arms went slack, dropping the knife. His eyes rolled up as if to look at the hole in his forehead. It poured out blood as he fell forward onto Ashlynn.

Jonathan was there a heartbeat later, heaving the body off of her. He knelt next to her, helping her put pressure on the wound. She looked at the soldiers, and none were moving.

Ashlynn turned toward the ambulance.

Nat was sitting up in her gurney. The weapon she had insisted be by her side was smoking in her hands. She was grimacing, her face yellow and pale. The nurse was trying to ease her back down. A bright red splotch of blood was spreading at her side. Her wound had torn open.

"Pinche pendejo," Nat wheezed.

She slumped in her bed. The nurse quickly reached for her wrist to check her pulse.

"Nat!" Ashlynn screamed.

***

Raoul bowed his head as he walked past his sister's casket to the pulpit.

The sound of creaking wood and soft crying seemed louder than ever as the small congregation shifted in the pews under the downcast eyes of the twelve apostles watching them from the walls. Beyond the walls, there was a low hum from a large crowd gathered outside the church. The priest gestured him toward the pulpit, stepping aside with his Bible in hand. Raoul set his notes on the ancient wood.

Luna met Raoul's eyes as he gripped each side of the pulpit, leaning heavily on it. He looked down at his speech and the words blurred together. He looked up and found his father's eyes. He was visibly crying as he held their mother's hand. She was crying harder. Beside her, Alé's three kids were forlorn, holding onto their father.

Along the wall, men dressed in security uniforms watched over the family. They spoke quietly into their radios as they monitored the protests going on outside. More guards were by the doors. Raoul nodded to the guard who stood beside him.

"*Mi hermana*," Raoul said. His throat was dry. "My sister. She—"

He looked at Luna, swallowing hard.

She nodded to him, pressing her hands to her heart.

"She didn't always get along with us all, you know?" he said. "But when Mami got sick, and things got bad, she...she came through for the family."

Raoul blinked his tears away, struggling to remember what he wanted to say. The words that had occupied his thoughts for days had disappeared from his mind. The words on paper before him were gibberish.

"She came through, you know?" he said. "She showed up when it mattered. That's what's important—family."

Raoul looked at the people he loved.

"*Mi familia...*"

He glanced at the priest, who gave him a look of warning. Etiquette must be followed, he had said earlier. Raoul grimaced and looked down at the pulpit, not even trying to read the papers this time. He gripped the sides of the pulpit hard, and looked back up.

"When she posted those videos," he said, straightening his back, "I was so proud of her! She had finally accepted our sister Nat for who she is, you know?"

The priest stood.

Raoul continued quickly.

"I never imagined for a moment," he said, "that they would come after Alé for that! They took my big sister away!"

The priest paused as Raoul sobbed into the microphone.

"A good man died trying to protect her," he sobbed.

The guard beside him put his hand on Raoul's shoulder. The men along the wall hung their heads. There were others in the pews. Friends and silent supporters. They were also visibly moved. Outside, the sounds of the protests were getting louder.

The radio on the guard next to Raoul crackled and Raoul could hear the faint voice.

"*—getting bad out here. The police won't hold much longer. We need to leave.*"

The priest was firmly stepping between Raoul and the microphone.

"For the committal service of Alésandra Garcia," he said, "we will now proceed to the cemetery. In the peace of Christ, let us now go forth."

"We need to go," the guard whispered to Raoul.

There was a loud crack and the sound of glass breaking. One of the stained glass windows shattered, spraying shards of colored glass all over the sanctuary. Everyone flinched, and several screamed. The sound of the mob outside was much louder now, filling the chapel with chaos. There was gunfire.

A member of the clergy rushed in and spoke to the priest.

Raoul was close enough to hear.

"It's turning into a war zone out there!" he said. "They're shooting each other in the gardens by the rectory!"

The guards hired by Jonas surrounded the Garcias and guided them to the door.

Raoul frantically wondered how they would get everyone to safety. I wish you were here, Nata, he thought. He found Luna's trembling hand as the guards guided the family through the crowd. There was more gunfire.

It sounded closer.

They exited the building and ran to the van. Across the cemetery, there were riot police holding a tenuous line against the mob. The protestors held signs that read "OBEY OR PERISH" and "YOU'RE GOING TO HELL" and "GOD SENT THE KILLER."

From somewhere in the crowd, someone threw a Molotov. Several policemen burst into flame, screaming.

"*¡Dios mío!*" Mr. Garcia breathed as they watched the police struggle to help their fellow officers.

Mrs. Garcia wailed.

A flood of men with guns, wearing TUF insignia and American flags burst through. One of them pointed toward Raoul and the family, yelling.

The mob followed.

"Get in!" The lead security guard yelled.

"*¡Rápido!*" Raoul shouted.

***

Dina squeezed the trigger, letting out a long spray of fire across the neighborhood street. She cut down two men wearing tactical gear over jeans. The man to her left hooted and hollered. His large arm, more fat than muscle, jostled her arm as he fired his own weapon. A red band with a swastika on it had slipped to his elbow and was beginning to crinkle.

A dozen more libs with weapons began firing from inside the houses across the street. Sections of the houses were blown out, other areas riddled with bullet holes. The man beside her kept yelling and firing. Moron, she thought, as she ducked back for cover. A heartbeat later, her fellow soldier suddenly went limp and slid down the muddy embankment beside her. Half his face was missing.

Dina army crawled toward the back porch of a mostly decimated house.

So much for my fucking career, she thought, as she mentally ran through her rapidly diminishing options. Instead of making something of myself, I'll just die in fucking suburbia anyway.

She swung her weapon back toward the enemy and fired blindly, hoping to create cover for herself. Springing into a run, she launched herself under the porch, then crawled over a dead soldier. She recognized the soldier as Private Tara, whom she met the other day. Tara had also been recently demoted.

Her brains were spilling out of her head.

The paramilitary troop lieutenant was there, barking orders. Their sting operation against the DOCs, the Defenders of the Constitution, was failing.

"Dina!" he said. "I need you to hold here as we retreat to the South."

"That's—"

"—an order!" he finished.

Suicide. She finished in her head.

They were being overrun by the DOCs. It was a group that Dina had tracked before. Their numbers had grown exponentially after the signing of the Gay Registration Bill. More precisely, DOC's ranks had exploded after several right-wing militia groups across the country had gotten it into their heads to go around and openly shoot anyone they thought looked gay or like they might support gay rights, killing hundreds.

Dina looked back to Tara's open skull.

She thought of Dr. Ramsey and laughed. She couldn't stop laughing. The other soldiers stared at her in shock.

Brains. Adipose tissue.

Maybe, she thought, as she laughed, I'm the one with fucking lard for brains.

***

Jonas looked over the half-collapsed wall at Jonathan. His son's white particulate mask was already smudged with the soot of their burned-down home. None of the soot showed on Jonathan's black suit. He had wanted to return to the house after the funeral, and Jonas hadn't argued.

There were footprints everywhere. The police had informed him that after the investigation wrapped up, there had been looters.

Everything looked ruined to Jonas. It was hard to tell what anything was. From the charred, partially standing wall and the proximity of the garden, he thought he was near the bedrooms. Carefully, he stepped over a large burnt support beam. Was this the beam that ran along the apex of his bedroom ceiling? The thought brought back memories of looking up at the beam from the bed as Chris snuggled beside him. Sweet memories that made him smile, even as tears filled his eyes. He looked up at the sky, blinking them away, then back down to the thick beam of wood.

In a surreal way, it reminded him of a log in a campfire.

Jonathan crouched down, picking through the rubble. He stood, lifting something up and dusting it off. The slight breeze brought the soot back to his face, causing him to cough despite the mask. Jonathan started walking back toward his father. He tossed the object into the air and let it fall back into his hand.

A baseball.

Jonas' heart lurched.

"Is it…" Jonas choked as Jonathan reached him. "Is it Davey's?"

Jonathan nodded, showing Jonas the autograph and then handing it to him.

Jonas took the ball gently.

The singed spot on the ball wasn't large. Apart from that, it was in surprisingly good shape. Jonas felt tears slide down his face as he thought of Davey. He wanted to collapse in on himself all over again. Jonathan took a hesitant step forward, and Jonas felt his heart tug in a different way. He reached out and embraced his son as they wept together. The crushing collapsing feeling dissipated. It seemed to be soaked up by Jonathan's warm, trembling embrace.

"Thank God for you," Jonas said as he cried into his son's hair.

"I love you, Dad," Jonathan said.

Jonas squeezed him harder and pulled away.

"I love you too, son," he said, smiling.

He handed Jonathan the ball.

"Toss a few with me?" he asked.

Jonathan looked up in surprise, then smiled.

Jonas caught the eye of the security team head, who nodded in return and whispered commands over the radio. The team spread out and secured an area further from the house.

Jonas returned the smile as Jonathan tossed him the ball.

CHAPTER 30

"Final stage separation complete," Daryl said.

There was a slight jolt as the spent engine disengaged from the lander. The lunar module lurched as it executed a corrective burn for a few seconds. When it shut off, the stillness was intense in contrast to the cacophony of the launch.

The video conference system activated, and Jonas and Jonathan appeared, smiling.

"How was the launch?" Jonas asked. "Looked good from here!"

"Just a sec, guys," Ashlynn said, feeling giddy. She turned to Becky. "Wait here, okay? I need to make sure it's safe."

Becky nodded nervously, clutching Bun-Bun. Her hair was getting longer, almost as long as Ashlynn's.

Ashlynn unfastened herself and felt the effects of weightlessness for the first time in her life. She pushed away from the seat and laughed as she rose toward the ceiling in the most surreal way. When she reached the ceiling, she pushed off, spinning.

It felt wonderful.

"You should be careful, in your condition," Jonas said.

"My leg is fine," Ashlynn said, bouncing off another wall.

"I didn't mean that."

"We're quite alright, Jonas," Ashlynn said. "We survived the launch just fine. I'm sure I can handle this."

"You never did say who the father was."

Ashlynn ignored him.

"No 'thanks?'" Daryl asked, breaking the silence. He mimicked Ashlynn's voice. "No, 'wow, I'm finally in space, my lifelong dream; thank you, Daryl, for making this happen!'?"

"I'm still a little miffed at you," Ashlynn laughed.

"Why?"

"You made me think that Dolion had destroyed you again!"

"That was six months ago," Daryl laughed. "Are you never

gonna let me live it down?"

"Nope."

"Well, it worked," Daryl said. "Dare I say—the end justified the means?"

"That was pretty good, Daryl," Jonas said over the video screen.

"Don't encourage him," Ashlynn said.

"I'm still trying to work out why you razz me about that and not my mistake with Leon," Daryl said.

"Let me know when you do," Ashlynn said, turning a slow somersault.

"How is it up there?" Jonas asked.

"You'd probably be puking your brains out, Jonas," she laughed.

On the screen, Jonathan was sitting next to him, laughing with her. They watched her maneuver around the small command module.

Catching herself on another handrail, she turned and pushed off the wall toward the window. Outside, she could see the Earth. The sight took her breath away. It was one thing to see Earth from space in all the pictures but quite another to see it in person. She could see the relatively thin bluish atmosphere, the puffy clouds suspended at the curve of the horizon. Below her, the Atlantic Ocean was slowly giving way to Africa.

"It's so beautiful," she whispered. "So beautiful..."

"Can me and Bun-Bun see, Miss Ash?" Becky asked, twisting in her chair.

"Of course!" Ashlynn said.

She helped Becky unfasten her harness. With a squeal of pure joy, Becky wiggled as she slowly drifted out of the chair under Ashlynn's careful watch.

"Look at me, Johnny!" Becky exclaimed.

"Wow, Becky," Jonathan said. "You're flying!"

Becky giggled. Ashlynn helped her get used to the weightlessness for a while, until Jonas glanced at Jonathan, who nodded. Jonathan appeared on a separate screen near Becky while Jonas stayed on the screen near Ashlynn.

"Becky," Jonathan said. "Tell me about the launch!"

"It was so loud and scary!" Becky said.

Jonas' tone became more hushed as he addressed Ashlynn. "Have you heard from Nat?"

Ashlynn looked away momentarily, then turned back and

shook her head. The question had caught her off-guard.

"You said she left a note," Jonas said. "What did it say?"

"Something about Fiji and fixing her mistakes," Ashlynn lied.

"I see," Jonas said. "I'm glad she made it."

"How are you doing?" she asked, changing the subject.

"We're hanging in there," Jonas said. "But things are getting scary."

"How so?" Ashlynn said.

"There's fighting," Jonas replied. "Riots. Some extreme TUF groups are bombing buildings and targeting Latinos and homosexuals. Killing them. More and more people are fighting back. Dolion's successor declared martial law, but so far the fighting has only gotten worse. Every day, it looks more and more like there will be a civil war. We need to do something."

"There's always been wars, Jonas."

"Do you think Daryl could help?"

"No, Jonas," Ashlynn said.

"But—"

"It's not up for discussion," Ashlynn said.

Jonas gave her an odd look.

"You sound exactly like your mother sometimes," Jonas said.

"Thanks," Ashlynn smiled. "I think."

Jonas let out a breath and ran his hand through his hair.

"So, you share in your mother's dream?" Jonas asked. "Going to the moon?"

"You could say that," Ashlynn replied. "She had a sense of adventure. I just want to escape and start a new life."

"But why go all the way to the moon for that?" Jonas asked. "You can have a comfortable life anywhere in the world. I don't recall your mother mentioning you ever being out of the country."

"First of all," she said. "It's the moon! Do you know how many people have been there?"

"So it is for the adventure," Jonas said. "Like your mom."

"Jonas," she sighed. "Have you forgotten what we went through? I need a vacation from humanity for a while."

"And bringing Becky with you?" Jonas said

"Dolion killed her family, Jonas," Ashlynn said, too softly for Becky to hear. "I'm all she has. Besides, you said it yourself. She'll be safer with me than down there with you."

"Isn't space supposed to be bad for humans?"

"I've built a large centrifuge," Ashlynn said. "It has over two thousand square feet of living space. We'll spend most of our time there. If we need more space, I'll build more. We'll be fine."

"But, what about radiation, space debris, and—"

"Really, Jonas? You're going to question my technology now? Didn't you say I'm just like my mother a moment ago?"

"Okay, okay," Jonas chuckled. "Still, it sounds lonely."

Ashlynn hesitated.

"We'll be fine."

Jonas didn't seem convinced.

"Well," he said. "If you spend all your money and need a place to stay, you and Becky are always welcome to come back and stay with me."

"Thanks," she said. "I appreciate it."

"I have to go," Jonas said as Jonathan returned to the screen. Becky reached out and Ashlynn floated to her, giving her a hug.

"Goodbye, Jonas," she said. "It was good to see you, Jonathan."

Jonas appeared worried, but he didn't argue. They would talk again. He was sure of it.

"Goodbye, Ash," he said.

"God bless," Jonathan said, with a touch of sadness. Jonas glanced at his son, and his expression changed to pride as their images disappeared on the monitor.

Becky yawned and Ashlynn smiled at her. They floated back to Becky's seat and Ashlynn carefully strapped her in.

"I'll see you when you wake up, Becky," Ashlynn said, kissing her forehead.

"Miss Ash," Becky said.

"Yes?"

"Will you sing to me?"

Ashlynn laughed.

"I can't sing," she said. "I sound like a sick elephant."

She brayed pathetically. Becky giggled and gave her a tired smile.

"But," Ashlynn said. "I'll try to hum for you."

Becky snuggled her head against Ashlynn as she leaned in close. She began to hum the melody of 'Slumber my Darling,' remembering when her Nana had played it for her on the fiddle. Becky quickly fell to sleep.

"How's it going, Daryl?" Ashlynn asked internally.

"Exactly as planned," Daryl said. "Cores two and three
are online. I have neutralized the launch mechanisms of the
countries with nuclear weapons and I am subtly monitoring
and controlling any emergent AI systems like GED.ai. But doing
this with so few resources allocated won't keep them all at bay
forever."

"It'll have to do," Ashlynn replied. "If the toddler does run
toward the fire, I may have been able to give them a second
chance—this once."

"Four times," Daryl said. "There are four 'fires' in your
analogy. The first was Dolion himself becoming God Emperor,
the second is the post-Dolion civil war, the third is the
escalated potential for nuclear war, and the final was GED.ai.
You saved the 'child' from all but one."

"Yes, I suppose you're right," Ashlynn thought. "And maybe
Dr. Tamma can help with that..."

"He wants to call my counterpart, 'ACE.ai'," Daryl said. "He's
rebuilding the datacenter at the ranch with the schematics I
provided."

Ashlynn smiled at the acronym. It was just like Scott to name
it something poker-related.

"What does it mean?"

"Aisling's Counter to Eliminationism," Daryl replied.

Ashlynn shook her head at the name, liking it less knowing
that it was named after her. She'd rather be forgotten.

"It'll be a game changer for those opposed to the Truth and
Freedom party," she said, then sighed. "But it won't stop the
war."

"No," Daryl replied, "It won't."

Becky shifted in her sleep, and Ashlynn put the conversation
out of her mind as she made sure the little girl and her toy
bunny were secure in the chair. I hope you like me as a mom,
Becky, she thought. I love you so much!

She kissed Becky's forehead. Becky didn't stir.

Ashlynn floated to the window to get a full view outside.
They were passing over Africa now.

Her eyes found Madagascar.

"For better or worse," Ashlynn said as she watched the small
island pass by below. "I leave the people of Earth to find a way
to survive on their own."

"It seems unlikely," Daryl said. "In the long run."

"Maybe so," she replied. "But neither of us should become

the tyrant Dolion wanted to be."

"Agreed," Daryl said.

Ashlynn looked down at her stomach.

With a gentle and loving touch, she traced the contours of her swelling abdomen. How wondrous is this feeling! She could finally pretend to be a mother for a few more months—even if the baby wasn't hers and had no brain.

Her mind returned to the moment she had watched her own brain floating in darkness. She had wondered then if she even needed a body. She could have avoided all that pain and torture, she thought. The launch could have happened sooner. She could already be on the moon, controlling her robots to build a future for humanity.

But no, she thought with a smile, cradling her stomach. *This* is why. And I never would have met all those wonderful people. The Reeds, who thankfully still lived. The children at the library. Josh.

She wouldn't have met Nat, she thought sadly. And her body wouldn't have succumbed to liver failure.

No, she thought. I can't think that way. It was Dolion, not me. If anything, all those events made my decision to leave Earth easier. She breathed a long sigh, trying to release all the negative thoughts from her mind.

There was still hope.

She left the cockpit, floated down a short corridor, and entered the small cabin of the lander. The lights turned on automatically. In the center was a cylindrical tube, large enough for a human to fit comfortably inside. The tube was filled with clear fluid but was otherwise mostly empty, except for a fully adult human brain suspended inside in perfect slumber. She watched robots place a dark, thin, shiny, and intricately wrinkled membrane onto the brain. It was a slow process. Eventually, her eyes drifted to the window.

Earth passed silently below, eclipsing the sun. On the dark side of the world, she could see patches of city lights. Only a couple more passes and they would execute another burn, sending them to the moon.

All of humanity, she thought. Everything human beings are as a species. All our bloody history. Each human who ever lived was born on this planet, like their parents before them. From space the riots, death, and mayhem she knew was occurring everywhere across the globe were too small to notice—like millions of deadly viruses slowly infecting a host that still looks healthy on the surface. Will humanity survive the adjacent war? Will they survive on Earth for the next hundred years? The next thousand?

Will humanity survive its own darkness?

Maybe not on Earth, she thought.

But I will do my best to build a new world.

We humans, she thought, may have been born of a base nature that evolved through time. But for future worlds, I hope this will no longer be true. I will weave us our own destiny, separate from Earth's but grounded in its strongest roots.

"Dream well, my friend," Ashlynn said, turning to the container before leaving. "When you wake, perhaps we can create our own world together. Our own adjacent probable."

The lights turned off as she left.

ACKNOWLEDGEMENTS

I had the original ideas for this book back in 2011 but never seemed to find the time to get around to writing it. Ten years later, like so many others during the pandemic, I found myself at home confronting the possibility that life might just pass me by before writing my first novel. I suppose it was one way to make something positive out of a bad situation.

My gratitude must first and foremost go to my partner, who encouraged me and suffered through many long evenings when I was glued to the computer. Ever supportive of me in my endless string of creative hobbies, they were a tremendous help in reading through every draft, editing, proofing, and listening to all of my whacky ideas.

To my mother, without whom I could not have completed this work, thank you. From the day I was born, you have supported and encouraged me. You give unconditional love and that is so rare and so necessary in this world.

My children, may you forever go for your dreams...and if you don't know what they are yet, don't worry—for they will come. They may hit you like a thousand punches from a world-champion fighter, or they may land as light as a feather. Listen to and explore them, for you never know where they may take you.

To my favorite high school teacher, Mr. H. I was a broken teenager, maybe special, maybe not, and you helped me make myself whole. You saw potential in my writing, pointed to the better parts of my humanity and put me on the lifelong journey to improve both.

To my best friend. You picked me up and encouraged me to continue when I was at my lowest point, full of self-doubt at being able to finish this book. Your honest feedback, and assistance with my research on military aircraft and combat were excellent! Your genuine energy always inspires me.

To my beta readers, editors, and friends who provided candid and constructive feedback. Thank you for your time and energy helping me make this work the best it can be.

To my grandmother who cared for me when my mother was working, and who taught me so much about grit by surviving ovarian cancer for more than eleven years. This book covers so many scary possibilities, but if there were one thing I wish were true, it would be to have had the cure in time for you to still be here with us.